DIVIDED BY TIME, BOUND BY LOVE

Engelina stirred, and Roan stroked the hand held within his. It was small and delicate, yet strong. He studied the rest of her—the pale shoulders illuminated in the flickering candlelight, the striking beauty of her face, the sublime entanglement of hundreds of raven curls. Outside, lightning struck again.

She moaned.

"Shh, it's only thunder," he said.

"Roan?" she called softly, then said something that he couldn't make out.

He leaned forward. "What?"

". . . your world," she said, slurring the two words together.

He leaned closer. "I can't understand you."

". . . take me . . . to your . . . world."

For the rest of his life, Roan would never forget the agony, the ecstasy, of her plea.

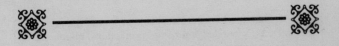

The Loving

Sandra Canfield

HarperPaperbacks
A Division of HarperCollinsPublishers

This is a work of fiction. The characters, incidents, and dialogues are products of the author's imagination and are not to be construed as real. Any resemblance to actual events or persons, living or dead, is entirely coincidental.

HarperPaperbacks   *A Division of* HarperCollins*Publishers*
10 East 53rd Street, New York, N.Y. 10022

Cover illustration by Renato Aime

First printing: June 1992

Printed in the United States of America

HarperPaperbacks and colophon are trademarks of HarperCollins*Publishers*

❖ 10 9 8 7 6 5 4 3 2 1

For Engelina Franquery who died so young.
You weren't forgotten.

The Loving

$\mathcal{P}$ROLOGUE

Like an intriguing woman, the house had secrets.

Roan Jacob sensed this the moment the two-story structure came into view. Even its location, in the famed Garden District of New Orleans, suggested this fact. While most of the other fashionably restored nineteenth-century houses stood proudly in plain view, this one sat far back from the street, completely hidden by a copse of huge old magnolia trees, as though it had been banished for committing some unspeakable deed.

The current residence of a doctor who was spending the summer in Europe, the house was small, at least compared to its massive neighbors, and shaped like a tall, rectangular box. Only a narrow right-hand balcony relieved the severity of the lines, that and four sets of double pipe columns joined together in an archlike fashion by lacy cast-iron tracery. Even here, though, in the shape, in the tracery, in the gate that offered further seclusion, there was a reticent austerity, which the house's hushed color—it wasn't white, it wasn't gray—only accented, as did the thin, draped windows and the heavy, dark wooden door that seemed designed to keep inhabitants in and strangers out.

Stranger.

1

Roan was a stranger to the house, a stranger to the house's owner, a stranger to himself. Less than two weeks before—eons ago—his life had fallen apart, and now he was left with the formidable task of fitting the shattered pieces back together. If he could. The truth was, though, he was uncertain that he had all the pieces or, more accurately, that he didn't have aberrant pieces of some other puzzle. Either way, he feared he wouldn't be able to make his life whole again.

In the beginning he'd denied the strange things that were happening to him, but slowly, as an educated man, as a doctor, he'd had to face the fact that something within him was different. Very different. If he'd harbored any illusions to the contrary, the incident at the hospital two days before had killed them completely and forever. He was not the man he used to be. That plain. That simple. That frightening.

So, he thought, as he shut off the motor of his Mercedes roadster, the house might have its secrets, but then he had a few of his own.

As he walked toward the gate, the summer heat swarmed about him, slamming against his chest, stealing his breath and fleeing into the sunshine-fired afternoon. At the same time, he was acutely aware of sounds and smells. He heard the twit-twitter of a bird, the drone of busy bees, the creaking of the iron gate as he pushed it open. He smelled flowers—roses and honeysuckle, he thought—the plush thickness of reedy grass, the rich, pungent fragrance of the earth.

Earth.

For a moment he thought he could hear it—it sounded like the thump-thump of shovelfuls of dirt falling on a newly laid coffin—and he feared that he was having another bizarre episode, but it didn't materialize. He was relieved. As relieved as he knew how to be these days.

Roan took the steps slowly, feeling the sun beating mercilessly down on his back. Houston was hot, but not as oppressively hot as this. It must be the humidity, he reasoned. The tropical climate nurtured growth—the flourishing flora attested to this—but the citizens of New Orleans paid a heavy price for their paradise. Once Roan attained the fern-bedecked gallery, a shadowed coolness enveloped him. So pleasant was it, so like standing beneath the drooping branches of a shady tree, that he simply stood and soaked it in.

Up close, he noted details that had escaped him before. A bougainvillea adorned with vanilla-white blossoms grew within a glazed oriental jardiniere, while a brass and glass light, suspended from a long chain, hung in front of the door. The narrow windows, two on the right of the asymmetrically set door, were sparkling clean and edged in teal-colored shutters. A woven mat proclaimed him welcome.

Fishing in his pocket for the key, Roan had just inserted it into the lock when he noticed the note taped to the door. He reached for it and read:

I'm glad the house will have a sitter. Make yourself at home. By the way, I forgot to tell Stewart that a cleaning lady comes in once a week. Oh, and will you feed the stray cat that stops in occasionally for a handout? There's cat food in the pantry. Again, make yourself at home.

The note was signed "David Bell."

"Thanks, David Bell," Roan said to his absent benefactor as he finished turning the key. The lock clicked. Slowly, Roan twisted the brass doorknob. Slowly, he pushed open the door. Shadows rushed in, striping the teal-and-apricot Aubusson runner, which strategically stopped short of the graceful curving staircase that floated upward in a cloud of elegance. An exquisite crystal and gold chandelier hovered overhead. Though the room was lovely and inviting, Roan hesitated. What if something strange happened again? But how could it if the house was empty? He reacted only to people and their emotional vibrations.

He stepped inside.

And waited.

Nothing . . . except the strong feeling once more that the house had secrets. Secrets which, thankfully, it didn't care to share. Roan gave a sigh of relief. He didn't need additional problems. He had enough of his own. In the next few weeks, he had to come to terms with his life. More important, he had to come to terms with his death.

ONE

He was going to die.

Roan Jacob accepted this harsh reality calmly and rationally, partly because he dealt with death on a daily basis—as a cardiac surgeon, he cheated the Grim Reaper every chance he got—partly because he took pride in a thorough presence of mind. He was a man who valued control above all else, and control demanded a clear head. Now exercising that control, that clear-headedness, with movements pantomime-slow in the salt seawater of the Caribbean, he checked his diving equipment for mechanical failure. No twisted hose. No faulty valve. Nothing impeding the flow of air. And yet the precious substance had ceased. Though he knew what he'd find, he rechecked the air indicator. It showed a safe seven hundred pounds. He shook the instrument, wishing the needle would drop into the red danger zone. At least that would logically explain what was happening.

He knew what was happening, though. Or rather what had happened. The guide he and his buddies, both fellow physicians, had hired in Cozumel had vowed, in broken English, that the diving equipment was new and top-notch. Well, it might be new and top-notch, but the equipment obviously had one minor flaw: It didn't work. But then, Roan thought on a wave of scalding sarcasm, for the money the

5

guide had been paid he'd have vowed that his mother was the Virgin Mary. Just wait until he got his hands on the son of a bitch!

Always one to appreciate ironic humor, Roan would have laughed if he could have. *That's the whole crux of the matter, Jacob ole boy, you're not going to get your hands on him.* On some heretofore unreached gut level, this thought penetrated, making him realize that he truly was about to die. This time, the realization unleashed an unfamiliar wave of panic.

Easy, Jacob, easy.

The survival instinct forced him to try the mouthpiece again. Nothing. Drier than dry. Like sucking on an empty soda bottle. The panic tried to make a reappearance, but Roan held it at bay. He couldn't prevent a slow burning in his chest, however. Whether it was from lack of oxygen or from fear, he couldn't say.

He looked around, searching for the entrance to the cave. Even as he did so, he realized that he had been as careless as the guide. He never should have separated from the others. It was the cardinal rule of diving: never go alone. But the cave had beckoned, an underwater paradise calling to him, and the others had been up ahead. What harm could there be in a brief peek?

"You arrogant bastard," he could hear Stewart Kesterson say the way he had a thousand times.

"Yeah," he could hear himself answering back, a cocksure grin on his face, "arrogance is what makes me the best damned heart surgeon in the U.S."

"How fucking modest, Jacob. You mean you're not the best heart surgeon in the world?"

"Well, yeah, I am, but I was trying to be fucking modest."

"Know what your trouble is?" Stewart would always ask. "Nobody's told you yet that you're just a mere mortal."

Yeah, well, he was about to learn that, and in spades, unless he could make it out of this cave. Maybe if he could, the others would be nearby. Then, he could bum some air.

He could feel his chest tightening even more as he started to swim in the direction of the cave's gaping mouth. He forced himself to make athletically strong, but unfrenzied, strokes. He forced himself to think calmly. A person could hold his breath for two, three minutes. Maybe longer. Even if he slipped into unconsciousness, he could live a few minutes before brain damage occurred. Surely his friends—they were doctors, for God's sake!—could revive him. But only if they found him. Sweet Jesus, where are you, Stewart?

The underwater scene that had been so intriguing only minutes before now held no interest for him. He marveled no longer at the water's turquoise translucence or at the phantom-shaped rocks. Roan noted only peripherally as a school of silver fish darted from his hurried path, as a flash of sunshine yellow unwisely came too near, as a brown grouper, its large, sleepy eyes wide in surprise, collided with him.

Dammit, get out of the way! Roan roared silently.

Easy, easy. You're losing it. Think calm. Think coherent. Think . . . think of Kay.

Willfully, he conjured up an image of the blond-haired woman awaiting him on the yacht. He could see her, her long, lean, suntanned legs projecting from crisply starched shorts so white that they blinded the eye. Her smile was just as dazzling. She was going to be royally p.o.ed to have her carefully arranged wedding plans screwed up, which was what a dead groom usually did to wedding plans. Sorry about that, Kay. Sorry about . . .

God, his chest hurt! It felt as if a fire were burning

in its middle, or a giant, heated hand were pressing down. Breath! He had to have a breath. Just one. That was all he asked. Just one more breath.

He stopped swimming. Adjusting the mouthpiece as though a new angle were what he'd needed all along, he sucked greedily, voraciously. Surely there was enough air left for one more breath. But there wasn't. There wasn't even a trickle. Just a profound nothingness, which in no way satisfied his hungry lungs.

He wasn't going to make it. In surgery, he had an intuitive gift for knowing when to keep fighting for a patient's life and when to give up. He experienced that same intuition now. He also experienced anger. Anger that this was happening. Thirty-six was too young to die. Too damned young! And his surgical talents were too damned rare!

His heart pounded wildly.

His flesh tingled with the numbing coldness of fright.

The absence of his breathing crashed against his eardrums with a deafening silence.

And yet, he forced himself to gather one last raiment of calmness about him. He would die in possession of his mind. He would die with dignity. He would die . . . He felt his head growing light, lighter. His thoughts were becoming hard to hold on to. Make it quick, he told himself. Remove the mouthpiece and swallow a lungful of water. Even as he told himself to do this, however, he found that he couldn't. Though the mouthpiece and air tank had become superfluous baggage, he couldn't shed them, simply because they represented his only lifeline.

The mouthpiece, bearing the marks of his teeth, slipped from his lips. Despite his resolve he panicked, flailing for, grasping at, anything. In the process he knocked the mask from his face and kicked a flipper from his foot.

His head grew lighter.

His body drifted downward.

Calm . . . calm . . . the word swam through his consciousness like a sleek silver fish. And then, the lightness in his head turned black, black like the yawning death hole into which he was falling. His last thought was that Stewart had been right. He was a mere mortal, after all.

"Quick!" Stewart shouted up to the three women on board the yacht catnapping in the full May sun. "Help us get him up!"

At the brusquely given order, three startled women appeared at the boat's edge, each wondering what could have happened to shatter the stillness of a sleepy afternoon. At the sight of Roan's inert body, his head lolling eerily to one side, one of the women, Mark Hagen's wife, Susan, cried, "Oh, my God! What happened?"

The blond-haired woman with long, lean, suntanned legs and dazzling white shorts whispered a husky, disbelieving, "Roan?"

The third woman, wearing a hot-pink bikini that was more suggestion than substance, an ER nurse trained for crises, rushed to the men's aid. Mark Hagen started up the ladder, hauling Roan's crumpled body up behind him as best he could. Stewart, standing on the ladder's bottom rung, pushed with his shoulder. Neither man was making significant progress. The woman in the bikini grabbed one of Roan's arms.

"Get the damned air tank off!" Stewart shouted.

The woman began to fumble with the straps stretching over Roan's shoulders. Susan hurried to help. The woman in the white shorts stood still, as though rooted to the spot.

"Pull!" Stewart shouted.

"I can't!" the ER nurse hollered.

"Get it off!" he bellowed.

She tugged again, ripping three fingernails and bringing a breast dangerously close to exposure. She was rewarded, however, by the strap's slipping from one of Roan's shoulders. It was a simpler matter to remove the corresponding strap, a feat which Mark accomplished quickly. The air tank fell into the sea, creating a spray that splashed everyone. No one seemed to notice, particularly the woman in the white shorts.

"Pull him up!" Stewart ordered, pushing as both Mark and the bikini-clad woman pulled. Susan grabbed a flipper that dangled half on, half off.

In seconds, Roan's lifeless body lay stretched out on the deck of the yacht. His brown hair fell across his face, leaving sea drops on his ashen cheeks and blue, lifeless lips.

As though galvanized by the grim sight, the woman in white shorts stepped forward, fell to her knees beside the body, and cried, "Roan?" It was a soft, plaintive sound, as though she were begging him to awaken and tell her that everything was all right, that he was not lying dead before her, after all.

"Get her back!" Stewart called, already elevating Roan's neck in preparation for CPR.

"C'mon, Kay," Susan said quietly, reasonably, "let them help him."

"No, I—"

"Kay, please," Susan said, forcefully removing her, though she was only half the woman's size.

Mark, having divested himself of his air tank, moved to Roan's side. "Ready?" he asked Stewart.

"Yeah," Stewart said, pinching Roan's nostrils together.

For what seemed like forever, Mark pushed on Roan's chest with the heel of his palm in an attempt to stimulate his heart, while Stewart breathed into his friend's lungs.

Finally Mark shouted as Roan's heart thump-thumped beneath his hand, "I've got something!"

"C'mon, man!" Stewart encouraged.

In one sharp breath, oxygen flooded Roan's lungs. With it came a gush of stinging seawater . . . and the welcome rush of life.

A week later, on a mellow May night, Roan, who'd just slipped from the shower and wore only a worn pair of jeans, stood on the balcony of his condo, located in a fashionably sequestered section of Houston. Here, amid tree-lined avenues and grilled gates, residents paid, and handsomely, for the privilege of privacy. What they paid for even more, however, was the right to discreetly, silently boast that they were able to afford such uncommon luxury.

Like his neighbors, Roan had plunked down his money with the same arrogant pride. In fact, he'd added further insult by bringing in one of the South's most celebrated interior decorators, an emaciated, wormlike man whose principal talent lay in spending other people's money. But the worm did it with flair and, in the end, his customers were satisfied because, after all, they'd hired him to spend their money so that they could complain about it and, thereby, crow about their wealth.

Roan, too, had complained, particularly about the claret-red silk wallpaper that had cost a hundred and fifty dollars a roll. He had equally resisted the twenty-four-carat gold Waterford crystal chandelier that hung in the master bath and the cut crystal bathroom faucets. Most strenuously of all, he'd objected to the twelve-thousand-dollar Ming vase that held a place of prominence on the black lacquered table in the living room. He always made certain, however, that a first-time visitor saw the vase and, while he never quoted a price—that would have been gauche—he did subtly, jokingly insinuate that it cost him an arm and not one but two legs.

Tonight, as he stood on the balcony staring into the burgeoning blackness, the condo, the Ming vase in particular, seemed decadent. Even vulgar. Like a two-bit whore selling her wares on the street corner. The truth was that the chirping cicadas, the blinking fireflies, the lone whippoorwill calling to its lost mate were the things of value, the things of worth.

Jesus, he thought, raking his fingers through his damp hair, where did all this philosophical crap come from suddenly?

The whippoorwill called again, and this time Roan could have sworn that the elusive bird taunted him. "You're different," the unseen creature seemed to say.

Yes, he was different, Roan had to admit. Ever since the accident, he'd been different. At first, it had been so minor that he thought he was only imagining it. After all, the change wasn't something that could be accounted for easily—or logically. How could he, as a doctor, explain the fact that his vital signs had altered? He probably wouldn't have noticed at all if he wasn't a committed jogger. As such, though, he was attuned to his body. He even had a fancy gizmo that measured his blood pressure and heart rate as he exercised. All three—his respiratory rate, his heart rate, his blood pressure—had been lowered, subtly but consistently.

At the same time, and just as baffling, though here the changes came and went, sometimes in the flash of a second, had been the heightening of his senses. Unexpectedly, shadows could glare, whispers could shout. He could barely tolerate perfume and cologne, and he'd given up spicy foods entirely. And touch . . . it seemed the strangest sense of all. He could sometimes imagine what something felt like without ever touching it. Conversely, he sometimes felt that he was being touched, when it was an impossibility. For instance, now he could swear he felt the starlight warming his bare chest.

Roan groaned. Was he losing his mind? No, he'd just experienced a trauma. A severe trauma. Nearly drowning would unnerve anyone, and nerves that were agitated took a while to calm down. If Stewart, acting more as his doctor than his friend, had let him go back to work when he'd wanted to, all of this could have been minimized. As it was, he'd had too much time to think. That was all there was to it. And the memories of floating out of his body, of dark tunnels, of white-bright lights were all part of some elaborate hallucination. What else could they possibly have been?

He knew what some of his colleagues would say, that he'd had a near-death experience, but he didn't believe in all that bunk. There was no real evidence to support it. When you died, you died. It was that simple. Hadn't he seen hundreds of patients draw their last breaths? And there had been nothing particularly noble or glorious about their dying. Certainly nothing mysterious and otherworldly. They had simply ceased to exist.

And as for God, well, all he could say was that atheism had served him well up to this point. Atheism, the religion of logicians, pragmatists, those who had the courage to tell it like it was. Sacrilege aside, he himself was the closest thing he knew to a god. In fact, he was descended from a long line of surgical deities. Both his grandfather and his father had been surgeons. Their temple was the operating room, their altar the operating table. They were the givers of life, not some shadowy God that got his kicks from hanging out in bright lights.

And yet, try as hard as he could to forget, he remembered the exquisite sense of peace that had come over him, an all-encompassing, all-pervasive peace.

There is yet something you must do before you can cross over.

Roan felt rather than heard the words. They blew across his memory like a gentle breeze traipsing across an arid desert. What did they mean? Roan wished that he could decipher the enigmatic message.

What he longed for most, however, was the one thing he'd somehow lost. Somewhere along the way, during the climactic course of the accident, he'd forfeited that which was most precious to him: control. It was how he wielded power, how he survived, how he manipulated his stressful, larger-than-life life. In the operating room, control was crucial. The lives of his patients depended on it. And no one was better at it than he. He controlled his mind when concentration was needed. He controlled his emotions when those about him were falling apart. He controlled his fatigue-ridden body when his hands threatened to shake. Stewart teased him about being a mere mortal, but the truth was that he couldn't afford to be human.

And yet, in Mexico he'd been all too human. For one brief moment, it seemed as if he'd died like any mortal man. No, he thought with his typical arrogance, even then he hadn't been mortal. Hadn't he cheated death of its final victory? What, then, had happened to his control? Why did his mind wander? What had happened to his body? What strange force was playing havoc with his senses?

The ringing of the telephone sliced through the silence. With his newfound sensitivity, it sounded like a thousand blaring bells, each vaingloriously trying to outdo the other. Cursing the noise, Roan checked his watch. Damn, he was late! He was never late—how could time have slipped by unnoticed?

He stepped to the phone and grabbed it on the third ring.

"I know, I know," he said without preamble, "I'm late."

There was a slight hesitation, then, "Well, hello to you, too, darling."

The sound of Kay's throaty voice, which always managed to be both church-sweet and motel-sexy, made Roan feel instantly contrite.

"Sorry," he said, brushing back a lock of hair that had fallen onto his forehead.

"Bad day?"

"No," he lied.

"Sounds like one."

"I'm just bored. I want to be in the OR."

"Darling, do I have to remind you that you nearly drowned—"

"No, you don't have to remind me that I nearly drowned. I've been reminded of it on a daily basis all week. And, frankly, I'm pretty sick of it!"

At the hurt silence that met his outburst, Roan could have cut out his tongue. One of the first sights that had greeted him when he'd regained consciousness was that of Kay. Overcome with relief, she'd been unable to speak. She'd simply fallen at his side and cried. He had known all along that she loved him—she'd never made a secret of that—but he hadn't realized the staggering depth of that love. He remembered thinking then, as though the accident had made him more sensitive to her feelings, that she deserved someone better than him, someone who wasn't a self-centered son of a bitch whose first love had always been, and always would be, medicine.

Roan breathed out a tired sigh. "I'm sorry, Kay. I guess it has been a bad day. Hell, it's been a bad week!"

Always understanding, she said, "If you don't want to go tonight, I'll call Stewart—"

"No, we'll go," Roan said, adding the blatant falsehood, "I want to."

Stewart had called earlier in the day to announce that he'd made reservations for dinner at a can't-get-in-without-being-on-a-waiting-list restaurant in the heart of the city. It had been an impromptu decision, the kind Stewart was the best in the world at making. Roan hadn't asked how Stewart had finagled reservations at the busy restaurant, and on a Saturday night to boot. He'd simply agreed to show up, though in his heart he'd wanted to decline. He just didn't feel up to company.

"Look, give Stewart a call and tell him I'm running late. I'll pick you up within the half hour. Okay?"

Another hesitation. "Roan, are you sure?"

Transferring the phone to his other ear—her voice had suddenly seemed overloud, though he knew she was speaking normally—he said, "Yeah, I'm sure."

Roan could almost see her lips piqued in naughtiness when she said, "I'm wearing the black dress. Does it give you any ideas?"

Ideas. Images. The vision of a woman dressed in clingy black walking toward him, hips swaying, her sea-green eyes unswervingly on him. The time had been a year before, at a party hosted by the head of

the radiology department. Roan recalled not wanting
to go to the party, but not having a polite out. So he'd
gone, made the required social chitchat, had a couple
of tasteless canapés and as many glasses of a decent
imported wine. It was as the wineglass was tipped at
his lips that he first noticed the woman staring at him.
And she was staring, openly. Roan did what any red-
blooded American male would have: he stared back.
Just as openly.

The game had begun.

Over the next hour the two of them watched each
other, stalked each other, made blatant sexual over-
tures, though not a single word was exchanged. He
later learned that her name was Kay Regan, that she
was the socialite daughter of one of the state's wealth-
iest oil men, that she'd been married at the age of
nineteen and divorced at twenty, and that she, now
twenty-nine, worked out religiously in the health spa
she owned, which was the reason she kept her blond
hair cropped close to her head. On anyone else the
cut might have appeared mannish, but not on the
curvaceous woman who finally crossed the room and
walked toward him.

"Would you like to take me home?" she queried.

"I thought you'd never ask," Roan replied.

"I've been asking for the last hour. I thought you'd
never answer."

Putting down his glass, he silently took her elbow
and escorted her from the house. Still without a word,
he assisted her into his sporty two-seat 500 SL. As they
roared through the hot Texas night, the wind blowing in their faces and through their hair, they once
more played their sensual game. The only thing that
was said en route was the location of her apartment,
which turned out to be in a nice but not ostentatious
area. When they arrived, still speaking only with their

eyes, they moved from car to apartment. Inserting the key in the lock, Kay led the way inside, but, before she could even reach for the light switch, Roan followed her in, closed the door behind him, and backed her up against it. His lips slammed into hers.

What happened next was indelibly etched in Roan's memory. They didn't even make it to the bedroom. They screwed right there in the living room, with their clothes on, he impaling her against the hard wood of the door. When it was over, and it had been quickly because each was hotter than a noonday sun in the prime of summer, the black dress was bunched around her waist and she still clutched the apartment key in her hand. They laughed and introduced themselves.

Later that night over coffee, she told him that she'd never done anything like that before. As naive as it seemed, he believed her. There was something about her pale green eyes that didn't lie. She'd seen him, wanted him, gone after him. He understood and appreciated that kind of forthrightness. And the forthrightness that had followed.

"Are you married?" she asked as the oyster-pink sun crept into the sky.

"Yes," he answered and was impressed by the fact that her face showed no reaction. She was ready to pay the piper for this stolen night with no sentimental regrets. It was yet another thing about her that he admired. "To medicine," he added. This time, he did see a twinge, but nothing more than a twinge, of relief.

She shrugged her bare shoulders—they were in bed, the black dress lying forgotten across a chair—and said, "I can stand the competition. What do you want to bet, Dr. Jacob, that before the year is out, you'll be married . . . to me?"

Roan was wise enough not to bet against determined green eyes. And, as it turned out, he would have lost had he. The two-carat flawless diamond on her hand and the wedding planned for the end of June were proof of that.

"Roan?"

At those times when he was honest with himself, he had to admit he had mixed feelings about marriage. He hadn't lied when he'd said he was wed to his work, and he knew that, try as hard as he would, Kay always gave and he always took.

"Roan?"

He knew he wasn't being fair to her. Even Kay occasionally complained that the emotional detachment he needed to perform as a surgeon bled over into his personal life. It was as though he kept a part of him only unto himself.

"Darling, are you there?"

Her voice filtered through to his consciousness, and he was surprised to find himself still on the phone. Such vagueness in the face of his usual clarity of thought troubled him anew.

"Yeah, I'm here," he said.

"Well, does it give you any ideas?"

"What?"

"The black dress. Darling, are you sure you're all right?"

The black dress. Now he remembered. And as it always did, the thought of it aroused him.

"I'm all right," he said, adding, "And, yes, the black dress gives me some very definite ideas."

Kay responded with a provocative, "Good."

Seconds later, as Roan hung up the phone, her sexy voice still ringing in his ears, he decided he was being foolish. Exceedingly so. A night of good loving—and Kay was good at it—was exactly what he needed to right a very wrong week. If anything, he should be rejoicing, not moping about. He'd almost died, for God's sake, but he hadn't. He was alive, thanks to his good friends. And there was nothing wrong with him except the emotional aftermath of the trauma. Any psychiatrist would agree. Furthermore, he'd go back to the hospital Monday morning and then his life would return to normal. Come Monday, he'd be back in control.

Right?

Fucking-A!

Within thirty minutes he'd dressed in navy-blue slacks and a matching blazer and was on his way out. He felt better than he had all week. He conveniently ignored the pile of clean shirts lying on his bed, all discarded until he'd found one whose starched precision he could withstand next to his sensitive skin. He also ignored the fact that he didn't touch the expensive cologne sitting on his dresser. And the fact that the claret-red silk walls seemed to scream—literally—with color.

Two

Roan had always heard that one should be grateful for small favors. Never had he so fully appreciated the sentiment as he did on the drive to the restaurant. Had he not been behind the wheel of a convertible, he was uncertain he would have survived. Even so, the smell of Kay's perfume swirled ruthlessly about his raw senses.

Just as annoying was the way that Kay constantly touched him. He hated himself for feeling as he did, but it didn't change the fact that he resented her continual stroking, caressing, fondling. He particularly hated himself for the intolerance because he understood the source of Kay's need. Ever since the accident, she'd needed to touch him, to feel him, to verify that he was, indeed, alive. The need was human enough, honest enough. Even flattering. And humbling. Why then couldn't he cut her some slack?

He knew the reason. It was because of the changes within *himself*. The inexplicable changes. Like her perfume, her touch now felt heavy, cloying, even suffocating, and it made him feel . . . He wasn't quite sure how it made him feel. Certainly it was in no way that made any sense. The best he could describe it was lonely. Her touch made him feel lonely, as if a part of him were missing, as if a part of him needed completing, but rather than finding the missing part of him, rather than completing him, her touch served only to point out, tauntingly, an emptiness he hadn't felt before.

To the contrary, he'd always seemed full—full of himself. Case in point: at their engagement six months before, Kay had wanted to move in with him. He'd hedged, reminding her that his hours were irregular. Would they be any more regular once they were married? Kay had asked. Well, no, he'd admitted, but . . . The list of buts had gone on and on and on until Kay had had her feelings thoroughly hurt and Roan had been annoyed—not with Kay, but with himself. Why did he insist on shutting part of himself away, as though to disclose too much would somehow lessen him or, perhaps, destroy him altogether? Even when she'd given him a key to her apartment, he hadn't been able to reciprocate, leaving her hurt once more, though she hadn't said a word, and him wondering once more why he clung so tenaciously to his privacy.

The accident had revived this tender, touchy issue. Upon returning home from Cozumel the day after the accident, Kay had started in again about moving in with him. The wedding, after all, was only weeks away. Besides, he didn't need to be alone right now. In truth, it was Kay who hadn't needed to be alone, but Roan hadn't pointed that out, although he had insisted he was fine and that, if he wasn't going to spend the week at the hospital, he needed to catch up on the medical reading he never seemed to have time for. She'd be bored. Trust him. Furthermore, he'd added in an attempt at levity, he couldn't risk her finding out what a lousy housemate he was going to be before he'd legally ensnared her.

Kay hadn't been placated.

Roan hadn't given in.

So Kay had had to settle for inventing excuses to touch him, which Roan had had to let her do. Granted, he could be a jerk, but not even he could be that big a one.

"Roan, you're not even listening to me."

Glancing over at her, he lied and said, "Of course I am."

"What did I say then?" she challenged.

Roan had no idea. If he was going to be shot the next minute, he couldn't have told her, but with bravado he faked an answer. "That the groom's cake is going to be chocolate."

"That was five minutes ago. Really, Roan, where have you been?"

He had no idea about that, either. His mind just roamed at will, leaving him to catch up as best he could.

"I said," she added excitedly, the subject too important to play immature games about, "that I found this marvelous black negligee. I thought under the circumstances that black might be appropriate for the honeymoon. What do you think?"

What he thought was that the hand on his thigh tightened, suggestively. In seconds he didn't have to think but knew with complete certainty that the hand was moving upward toward his crotch. In the past he would have welcomed such sexual intimacy, but now he surprised himself by intercepting her hand and intertwining their fingers. She accepted the action as a positive vote for the black negligee. She didn't seem to notice that she'd been stayed in her erotic quest.

Nor had she seemed to notice the blandness of the kiss they'd shared earlier. More than participating in it, Roan had merely, passively, allowed her to kiss him. The truth was that, though he'd wanted to feel his usual passion and desire for her, he'd felt nothing. He might just as well have been kissing a relative. His lack of response was yet one more thing to baffle him, to trouble him.

"It's sheer," Kay said, "and it has all this gooey lace and satin and the most sinful slit right up the front."

He tried to imagine her in the gown, could, and felt the image stir his libido in a purely masculine way. Relief flooded him. "Sounds sexy."

"You think I ought to get it?"

"I think you ought to get it. Maybe even two of them."

She laughed, a throaty, sultry sound. "You need only one gown to take off."

Roan squeezed her hand, realizing as he did so that he felt like his old self. It was a damned good feeling. So good, in fact, that the second he parked the car in the restaurant lot and shut off the motor, he reached for Kay, pulled her to him, and planted a kiss on her shiny fire-engine-red mouth. He opened his lips wide, coaxing Kay's to follow. His tongue sought hers; hers sought his. He kissed her hard, as though to punish her for not making him respond earlier, as though to punish himself for the same transgression. By the time he pulled his mouth from hers, he realized that her perfume was no longer bothering him. The overreaction of his senses came and went, without rhyme or reason, without the slightest hint of why or how. With optimism flowing in his veins, Roan found it easy to believe that he could keep it from returning again. After all, wasn't he the man with the steel-plated control?

"What was that for?" Kay asked breathlessly.

"A deposit, on the end of the evening," he said, flinging wide his car door and adding, "C'mon, let's go. I'm suddenly starved."

Before he could get out of the car, however, Kay grabbed his arm. She had a dead-earnest look on her face. "Roan . . . " She hesitated, then said, "You *are* all right, aren't you?" Without giving him a chance to answer, she said, "I couldn't stand it if you weren't all right. When I thought you had drowned, I . . . " Her voice trailed off as her eyes misted with tears.

Roan cradled her cheek with his palm. He felt a tear slip onto the back of his hand.

"I'm all right, Kay," he said, moved by the depth of her feelings. He envied her, because she had just forced him to face a truth he guessed he'd known all along: He simply did not have her capacity to love. And, clearer yet, he understood that it was infinitely more important to love than to be loved. For only in loving was the empty heart filled.

Mark Hagen, lank and lean, was physically the most unattractive person Roan had ever seen. At least that was what Roan had thought at their first meeting six years before. Now, however, instead of his acne-scarred face, limbs that seemed monkey-proportioned, and hair that was a soiled yellow-white, Roan saw only his brilliant mind, his generous spirit, and his quick wit. He was a damned good person, a damned good friend, and a damned good doctor. In fact, he was the best oncologist on staff at the hospital; many said, and Roan believed, that he was one of the best in the country.

Mark's wife, Susan, was uncommonly attractive, with short curly black hair, a bobbed nose, and a doll-like stature. She adored her husband, every bit as much as he adored he. They were the only truly happily married couple that Roan knew, which frightened Roan more than a little, particularly since he himself was about to take the plunge.

In diametric opposition to both these relatively quiet personalities was flamboyant Stewart Kesterson. Broad-shouldered, with a stomach seriously thinking about spreading into a paunch, the ob-gyn was, as his friends readily attested, a one-of-a-kind original. No one lived life any harder than ole Stew K. Nor did anyone break more rules. He cheated on the golf course, smoked like a chimney, and womanized outrageously. His current interest was Jacqueline Orantas—Jackie O.—a brunette from the ER. She was competent, pleasant, and pleasing to the eye, with more curves than a twisting roadway, all of which the hot-pink bikini she'd worn in Cozumel had blatantly revealed.

Mark, Susan, Stewart, and Jackie came into view as Roan, with Kay close at his side, walked into the restaurant. The four sat chatting at a small knees-together table in the bar. Jackie O. looked about ready to spill out of a daringly cut sapphire-blue dress.

"Gee," Kay said under her breath, "I wonder what two things Stewart sees in her."

Such catty comments were so unlike Kay that Roan glanced over at her with a raised eyebrow. "You don't like her?"

"A small-breasted woman never trusts a big-breasted woman. It's a fact of life."

Roan grinned. It had been so long since he had that it actually hurt. The hurt felt good, though. The positive mood that had begun minutes before in the car had been reinforced at the sight of his friends and at Kay's deliciously malicious remark. He was suddenly glad that Stewart had forced him to accept an offer of an evening out. It was precisely what the doctor ordered.

"I'm not a tit man. You know that," Roan remarked

as they started toward the foursome.

"Well, it's a good thing, isn't it?"

Stewart was the first to see them coming. When he did, he stood. "It's about damned time!" he said, slapping Roan on the back and kissing Kay's cheek. "Where the hell you two been?"

"Sorry we're late," Roan said. "It was my fault. Time got away from me."

"Time got away from *you?*" Mark asked. "I thought they called you each day to set Big Ben."

"Yeah, well, they didn't today," Roan said, absently running his finger around the stiff, starched collar of his red-striped shirt.

"Well, you're here now," sweet-eyed Susan said, adding, "I love your dress, Kay."

Kay smiled and tightened the possessive hold she had on Roan's arm. "Thanks. It's one of Roan's favorites, isn't it, darling?"

"Yeah," he said, glancing quickly into her eyes and lowering the hand at her waist until it rested with just a hint of intimacy on the beginning swell of her hips. The gesture was familiar, pleasant, making Roan feel that whatever had been out of kilter heretofore was righting itself.

Brown-haired Jackie had just started to scoot her chair around so that two others could be added when Stewart halted her. "Let's go on to the table. They're holding it for us." This he said as he flagged down the maitre d', spoke a few quiet words to him, then added to the others, "C'mon. The table's ready."

"I won't ask how you got last-minute reservations here on a Saturday night," Kay said as the six of them trooped into the dining area. "Or how you got them to hold a table."

"Barter," Stewart answered. "I scratch their backs, they scratch mine."

"Which translates," Mark said, "to he promised a free Pap test to the maitre d's significant other."

Everyone laughed, but Roan wasn't sure that there wasn't some truth to the comment. There had to be a logical explanation for the impossible feats that his friend accomplished.

Seconds after they were seated, the waiter asked what he could bring them to drink. Stewart took the lead. "We'll have a bottle of your best champagne."

"Yes, sir," replied the man, who wore a tuxedo and a crisp white shirt.

"What's the occasion?" Jackie asked.

"Just want to pay tribute to the gathering of friends," Stewart answered.

"Can't think of a better reason," Mark commented.

"Works for me," Susan added.

Roan knew that the events of the preceding week had inspired Stewart's gesture. After what had happened, or nearly happened, a celebration of friendship seemed appropriate. Roan also knew that Stewart wouldn't want a sappy display of emotions. Any more than he did.

"So how are you feeling?" Susan asked Roan, proving that the near-drowning was still very much on everyone's mind.

"Great," he added, unknowingly rimming his collar again.

"What did you do this week?" Mark asked.

"Grumble," Roan replied. "I wanted to be in the OR."

"I take it that as a patient he left something to be desired," Stewart said, directing his remarks to Kay, who sat between him and Roan.

"Actually, I don't really know," Kay said softly, her eyes uncharacteristically avoiding Roan's. "You know how Roan is. He doesn't like anyone pampering him."

Roan heard the hurt in her voice and wondered if anyone else did. Obviously she hadn't forgotten their discussion about moving in. But then, had he really thought she had? Once more, he felt like the heel of the year. Running his arm along the back of her chair, he drew a single finger along her shoulder blade.

"I can't risk running her off before the wedding," he said.

Kay said nothing, though no one seemed to notice the strain that had sprung up between them. Roan made a mental note to send her flowers, then thought better of it. Kay wasn't the type of woman to be bought off.

Thankfully—at least Roan was thankful for the diversion—the waiter chose that moment to reappear with the champagne. After allowing Stewart a taste test, the waiter filled the champagne glasses and iced down the bottle in a long-legged brass bucket.

"Toast," Roan declared, and everyone gave him their full attention. Again, not wanting to be melodramatic, he said simply, "To good friends . . . who're there when you need them most."

"Hear, hear," Stewart said.

"I'll drink to that," Mark said.

Glasses tinkled together, the sound of human communion, the sound of fine crystal speaking an age-old conversation. As though the toast had caused her fear to resurface, Kay slid her hand onto Roan's thigh. Roan noted it as he brought the glass to his lips.

He sipped.

The tawny-colored champagne exploded upon his tongue in a way that no champagne ever had before. Bubbles burst forth with a purity, a clarity that was astonishing but frightening in its strength, frightening in the way it took him prisoner, for he seemed unable to focus on anything else. He could taste the wine's dryness, a crisp sharpness that stabbed at his senses. Lacing that was the fruity flavor of sweet grapes and, unbelievably, the warmth of the sun that had ripened them to maturity. He could taste the sun's warmth! Yet the wine felt not cool, but glacier-cold. A frigid, fermented cold.

He swallowed.

Instantly, like a bolt of lightning, and with the same sure power, the sip of champagne rushed to his head, causing it to feel as light and airy as fluffy, floating clouds. The only thing he could compare the swift action to was the intravenous injection of a potent, mind-altering drug. And then he couldn't compare it to anything, because he suddenly grew tipsy, as in fuzzy-headed, wobbly-kneed drunk. He wasn't so drunk, however, that he didn't know that what was happening was totally abnormal.

But then, all week has been abnormal, he heard a voice in his woozy head remind him.

Yeah, well, another voice answered, *this was our first brush with liquor. Who would have thought . . . thought . . . thought . . .*

Abruptly, with the same speed that his mind had clouded, it cleared.

"Are you all right, darling?" Kay whispered.

Roan glanced around quickly to see if anyone else at the table shared her concern. No, thank God. No one was paying him the least attention. They were caught up in some hospital story that Stewart was telling.

"I'm fine," Roan whispered, setting the glass back on the table and wondering how he was going to get out of drinking any more of the champagne.

"So, how're the wedding plans coming?" Susan asked Kay.

Predictably, the question was one of Kay's favorites, leaving no room for her to think about anything else, not even something that might have concerned her seconds before. She smiled. "Great. The church is all arranged—"

"Church?" Mark asked. "Don't tell me the heathen has consented to a church wedding."

Fingering the stem of the glass, Roan cautioned, "Don't make more out of this than it is."

"Where's the reception going to be?" Susan asked.

"At the country club," Kay said. "Nothing real elaborate, just something small and intimate."

"If you call a thousand people small and intimate," Roan interjected.

Kay elbowed him playfully. "There're not a thousand people invited."

"Excuse me. Nine hundred ninety-nine," Roan conceded.

Everyone laughed.

"What about your parents?" Stewart asked Roan. "Will they be able to make it?"

Roan's parents lived in Atlanta, where his father had only recently retired from medicine.

"Oh, yeah," Roan said, still fingering the glass, "you don't think they'd let their only child get married without them, do you?"

"To the almost newlyweds," Mark said.

"Hear, hear," Susan said, and Stewart added, "Though why in heaven's name Kay wants the arrogant bastard is beyond me."

Everyone laughed and began to clink glasses. Roan had no option but to join in. So he picked up the glass, tapped it first here then there, and brought it to his lips. He braced himself, even though the sip he took was minuscule.

Nothing.

Nothing happened, except a cool, effervescent taste tingling across his tongue. Emboldened, he took another swallow. This one, too, tasted precisely as it should. No, wait, a tiny delayed kick, but none of the woozy, drunk feeling he'd experienced earlier. As always, whatever the bizarre something was, it had passed. Relieved, he settled back in his chair.

"You should have been at the staff meeting yesterday," Stewart began and held center stage for the next few minutes as he related how two doctors had almost come to blows.

Roan smiled in the appropriate places, or hoped he did, and occasionally took a sip of champagne, mostly to see if it tasted normal: it did. Occasionally, however, there was a second's worth of a buzz, which wasn't altogether unpleasant.

"So these two guys were getting ready to go at it when . . ."

Roan heard the steady, quiet drone of Stewart's voice. The voice receded, as though traveling through a tunnel, then drifted back in full force. The variance didn't disturb Roan, though, for he'd begun to feel warm and fuzzy and wonderfully tranquil. He took another sip.

Roan blinked to steady the image of Stewart. His friend had blurred slightly but quickly jumped back into focus. Maybe he needed to get his eyes tested, Roan thought. He took another sip of the cool, bubbly wine. It wasn't tasting half bad by now.

"Kepler told them to stuff it or take it outside?" Stewart went on.

Right.

Left.

Had his hands begun to tremble? Roan wondered, setting the glass back on the table. Yes. No. Maybe. What did it matter? What mattered was that this shirt was scratching the hell out of him. Without any thought of how it would look, he loosened the tie and unfastened the first button of the shirt. It took more than one attempt because his hand was shaking. He could feel the red chafe marks ringing his neck. They felt hot, as though he'd been branded.

"Naturally, we all followed them out into the hall-way," Stewart intoned.

Stewart's voice sounded as though it came from some faraway mountaintop. There were other sounds, too—the muted clanking of silverware and china, the muffled notes of countless conversations blending into a quiet, surreal symphony. And there were dozens of smells—food, flowers, a mélange of perfumes. The sounds and the smells mingled eerily until Roan could no longer tell one sense from another. He smelled the voices; he heard the fragrances. Stewart's voice smelled like the dark-roasted coffee being served around him, while Kay's perfume sounded like the solitary whippoorwill he'd heard earlier that evening.

Was he drunk?

Maybe.

For the buzzing in his ears had grown louder, and his head felt as light as a helium-filled balloon.

"So there they stood near the elevators," Stewart said, adding, "You're going to love this, Roan . . ."

Roan heard his name, tried to focus in Stewart's direction, but instead found his attention drawn to a woman three tables away. She was middle-aged, brunette, not beautiful but attractive. She was smiling at the man beside her. The man was her husband. Roan had no idea how he knew, but he did. Roan also knew that, despite the smile, the woman was sad. Her husband was having an affair, and the woman didn't know what to do about it. The husband felt guilt, an overwhelming guilt. He wanted to tell his wife that the affair was over. He wanted to beg her forgiveness, but he was afraid. Roan could feel the woman's sadness, the man's guilt and fear, as if they were his own. They felt heavy on his heart. Heavy and hurtful.

Roan would have gotten up and gone to the couple, but at that moment his head swirled, as though a troupe of dervishes were dancing inside his skull—dancing, prancing, whirling to the shrill beat of silent music. Another feeling, this one happy, intruded. Roan raised his head, seeking the source of this brightness. It came from a man halfway across the room. He was happy about some big business deal. Happy and hungry.

Suddenly, Roan was bombarded with feelings. The woman across the way was pleased about a pregnancy, someone else was grieving, another person was excited about a loved one that he'd soon see. Even at his own table, Roan began to pick up emotional vibrations. These flew at him like bats out of a black night. Mark and Susan were happy, at peace, enviously content with their lives. Kay was in love with him, deeply, abidingly. Jackie O. was hot and bothered and wondered what he—Roan—was like in bed. Stewart was in love. Stewart in love? Even in Roan's drunken state, the unexpectedness of this find made an impression. With whom? he wondered. Jackie O.? No, Kay. The realization came softly, sweetly, surprisingly.

He wanted to consider this last, but emotions were now coming from everywhere, from everyone, each piling on top of the other, each entering his body, his spirit, conversely filling him and draining him with its intensity. It hurt because he cared. He cared about these people's feelings, especially those who were suffering.

Stop, he thought.

"So there they stood near the elevators," Stewart

repeated, "with the doors opening and closing and Littleton choking Graves with his stethoscope."

Please stop, Roan begged.

"I swear to God he was choking him with his stethoscope!"

Stop! Roan screamed silently as the emotions tore at his senses.

Laughter erupted around the table.

Dammit, I said . . .

" . . . stop!"

The slurred word doused the laughter. Five pairs of eyes were instantly riveted on Roan. One by one, surprise claimed each viewer.

"Stop," Roan repeated at the same time he tried to stand. His knees buckled, though, and he fell back into the chair, knocking over the glass of champagne as he did.

Kay gasped.

Susan cried out.

Mark and Stewart rose in tandem.

People at the nearby tables glanced over.

Stewart reached Roan first.

"Make 'em stop," Roan said.

"Make what stop?" Stewart asked

" . . . inmyhead," he said, slurring the words together.

"Good Lord, he's drunk!" Mark said.

"He can't be," Stewart said. "He didn't even have a full glass of champagne."

"Drunk?" Roan seized the word. "Am I drunk?"

"Easy," Stewart said when Roan tried to stand again. Stewart took one elbow, Mark the other, and they assisted Roan to his feet.

"Is there a problem?" asked the waiter, who'd appeared suddenly.

"No problem," Mark said. "Our friend's just not feeling well."

"Let's get him outside," Stewart said. "He needs some air."

"Air? Ineedair. Kay?" Roan said, catching sight of her. He wanted to tell her to make the feelings go away, but the confusion in his head left him unable to find the words he wanted.

"I'm here, darling," she said calmly, though her expression was one of concern. Snatching her purse, she said to the two men, "Let's go." Kay led the way while Mark and Stewart, struggling with Roan, followed closely behind. Susan and Jackie brought up the rear of the solemn group. Roan knew only that he seemed to be propelled along, as though skimming the surface of water. The feelings still crushed him with their weight—sadness and happiness, fear and excitement all mixed together. Suddenly, as he passed through the dining area and out into the foyer, which was empty, the feelings disappeared, fled as though they'd never come.

Gone, he tried to mumble, but he was uncertain he made a sound. Maybe the thought had just rolled around in his alcohol-thick mind. Drunk. Was he drunk? But he never drank to excess. He hadn't been drunk since . . . He couldn't even remember the last time he'd been drunk, leading him to reason, as best he could, that he was drunker than he thought.

In the end, because it was doubtful that Kay could manage Roan alone, they decided that Stewart would drive the Mercedes, Kay would drive Stewart's car, and Mark and Susan would take Jackie home. En route to his condo, Roan passed out, reviving only as Stewart carried him, almost literally, into the house.

"Sorry, buddy," Stewart said as he ran Roan into a wall.

Roan moaned.

Once in the red-and-black bedroom, Stewart eased

Roan onto the side of the bed and began unbuckling his belt. Flinging her purse aside, indenting the mattress with a black-stockinged knee, Kay loosened the already-loose tie and started unbuttoning his shirt. As she dragged it from his shoulders, which was a difficult job at best since Roan kept slumping over, she noticed the red ring around his neck.

"What's this?"

Stewart looked up from where he was squatting on the floor. He'd just removed Roan's shoes and socks. Standing, he investigated the welted area by running the pad of his thumb over it.

"Looks like the shirt scratched it. Probably too much starch." Dismissing the subject as though it were nothing of any real importance, Stewart said, "Okay, buddy, let's stand up where we can get these pants off, then tuck you in." As he was trying to hold Roan and turn back the bed, Stewart first noticed the mile-high pile of shirts in the bed's middle. "What the hell?"

With a rake of her hand Kay scraped them to the floor, then helped Stewart settle Roan, who now wore only cotton knit underwear, between the sheets.

As she pulled the cover midway to his bare, hair-dusted chest, Roan opened his eyes. Seeing Kay—actually, he saw two of her—he said, "Light. Bright light."

Thinking that he meant the overhead light, she shut it off, leaving only the light from the hallway to illuminate the room.

"No," Roan mumbled. "The light . . . bright . . . died. I died."

"Don't think about it, darling. It's over. You're all right."

"You . . . don't . . . .understand. There's something I must do . . . " As he spoke, Roan tried to sling the covers from him and attempted to sit up.

"No, darling," Kay said, urging him back, "you can do whatever it is tomorrow."

"No . . . I have to do something . . . before I can cross over."

"Easy, buddy," Stewart said, restraining Roan.

"Stewart?" Roan said, as though just realizing his friend was there.

"Yeah, it's me. Why don't you just go on to sleep?"

"I think I'm drunk," Roan announced.

"I think you are, too."

"Stewart?"

"Yeah?"

"It's okay."

"Yeah, it's okay."

"It's okay about Kay."

"Fine. Go on to sleep."

"What did he mean?" Kay asked.

Stewart shrugged. "I don't know."

In minutes, Roan's even breathing filled the room.

"He's out like a light," Stewart said as the two of them stood at the bedside. "You're going to stay with him, aren't you?"

"Yeah," Kay answerd, not voicing her belief that Roan probably wouldn't like it.

Stewart nodded. "C'mon, walk me to the door."

As the two of them started down the hallway, Kay said, "He is all right, isn't he?"

"He's just drunk."

"But how can he be drunk? He didn't have even a full glass of champagne. And he hadn't had anything earlier."

"I don't know," he said, wondering the same thing and trying to placate both Kay and himself by adding, "Except that liquor affects people differently."

"But it's never—"

"Kay." Stewart turned as he reached the door and placed both hands on her shoulders. "Will you stop worrying?"

She smiled. "Yes, sir."

"Now, try to get some sleep yourself."

Leaning into him, she kissed his cheek before saying, "What would I do without you?"

Stewart's dark eyes darkened even more, but he said nothing. He simply tightened his fingers, then slid them quickly—as though if he didn't do it quickly, he wouldn't do it at all—from her shoulders. Once on the porch, he turned around and said a hasty, "Call me if you need me," and then he was gone.

Kay watched him climb into his car, watched the headlights flash on, watched the taillights disappear into the night. She closed the door. Quietly, shutting the lights off behind her, except for the one in the hallway, she stepped back to the bedroom. Roan was still sleeping. On a sigh, she sat down in a claret-and-black plaid chair, eased out of her black heels, and laid her head back. She was suddenly aware that the front of her dress, the black dress she'd had such high hopes for, was wet and smelled of champagne. She was aware, too, of a great heaviness in her heart. Something was wrong. Something was very wrong. And she hadn't the least idea what that something was.

$\mathcal{T}$HREE

Roan awoke with a blinding headache. He couldn't remember ever having a hangover of this magnitude. The closest he'd come to it was back in college, when he and a half dozen guys had decided to celebrate a Texas A&M football victory. He'd drunk until the wee hours of the morning, puked his guts up, and passed out. Even then, though, when he'd come to, he hadn't felt this bad. After nearly a bottle of whiskey, he hadn't felt as bad as he did this morning after only a single glass of champagne. He vaguely remembered spilling the champagne, so he couldn't have consumed even a full glass.

He couldn't recall exactly why he'd spilled the champagne. No, wait. Some crazy thing had happened to him, he realized as he pushed up against the bed's headboard. The sitting position made his head swim. His head swim? Now he remembered. As though he'd been some sort of receptor, he'd picked up on all the emotions seemingly scurrying around the restaurant. There'd been a woman whose husband was having an affair, another who'd just found out that she was pregnant. He'd even felt his friends' emotions—Mark's and Susan's happiness, Jackie's lust, Kay's love for him, Stewart's love for Kay.

My God, what was happening to him? he wondered, ramming his fingers through his hair and plowing up what felt like exposed nerves. He winced.

"Well, I guess I don't need to ask how you feel," Kay said softly, appearing at his side with a steaming mug of coffee.

Roan jerked his head upward, sending fireworks sparking inside his head. He hadn't realized he wasn't alone, though he supposed he should have. Kay wouldn't have left him in the condition he was in, especially since she wanted so desperately to stay with him. Even if he hadn't realized that, he should have noticed that the other side of the bed had been slept in and that her clothes were strewn about the room. Barefoot, she was wearing the emerald-green silk robe she'd given him for Christmas.

"Here," she said as she passed him the mug.

The thought of swallowing anything was nauseous, but then again he was nauseated anyway, so what the hell?

"Thanks," he mumbled, molding his fingers around the warm porcelain and forcing down a sip. His stomach turned over in rejection. To show it who was boss, Roan took another swallow. This resulted in a gag. Properly chastised, he set the mug on the bedside table and, angling his knee, rested his elbow on it and simply held his head.

"So, how *do* you feel?"

"Don't ask," he said, trying to speak without moving his lips. Even that little bit of motion hurt, from the top of his head to the bottom of his feet.

"That bad, huh?"

"That bad."

As she spoke, Kay moved about the bedroom, gathering up their clothes.

"You don't have to pick up my things," he said.

"I know, but I don't mind."

Once again, Roan thought that Kay deserved someone who could give her more than he could. Someone like Stewart? Why had he never realized before how Stewart felt about Kay? For that matter, how did he know it now? What had happened last night that had made him privy to people's feelings? It wasn't something that he wanted to experience again. It wasn't—

"What do I do with these?"

Roan glanced up to find Kay holding an armful of shirts. "Just leave them on the floor. They go to the cleaners."

"But they look clean."

"They, uh, they are, but they have too much starch. I've got to have them relaundered."

"Is that what's wrong with your neck?"

For a second, Roan didn't understand the question. His hand went to his throat. His tender, chafed throat.

"Yeah," he said, "the shirt had too much starch." Before she could make any further comment, Roan said, "How did I get home?"

"Stewart drove your car. I drove his. He helped me get you inside and into bed."

Roan nodded. He could imagine the scene all too vividly. He hated the thought that he'd been out of control. He particularly hated that someone else had witnessed it. Like an entire restaurant full of people.

Such troubling thoughts were still rambling through Roan's mind when he realized that Kay had eased onto the side of the bed. When her thigh brushed his, he looked up. He had the feeling that maybe all her straightening of the room had simply been a way of forestalling what she wanted to say but perhaps didn't know how. He saw her searching for the words.

"Roan." She began, hesitated, then said bluntly, "I

don't understand about last night."

Last night was not a subject he wanted to pursue. "What's to understand? I had too much to drink."

"That's just it, you didn't. You didn't even have a glass of champagne. A good half of a glass went on the table and my dress."

Roan's pulse quickened; he heard it tapping in his head. This was not something he wanted to go into. Not when he was feeling like yesterday's garbage. Even if he knew the answers, she was posing questions he wanted to avoid.

"I obviously had enough," he said vaguely. "Look, Kay, I'm sorry I embarrassed you."

Kay's eyes flashed annoyance at the implication that she was concerned about something so petty. "That's not it, and you know it!" Instantly contrite at her outburst, she said softly, "I just want to know what's wrong."

"I don't know what you mean," he said, afraid that he did indeed know.

"Something's wrong. I sense it. You haven't been yourself since the accident."

So she'd noticed. But then, how could he reasonably expect that she hadn't. Still, it wasn't something he wanted to go into. How could he explain what he himself didn't understand?

"Don't you think that nearly drowning"—even as he said it, he wondered why he always phrased it that way; the truth was, he *had* drowned—"is enough to make someone a little less than himself for a while?"

"Of course it is, and I've tried to believe that that was all there was to it, but"—she stood and started pacing the room—"I don't know, you just seem different. I talk to you, but you're not there. You look at me, but you don't see me. You've shut me out. Dammit, Roan, don't shut me out!"

The agony in her voice ripped at his heart. Even so, he couldn't give her what she'd asked for; he couldn't go into what was happening to him. He gave her what he could, however.

"Come here," he said. She hesitated and he patted the bed beside him. Slowly she crossed to him, eased onto the bed, and turned her sea-green eyes to him. "You're right," he said, brushing her cheek with his knuckles, "I have been distracted. And I'm sorry if you've felt left out. I guess the accident shook me up more than I thought, but everything'll be all right now that I'm going back to work. You'll see."

There was conviction in his voice because he believed what he was saying. Medicine, surgery, was the panacea for everything that ailed him. And at moments like this, when he felt in control of his life, he was convinced everything that had happened could be explained away by stress. Well, maybe that didn't explain his inebriation after only a few sips of champagne, but the inebriation could have explained the emotional overload he'd experienced. He'd been drunk and had only thought he'd picked up on the emotions. He forced himself to believe this premise.

"Everything'll be all right," he repeated. "I promise," he added, pulling Kay down beside him. He didn't kiss her, he didn't make love to her, he simply held her. It was enough for Kay, however. And so was his promise. If he said everything would be all right, then it would. She clung to this thought.

Almost as tightly as Roan.

Come Monday morning, Roan was glad he didn't have surgery scheduled. He felt washed out, as though he hadn't slept well for days, which, in fact, he hadn't, unless being snockered into a comatose state qualified as sleep. He no longer had a hangover, though his mind still wasn't as sharp, as clear, as he liked—as he demanded—for surgery. Fortunately he had a day filled with consultations, including one with a wealthy, influential Arab businessman who'd flown to Houston solely to see him about bypass surgery. Purportedly the man wouldn't let another doctor touch him. Roan didn't blame him. If he were the man, neither would he.

God, it felt good to be back! Roan thought as he walked the hospital's white-walled corridor en route to his office.

"Hey, Roan," a cohort called out, "good to see you."

"Thanks," Roan acknowledged and opened the door of his office.

Though small, his office was efficiently arranged and tastefully decorated in forest green and shrimp pink. A massive desk ornamented with scrolls sat in the back half of the room, with only a brass lamp, a floral arrangement, a telephone, and a photograph of Kay on its surface. He hated clutter, on his desk or in his life. He had just started reading through a massive stack of messages when there was a brisk rap of knuckles on the door seconds before it opened.

James Kepler, chief of staff of the hospital, stuck his head in. "Busy?"

Though only middle-aged—he couldn't have been more than forty-five, forty-six, Roan thought—James Kepler had a full head of cloud-white hair. He also had a noticeable limp, the result of his heroic service in Vietnam. There were those who didn't like the chief of staff because he was too regimented, too fixed, too conservative, in his thinking. He was a man who would never change his mind once it was made up. Roan liked him, though, mainly because he was fair and honest and dedicated both to medicine and to the running of a prestigious hospital. As to Dr. Kepler's feelings for him, Roan had always suspected that the man admired his surgical skills but didn't much care for him on a personal basis. Roan's guess would be that his superior thought him just a little too cocky.

"No," Roan answered, "just going through my messages."

Dr. Kepler limped in. "How're you doing?"

"Fine. Now that I'm back."

The man smiled. "I wondered if you weren't chafing at the bit."

Roan smiled, thinking that the good doctor didn't know the half of it. "Let's just say it was a long week."

"Well, I won't keep you. Just wanted to tell you that we're glad you're back and that everything worked out as it did. That was a damned freaky accident."

"Yeah," Roan said, wondering why the memory of it, instead of fading, only seemed to grow brighter, like the radiant incandescent light into which he'd been drawn. He remembered struggling in the final throes of death, then stepping into some kind of life after death. He remembered a light, a tunnel, silent voices.

There is something you must do before you can cross over.

What? Roan thought, then realized he'd obviously spoken that word aloud, for Dr. Kepler repeated himself.

"I said, have a nice day, and welcome back."

"Thanks," Roan said and watched as the man crossed the room and closed the door. For long seconds Roan sat staring at it. He wondered what his boss would think if he knew that his heart rate, respiration, and blood pressure had not returned to normal following the accident. He wondered what Kepler would think if he knew that perfume drove him crazy, that starched shirts left his neck raw, that he'd gotten skunk-drunk on a fraction of a glass of champagne. He'd probably think what *he* did, Roan surmised— nothing—because he simply wouldn't know what else to think.

The morning passed smoothly. Roan had two consultations, both of which ended in recommendations for surgery. One would entail a mitral valve replacement, the other a simple single bypass. At noon, Roan joined Stewart and Mark in the hospital cafeteria for lunch. It was just like old times, and Roan felt good. More important, he felt in charge of his life once more.

That afternoon at two o'clock he met with Fahid al-Saqqaf, who wore the traditional robelike *thobe,* and the *keffiyeh* and *akal* on his head as he sat across from Roan. Roan didn't even bother to check the chart before him. He'd already committed it to memory. The man was fifty-eight and had no previous history of heart trouble, nor was there any in his family. Two weeks before, however, while on a business trip to Atlanta, he'd suffered chest pain. The man had been hospitalized; tests were run and surgery was recommended. He'd insisted on Roan's performing the surgery.

"As I'm sure you've already been told," Roan began, "you have two minor arterial blockages and one major one."

"That is precisely what I have been told," the man said. Because of an extensive education in the United States, he spoke flawless English.

"The surgery is routine, though of course I'm obligated to tell you that no heart surgery is ever risk-free. For that matter, no surgery is risk-free."

"I understand completely."

"I must also tell you that walking around with this condition is even more risky."

"I am resigned," the man said. "I need to know only when you can perform the surgery."

"I'd like to do it as soon as possible," Roan said, consulting his schedule.

Non-emergency surgeries had been rescheduled from the week before, making his calendar for the second half of the week look crowded. Even as he saw his busy week, adrenaline-filled excitement raced through him. He'd been born for surgery. He liked the pressure, the drama, the way he was called upon to function in a superhuman capacity.

"I have an opening Wednesday afternoon." He looked up to find Fahid al-Saqqaf mopping his perspiration-beaded forehead with an expensive linen handkerchief. To Roan, the room didn't seem particularly hot. "How does that sound?"

"Acceptable," the man replied.

"Fine, I'll call right now and reserve an operating room." As Roan spoke, he reached for the phone and punched in the appropriate extension.

"May I have some water," the man asked, nodding toward a carafe on the nearby counter.

"Of course. Please help yourself."

Fahid al-Saqqaf rose, crossed the room, and poured a glass of water. He took a sip, then another, and then, with the glass still in his hand, he started back to his chair. He stopped midway. The halting action caught Roan's eye, that and the way his face blanched.

"Mr. al-Saqqaf, are you all right?"

The businessman opened his mouth to speak, but nothing came out except a gasp. At the same time, he grasped his chest. The glass dropped from his hand, spilling water all over Roan's oriental rug. Roan noticed nothing except the way Fahid al-Saqqaf, in a macabre slow motion, collapsed onto the floor.

"Call in a code blue!" Roan bellowed into the phone. "My office!"

He didn't wait for a response but slammed the phone down, missing the cradle entirely. In a flash, grabbing his stethoscope, he rounded the desk. He stopped dead in his tracks as a wave of nausea struck him. Then another. That was closely followed by a whirlwindlike dizziness and a weakness that dropped him to his knees. A cold, clammy sweat popped across his brow in seconds. It crossed his mind that he, too, might be having a heart attack, but he dismissed that with what rational thought he had. There was no pain in either his chest or left arm, and his heartbeat was as steady as a rock, as even as a saint's temperament.

In the distance he heard voices and the rush of lifesaving equipment to his office.

Someone shouted, "Hurry!"

Another someone hollered, "Get out of the way!"

The door flew open. Weak, wanting to speak but unable to, Roan watched as the crew took in the scene before him. He saw their surprise, then their shock. Finally, he heard someone rally enough to cry, "Holy shit!"

"I did not have a heart attack!" Roan bellowed three hours later as he sat in James Kepler's over-sized, richly appointed office. "I told everyone I wasn't having one, and I wasn't."

His denial at the time had done Roan no good, however, and he'd been put through a battery of tests guaranteed to make one ill if one wasn't already. Curiously—in fact, it boggled Roan's mind—the symptoms had abated the very moment that Fahid al-

Saqqaf had been wheeled from the room. As long as he wasn't present, Roan was fine.

"Then what do you think happened?" a second voice asked.

Roan shot a glance toward Paul Sandman. The significance of the psychiatrist's presence at the meeting did not escape Roan, any more than the carefully asked question. God, he hated psychiatrists with their wolf questions disguised in sheep's clothing!

"Gee, Paul, I don't know. What do you think happened?"

Paul, whose most notable feature was a pair of ice-blue eyes that could stare down the most obstinate of patients, now peered at Roan. "Well, if you didn't have a heart attack, and you obviously didn't—in fact, your heart seems remarkably strong, although the rate is a little below normal," he said in a voice that was totally unruffled despite Roan's agitation, "well, then I'd say you had some sort of empathetic reaction to this Fahid al-Saqqaf's heart attack."

"What does that mean exactly?" Dr. Kepler asked.

"Some people have the ability to empathize to the point of simulating physical symptoms."

"I didn't simulate his symptoms," Roan threw in. "My symptoms weren't those of a heart attack."

James Kepler ignored Roan. "You mean like a man having labor pains because his wife is having them?"

"Precisely," the psychiatrist said.

"I'm telling you guys that I didn't mimic the heart attack."

The psychiatrist shrugged in response to Roan's statement. "It wouldn't have necessarily had to be an exact mimicking. You could have simply reacted to his suffering with your own individually selected physicality." Before anyone could speak, the psychiatrist added, "While empathizing isn't altogether a common phenomenon, it's not altogether uncommon, either. I've seen mothers in pain because their children were; I've seen men have morning sickness. The truth is that most of us have the ability to empathize to some extent. Most of us can imagine what it's like to lose a loved one, so that when a friend does, we cry along with him."

"Well, you're overlooking one thing," Roan tossed in. "In every scenario you just spoke about, the empath had some relationship with the person in pain. I'd never set eyes on Mr. al-Saqqaf until he walked into my office."

Even as Roan presented his argument, he wasn't sure it carried much weight. He remembered how, at the restaurant Saturday night, he'd reacted to the feelings that he'd picked up on. He'd felt like rejoicing with some people, or sharing others' misery. The point was that he'd cared. He'd cared for people who were total strangers. For that brief moment in time, he'd felt depersonalized, a conduit for others.

Paul Sandman shrugged again. "You've undergone a trauma," he said, adding, his steel-trap eyes caging Roan, "I've even talked to a couple of people who claim to have had near-death experiences—all that lights and tunnels and floating-out-of-your-body business. Both of the people seemed inexplicably attuned to the feelings of others afterward."

This time it wasn't a wolf question but rather a sly statement. Paul Sandman was testing the water, giving Roan the entree he needed to bare his soul. A part of Roan wanted to shout, "Yes, something strange and wonderful and damned scary happened when I drowned, and I want you to help me make some sense out of it," but another part of him, the private part that always had to be in control, said he couldn't risk the disclosure, that it would be the same as admitting he was no longer in the driver's seat of his life. Besides, he didn't believe in all that near-death garbage. And so, Roan met the psychiatrist's gaze openly and fully and said absolutely nothing.

". . . some time off."

James Kepler's words seized Roan's attention. "But I just had some time off."

"I want you to take some more," the chief of staff said.

"I don't need—"

"You're missing the point here, Roan," his boss interrupted. "You don't have a choice."

Roan came out of his chair. "Now wait just a minute—"

"No, you wait just a minute. I have a hospital to run. I have the safety of patients to consider. What if that episode had happened during surgery?"

"But it didn't!" Roan shouted.

"Can you guarantee me that it won't?"

Of course Roan couldn't, and deep in his heart the same thing was worrying him. He'd thought if he could only get back to work, everything would be all right, but the events of the past few hours had proven the inaccuracy of that. Something was wrong. Very wrong. He had lost the detachment necessary to the performance of his job. And yet, he didn't want to take any more time off.

"Okay, I can't make that kind of guarantee," he said, reluctantly. "But there are a lot of things I can do in my office. I'll just stay out of surgery for a while."

James Kepler shook his head. "Take a couple of weeks off—however long you need. Give yourself some time to heal. Paul's right. You've had a whale of a trauma."

In the end, Roan realized, Jim was right. He'd never really had a choice. As he drove home, after all of his appointments were canceled and all of his work allotted to fellow surgeons, Roan kept asking himself two questions: What in hell had happened today? And what in hell was he going to do with himself for the next two weeks?

Roan should have known that Stewart would have an answer—at least to one of the questions.

"Hi," Stewart said when Roan opened the door of his condo late that afternoon.

"Hi," Roan returned, stepping back to allow his friend entrance. The last time he'd seen him had been at the hospital. Once the news had spread—the hospital had a remarkably healthy grapevine—both Stewart and Mark had been at Roan's side in minutes. Stewart had wanted to call Kay, but Roan had persuaded him not to, using the argument that she'd only be upset, and for no good reason, because he was fine.

"How ya doing?" Stewart asked, sitting down and automatically reaching for an ashtray. He slipped a hand into a pocket of his snug-fitting shirt and pulled out a pack of cigarettes.

"Those things are going to kill you," Roan said.

"Probably. But forget about me. I asked how *you* are."

A jeans-clad, barefoot, bored-already-and-about-to-scream Roan plopped down on the damask-covered sofa in such a careless fashion that his designer, had he seen, would have cringed. "I'm fine. I told everyone I was fine, and I am."

Through an acrid stream of smoke, Stewart said, "I believe you, I believe you."

Roan dragged his fingers through his already tousled hair and stood, partially because he couldn't be still—he hadn't been for five minutes since coming home—partially because the cigarette smoke bothered him.

"Sorry I shouted," he said, moving to a window and sliding his hands into his back pockets.

Outside the world looked so normal. There was a sun about to set. There was a sky getting ready to turn wondrous shades of pink and purple and yellow. Men and women were driving home from work to greet their families. Insects were buzzing, flowers were closing, grass was growing almost as one watched. Normal. Everything was so normal. Except in his life, where nothing seemed normal anymore.

"What happened today, Roan?"

The words weren't unexpected, just dreaded. "I don't know. I honestly don't know. The patient went into coronary arrest and the next thing I knew I was nauseated and dizzy. It was as if . . ." Roan hesitated, not wanting to give voice to the words.

"It was as if what?"

Roan turned. "It was as though I was somehow connected to his pain. The moment he was wheeled away, I was fine. As if nothing had happened." He laughed mirthlessly. "Paul had a field day explaining how I was empathizing."

"Stranger things have happened."

"Not to me!" Roan cried, swinging back toward the window and letting out a weary sigh. "Sorry. I don't mean to take this out on you."

Stewart said nothing. He knew that Roan knew he understood.

Quiet, turbulent seconds passed before Roan said, "Did you hear I got kicked out of surgery? Actually, I got kicked out of the hospital, period."

"A leave of absence doesn't sound like getting kicked out."

"Yeah, well, it's a matter of semantics, isn't it? Either way you look at it, I won't be there in the morning."

Stewart didn't answer. There was no need to engage in a quarrelsome battle that was unwinnable considering Roan's dark mood.

"So what are you going to do with yourself?" Stewart asked.

"Go crazy," Roan answered without even a pause. "No, make that 'go crazier.'" He whirled around, his face tormented by what he knew lay ahead of him. "I swear, Stew, I'll go slap-dab, lock-me-up-behind-bars crazy if I have to stay in this house for the next two weeks."

"Why stay here?"

Roan looked as though this possibility hadn't even entered his mind. The moment it did, though, he discarded it. "And where would I go?"

"How about New Orleans?"

If Roan had been struck upside the head, he couldn't have looked more surprised. "Why New Orleans?"

Stewart stubbed out his cigarette and stood. "Just hear me out before you reject my idea. Okay?" When Roan didn't answer, Stewart repeated, "Okay?"

"Okay," Roan agreed grudgingly, thinking that his listening to Stewart only proved how desperate he was.

"I have a friend, David Bell—we went to med school together—anyway, he teaches at the Tulane Medical School, and he's been sent on some exchange program to Switzerland for the summer, which—and this is of paramount importance to you—means his house will be empty. I talked to him a little while ago, and he loves the idea of a house sitter. For a week, two weeks, however long you want to stay."

"I don't know—"

"What don't you know? For God's sake, I'm offering you some time in New Orleans. If nothing else you can go down and gain twenty pounds eating some of the best food in the world, listen to a little jazz, swig down a little café au lait, and take life easy. And this house is no slum. It's in the Garden District. David bought it a while back—a real dump that was going to be torn down—and restored it. It's got"— Stewart searched for a word and settled on—"character. It's a house with a lot of character." When Roan didn't exactly jump at the invitation, his friend added, "Look on the bright side. It'll give you some different walls to look at. Might actually slow down the going-crazy process."

"I don't know—"

"Yeah, you said that before. Look, just think about it."

Which was precisely what Roan did during the time it took Stewart to walk the distance from the front door to his car. Suddenly, Roan's survival instinct kicked in. Besides, what did he have to lose? Only his sanity, which he was bound to part with if he stayed in this house.

"Hey, Stewart!"

His friend turned.

"I'll go."

Stewart grinned. "The key's on the coffee table."

Roan grinned back as he lazily leaned against the doorway. "You presumptuous son of a bitch!"

"Yeah, well, at least I'm not an arrogant son of a bitch."

Within thirty minutes of Stewart's leaving, Kay arrived. It seemed that someone had told someone who had told someone else who had told yet another someone about Roan. This last someone had wagged the news all the way to the Fitness Emporium, where this garrulous individual had a membership. Kay had rushed over the minute she'd heard.

"I'm all right, Kay. I swear it."

She wasn't about to be placated so easily. "You're sure you didn't have a heart attack?"

"Kay, I'd know if I had."

"But they tested to see if you'd have one?"

"They tested me, but I was fine."

"You didn't have a heart attack?"

Forcing himself to be patient, Roan asked, "Don't you think they would have kept me in the hospital if the tests had indicated that I'd had a heart attack?"

There seemed to be enough logic in the statement to satisfy Kay, though only momentarily. "Then what happened? I heard you collapsed."

"I didn't collapse," Roan said, fudging on the truth. "Look, I'm fine. See for yourself."

Actually, she'd been feeling for herself. From the second she'd flown through the door, she'd had her hands on him, trying to reassure herself through touch that he was, indeed, all right. When she had, her anger exploded. "Dammit, Roan, why didn't you call me?"

"There was no reason to call you. I was fine."

"You didn't know that in the beginning. I could have been with you. I could—"

He took her firmly by the shoulders. "I'm sorry. I should have called you."

His apology, his admission of guilt, took the wind from her sails. Pulling from him, she sighed and ran her long nails through her short hair. "Oh, Roan, what am I going to do with you?"

He smiled sheepishly. "You sure I'm worth it?"

She smiled, too, walked back to him, and, leaning into him, kissed him. The kiss was sweet and simple, but Roan, although he had no idea why, felt uncomfortable with it. No, he did know why. It had something to do with its underlying possessiveness. He eased his mouth from hers, wondering why he suddenly had these unwelcome feelings toward Kay. In his own way, he loved her, and yet somehow, ever since the accident, she no longer seemed to fit his life. Maybe the truth was that *he* no longer fit his life. Or maybe the truth was simpler yet. Maybe he was going crazy.

"What is it, darling?" Kay asked, sensing his mood.

Since the last thing he wanted to go into was what he was presently thinking, he chose instead the second-to-last thing he wanted to go into. "I'll be taking a leave of absence from the hospital. Probably a couple of weeks."

Surprise raced across Kay's pretty face. "Why?"

Roan made a sound that was intended as a laugh but fell far short. "Dr. Kepler thinks I'm a liability."

"What does that mean?"

"He's afraid to send me into surgery, afraid that there'll be a repeat of what happened today." As much as Roan hated admitting it, he added, "He's right. I need some time to get my life back in order."

Kay said nothing. Obviously the idea of Roan's not being in the operating room didn't compute.

"I'm, uh, I'm going to New Orleans for a couple of weeks," Roan threw in nonchalantly. This got Kay's attention like a red flag draws a bull's. Before she could say anything, however, Roan said, "Stewart has a friend there who's in Europe for the summer. I'm going to stay in his house."

Roan could see Kay sifting through all the information. Finally, she said, "Yes, getting away from here might be a good idea. You'll go crazy if you stay here."

That she understood him so clearly didn't surprise him. What she said next did.

"When are we leaving?"

"Hey, wait, wait!" Roan said. "I can't ask you to go with me."

"Of course I'll go."

"Kay, you can't just walk out of the Fitness Emporium."

"There are a couple of people who can fill in for me."

"No!" The word was said far more sharply than Roan had intended, and he hated himself for the slip when he saw its harshness reflected in Kay's face. He hated himself, yet it was imperative that he have this time alone. He wasn't quite certain why. It just was. He knew, too, that he would do what he had to to get the time alone—it was that elementally important—yet he tried to soften his tone when he added, "Kay, be reasonable. I'll only be gone a couple of weeks. I'll call you every day."

"That's not the same—" she began, but she was cut off by the most persuasive argument Roan had. If this couldn't convince her, she couldn't be convinced.

"How are you going to finalize the wedding from that far away?"

"They have telephones in New Orleans."

"True, but I thought you had a last fitting for the gown."

"I could do it before I left, or drive back for it."

"Driving back is ridiculous. It's not only ridiculous, it's—"

"You don't want me to go, do you?" she asked, cutting to the chase.

"It's not that," Roan lied. "It's just that it isn't necessary, and it's going to inconvenience you."

Kay said nothing. She simply stared at Roan until he began to feel uncomfortable. Finally, she said, "Okay. We'll do it your way."

He could tell, though, that she didn't want to. He could tell that she'd relented only because she'd had to.

Dammit, Kay! I don't want to hurt you, he thought. But he had. And for that he was sorry. But not sorry enough to change his mind. As inexplicable as it was, he knew that he must go to New Orleans alone. Of that he had no doubt. Not even so much as an iota's worth.

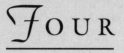

FOUR

The house, hidden by its copse of magnolia trees, was called Lamartine House. Roan wasn't certain why; probably the name of the previous owner. What he was certain of, however, was that the house had a certain atmosphere. Stewart had called it character. Roan thought it something more, some nebulous ambiance he couldn't put a finger on, except to say that, as odd as this admission was, he was left feeling that the house had a secret. There was once a time when such fanciful notions would have had no place in his pragmatic life. Now, however, they seemed all too familiar. Not comfortable. But familiar.

Getting out of the car, he saw that the magnolias were in bloom, yellowish-white blossoms as big as a man's hand nestled among green leaves so shiny they might have been waxed. He saw one other thing as well: the house, though tall and gaunt, was pretty in its own austere way. Uninviting, uncordial, but pretty. And he felt drawn to it, much as one does to a mystery. Letting himself in through the creaking iron gate, he took the steps slowly, feeling the sun's wrath, like a burning poker, brand his back. He also heard the sound of birds and bees and smelled flowers and grass and the rich brown earth. For a moment he thought his senses were blending again, that he could smell sounds and hear fragrances, but no such peculiar episode was forthcoming. Roan was relieved.

Once he moved into the blue shadows of the porch gallery, Roan halted, luxuriating in the coolness, in the stillness. Peace. Standing here, he could vividly remember the peace he'd felt in the white-bright light. How he longed for just a portion of that peace, just one tiny portion to hold on to until his out-of-control world settled back down.

Roan glanced at the crescent-shaped welcome mat lying before the door. Maybe he could find some peace here, he thought, fishing the house key from the pocket of his khaki slacks. As he inserted the key into the lock, he noticed the note taped to the door. He reached for it, read it, and looked around for the stray cat that occasionally, presumptuously, stopped by for a handout. There was no four-footed moocher in sight.

Turning the doorknob, Roan pushed open the heavy wooden door and stepped cautiously over the threshold.

The house was hot. The air-conditioning had been turned off, probably since the day before, when the owner had left for Europe. Only two days had passed since Stewart had suggested that Roan house-sit. Once Roan had made up his mind, he had been eager to get away, eager to try and make some sense out of his life, out of his death. But right now, he had to deal with the heat.

Leaving the front door open on the off chance that a breeze might brave the sun-doused afternoon and wander in, Roan searched along the hallway, which ran the entire length of the house. A couple of chairs, a settee, all in shades of blue and apricot, graced the hallway as though it, too, were a room of the house. Roan found the thermostat beside a rococo gilt mirror. Curious as to the rest of the downstairs area, he poked his head into each room, only to discover that the house was larger than he'd thought. Though narrow, it was long.

At the very end of the hallway there was a kitchen, a white-on-white room—white tile and ceiling, white walls, white curtains, white appliances. A cream-colored magnolia blossom floated in a white bowl sitting in the middle of a white table over which had been laid a white tablecloth edged in Battenberg lace. The severity of the room, which, though lovely, vaguely reminded Roan of an operating room, was broken only by copper, whose gleam far outshone any new penny. Copper pots and pans hung from a rack suspended from the high ceiling by massive chains. Copper appointments, an oilcan on the counter by the range, a planter filled with green-and-white ivy, a collection of molds mounted on one wall, appeared here and there.

Adjacent to the kitchen, its entrance off the hallway, was an enormous high-ceilinged, wooden-floored room that had been sectioned in two by the placement of furniture and area rugs. The far end housed a black walnut desk, file cabinets, all the amenities of an at-home office, while the end nearer the door obviously served as a library. Book-filled shelves covered one whole wall, rising so high that a sliding ladder was necessary to reach the furthermost heights. The room was done in the color of wine and smelled of leather, both in the furniture and what had to be expensively bound books, many of which Roan suspected were first editions. What impressed Roan most about the room was its lack of light. Again, there were only narrow windows, heavily draped with velvet. He had once more the fanciful feeling that the house was trying hard to contain something within its walls.

Next door was a room—a living room, a parlor, whatever the proper designation—that had an entirely different character. It had a brighter, more feminine touch, leaving Roan to wonder if David Bell had a wife, though for some reason he didn't think so. Perhaps the owner had simply tried to be true to history in his restoration of the house. The room was done in salmon and blue and had full, billowy ivory damask drapes at the windows. A white marble fireplace held center stage. Two vases of pastel-shaded roses rested on the mantel, one at each end, along with two candleholders of a pale blue glass. In front of the fireplace stood a summer cover, a petticoat mirror, designed so the nineteenth-century ladies could check the hems of their long gowns.

This Roan knew because his grandmother had been interested in antiques and had owned such a fireplace cover. The young Roan had been fascinated by the antiques in his grandmother's house. The truth was, he'd always enjoyed history. He imagined— and it was quite easy for him to do so—that he'd once been a part of it.

He was still taking in the room, objects here and there, when he stopped cold, dead on a dime, as his gaze connected with the portrait hanging above the fireplace. It was of a young woman who couldn't have been more than twenty-one or twenty-two years old. He fleetingly thought he'd seen her before, then realized how stupid the notion was. This woman had lived in another time, in another century. Besides, her beauty was unforgettable. If he'd ever seen her, nothing could have made him forget her. Even now, her beauty captivated him.

Hair, as blue-black as a raven's wing and as long as a winter night, fell about her heart-shaped face in a wild, wondrous tangle of waves and curls. In sharp but beautiful contrast, her skin shone with an alabaster perfection—whiter than white, clear and flawless. Her cheeks rose high and her chin was pointed slightly, while her nose was small and delicate. As arresting as these features were, however, none could compare with her eyes. They were dark, darker than a moonless eve, darker than a midnight dream, darker than a lonely heart.

Surely the artist had taken liberties. Surely no pair of eyes could be as black as onyx. Could they? No. Even as he denied it, however, Roan knew that her eyes were, indeed, purest black, though how he knew he could not say. Any more than he could say why the sadness in those eyes troubled him so. Actually, it wasn't the sadness itself that bothered him, but her brave attempt to hide it. For long uneven heartbeats, Roan stared at her eyes. They were distant, as though she gazed at unseen things she wished for but knew she could never possess. Even her lips, pretty, pink, pouty with an understated sensuality, smiled enigmatically.

Slowly, as though he were a vessel being filled, Roan became aware of her sadness. Physically aware. The way he'd sensed emotions in the restaurant. Her sadness was oppressive, dark, and heavy. So heavy that he felt he would be crushed beneath its weight. In a reactive motion, he flattened his hand against his chest, as if the gesture might help him breathe more easily.

It was then that he sensed the presence.

Someone, something, had entered the room.

Roan's heart began to pound. Part of him wanted to turn around, part of him didn't. Before he could belabor the decision, he whirled, uncertain what to expect. He immediately caught sight of his visitor and smiled at his foolishness.

A Siamese cat, which had obviously invited itself in when it found the front door open, sat on its haunches quietly taking in Roan with its wide blue, almond-shaped eyes. The tip of the cat's long pointed tail, which looked as though it had been dipped in melted chocolate, flicked like a whip.

Roan let out a relieved sigh and said, "So you're the bum."

The cat cocked its wedge-shaped head and twitched a large ear.

Roan hunkered down and stretched out a hand. "Come here, boy."

The cat didn't move, but returned a look of indifference.

"Okay," Roan said, rising, "have it your way. But I know where the food is."

As he spoke, Roan crossed the room and, pausing at the doorway, stared back at the portrait. Curious eyes met sad eyes. Had he only imagined that he'd felt her sadness? Wouldn't anyone staring into her bleak eyes have felt the same? Roan stepped from the parlor, leaving woman and cat behind. Making his way to the kitchen, he rummaged through the pantry until he found a bag of cat food. He poured the pellets into a bowl. The crunchy sound brought the cat running, though the animal slowed, seemingly so that it could preserve its dignity, its aloofness, by nonchalantly sauntering in on its snow-silent footpads. It began to eat slowly, quietly, with nothing akin to crass hurriedness.

"You're welcome," Roan said to the cat as he went to the refrigerator and took stock of its contents. Just as he'd expected, it was virtually empty—an egg, a few jars of pickles, olives, jam, and a pitcher of water.

Checking his watch—it was nearing four-thirty—he decided he'd do the shopping now and call it an early evening. He was exhausted from the tiring drive. Within ten minutes, Roan had hustled an affronted cat onto the front porch and was locking the door behind them. He had fought the urge to take another look at the portrait. He'd fought and lost. He'd excused his action by telling himself that he was checking to see if there was a plaque revealing the woman's identity. But there wasn't, and he was left to wonder who the sad-eyed beauty was.

Cursing the heat—God, New Orleans was hot!—a sweat-damp Roan returned within the hour, stored the two sacks of groceries, and settled himself in an upstairs bedroom. He'd been given no instructions regarding which room to use, so he took the first one he came to. Large and high-ceilinged, it had an enormous four-poster bed and a massive armoire made of what Roan thought was rosewood. The bold color scheme was gray-blue and poppy-red. Poppy-red. Claret-red. The color reminded him of home. He longed to be there, yet he didn't. He missed Kay, yet he didn't.

He had to call her.

The conversation was awkward. Kay was still hurt, even quietly angry, that Roan had forced her to stay behind in Houston.

At the end of the conversation, she said, "I love you."

Roan hesitated, not because he didn't love her, but because those three words had never come easily to him. They demanded that he relinquish his control by admitting that someone else had power over him. If only for the time it took to say them. But say them he did.

"I love you," he said. Curiously, his mind chose that time to wander to the portrait downstairs. To blue-black hair, to coal-black eyes.

"Roan?"

He roused himself. "Yeah?"

"Where are you?"

"I said I love you, too."

"I asked if you miss me."

He hadn't heard the question. Instead, he'd heard silent, sad eyes. Switching the receiver to his other ear, he answered, "Of course I miss you."

"You sound tired."

"I am. Look, I'm going to call it a night and go to bed early."

"Roan . . ." Kay hesitated, then said, "Good night, darling."

Roan slept poorly, awakening periodically to the creaking, rustling sounds of the unfamiliar house. Once he even thought he heard the cat meowing to get in, but when he went grudgingly downstairs, the cat was nowhere to be seen. Either it had grown tired of waiting or had never been there at all. Roan crawled back into bed and finally fell into a restless sleep around three o'clock.

The dream began immediately. Once more he was drowning. His lungs burned with the need to breathe; his limbs fought to cover the watery distance to the cave's mouth. But he knew he wasn't going to make it. He was going to die. Here. Now. Without getting a reprieve. He began to struggle. Blackness. Then a white light, followed by calmness and peace.

You must return. There is yet something you must do before you can cross over.

And then, in the dream, Roan was standing before the portrait downstairs. He couldn't shake the feeling that he'd seen this woman before. But where? He knew, though, as in absolutely certain, that whatever he must do had something to do with her. He reached out his hand to touch the portrait, but it mysteriously began to travel away from him, as if it were being drawn at high speed into a black tunnel.

"No!" Roan shouted in his sleep, feeling a tremendous sense of loss at the woman's disappearance. Moreover, he feared for her. His helplessness, which bound him in its shackling chains, angered him.

Abruptly, with a jolt, Roan came awake. There was someone in the room with him. He felt the presence as surely as he felt his own heartbeat, which thumped savagely in his chest. The cat? No, it wasn't the cat. Besides, whatever the presence was, it had a desperate aura about it.

Beads of sweat had popped across Roan's brow and dampened his bare chest. In the air-conditioning, he suddenly felt chilled. Or was it possible that he was just afraid? Slowly, silently, he eased to an elbow and stretched toward the bedside table. One flick of the lamp switch and light danced across the dark room.

No one was in the room except him.

On a deep sigh, Roan collapsed back onto the bed, slinging his arm across his eyes. What had he expected? He honestly didn't know, though the desperation he'd felt had been all too real.

Worn, weary, and just a wee bit grumpy, Roan plowed his way through the next day. He ran a couple of miles in the cooler early morning hours and, when the heat set in, which it did with a humid vengeance, he settled down with some medical journals. By late afternoon he was stir-crazy and began to roam the house. He rummaged through the well-appointed bookshelves in the library, then ambled toward the parlor. Which was where he'd wanted to go all day. To the parlor. To the portrait. It was still there, as beguiling as ever, though Roan forced himself to divert his attention elsewhere.

He found a door that led, via the parlor, to a closed-in courtyard. The wall ran neck-high on three sides, the fourth side being the house itself. Trees, banana and palm and a single magnolia, grew well beyond the wall, making the courtyard appear even more sequestered, even more shut off from the world. The trees, however, did provide shade. Blessed shade. Camellias, azaleas, bougainvillea, and rosa-de-montana added color, each in its own blooming season. At present, the bougainvillea blushed bloodred, while lavender-clustered wisteria climbed over the wall as though trying to escape.

The courtyard, though beautiful, was a prison, a sweet-smelling, cool-shaded prison. Shadows crouched in the verdant corners, while fallen, decaying leaves muffled sounds. Branches and vines hung downward as though draping their symbolic arms about the courtyard, not in protection but in prevention. No one was free to leave without permission. Had the woman in the portrait walked here? Had she, too, sensed the cloistered confinement? Once more, there were no answers, only Roan's solitary footfalls on the moss-edged brick floor, only the gossipy gurgling of the nearby fountain bordered in grotesque gargoyles.

That night, Roan awoke to a wave of nausea. It was not as great as when he'd witnessed his patient's heart attack, but nausea just the same. He was certain he was keying into someone's pain. But whose?

Another bizarre occurrence happened that night. A drizzling rain had moved in, peppering windowpanes and pattering the thirsty earth. Cat—Roan simply called him Cat—woke Roan up wanting its usual handout. The animal appeared highly miffed at the rain's audacity to dampen its beautiful sleek fur. After eating, it refused to go back outside and proceeded to follow Roan upstairs, where it jumped onto the foot of the bed and began to bathe itself. That finished, it curled into a ball and went to sleep, as though the house, the bed, were its to do with as it pleased. Roan didn't have the heart to disturb the cat. Besides, the idea of not being alone was appealing. Roan turned out the light and went back to bed.

At a quarter to two, he awoke abruptly. This time, the smell of smoke was thick in his lungs. It pricked, stung, blistered. Gasping for breath, Roan rolled from the bed to the floor. Wasn't that what one was supposed to do during a fire, keep low to the floor? Fumbling for the lamp, he turned on the light.

The cat looked up with sleepy, half-masted eyes.

Roan paid no attention to the animal. He was too intent on finding the source of the fire. The bedroom obviously wasn't it, however, for not a spiral of smoke could be seen there, although the acrid smell filled the room to capacity. How was that possible? he wondered vaguely as he risked standing and opening the bedroom door. This latter he did with extreme caution.

Nothing in the hallway. Nothing in any of the other three bedrooms. Nothing downstairs. Nothing! There was no fire anywhere in the house. Plus, the smell of smoke vanished as abruptly as it had appeared. Roan went back to bed but he didn't sleep. Instead, he listened to the falling rain and the rumbling thunder. He listened and wondered.

Friday morning dawned with a bright, clean, rainwashed sun. The world looked alive and inviting and, despite his unsettling night, Roan felt . . . well, he wasn't quite sure how he felt. The world, his life, seemed to have taken on a Daliesque surrealism. It was like walking through the mirror house at a carnival. Everything was distorted, contorted, but down the road everything would snap back into its proper perspective. Roan believed this. Because the sun shone so brilliantly after a stormy night. Because he was arrogant enough to think that he could make things right if only he wished it long enough.

Tired of medical journals, he scoured the downstairs library for something to read. He found a book on the history of some of the older houses in the city. To his amazement and delight, Lamartine House was mentioned, though only briefly. The house had been built in 1856, but, apparently, there was no record of the original owner, though one Galen Lamartine bought the house in 1875. In a couple of succinct sentences the book described him as a handsome man, a French aristocrat. He had arrived in New Orleans several years before purchasing the house. Though history recorded little of him during those early years, it did hint that he was quite the ladies' man and that he had political aspirations.

Had the woman in the portrait known him? Had she been one of his women?

Out of sheer boredom, Roan took a tour of the historic, picturesque French Quarter. Back at the house, he settled down with a cool glass of tea and read the *Times-Picayune*. The city was having a heat wave though it was only the first week of June, and the grounds of the famed St. Louis Cathedral were being excavated. According to the newspaper, a secret tunnel had been found.

The weekend passed uneventfully, and Roan was beginning to believe that his life finally might be falling back into place as he went to bed Sunday night. He fell asleep instantly, a dreamless, intoxicatingly peaceful state. Sighing, he rolled to his side. His foot struck a ball of fur. Both he and the cat found new positions and settled back down.

The scent of rosewater began to waft through the room. Roan stirred. Sighed again. Wondered when he'd ever smelled anything as sweet. The fragrance filled the room, his lungs, his senses. Slowly, though, like a symphony swelling to its conclusion, the scent grew stronger, and stronger yet, until Roan moaned in discomfort. He came awake and reached for the lamp. The experiences of the past had conditioned him to expect no one to be in the room. He wasn't disappointed. It was just he and the cat. Just he and the cat and the overwhelming, now sickening fragrance.

He had to get out of the room or suffocate. The smell already seemed to have invaded his every pore. His eyes stung, his head throbbed, his heart pumped the sweet scent. Throwing back the covers, Roan staggered from the room and slumped against the hall wall.

He drew in a deep draught of clean, roseless air. As he did so, his gaze wandered to the stairway. Though the carpeted wooden stairway curved into a graceful S shape, it was possible to see the foot of the stairs from its head. At the sight that greeted him, Roan's freshly drawn breath hitched in his chest.

A candle.

A woman holding the candle.

In the darkness, the candle glowed brightly, its golden flame flickering as though some unseen breeze teased it. The woman . . . Roan couldn't see her clearly, though he could *feel* her. She had now invaded his senses as the rosewater had only moments before. Roan wondered—no, he knew!— he'd been driven from the room just so he could witness this.

But what was he witnessing?

Or rather, whom?

As though to answer his question, the feminine figure started up the staircase, slowly though resolutely. Closer and closer she came, her face hidden behind the brilliance of the candle she carried. In the mottled firelight, Roan saw flashes of black hair, spilling in ringlets about her shoulders and past her waist to hang even with her hips. He saw glimpses of pale skin. She wore an old-fashioned white nightgown, buttoned high at the throat with prim pearl buttons and hugging her trim ankles, which lingered in view with each step she took. Her bare feet peeked from beneath the edge of the gauzy garment. Within the filmy folds, Roan could see the silhouetted outline of her body—spare, willowy, gentle curves defining her femininity.

Roan's heartbeat quickened, not only because of her sensual beauty, but because she had stopped only steps away from him. The faint scent of rosewater, like a zephyr of spring, clung to her. His heart pounding, he let his eyes meet hers. Winter-brown eyes met those that were ink-black. And sad.

It was the woman in the portrait, though in truth he wasn't really surprised. Had he known all along that it was she? He once more had the feeling that he'd seen her before. Even more curious than that, he sensed that she recognized him.

"*Aidez-moi,*" she whispered.

Her voice, melodious with the notes of fluent French, sounded like starlight—light, airy, far away.

"I-I don't understand," Roan whispered back as he watched the candlelight wash across her lily-white skin.

"*Aidez-moi,*" she repeated, and this time a lone, plump tear fell from a mournful eye and rolled down her fair cheek.

Instinctively, Roan reached for the tear, but, before he could touch it or her, she stepped forward, passing through him as though he weren't there— spirit merging with substance. At the moment they were one, a feeling jolted Roan, a feeling that dropped him to his knees. He was vaguely aware that the cat stood beside him, swatting at the hem of the woman's gown. All that really registered, however, was the desperation he felt, the sadness. The woman's desperation and sadness. He felt one other thing as well: a fusion, a binding, a split-second bonding of their souls.

And then the woman disappeared before his very eyes, leaving him to feel that she'd taken a part of him with her.

ƒIVE

The aroma of coffee drifted upstairs.

Roan sensed it the second he awoke, or maybe even before. His first thought was that he was dreaming or that something strange was happening again, but the smell was accompanied by the abrupt rattle of a pan. The noise sounded real. Very real. But then, the woman last night had seemed real, too, yet she had vanished in the span of a heartbeat.

Had she returned?

The possibility set Roan's heart to racing, and, throwing back the sheet, he rolled from bed, yanked on a pair of jeans, and combed his rumpled hair with his fingers. He took the stairs swiftly, though cautiously. As he traversed the long downstairs hallway, his bare feet padding against the Aubusson runner, the smell of coffee grew stronger and was accompanied now by the tantalizing fragrance of frying bacon. Roan heard the clang of silverware, the clatter of china, the off-key hummimg of an unrecognizable tune. The voice sounded soft and sweet. And familiar?

Roan stepped into the kitchen, not at all certain what he was expecting to find. A beautiful woman in an old-fashioned white nightgown? Or maybe white-coated men who'd cart him off to the funny farm? He found neither.

The middle-aged woman, whose back was to him, stood as tall as she was wide, with broad shoulders and broader hips and nothing even resembling a waistline. Short legs extended from a white uniform, and on her feet she wore matching white lace-up shoes, obviously manufactured not for their chic look but for comfort. A lace-edged handkerchief covered the crown of her head, sprigs of faded brown hair crawling out from beneath. It crossed Roan's mind that maybe the woman was a nurse. Maybe he'd already been picked up by the men in white coats and taken to some institution that he just thought was Lamartine House.

The woman turned and gasped at the sight of a half-clothed, disheveled Roan. Her hand, holding a fork, flew to her ample bosom. "Sweet Mary, Mother of Jesus!" she said. "You done gave me the powerful fright."

Roan noted a number of things at once—that she spoke in a Cajun dialect, that she had a pretty face, and that she'd just come from mass. Why else would she be wearing a handkerchief on her head?

"Sorry," he said, "I didn't mean to startle you. I smelled coffee . . ."

He trailed off, as though that were excuse enough for him to seek out the kitchen. Disappointment shafted through his heart, followed by self-disgust. Had he really thought he'd find the woman in the white nightgown? For that matter, had he only imagined her the way he had the smell of rosewater, the smell of smoke? No, the smell of smoke had been real. The smell of rosewater had been real. The woman had been real—even the cat had seen her. Roan didn't know whether this fact comforted him or scared the hell out of him.

". . . Eutta Lee Fontenot."

Roan reigned in his renegade thoughts.

"I'm the housekeeper. I come every Monday. Dr. Bell, he said you'd be staying in the house." She motioned back toward the stove. "Thought you might like breakfast."

"You shouldn't have bothered," Roan said, adding, "I'm Roan Jacob."

"It's no bother, Mr. Jacob. I like to see a man eat. Me, I have three sons of my own and not a one of them weighs beneath two hundred pounds." The pride in her voice was unmistakable.

Roan did as bade when she gestured toward the table.

"Now, you sit down and I'll serve you right up, yeah?" The cat had appeared from nowhere and began weaving its way around the housekeeper's stubby legs. "*Couri!*" she cried, shaking a dishtowel in the animal's face.

Indignant, the feline fell back, seeking solace at Roan's side. Perhaps, because of the experience they'd shared the evening before, Roan felt a bond with the cat. He reached down and scratched behind the animal's large ears. The cat, so standoffish in the past, nuzzled its head against Roan's hand, as though it, too, felt this new camaraderie.

"I was mighty glad, I can tell you, when I found out there'd be someone staying in the house. It don't do for a house not to be lived in. Yes, sir, I was mighty glad."

"Have you worked here long?" he asked with what he hoped was nonchalance. If she'd been here awhile, perhaps she knew something about the history of the house. Maybe she knew who the woman in the portrait was.

"Ever since Dr. Bell restored it," the housekeeper answered.

"Why's it called Lamartine House?" Roan asked, knowing full well why it was.

Eutta Lee Fontenot looked up, her clear blue eyes meeting Roan's. She glanced back at the bacon, took it up, and drained the grease from the skillet. "A man named Lamartine used to own the house," she said at last, removing scrambled eggs from yet another skillet. "Leastways, that what people say."

Roan could tell that she'd given the information grudgingly.

"How long ago?" Roan asked.

"A long time ago," she said, adding, as though this closed the subject, "Here be that breakfast."

She put a plate before him heaped high with eggs, bacon, grits, and toast. The sight made his stomach rumble with hunger.

Breaking off a bite of the bacon and handing it to the cat, Roan thanked the woman for breakfast, then asked, "How long did he live here?"

The housekeeper hesitated again and answered vaguely, "Not long, they say."

Roan found the information intriguing, but even more fascinating was the housekeeper's reluctance.

"Why, what happened to him?" Roan asked.

Her blue eyes suddenly looked troubled. "The house burned. I can't say no more," she said, making the sign of the cross. "To speak about this house is *mauvaise fortune* . . . bad luck."

"I don't understand. Why is it bad luck to talk about the house?"

"Dark things happened here, they say. Evil things. Godless things."

"What kind of dark things?"

"I can't say," she said, giving the lie to the statement by volunteering, as though warming to the subject, "Satan never dies . . . and Galen Lamartine was

Satan hisself. All handsome on the outside he be, all evil within. No, sir," she added at her righteous best, her face florid with fervor, "once that kind of evil lives in a house, you can never get it out. No wonder the house is haunted." Again she made the sign of the cross. "I won't come here without going to mass first. God protects the righteous, yeah?"

"Haunted by what? Whom?"

"Her," the woman replied simply, softly, looking toward the doorway as though expecting a specter to float in.

Roan's heart quickened. "Her? Her who?"

Still staring at the doorway, the woman said, "His wife." Then, she added, "Engelina D'Arcy Lamartine, God rest her soul."

"The woman in the portrait," Roan said, with a certainty that passed all understanding.

Eutta Lee lowered her gaze from the doorway to Roan. "I told Dr. Bell not to hang the portrait in the house, that it would only upset her spirit, but he said it would end the bad luck. He said that finding the portrait was good luck. That bringing her home would appease whatever spirits are in the house." Eutta Lee Fontenot smiled indulgently. "Dr. Bell doesn't believe in ghosts."

Neither had he, Roan thought. Until last night.

"But you believe," he said.

The woman's eyes were clear with certainty. "Everyone believes if the night is dark enough."

Yes, Roan thought, and everyone believed if he'd seen. A vision of a white-gowned woman flashed into his mind. She was carrying a candle and shedding a lone tear. She was passing through him, uniting the two of them, making him feel things he'd never felt before.

"What happened to this Engelina D'Arcy Lamartine?"

The question was the single most important question he'd ever asked. It was something he had to know before he breathed another breath, before his heart struck another beat.

"She died in the fire. And maybe Lamartine, too. No one knows what happened to him."

Died in the fire.

The phrase burned Roan's senses. He remembered vividly the night he'd awakened with the smell of smoke permeating the house. Now, as then, he could feel the caustic gray-white vapor shoving its way into his lungs, suppressing his breath, stinging his eyes. The thought that the woman in the portrait had died in a fire filled him with grief. The agony of her death, her fear, were almost more than he could bear.

Eutta Lee Fontenot noticed none of Roan's misery. As though embarrassed, perhaps even frightened, that she'd revealed too much, she gathered up a bucket of brushes and cleansers. "I've got a house to clean. And legend is only legend, yeah?"

"What does she want?" Roan asked as the woman started for the door. His voice was tight, strained, full of feelings that he couldn't begin to understand.

Eutta Lee Fontenot stopped, turned, and stared at the man seated at the table. His question needed no clarification.

"Someone who will help her escape from this house. Or so the legend goes."

Unwilling to say more, the woman again started from the room, but Roan again stopped her. "You speak French, don't you?"

Eutta Lee nodded. "We Cajuns we have our own French."

"What does *aidez-moi* mean?"

The housekeeper said nothing for so long that

Roan began to believe she wasn't going to answer him. He was uncertain whether she, too, had glimpsed the beautiful specter, but he was confident that she knew he had.

"Help me," she said finally, then repeated the sign of the cross and walked resolutely from the room.

Help me.

The words stayed with Roan like dark, brooding companions. Over and over, they whispered to him. Over and over, he saw the sadness in Engelina's eyes. Over and over, he felt her desperation, her despair. But what could he do to help her? How could he help her when her life had ended before his had even begun?

He walked the house in search of answers that would not be found, though, in truth, he searched the house for something else: Engelina's ghost. Throughout the course of the day, he checked the foot of the stairs a hundred times. There was never anything there, however, except occasionally the housekeeper, who always glanced up at him, as though she knew precisely what he was looking for. A couple of times the reality of what he was doing struck him so forcefully that he felt as though someone had poleaxed him right between the eyes. For God's sake, he was hunting for a ghost!

When he wasn't prowling the house, he was sitting before the portrait in the parlor. With his newfound knowledge, after what had happened on the stairway last night, the portrait looked different somehow—more personal, the woman's expression sadder, her midnight-black eyes more beseeching. And, try as hard as he would, he could not shake the feeling that he'd seen her before. Or the feeling that, for a fleet-

ing second as her specter had stood staring at him on
the stairway, she'd recognized him.

The housekeeper left at three o'clock. Afterward,
the house seemed quieter than usual. Unbearably
quiet. Even the cat abandoned him for neighborhood
adventures. Roan rummaged again through the books
in the library, hoping he'd missed one that mentioned Lamartine House, yet he could find nothing
beyond the one volume he'd already read. He reread
it. It was still as unenlightening as the first time,
though it did give him an idea, which, frankly, he
wondered why he hadn't thought of before. At four-
thirty he left the house in search of the public library.

After long hours of dragging every book that had
anything to do with New Orleans off the shelves,
Roan had learned little more than he already knew.
Oh, several books had a smattering of information,
and almost all mentioned the sensational legend that
Lamartine House was supposedly haunted. Roan
came to learn that New Orleans loved legends, the
bigger the better, legends that apparently grew with
each telling, for one account had the house haunted
by no less than half a dozen ghosts, ranging from servants to Galen Lamartine himself. All were reported
with an obvious tongue-in-cheek attitude. It was a flip-
pancy that Roan couldn't share.

He did learn a number of new things, each sup-
ported by enough repeated references to suggest at
least some accuracy. Galen Lamartine did purchase
the house in 1875 and, apparently, he was quite the
ticket with the ladies, so much so that, when he sailed
for France in 1878 and returned that same year with a
wife, the females of New Orleans—and not all of
them single—swooned with dismay. Accompanying
the newlyweds was Engelina's younger sister, a frail
young woman of sixteen.

And then came a hodgepodge of facts, which the reader was free to believe at will. Galen Lamartine was referred to as a sadist, a practitioner of voodoo, Engelina's jailer. The young sister's health had worsened and a fire had occurred. One source reported that Engelina had started the fire herself as a diversion in an attempt to escape her husband. Another source said that the fire had been accidental. Both Engelina and her sister had died in one account, while in another the sister survived. The fate of Galen Lamartine could not be substantiated. Some sources said that he, too, died in the fire, others that he escaped and fled back to France.

Roan slammed this last book shut with such force that the stern-faced librarian looked up. But what about Engelina herself? Other than her beauty, other than the fact that she was a devout Catholic, other than that she died in the fire, Roan knew little about her.

"The library's closing," the librarian said at Roan's elbow, looking disapprovingly at the books he'd scattered across the desk.

Roan glanced at his watch and was surprised to see the hands at nine o'clock. He'd been at the library for hours, not even being diverted from his task long enough to eat. Considering that he'd had nothing since breakfast, he should have been hungry. But he wasn't. He pushed back his chair and stood, starting to gather up the books.

"I'll get those," the librarian, a young woman with an old disposition, said. Her tone suggested that he couldn't be trusted to return them to their proper slots.

Roan thanked her, though he wasn't certain why he had. Her attitude had been surly. Thirty minutes later, carrying a hamburger in a bag, Roan entered the house. The phone was ringing.

"Hello?" he answered, picking up the telephone in the hallway.

"Where've you been?"

At Kay's voice, which sounded only pennies away from panic, Roan realized that he hadn't placed his expected daily call to her. It was hard for him to believe that only twenty-four hours had passed since he'd last spoken to her. It seemed like forever. Worse, Kay seemed like someone from his past.

"I was out," he said.

"You've been out all evening. I started calling about five."

And God alone knew how many times she'd called since.

"Yeah, well, I just walked in."

"Where've you been?" she repeated.

He told himself that she had every right to ask, that under the circumstances he'd probably have asked, too. After all, they were engaged to be married. Why then did he have to force himself to answer her?

"I, uh, I went to the library."

Kay's hesitation clearly said that his response had taken her by surprise. "The library?"

"Yeah, I, uh, I was doing some research." He knew that she would assume that the research was of a medical nature.

"You were at the library all this time?"

"I got something to eat, too, okay?" He heard the testiness in his voice, rubbed the bridge of his nose with his forefinger and thumb, and said, "I'm sorry."

Kay's "I'm sorry" merged with his. "I'm sorry," she repeated, adding, "It's just that I've been worried about you."

"You worry too much," Roan answered, though in truth he was worried about himself. His sojourn in New Orleans was supposed to simplify his life.

Instead, it had only complicated it.

Kay talked on and on for what seemed like an eternity before she finally said, "Well, I guess I ought to let you go. You sound tired again. Aren't you sleeping well, darling?"

"So-so. You know how being in new surroundings can be."

"What *is* the house like? You've never said. Is it pretty?"

"Yes and no. It's . . . It's unique." Not wanting to pursue this subject any further, he hastened to say, "We'll talk tomorrow. I promise I'll call you."

"Promise?"

"I promise," he said, once more feeling strangled by her demands, though he knew that she was acting like every other woman in love. The problem was with him, not with her.

"I love you," Kay said, beginning the farewell ritual.

Roan tried to say the words—he really did—but in the end he heard himself sidestepping with "Me, too."

He could tell that his response disappointed her, but she didn't push him. Kay never pushed. Sometimes he wished she would.

"Well," she said, "I'll talk to you tomorrow."

"Good night," Roan said.

"Good night."

"Kay?" Roan said suddenly, surprising himself.

"Yes?"

He honestly didn't know what he wanted to say. He just didn't want to let go of one of the few things that was safe and secure in his topsy-turvy life. He didn't want to let go of something familiar. Yet, he realized, sadly, that Kay seemed a stranger. Inexplicably, it was Engelina D'Arcy who seemed familiar.

"Sleep well," Roan said finally. He pretended not to hear Kay's disappointment.

Later, he ate the cold hamburger, not because he wanted it but because he knew he needed it. Afterward he showered, then did what he'd wanted to do since arriving back at the house. He went to the parlor, sat in a blue-and-peach flame-stitched chair, and stared at the portrait. Just stared at it. Second bled into second, minute into minute, hour into hour. A thousand things crossed his mind: how beautiful this woman had been, how tragic her life had been, how he couldn't escape the feeling that he'd seen her before. He also realized that she was quickly becoming—no, she'd already become—an obsession with him. A full-fledged, see-your-local-psychiatrist-as-soon-as-possible obsession.

Get out, Roan told himself. Get out of this house as quickly as you can. And yet, even as he gave himself this order, he knew he would not obey. It had everything to do with the way the woman in the portrait stared back at him. It had everything to do with what he'd witnessed on the stairway last night. It had everything to do with that heart-bursting feeling he'd felt as she'd passed through him.

No, he'd stay, because somewhere deep inside him, in that corner of the heart that was wise enough not to question why, he knew that he'd been allowed to live because of Engelina D'Arcy. Whatever he had to do before he could "cross over" had to do with her. That he would stake his life on.

Roan fell asleep where he sat. He awoke sometime during the night, shifted positions, and glanced up at the portrait. In the murky lamplight, he thought he saw a tear seeping from the corner of the woman's eye. He told himself that he was dreaming.

New Orleans in June of the year 1880 was, as the

newspaper announced, so hot that it was fit only for the Devil, and even he was carrying a fan and secretly praying to God for relief. To make matters worse, recent rains had bred mosquitoes by the thousands, by the millions, until one was forced to choose between suffocating in closed quarters or slapping at pesky, blood-sucking insects. At the moment, standing at the open window, Engelina D'Arcy—she never referred to herself by her married name—opted for the stinging beasts. In truth, she barely noticed them, or the oppressive heat, for that matter. She was aware only of the fear in her heart.

How she hated the night, for it was then that he came to her. She never referred to him by name, never referred to him as her husband. If he had no name, if he held no position in her life, it somehow made him less than real. It was a game she played, a game that in no way balanced his sick game, but it did give her a manageable edge. It gave her a means of holding on to her sanity. And it was important that she hold on to her sanity. Not for her sake—the good God above knew that she no longer cared what happened to her—but for her sister's sake.

Beneath her, in the courtyard below, she heard the fountain burbling and could imagine it as the chatter of the hideous gargoyles that guarded it like sentries. Their chatter mocked her. Only two years before, as she'd stood at the candlelit altar of the small Catholic church in her hometown of Rouen, dressed in lace and satin, vowing her love before God and man, she'd thought that the stranger who'd so unexpectedly come into her life had been a gift from God. She'd soon learned, however, that he was a gift from Satan. A Janus-faced gift.

Memories of their wedding night, memories of the nights that followed, sluiced over Engelina, leaving her cold despite the sweltering heat. She hugged her white cambric dressing gown about her, as though keeping the knowledge, the pain, close to her. Her sister must never know. Never! Chloe must never know the price she was paying for her. Engelina felt her eyes sting with tears, tears she could not shed before her sister, tears she had never shed before *him* because she would not give him the satisfaction.

"Sister?"

With the heel of her hand, Engelina swiped at a single tear that defied her best intentions, plastered a smile on her lips, and turned. "Yes, *ma petite*?"

No matter how many times she thought she was prepared for the sight of her sister, Engelina never was. Chloe's chalky paleness always startled her, always caused a heartsick feeling. Perhaps the paleness only seemed accentuated by the black of her hair, which presently was plaited into a single braid that lay draped over one thin shoulder. At eighteen, Chloe should have been racing through the exciting days of her youth, dancing her way into the hearts of admiring beaux, but instead she lay in her bed most of the time. And when she wasn't in bed, she was confined to a chair or settee. On good days, a pallet was laid for her in the courtyard. On any day, good or bad, Engelina was by her side.

"You seem sad tonight," the young woman said, her eyes as dark blue as her sister's were black. She lay back against pillows that had been fluffed and propped against the headboard. A cup and saucer, in a delicate rose pattern, rested in her frail hands.

"And what would I have to be sad about?" Engelina asked, smiling hugely and stepping forward.

About the bed, a mammoth four-poster with intricately carved cherubs, fell yards and yards of a pale pink netlike fabric, a *baire*, whose sole purpose was to keep out mosquitoes. The *baire* was currently draped back, allowing Engelina easy access to the side of the bed. She sat down, gingerly. Her eyes caught sight of the crucifix hanging on the wall behind the bed. As always, the sight strengthened Engelina.

"How about my win at cards this afternoon?" Chloe asked, with a minxlike grin.

Regardless of how bad she felt, Chloe more often than not managed a smile. Engelina knew the courage this took. It was yet another reason why she had to hide her own misery. How could she be any less courageous than her little sister?

"Won, yes, but a tainted victory," Engelina said. "The squirrels stole my best cards."

"You always say that when you lose, but I didn't see any squirrels. Did you, Lukie?"

The young servant, with skin the color of soft brown velvet, arranged a pitcher of water on the bedside table. "I didn't see any, Miss Chloe, but I was trying to keep the blue jays from getting my best cards." The black woman's voice was smooth, refined.

Chloe started to smile, but it faded before it had begun. She held the cup and saucer out for the servant to take. "I can't drink any more."

Engelina intercepted the china. "You must, *ma chère*," she said quietly but insistently. "Dr. Forsten says it's good for your heart."

"But I—"

"Drink," Engelina ordered, placing the cup at her sister's lips.

Begrudgingly, Chloe took a sip. Engelina felt her own heart beating as fast as Chloe's, maybe even as erratically, and wished that the foxglove tea would bring her relief as well, but it would take more than the digitalis leaf from the foxglove tree to administer to her ills. It would take a miracle. But then, as a good,

devout Catholic, she believed in miracles. She prayed
for one each day at mass. Surely God would not turn
his back on her. Surely he would find a way to liberate
her and Chloe. Engelina only hoped it would be soon.
She was uncertain just how much longer she could
hold out.

"You drink the tea," Lukie said, "and I'll brush out
your hair. You know how that puts you right off to
sleep."

"Ah," Engelina crooned, addressing her sister,
"how can you refuse that?"

Chloe's summer-blue eyes narrowed, while a grin
nipped the corner of her mouth. "This sounds like *le
chantage.*"

At the word *blackmail*, Engelina's heart speeded up its
pace. She knew every dark corner, every miserable
nuance of that word. "But of a gentle kind," she said,
adding, "Hurry, hurry, before Lukie changes her mind."

Chloe drank the remaining tea in a single gulp,
then grimaced.

Engelina slid from the bed. She set the cup and
saucer on the bedside table and gave her attention to
Lukie. "I'll leave the windows open, else she will bake
in this heat." As she spoke of the fire-hot weather,
Engelina could feel her wrapper clinging to her
damp skin. Hot weather or no, mosquitoes or no, the
windows were most often left open so that Chloe
could breathe. "Be sure and leave the *baire* down,
though, or the mosquitoes will eat her alive."

"Yes, ma'am," Lukie said and swatted at one of the
vexatious creatures. "Mercy, they're big enough to
carry a person away."

"Or all your good cards," Chloe said, her eyelids
already growing heavy with sleep.

Engelina smiled and leaned over her sister. She
planted a kiss on her forehead, fighting the urge to

haul her into her arms and cry her heart out for the both of them. "Don't forget your prayers," she said instead.

"I never forget my prayers."

"Good. God honors devotion."

"May we play cards again tomorrow?" Chloe asked.

"If you like," Engelina answered, brushing back wisps of hair from her sister's sticky forehead. "You ring for Lukie if you need anything during the night. All right?"

Chloe nodded.

Engelina's gaze met that of the young servant.

"I'll check on Miss Chloe," Lukie said.

"*Merci,*" Engelina said and left the bedroom. Her last view was of Lukie, her dress of yellow calico cascading about her, as she pulled the ivory-handled brush from the dresser and started to unplait Chloe's braid.

With each step that Engelina took toward her room, her heart began to pound faster until it felt like some wild, frightened creature trying to flee her chest. Would he come to her or wouldn't he? His keeping her guessing was part of the cruel game he played. As always in the presence of others, he'd been divinely charming at dinner, complimenting the cook and Engelina herself on everything from her looks to the beautiful floral arrangement in the table's center. He even touched her often, gently but with an underlying possessiveness. She found his silken caresses more loathsome than the bite of a viper, for they were nothing more than lies, nothing more than part of a diabolical game.

And then he had retired to his study, a feebly lit room with a collection of weaponry on one whole wall, for his usual after-dinner port and cigar. As was often her task, she played the part of his personal servant. She began by pouring his port. As she'd held the match for him to light his smoke, he'd clasped her wrist, at first lightly, then tightly. His fingers produced pain, but Engelina knew there would be no bruise marks to betray him. There seldom were. Their eyes met and held. Then he eased his grip and brought her wrist to his lips, where he delivered a slow kiss. Even now, the thought of the kiss sickened Engelina, and she rubbed her wrist as though trying to remove his vile touch.

Having reached her room, she stepped inside and closed the door. The room was beautiful, a dream of a creation in rose and pink and springtime green, but it was a prison—as was all of the house, even the courtyard. She could not come and go as she pleased, only as he willed.

Oh, God, how she hated him!

Quickly, guiltily, she glanced at the small altar she'd arranged in the corner of the room. A crucifix hung on the floral-papered wall. On the table beneath it stood votive candles. She quickly lighted one and asked forgiveness. To hate was a sin. However despicable he was, she would not jeopardize her own immortal soul. Reaching for her pink-and-silver rosary, she began saying the penance she knew Father John would exact when she told him of this transgression in confession, though she would give no name to the object of her hate. Somewhere in the penance as she prayed for forgiveness, it became a plea for something else entirely. *Please, God, don't let him come tonight. Please, God, send someone to save me and Chloe.*

Her prayers said, Engelina brushed her hair, removed her wrapper, and moistened her hot skin with a cool damp cloth. She slipped on a white lawn gown. When almost an hour had passed and still he hadn't come, she breathed her first sigh of relief.

Maybe he wasn't coming. Maybe tonight the cup would pass from her. Maybe . . .

She heard his footsteps as he slowly mounted the curving staircase. She held her breath. Please, God, please! Onward his footsteps came—one, then another, then another after that. They stopped at the door to her room. Nothing. Silence, except for the pounding of Engelina's wayward heart. And then, his footsteps moved on down the hallway to his room. Engelina let out a sigh. The relief was so great that she had to grasp hold of the bed to keep from falling.

She closed her eyes.

When she opened them seconds later, her heart jumped into her throat; sickness crawled through her stomach. He had learned a new game to play, the game of doubling back quietly.

The door of her room was open. In the dim light stood Galen Lamartine, a handsome, dashing figure that caught every lady's eye. He had once caught Engelina's. Now, however, all she saw were his pale gray eyes, eyes the cold color of steel, eyes that cut like the blade of a knife.

Wordlessly, with no emotion whatsoever, he closed the door behind him and started toward Engelina.

She would not cry out, Engelina promised herself. The windows were open and Chloe would hear. No, she must not cry out whatever he did to her. Nor would she cry a single tear in his presence. That vow she would keep above all others.

S IX

Roan wasn't exactly certain as to the source of his discomfort, but he was aware of its existence. A cramp in his leg? Yeah, he definitely had a cramp in his leg, he thought, shifting his numb hips in the chair and stretching his long legs out before him. That helped greatly, but he was still aware of . . . of what? A dull, misty-gray nausea bubbling in his belly. He was keying in to someone's pain, someone's fear. But whose?

"*Aidez-moi,*" said the soft, lyrical but plaintive voice.

Engelina.

The realization sent Roan clawing at the last vestiges of sleep, shredding slumber until it was nothing more than tattered dreams. His drowsy eyes tried to focus on the portrait above the mantel. He vaguely remembered dreaming that he'd seen a teardrop on the canvas, but he didn't have time to consider this because a flash of white drifting by the parlor door caught his attention. It was the white of a nightgown.

Springing to his feet, he hobbled forward on muscle-bunched legs. He arrived in the hallway just in time to see the white-garbed woman ascending the spiral staircase. Her back, cloaked in ebony curls, was to him. As before, she carried a taper, the flame of which speared the somber darkness.

"Engelina?"

His voice startled him, as did her name so familiarly spoken aloud. He wasn't certain what he expected her to do—turn around? acknowledge him? She did neither. She just kept mounting the steps, slowly, steadfastly. Once at the top, however, she turned. Her gaze fixed his.

"*Aidez-moi*," she repeated as a single tear slid down her alabaster-white cheek.

She then disappeared, a vapor vanishing into the jet-black night. Roan was left with nothing except a dull, rumbling nausea, and the certain knowledge that somewhere in time Engelina D'Arcy Lamartine was in pain.

Engelina fought wakefulness. She didn't want to leave the sweet oblivion of sleep, even troubled sleep, for it was only here that she could escape. And sometimes not even here, for bad dreams often plagued her. But not this morning. This morning she felt herself floating like airborne clouds. She felt the sunlight, toasty-warm and enviously free, streaming through the fanlight above her balcony door. With her memories held at bay, she could believe that the day would be glorious and well worth living. Her memories, like all memories, however, would not be long denied.

They began to return—slowly, hurtfully.

Last night. *His* touch, menacing and odious, abrading her skin. His fingers pinching, pulling, producing pain. His mouth, hot and hungry, at her lips, her throat, her breasts—nipping, nipping, making her wait for what she knew was coming. Then, just when she thought that maybe this time would be different, his biting her until she clenched her teeth against the cry that welled in her chest. Anything to demean her.

Anything to exert dominance over her. Anything to humiliate and frighten her. And he had frightened her last night. He hadn't brought his snakelike whip, but he'd brought something far more dreadful: a threat.

Engelina closed her eyes to the sudden tears that filled them. He had always manipulated her through Chloe, through clever insinuation. Never did he come right out and say anything. Oh, no, he was too shrewd for that. Besides, there was something far more sinister in suggestion than in statement, for in suggestion, one was compelled to play and replay the words, hoping to convince oneself that one had misunderstood when all along one knew one hadn't.

Ever since their marriage, he had implied that, if she didn't do his bidding, if she didn't play his sadistic games, he would send Chloe away, ostensibly to a place where she could get the best medical care, but Engelina knew that it was only to separate the two of them as punishment. He wasn't concerned about anyone's welfare, short of his own. And then last night he'd made a new, and ugly threat. He'd suggested, oh so meaningfully, that eighteen-year-old Chloe was blossoming into adulthood, and her pale frailty lent her a beauty that some men would find appealing . . . along with the generous dowry he would provide for her.

Surely he did not intend to marry Chloe off!

Once more, suggestion had proven more vile than statement, and Engelina, repulsed by this last thought, rolled from the bed. As always, she had spent the night alone. As always, he had left not only her bed, but also the house. She had no idea where he went, and she didn't care. She could not keep the hate from her heart, though she knew it was far from what God wanted.

Except for Chloe's sake, she would not have bothered with her toilette, but she must keep up the appearances that he demanded. He'd once told her that he'd married her simply for her beauty, that he wanted a wife that other men would covet. He took great pride in the covert glances other men, both single and married, slipped her. On occasion he even forced her to flirt, though she was not good with such deceit and knew that the men saw right through her. Or maybe they didn't. People saw what they wanted to see, which was why no one, certainly no woman, would have believed him to be anything other than the handsome personification of decorum.

Sweeping her hair up as tightly as the rebellious curls would allow, Engelina donned a flounced gown of black-and-white Chambéry gauze. Its neck, high and edged with lace, reached just beneath her chin, fortuitously covering the faint markings of a purplish-blue bruise. He was usually not so careless. He was a master at knowing just how much pressure to apply to inflict pain but leave no evidence. She didn't have to be told to hide the bruise. Her own shame demanded it.

In her haste to see Chloe, Engelina almost forgot the rosewater that her sister liked so much. As Engelina tilted the cobalt-blue bottle, the sweet rosy fragrance floated upward. She placed a dab behind each ear. Chloe loved the scent. She loved the fragrance of any flower. In truth, she simply loved flowers—their smell, their beauty, their delicacy. Though she'd never said so, Engelina thought the young woman equated her own life with that of a blossom: fragile and short-lived.

Chloe's health had been poor since the summer she was eight, when she'd contracted a high fever. That Chloe's life, in all probability, would be cut short was a bitter pill for a healthy Engelina to swallow. What Chloe needed was a miracle. What Engelina herself needed was a miracle.

"Good morning, *ma petite*," Engelina said minutes later as she entered Chloe's bedroom.

The smile on Engelina's lips was just a little too wide, her voice just a little overbright, but Chloe didn't seem to notice. She was too busy being pampered by Lukie, who had just finished braiding her hair and was now fluffing the pillows at her back.

"Ah, how pretty you look," Engelina said, throwing wide the shutters of the windows to allow in the brassy, bold sunshine. "And how did you sleep last night?"

"Fine," Chloe said with her usual smile, but it was to Lukie that Engelina's gaze went for confirmation.

"Miss Chloe awoke only once," Lukie replied. "I gave her some more tea and she fell back to sleep."

It went without saying that the tea contained digitalis. Other than Engelina herself, Lukie was the only person Engelina trusted to administer the powerful drug to Chloe. Helpful in controlled dosages, it could be fatal if overdone. Lukie, only sixteen, was mature and bright. Of Santo Domingan descent, of mixed blood, she'd been educated and could read and write.

Lukie was rumored to be the niece of the respected but feared Marie Cambre. It was the only thing about Lukie that troubled Engelina. Marie Cambre's reputation was less than sterling. Some said she was the reigning voodoo queen and presided over lewd, orgiastic meetings. She was a heathen who dispensed black and white magic, and this, so in contrast to Engelina's devout Catholicism, could not be tolerated lightly. It was a sin, pure and simple. A sin for which the priestess, if that's what she was, would one day be punished. Though she had never found proof, Engelina worried that Lukie, who worshipped in the Catholic Church, nevertheless hedged her bets in both religious courts.

"Shall I bring up breakfast?" Lukie asked, breaking into Engelina's reverie.

Engelina's gaze leveled on the pretty young woman with fawn-colored skin and gentle green eyes, and in that moment Engelina realized that she could forgive Lukie for almost anything. Her devotion to Chloe guaranteed that. Though she was well paid—all Lamartine servants were—Lukie might not have stayed were it not for Chloe's need of her. There was a dark undercurrent in the house that, although nothing had ever been said, Engelina suspected the servant could feel. She might not understand its source, but surely she felt its presence. There were even times when Engelina thought she saw *his* eyes roving over the beautiful black woman, though here she might be mistaken. Maybe he had conditioned her to see things that just weren't there.

"I'm sorry," Engelina said, realizing that she was staring. "Yes, bring Chloe's breakfast, *s'il vous plaît.*"

In fifteen minutes a banana, fresh that morning from the wharves, fresh-baked biscuits, ham, and red-eye gravy sat before Chloe. A similar tray, unsolicited, sat before Engelina.

"Eat," Engelina demanded when it became obvious that Chloe was only picking at her food.

"I am," Chloe insisted.

"Like a bird," Engelina countered.

"You both eat like birds," Lukie said, nodding toward Engelina's hardly touched plate.

Engelina had tried several bites, but her nervous stomach had not taken kindly to the intrusion. She knew she was growing thin, perhaps too thin, but how could one eat when one's life was in chaos? The evening before was still too fresh in her mind, her heart.

Forcing a smile, Engelina said, "Lukie's right. We're eating like tuft-titmice."

This brought notes of laughter from Chloe, an occurrence that, because of the energy it took, was rare, but more precious than gold. The sound warmed Engelina's troubled heart.

In the end, Engelina was able to coax Chloe into eating an entire biscuit covered with gravy and part of the ham, but only by example. When Lukie took the trays downstairs, Engelina followed after kissing Chloe good-bye. As was her daily custom, Engelina went to the courtyard and plucked a flower for her sister—this morning a scarlet rose. This she would send upstairs by Lukie, while she went to mass. It was the only place she was allowed to go alone, though even then she was not alone, for the carriage driver, a burly Irishman with beefy arms and a red beard, was always with her. Standing guard, Engelina thought. Always quietly prompting her to a hasty departure.

Handing the dethorned rose to Lukie, Engelina said, "Stay with Chloe until I return. Don't leave her for any reason." The talk of Chloe's pale beauty being appealing still troubled Engelina.

"Yes, ma'am. Oh," Lukie added, as though just remembering, "Mr. Lamartine said to remind you of the party tonight. He said to tell you that he'd be out this morning."

The mention of his name caused Engelina's heart to skip a beat. She hadn't even known that he'd returned home, much less that he'd gone out again. "I see. And when did you speak with him?"

"This morning, ma'am. On the stairway. He was on his way out."

Was it Engelina's imagination or did the servant seem relieved?

"I see," Engelina repeated, trying to remember which party was scheduled for this evening.

She loathed the gatherings that he planned, but

he had his eye on politics and more than once had told her that, at election time, one could not have too many friends. The Gastons? Were they coming tonight? Or was it the Pontalbas? She remembered of a sudden that it was neither, but instead a couple of his cohorts, Messieurs Desforges and Harnett, and their tiresome wives, who spoke of nothing but clothes and the opera. Engelina thought that the three men were in some kind of business together, but *he* was most careful not to discuss business with her. It was not in a woman to understand business, he said. Besides, he never ceased to tell her that the only thing he required of her was for her to be beautiful, and to be at his side. She did not even have to plan the parties. That he did himself.

Again, Lukie remembered something else. "He said to tell you to wear the new red dress."

At the thought of the red dress, a Parisian creation which he'd sent to Europe for and which had only recently arrived, Engelina's hand rose to her throat. The red gown fell scandalously off her shoulders, threatening propriety by mere inches.

Deliberately drawing her hand away, she said with a forced smile, "Thank you, Lukie."

Minutes later, with a white bonnet perched atop her head, holding her prayer book and rosary in one lacy-gloved hand while in the other she held a rose, Engelina sat inside the Lamartine carriage, a smart-looking conveyance of polished black drawn by two midnight-black steeds. A gold crest, the Lamartine coat of arms, emblazoned the carriage door.

From within the jostling carriage, Engelina absorbed the smells, the sounds, the sights that were New Orleans. Some said that the city reminded one of Paris, especially Canal Street with its promenading people, its imposing and elegant buildings, its busy coffeehouses and restaurants, but Engelina could not see the similarity. Not that she was that familiar with Paris, but the two times her papa had taken her there, she remembered the city as being outrageously gay. New Orleans seemed simply outrageous—a lady on the one hand, a trollop on the other, pretty here, ugly there, both civilized and savage. Maybe the truth was that it had been she who had been gay in Paris, not the city. If so, it explained her solemn feeling for New Orleans, for gay was something she'd never been here.

Engelina closed her eyes, trying to remember what happiness felt like, trying to appreciate the city for what it was. She heard the rattle of another carriage, the snorting of a horse. She heard the morning quietness as it fell upon a night-tired, night-noisy city, for there were sections of the town that never slept. In the stillness, birds chirped, an insect buzzed, the sun blared its blazing message.

Here in the Garden District, the smell of flowers prevailed, a rich admixture of scents that lay thickly, though pleasantly, upon the senses. The closer they came to the heart of the city, however, the rarer these smells became. Instead of nectar-filled flowers, Engelina now smelled garbage, a dank, foul odor that came and went with the capricious stirring of the warm wind. In parts of the city lay open cypress-lined drainage ditches into which refuse was thrown— orange and banana peels, kitchen waste, bottles and tins, rotting rags and decaying rats. Reigning even more supreme was the hot and heavy fragrance, the sultry smell, of summer.

Like a blessed mirage rising from a shimmering desert, the St. Louis Cathedral appeared. With its two bell-topped hexagonal towers, one on each side of the massive brick and stucco structure, with its central spire and belfry, which seemed to pierce the clouds, with its columns and pilasters, it stood a tall and proud place of worship. It was Engelina's haven, and she could feel it beckoning to her.

The burly, red-bearded Irishman, her hateful sentry, wordlessly helped Engelina from the carriage. As was his habit, he did not accompany her, though she felt his gaze on her back the whole of the walk to the cathedral. Garbed entirely in black, which he always wore, he would be waiting for her, his golden-colored eyes ferreting her out in the throng, his silence ordering her back to the carriage.

Once inside the cool, shadowed building, Engelina moved briskly toward the confessional, which was to the rear of the cathedral on a side wall. The center stall contained the priest, while on either side rested a cubicle. Stepping into the one on the right, she kneeled and waited. Her mind rambled. How odd, she thought, that in such tight, close quarters she felt freer than she did in the far larger house she shared with *him*. This thought had but barely solidified when it was replaced with her awareness of the rose in her hand. Its strong, sweet scent came to her, urging her to bring the flower to her nose and inhale, but she didn't. Flowers for the altar must never be sniffed. Flower. Had Chloe smelled the rose she'd sent her? What was Chloe doing? Would it be Father John who heard her confession? Would it—

The partition to Engelina's cubicle rasped open. Even though she could see no one behind the metal latticework, she knew that she had the priest's undivided attention.

"Bless me, Father, for I have sinned," Engelina said as she made the sign of the cross. Her voice was as penitent as her words.

"How long has it been since your last confession?"

the priest asked.

Father John. Engelina recognized his soft, kind voice. In her mind's eye, she saw his white-blond hair and his cherub-round face with its understanding, compassionate blue eyes, its apple-red cheeks, its chin that had been flattened from long and repetitive rests in his palm during contemplation.

"A week, Father."

"And how have you sinned, my child?"

Each time she confessed but a single sin. The same sin. She knew she sinned in other ways—spoke too sharply at times, envied those women with gentle men in their lives, grew impatient waiting for God to answer her prayer—but none compared to the blackness of one particular sin.

"I have hate in my heart, Father."

In the beginning, the priest had questioned her as to the object of this hate, the reason for it, but she'd refused then, and now, to reveal anything more. She could not risk anyone's knowing more, not even a man of God. Father John no longer questioned her; he just absolved her, though his continuation to do so surprised her. She thought that after a while, when she repeatedly confessed the same sin, he would doubt her sincerity, but he never did. Perhaps he sensed what was in her heart. At each confession she was penitent, at each confession she vowed not to corrupt her soul again by letting hate in, but then *he* would touch her and her resolve would shatter.

Did Father John know which of his parishioners she was?

She hoped he didn't.

She hoped he did.

"Meditate on your sinfulness," Father John said, "and recite a dozen Hail Marys."

"Yes, Father," Engelina said, bowing her head in

thanks for his absolution. Once more, her heart, her soul, had been cleansed.

Silence, like a prayer to deaf gods, whispered through Lamartine House that Tuesday evening. Twilight had long since fallen, leaving lavender shadows to collect in the corners of the rooms and ghostly phantoms to hide beneath the stairwell. Bored and restless, with not even Cat to keep him company, Roan had retired to his bedroom with a stack of medical journals. They remained untouched. Earlier he had called Kay. He'd wanted her voice to make him homesick, to make him miserable with longing for her, but it hadn't. He didn't know why, but it hadn't.

There were times of late when it was Kay, and the life he'd left behind in Houston, that seemed unreal, even surreal, while this house, the portrait, the sad-eyed specter were the tangible things of reality. Reality. He, Roan Jacob, the man who prided himself on logic, was no longer sure what reality was. For that matter, he was no longer certain what sanity was. He knew his conduct was questionable. He spent most of his days staring at a portrait, most of his nights hoping to see the ghost of a woman who'd been dead for over a century. He laughed. The sound was hollow and brittle and seemed to echo not only about the room, but also the house. For just a moment, he thought he heard other laughter join with his. He stopped, listened, but heard nothing beyond the silence.

Reaching for the remote control, Roan turned on the television. A fanfare of noise blasted forth. A cop show. Sirens blaring. The obligatory car chase with brakes squealing. Roan grimaced as the racket played havoc with his supersensitive hearing. He turned down the volume and changed channels. A love story. Sighs and kisses, and an emptiness that suddenly welled within Roan. He was reminded of the heart-fullness he'd felt when the apparition had passed through him. The incident had made no sense logically. He knew only what he'd felt—which, he thought, was maybe what reality translated to. It wasn't what one could see or reasonably explain. It was what one felt.

Roan cut off the TV, closed his eyes, and lay back against the pillow. He heard the scratching of a tree branch against a window, a slow creaking of the house, voices. Hushed, muted voices. Voices that faded in and out like distant chatter.

Voices?

Roan opened his eyes, halfway expecting to see that the television was still on, but it wasn't. The screen was black. Then where were the voices coming from?

Roan eased from the bed and walked out into the hallway to the head of the stairs. He stopped. Waited. Listened. Nothing. He heard nothing. No, there they were again. It sounded as if the voices were coming from downstairs. As though he had no will of his own, Roan began the descent—slowly, one careful, quiet step at a time. At the foot of the stairs, he halted. He was aware of his breath growing shallow, of his heart pounding. He was aware that the voices were coming from the parlor, from behind the closed doors of the parlor.

Something compelled him forward. His heart striking a faster rhythm, he stepped toward the double doors, gripped the doorknobs, and pushed wide the portals. As though he'd wandered into a dream, Roan saw the shadowy figures of three men and three women, each sex gathered in its own discreet group.

The figures, chatting quietly, gaily, were garbed in elegant dress clothes, the men in cutaway jackets, the women in long full-skirted gowns. Both figures and clothes were clearly from another era.

The room itself Roan recognized as the parlor, yet it was different, subtly different. The furniture had altered. The sofa fabric was now striped instead of printed, two chairs had given way to three, small tables replaced larger ones. The color scheme, however, was the same salmon and blue, telling Roan that David Bell had tried to be as authentic as possible in his reconstruction of the past. In addition to the colors, one other thing was the same: the portrait above the fireplace.

In the golden glow of the gas chandelier, the portrait was the only thing in the room with any substance. Though colors were discernible, everything else—the room, the people—appeared nearly transparent, with a see-through clarity that was eerie. To add to this strange unnaturalness, fog, like a smoky serpent, coiled and curled around the feet of the figures. The figures seemed totally oblivious of him as he stood on the threshold and peered inside.

The logic that Roan so loved demanded that he deny everything. He could not be seeing what he thought he was seeing. Could he?

One of the men laughed, drawing Roan's attention. The man, lean and fit and picture-perfect handsome, stood a head above his companions, with wavy dark brown hair and pale gray eyes. There was something familiar about the man. Something disturbingly familiar. Even as Roan watched, the man brought a snifter of brandy to his lips and sipped. Covertly, as though he didn't want his cohorts to see, he glanced toward the group of women. His gaze singled out the one standing with her back to the door. The woman didn't look up, though Roan would have sworn she'd sensed the man's scrutiny of her. Just how he knew that he had no idea.

Nor did he know why he found the man's gaze so unsettling. It had something to do with the clandestine way he'd sought out the woman, as though he would not long tolerate her out of his sight. It had even more to do with the color of his eyes, or rather their colorless shade of gray. They were the kind of eyes that looked right through one, eyes that saw only what they wanted to see, eyes that looked selfishly inward rather than outward, eyes that could be cruel.

Galen Lamartine.

The realization pierced Roan like a needle-sharp rapier. Yes, this had to be Galen Lamartine. Everything fit, from his handsomeness to the sadistic glint in his eyes. From out of nowhere came a hatred so pure it was startling. And painful. Roan had never realized hate could be painful, but it was. It swelled within him until it consumed him like a fiery flame. He and this man had been, were, would be—Roan wasn't certain which verb tense applied—adversaries. Fight-to-the-finish adversaries.

Roan watched and listened as Galen Lamartine disengaged himself politely from the other two men and moved to a sideboard where he freshened his drink. Galen surreptitiously cast his gaze back at the women, one of whom was talking about the latest style in clothes, while another, out of the corner of her eye, checked her dress in the petticoat mirror fanning the opening of the fireplace. This second woman then let her gaze drift to Galen Lamartine. Roan could see the admiration in her eyes. She obviously thought Galen handsome. The third woman, her back yet to the door, still did not glance up, though Roan once more *felt* her. He felt the racing of her heart as Galen Lamartine stepped toward her. He felt her fear as the man's arm slipped about her slim waist.

"Ah, my pretty, might I steal you away for a moment?" he said, but he didn't wait for her reply. Instead, he smiled up at the other two women. "Would you excuse us?"

Polite murmurs of acquiescence followed, though Engelina—the woman had to be Engelina—said nothing. She simply turned as her husband directed her, which was to say away from the room, away from their guests, and toward Roan.

At this first real sight of her, Roan felt as if the air had been knocked from his lungs. The woman wasn't merely beautiful. She was exquisite. More beautiful than portrait or specter. More beautiful than any woman Roan had ever seen. A gown of the palest pink, in a fabric that shimmered in the shadowy light, touched her high at the throat and fell in gathered folds about her ankles. Pink slippers graced her feet, while a wreath of pink rosebuds nestled in her hair. The latter had been left to trail about her shoulders in a wild display of corkscrew curls. She carried a pink point lace and needlework fan, a tassel from which brushed against the back of her porcelain-pale hand.

Her hand shook. Slightly, but noticeably. Though perhaps only Roan, who was so in tune to her, noticed.

"Your lips are frowning, my pretty," Roan heard Galen say softly to his wife. "We don't want our guests to think that you are unhappy, do we?"

As though by magic, a smile spilled across Engelina's lips. It was a pretty smile, but forced.

"Ah, that's better."

With that, Engelina started to draw away from him, but his fingers tightened about her arm. Roan could feel the pressure, could feel her immediate reaction. Her gaze, as dark as midnight, rushed to her husband's eyes.

"You have displeased me, my pretty," Galen said, sweetly, menacingly, as he drew the knuckle of one finger across her cheek.

Fear dashed through Engelina. Roan felt it as though it were his own.

She clung to her brave smile, but the corner of her mouth trembled. "But I am smiling," she said. "See, I am smiling."

"I know you are, my pretty," her husband returned, adding, "but you have disobeyed me. You did not wear the red dress as I asked you to."

Though the smile remained at her lips, Engelina's chin tilted defiantly. "I did not think you would thank me for it."

A look of query flashed across Galen's pale gray irises.

Engelina pressed her advantage. "I did not think you'd want to spend the evening explaining to our guests how I got the bruises at my throat."

Roan heard the words. He even saw the momentarily startled look on Galen Lamartine's face, but he couldn't make the words, the look, make sense. Or maybe he could and was fighting against it. Whichever, he watched closely, as one does the sway of a serpent, as Galen's hand released his wife's arm and rose to her throat. Slowly, unobtrusively, he eased aside the ruffled collar of her gown.

For one brief moment, the victory was Engelina's. If the victory was hers, however, the defeat, the anguish, belonged not to her husband, who seemed surprised and nothing more, but to Roan. At the sight of the purplish-blue marks marring her lovely skin, something snapped inside him. He felt despair, the likes of which he'd never known before. He also felt rage. Like the hate he'd felt only minutes before, this rage hurt. Deeply. Horribly. And it was borne along on the heels of frustration. A frustration of such magnitude that it demanded action. Not thought. Just action. Impulsively, acting only on gut instinct, he stepped toward her . . . and ran headlong into an electrical field that zapped him flat on his fanny. Worse yet, the peopled past disappeared instantly, leaving him once more alone in the empty present.

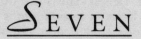

$\mathcal{S}$EVEN

The past caved in around Crandall Morgan. Literally. And it took the form of Louisiana black mud laced with brick.

The noise, somewhere between a rumble and a roar, sounded a lot as if the world had just come to an end. In seconds, though, a dusty silence descended, and Crandall found himself standing boot-high in mucky clods of cool earth and chunks of henna-red bricks. Ebony streaks of southern soil, the result of long hard hours of work, already stained his khaki shirt and slacks. The same soil smudged his sunburned face and clung to his sun-bleached blond hair, which was tied in a ponytail and secured around the forehead with a white—at least it had been white at the start of the day—handkerchief.

"Shit!" Crandall said, standing in the midst of the caved-in tunnel.

"Don't you just wish," the coworker beside him drawled, "it'd be easier to clean up."

"Ya'll all right?" a third voice, this one belonging to a woman, called.

"Yeah," Crandall answered. "How about you?"

"If you don't count a brick to the noggin, I'm fine," the woman replied with syrupy sarcasm as she rubbed a spot on her head that a fragment of brick had grazed.

Her blond hair, long and straight, was pulled back in a ponytail, too. Her nose was long and straight, as well, and, like a sharp knife, sliced her face into equal proportions. Her cheeks rose a little too high, while her chin dropped a little too low. She should have been unattractive, but she wasn't. It was as though the wide brown eyes and easy smile made up for all her other physical imperfections.

"Thank heaven it was your head, Evans, or you could have been seriously injured," the guy beside Crandall teased.

"Cute, Robinson," the woman called back, adding, "What do we do now?"

Resting his hands on his lean hips, Crandall surveyed the debris and sighed. "Call it quits for the day. It's too damned hot to be out here anyway."

The archeological team from Louisiana State University in Baton Rouge—Dr. Crandall Morgan, his assistant Wade Robinson, and Julie Evans, who was working on her graduate degree—crawled from the dark tunnel out into the bright sunlight of Wednesday afternoon. Ten days before, they had been sent to excavate the tunnel that had been found beneath the meditation garden of the St. Louis Cathedral. The accidental discovery had come about as a result of the installation of a new water main. This was the second time the tunnel had caved in. The first time it had taken days to dig out. This time looked no different. All in all, delay was part and parcel of an archeologist's life, but in this instance it created a particular impatience. Everyone was eager to see where the tunnel led.

"Secure the area," Crandall said. "We don't want any curious spectators falling in the hole."

Even though the area had been declared off-limits to the cathedral's countless visitors, some nonetheless dared a peek. The hole in the ground drew people in a way that the exquisite statuary, the blooming plants, and the pudgy trees, their branches filled with a chorus of singing birds, did not.

"Right," Wade answered.

He took one end of a sawhorse while Julie took the other. They dragged it into place and joined ropes to another sawhorse until they'd cordoned off the section. A sign blared NO TRESPASSING in bold black letters. All three people set about collecting their implements—shovels, trowels, a screen box that contained bits of candles and an assortment of religious paraphernalia such as rosary beads, a crucifix, and a leather-bound Bible. All things that one would expect to find, given the location. As for the tunnel, it seemed to be commonplace. What made it so intriguing was that no plan of the cathedral showed it. It was almost as if it were meant to be secret and hidden.

"There," Julie said, tossing in the last trowel. "I couldn't interest you guys in a beer, could I?"

"Is the Pope a Catholic?" Wade answered.

Julie looked over at Crandall. He swiped a crooked elbow across his sweaty brow. Patches of perspiration spotted his shirt, as they did those of his cohorts.

"I, uh, I think I'll pass," he said. "I've got a couple of things I need to do."

Julie hid her disappointment. She'd tried repeatedly to break through to her boss, her teacher, on a personal basis. She'd thought she was making headway until a couple of months ago. His father had died after a lengthy battle with cancer, leaving Crandall changed in a way that friends and associates had noticed, but hadn't necessarily been able to explain. Losing a parent was unquestionably traumatic, especially if one was an only child, especially if one had lost the other parent as well, but Crandall had taken the death harder than anyone had imagined he would. It was as though he hadn't expected it at all, which, of course, couldn't have been the case.

Crandall saw Julie's disappointment and regretted it. It wasn't that he didn't like her. To the contrary, he did. She was the first woman since his divorce, a couple of years before, who had sparked an interest in him, but he had other things on his mind right now. Things he couldn't explain to anyone else. Things he couldn't even explain to himself. The past had closed in around him only minutes before in the form of a tunnel. Two months ago, his personal past had closed in around him, too. On his deathbed, his father had told him something that he'd never in all his thirty-two years suspected. His father had told him that he'd been adopted.

The word still seemed foreign, as though it were valid enough, but only when applied to someone else. For weeks afterward, like a man possessed, it was all he could think about. And then, out of the clear blue had come the choice assignment of excavating the newly found tunnel at the St. Louis Cathedral. Not only had the job fascinated him professionally, but it would take him back to the city of his birth. He'd always thought he'd been born in Baton Rouge, but he now knew that he'd been born in New Orleans. It was from here that he'd been adopted at four weeks of age.

"Another time, okay?" Crandall asked, thinking of where he'd spent most every night since arriving in the city. His plans called for spending tonight there as well.

"Sure," Julie said.

"Want me to drink a beer for you?" Wade asked.

"Yeah. Drink two."

"I was hoping you'd say that," the man returned

with a wide grin. Wade Robinson, short but sinewy, with light brown hair cut soldier-close, was more than Crandall's associate. He was his friend, and Crandall longed to tell him his latest discovery, but something held him back. In fact, he hadn't told anyone. It was something he had to come to terms with himself first.

Thirty minutes later, Crandall stepped from the shower of his room at the downtown Holiday Inn. As he dried off, he placed his nightly call to his four-year-old son, whom he'd missed terribly since the divorce and who could speak of nothing beyond the Mutant Ninja Turtles. Following that, Crandall dried his hair and secured it in its usual ponytail. His wife—his ex-wife—had told him that he was too old for a ponytail. She'd also told him that he was never home, that he always had too much dirt on him, and that he was a lousy lover. Her new husband, whom she'd married with suspicious swiftness, was nearly bald, underfoot like a hound dog, and squeaky clean. As for being a good lover, the man didn't look as if he could screw a light bulb.

But then what did he know? Crandall thought sarcastically. He hadn't even known that he'd been adopted.

After grabbing a quick sandwich, he headed for his usual nightly destination. It was nearing seven o'clock, but traffic was still heavy. Crandall had visited the city dozens of times in the past, but he'd never felt about it as he did this visit. He felt as though the city was somehow his now, as though he were here on some sort of pilgrimage. This assignment at the cathedral had fallen from the sky like manna, putting him in the city of his birth, his adoption, at a time when he was trying desperately to decide what to do with his newfound knowledge.

How odd, he thought, that a man who respected

the past suddenly had no personal past of his own. That fact left him feeling incomplete, at loose ends. It left him uncertain as to exactly who he was.

Parking the car, Crandall walked toward the library and entered the building through its massive doors. He knew exactly where to find what he wanted. The genealogical section, he'd been assured, was one of the best in the state. He hoped so, though the truth was that he had so little to go on that maybe nothing, or no one, could help him. At the desk, Crandall requested the microfiche documenting house purchases in the 1950's. He'd already checked those made in the sixties, plus a slew of other things, including tax rolls, marriage licenses, and birth certificates. So far his search had proved fruitless. He could find no mention whatsoever of the name Drexel Bartlett. Drexel Bartlett, the name of his biologic father. It was the only lead, paltry as it was, that Crandall had to his past, and somewhere along the line discovering his past had become all-important. More to the point, it had become a full-fledged, all-consuming obsession.

Roan could feel his obsession growing. Ever since last evening's occurrence he'd been desperate for . . . For what, he wasn't certain. Desperate to see the past again, or rather to see Engelina again. To learn more about what had gone on in this house. This last desperation had driven him once more to the public library, but, as he suspected, there was nothing to discover there beyond what he knew already, which was too little.

En route home, however, a thought occurred to him. The housekeeper had said that the portrait of Engelina had been an unexpected acquisition. Where had it come from? Did whoever had possessed it know something about Engelina? It was weak, but it was his only lead, one he would pursue. The housekeeper had left her phone number should he need it. He couldn't think of needing it any more than he did now.

Parking the car in the magnolia-lined driveway, he started for the house. Funny, he didn't remember leaving the parlor light on, but he guessed he must have. But why would he have had the light on when he left during daylight? At the sudden thought that crossed his mind, his heart began to palpitate and he hastened his footsteps. Was it possible? As he bounded up the gallery steps, Cat appeared out of the shadows and raced inside the house once the door was opened. Roan ignored the mewling feline.

A wedge of dim melon-colored light spilled across the hallway. Quietly, hopefully, Roan approached the door, which was ajar. Please, he begged whatever powers that governed such moments, let whatever happened last night happen again. As he stood at the door, afraid to push it wider, afraid to look inside, he heard a soft swishing sound. It fell gently upon his ear. It appealed irresistibly to his curiosity. Inching open the door, Roan peered inside. His gaze went immediately to the woman moving so femininely about the hazy room. Her high-necked, full-skirted gown in pastel blue whispered about her ankles.

Engelina.

Once more she appeared shadowy, transparent, but not as shadowy and transparent as the evening before. Both she and the room appeared more substantive. Colors were darker, deeper, angles and corners more pronounced, and the serpentine smoke of yesterday was now but thin, isolated cloudlike patches. The most remarkable change was in Engelina herself, however. If possible, she was more beautiful. The sight of her stole Roan's breath away.

Lowering the wick of the lantern, she looked

furtively about her, then disappeared out into the adjacent courtyard. When she appeared again, she carried a small book in her hand. Easing onto the side of a chair in front of a small, curve-legged desk, she quickly dipped a quill pen in a crystal bottle of ink and began to write in the book. A diary? A journal? Roan didn't know. He knew only that she wrote hastily, as though afraid of being caught in the act. To confirm this, she looked back over her shoulder constantly. At one point, a noise must have frightened her, for she glanced quickly in the direction of the door.

Had she heard him? Roan thought. Could she see him?

No. She had looked right at him, right through him.

"Engelina?" he called softly, but she didn't raise her head. She continued to write. Furiously.

Exercising caution, Roan reached out his hand, bringing his fingertips into contact with the same energy field he'd encountered the evening before. Tiny tremors of electricity shimmered through his fingers, while a faint noise crackled and popped. Intrigued, Cat came running but instinctively stopped short at the invisible shield. The animal pawed the air. At what was obviously the same bolt of electricity that Roan had felt, the cat hissed and yanked its paw away.

As though she'd heard the cat, Engelina glanced back up. When she obviously saw nothing, however, she scrawled one last thing into the book, then shut it and stepped once more into the darkness of the courtyard. She returned without the book, leaving Roan to conclude that she kept it hidden there. But what was written inside it—thoughts that she could share with no one?

Suddenly she must have heard another sound, this one real, for she raced to the lantern. In the process, she hit her toe on the edge of the desk. Roan heard a startled gasp. He also felt her pain. He experienced it in a slight wave of nausea. And then she lowered the lantern wick, plunging the room into total darkness.

Roan waited, wondering if she were still in the room, wondering if he would feel her if she passed through the doorway. When he could stand the suspense no more, he carefully groped for the energy field. Nothing. He felt nothing. Walking into the room, he turned on the light. The room was empty, except for Cat, who was wandering about, smelling curiously around the chair that now stood where a desk had only seconds before.

Overwhelmed, Roan plopped onto the sofa and buried his head in his hands. She had vanished again, leaving him to feel extraordinarily alone, leaving him to feel extraordinarily helpless. Twice he'd witnessed the past, but neither time had he been able to help her. How could he, unless he could find a way to go back into time. Was that possible? And, if it were, was he willing to risk all that he called his present? As for time travel being possible, he had no idea. It wasn't exactly the type of question medical school had prepared him to answer. As to whether he would go back if given the chance . . . Roan thought of how Engelina had no one to confide in. He thought of her husband, the man who'd left bruises at her throat. He thought of that man's cold gray eyes and of the fear mirrored in Engelina's.

Would he go back?

With a start, Roan realized that the choice was no longer his. Maybe it never had been his. Yes, he would go back. Simply because it was the way it must be.

* * *

If Micaela O'Kane had learned one thing in her twenty-nine years, it was that there was no use fighting destiny. What would be, would be. Yes, she thought as she studied the tarot cards spread before her, events were going to happen that no one could stop. The Wheel of Fortune card—*La Roue de Fortune*—spoke of this inevitable fate. The wheel, which represented the sequence of events from beginning to end, from sorrow to joy and back again, was the perpetual motion of a continuously changing world and the forever flow of human life. What was, is, and shall be were intricately woven together until it was hard, even foolish, to deal with life in terms of time. The proof of that was in what was about to happen. It had started long before anyone today had drawn a breath of life.

Micaela's gaze drifted once more to the strength card—*La Force*—which depicted Hercules restraining a lion with his bare hands. On the ground beside him lay a red club, discarded as a sign of inner strength and self-confidence. Yes, someone with a spiritual power was coming, a stranger who would make love triumph over hate. This person would bring the wheel of life full circle, but not without personal risk. The death card—*La Mort*—told her this. There was also the enslavement or black magic card *Le Diable,* the Devil, and the Moon card, *La Lune,* which stood for trickery. Yes, this man's mission would be a treacherous one.

The cards told her one other thing. Unknown to the stranger was yet another stranger. This second stranger had his part to play as well, though Micaela was uncertain just what that part was. It had something to do with atonement. That much she sensed, felt in a way that she no longer questioned. Some things she just knew. The way her great-grandmother had known things. Yes, she'd inherited her powers from her great-grandmother, just the way she'd inherited the role she would play in the drama that was about to unfold.

Dressed entirely in black, with not a bangle or a bead of jewelry about her except for a silver cross at her neck, a barefoot Micaela rose and, gathering the cards, stacked them neatly together. Her hair, a bright and natural carrot-red, frizzed about her head in wavy ringlets that trailed all the way to the floor. Though both black and white blood ran in her veins, her skin held only a hint of yellow. She could have passed for white, though it never occurred to her to do so. She liked who she was, what she was, and she wasn't in the habit of caring what anyone else thought. This was why she wore no makeup, not as much as a hint of blush or a swipe of mascara. Even so, perhaps because of her stark beauty, her amber eyes, as golden as the moon that ruled the nighttime sky, ensnared everyone's attention. They could be as calm, as serene, as a baby's dream. Then again, she had an Irish temper that could make them flash with gilded fire.

Those eyes now sought out the clock. She hated clocks, but they were necessary to keep her clients organized. The clock read ten minutes of eight on a sweltering Thursday evening in June. In the background, Rod Stewart sang some throaty love song, while her cat Satan, soot-black with slanted eyes of golden topaz, lay watchfully on the back of a sagging sofa. The room itself, cooled only by an oscillating fan sitting on a scratched desk, needed a coat of paint. For that matter, several coats of paint. Even so, a vase of fresh flowers, a myriad profusion of gypsy colors, their fragrance a sweet commingling of scents, rested on the desk. The room was a curious blend of mindless neglect and meticulous attention. But this room, no room, really mattered. Nothing material mattered. Though, occasionally, something material held a fleeting importance.

Moving with the grace and elegance of a ballet dancer, Micaela walked to the desk and, opening a creaky drawer that threatened to stick, pulled out a small black book. Its edges were worn, its leather cracked like the face of an old woman. With long slender fingers, Micaela opened the book at random and, easing into a chair, began to read.

> *I am uncertain how much more I can bear. I tell myself that I must withstand all for Chloe, but I do not know if I am that strong. I pray—daily, hourly, with each heartbeat. I know God hears. I feel His presence. I know He will send someone. But I grow impatient. Please, God, forgive my sin of impatience.*

Micaela looked at the hastily scrawled handwriting, then reverently traced a fingertip across it, as though she were touching something holy, something sacred. A knowing and satisfied smile gently lit the corners of her mouth.

"He's coming," she whispered.

The downstairs tinkling of a bell captured Micaela's attention, and she unhurriedly replaced the diary in the desk. Rising, her shoulders straight, she started down the stairs with the cat close at her heels. Once there, she parted the beaded curtain and entered the living room. Still barefoot, she opened the door. A short, squat man stood there. Perspiration dotted his forehead and bald pate. Micaela suspected that the sweaty drops were as much the result of nervousness as they were the heat.

"Miss O'Kane?" the man asked tentatively.

"Yes," Micaela said, quietly and with great composure.

"I'm Ian Stein. I have an appointment."

Micaela smiled and stepped aside. She motioned the man into the adjacent room and indicated for him to sit down.

"I'm a businessman," he said, sitting in the worn chair. "I have my own little business. And I need to know about this investment I just made. I need to know about the future."

"Of course," Micaela answered as she seated herself at a nearby table, picked up a deck of tarot cards, and passed them to the man for him to shuffle. He did—nervously—then passed them back to her. She began to deal them.

The future, she thought as the colorful cards appeared one by one on the table. Why was it that no one ever wanted to have his past read?

Midnight.

She hated the midnight hour, Lukie thought as she tiptoed through the house and stole quietly out the parlor door and into the murky courtyard. She always felt as if the world stood still at that hour and that all the godless demons roamed the earth. She knew that God protected His children. The priests said so, and everybody knew that priests didn't lie, but still she wasn't certain that God could see everywhere at once. What if He turned His head for just a second? What if somebody else's need was greater than hers and He had to devote His attention to him? That was why she carried the voodoo charm. It was her protection for those moments when God was busy elsewhere. Plunging her hand into the pocket of the apron she still wore, she closed her fingers around a tiny bag in reassurance. Inside the dirty red cloth, held together with a bit of twine, was a chunk of coal-like black stone, a snail's shell, and a fragment of gleaming white bone. Yes, Lukie thought, her aunt made powerful protection.

It wasn't a protective amulet she sought tonight, however. It was one of healing. Miss Chloe had not had a good day. When Lukie had seen her that morning, her young friend had looked paler than usual, though, as always, she had smiled and tried to minimize how she felt. But she'd been so tired, so wilted, by afternoon that the missis had sent Lukie to fetch the doctor. He had said what he always did, that Miss Chloe must be kept quiet and comfortable and propped on pillows so that she could breathe better. If only it weren't so hot, maybe Miss Chloe wouldn't be so hungry for air. If only it would rain.

Lukie removed her shoes and, hiking up the hem of her skirt, reached for a low-hanging branch of the magnolia tree. Hoisting herself up, she began to climb. The short, close branches made the task difficult, but she persevered and soon found herself at the top of the brick wall. From there, it was a matter of finding the familiar footholds that led to freedom.

Hastening her steps once she was on the ground and again wearing shoes, Lukie started for the outskirts of town. Nearing the city, she cut through an alleyway. Alleyways were dangerous, oftentimes inhabited by ruthless riffraff, but she had no choice. This was a quicker route and, if she were found missing, there would be the devil to pay. Tins and trash littered the dirt pathway, and the stench of steamy garbage rose from seemingly everywhere. She held her breath and hurried on to the accompaniment of caterwauling cats.

Lukie's aunt was rich, or at least Lukie had always surmised that she was, for she wore beautiful gowns and glittering jewels, yet she lived in a simple house. The house, blue and two-storied, rose directly from the banquette. Adjacent to it on each side, as close as pearls on a necklace, stood its neighbors, creating a long row of structures in pastel shades of peach and pink, purple and blue. Delicate ironwork galleries, lacy etchings of leaves and flowers, surrounded both stories of her aunt's house.

There were those who said that her aunt, Marie Cambre, was part-owner—a silent partner—of some of the businesses on Canal Street. Others said that she operated a brothel. Some even went so far as to say that she was behind the beautiful young women, colored and white, who occasionally disappeared and were never heard from again. In terms of this latter, rumor said that they were procured for the Hell-Fire Club, an elite group of some of the city's most prominent men. Though the group's existence had never been proved—New Orleans loved scandal!—the grapevine said that their meetings were wild bacchanalian orgies. Lukie didn't believe a word of any of the rumors circulating about her aunt, except that she was a voodooienne. But she wasn't evil. That Lukie knew. She was too kind to her to be evil. And maybe she owned some of the businesses, because she did have money, even if she did live in a modest house.

Lukie rapped upon the door of that modest house and waited. Clouds trailed across a three-quarter moon, while a dog howled into the unsure night. Lukie knocked again, this time with impatience. She glanced about her, searching uncertainly for something, perhaps those godless midnight demons. Presently, the dim glow of a lantern appeared from within, and the curtains fluttered at the window.

"It's me, Auntie."

The door rattled open, revealing a statuesque woman with straight black hair, chocolate-colored skin, and fierce dark eyes.

"Good Lord, child, what are you doing out this time of night?" she asked, dragging her niece into the sparsely adorned house, which smelled faintly of incense and the lavender perfume she wore.

"It's Miss Chloe," Lukie said breathlessly. "She's had a bad day. I need a good gris-gris for her."

As though there was nothing strange about the request, Marie Cambre, the hem of her saffron-yellow dressing gown flouncing with her every step, moved to a table on which sat a variety of containers and vials. Above the table hung a crucifix, while to the right had been erected a small shrine to the Virgin Mary. Marie Cambre took great pride in saying that she was a voodoo Catholic and in taking all her gris-gris to the St. Louis Cathedral for a special blessing. She claimed that was what made them so powerful.

She mixed a dash of white powder with an equal dash of whiskey, then wrapped the doughy mixture in a white, lace-edged handkerchief. Closing her eyes, she prayed. Her lips moved slowly as her body swayed slightly. Opening her eyes, she handed the handkerchief to Lukie.

"Put this under her pillow."

"Thank you."

The dark-skinned, dark-haired woman studied her niece. "Are you all right?" The question was general enough, but both women understood its specificity. Beneath the question was implied another: Are you all right in that house?

"Yes," Lukie answered, hiding her fear.

Marie Cambre saw her fear, however, saying, "You could always work somewhere else."

"I can't leave Miss Chloe."

Her aunt smiled and laid her light-skinned palm across Lukie's cheek. "You are too good, my sweet."

"I do only my Christian duty." The comment was curious considering she'd walked the dark, unsafe streets to get a heathen gris-gris.

"Give me your protective amulet," Marie Cambre said, taking it for granted that her niece carried the charm.

Lukie produced it; Marie took it. Walking back to the table, she opened the scrap of cloth, placed in a coin, and retied the string. She handed the amulet back to Lukie.

"This is stronger gris-gris. It will protect you." Again, there was no mention as to from what. Or whom. There never had been; there never would be. It was a tacit understanding. "You must run along now. It is late. The mistress of Lamartine House would not take kindly to your being here."

Lukie nodded. "I must not be gone long from Chloe. She wakes often."

"Put the charm under her pillow," Marie repeated as she ushered her niece to the door. There, she bent and placed a kiss on the young woman's cheek. "Go," she said, shooing Lukie out before she could say another word.

Marie watched from the doorway until her niece disappeared from view. She made the sign of the cross for added protection. The house that the child-woman was returning to was evil. She'd sensed it the moment she'd seen it. But then what was evil? There were those who called her evil. And perhaps she was. Though she attended mass, though she practiced voodoo, the truth was that she practiced her own private religion. Based on the theory that people believed in what they wanted to believe in, she always made a habit of giving her customers what they wanted, from love portions to feared fixes. As a lucrative sideline she also occasionally served as go-between and letter-carrier in clandestine love affairs among married clients. As for the notorious Hell-Fire Club, she was personally offended at her name being linked with it.

Closing and locking the door, she took lantern in hand and began to ascend the staircase. At the landing, she didn't hesitate but walked straight to her bedroom. Her eyes went immediately to the naked man in her bed.

"Who was it?" her lover asked.

"Lukie," Marie replied as she set the lantern on the bedside table.

The man frowned. "What did she want?"

"A healing gris-gris. Chloe wasn't well today."

"That she wasn't," the man replied, adding, "Lukie shouldn't be out alone this time of night."

"I know."

"You want me to follow her back?"

"No. I strengthened her protective amulet."

The man grinned, displaying a line of pearl-white teeth. "Don't tell me you're beginning to believe in all this falderal you dispense."

Marie Cambre shrugged. "Maybe it's better to believe in anything than to believe in nothing."

The grin on the man's face faded, and he reached out a hand in order to unfasten the belt of Marie's robe. With just a hint of provocation, the silken fabric slid from her dusty-brown shoulders and slithered to the floor.

$\mathcal{E}$IGHT

Bright and early Thursday morning, Roan called the housekeeper. Regrettably, she knew nothing about the identity of the portrait's owner. She knew only that the portrait had unexpectedly come into her employer's possession. Well, did she have a phone number at which Dr. Bell could be reached in Switzerland? Roan had been stunned at his own audacity. Was he really considering calling David Bell and asking where he got the portrait? Yes. He was not only considering calling David Bell, he actually *was* calling him. Ten minutes later, Roan hung up the phone with a name and an incredible story.

According to David Bell, who'd been more than a little surprised to hear from his house-sitter, particularly in regard to this subject, a woman had mysteriously shown up on his doorstep with the portrait. She had told him that the woman who was captured so eloquently on the canvas was Engelina D'Arcy Lamartine and that she'd once lived in the house. The stranger had further said that she was giving the portrait to him, with the single request that it be placed over the fireplace in the parlor, where it had resided originally. It had taken little effort to authenticate the painting, and David Bell, interested in restoring the house as accurately as possible, gladly hung the portrait as requested. He had tried to pay for it, but the young woman had refused adamantly and had disappeared while he'd been called to the telephone.

Had the stranger given her name?

As a matter of fact, she had.

With the name of the benefactor before him, Roan searched Lamartine House for a telephone book. He was vaguely aware that the frenzy of his search was not altogether normal. One did not usually seek out a telephone book with such zealous impatience. Nor did one usually feel so emotionally elevated when the commonplace book was finally found. Tearing through the pages, both literally and figuratively, he found the section he sought. His gaze raced down the column of names.

Nothing.

There was no listing for this name. Or for any similar name.

Dammit! Roan thought, only marginally restraining himself from throwing the book across the room. He plopped into the parlor chair, raked his fingers through his hair, and looked up at the portrait. What in hell was he going to do now?

What was she going to do now? Engelina wondered as she looked up at the magnolia blossom taunting her from a limb just beyond her reach. If it weren't so beautiful with its petals of creamy velvet, she'd have long ago given up on it, but it was perfect to send to Chloe. The young woman had had another restless night, and Engelina wanted to do something special for her, something that for one fleeting second might divert her attention away from herself. Engelina was going to be late for mass, but it didn't matter. She had to have this flower for her sister.

Looking about the courtyard, she spotted a wrought-iron bench next to the hideous gargoyle fountain. Maybe if she stood on the bench, she'd be tall enough to reach the blossom. Once more, however, she ran square into a problem. The bench must have weighed a ton, for it was all she could do to scoot it a scant inch. When Lukie appeared unexpectedly, Engelina considered her arrival a godsend.

"Thank goodness," Engelina said. "Can you help me move this?"

"Yes, ma'am," Lukie said as she took one end of the long bench, while Engelina took the other. Together they managed to move it another inch. Then another. Followed by one more before they both doubled over. Sweat dampened their brows. Breathlessly, Lukie asked, "Where are we moving it to?"

Wiping her forearm across her forehead, Engelina replied just as breathlessly, "Beneath the tree. I want that flower."

At her employer's statement, Lukie's gaze raised to the blossom still perched inviolate in the branch. Without a further word, the young woman sat down on the bench and began to unlace her black leather shoes. Next, to Engelina's astonishment, she removed her stockings.

"Whatever are you doing?"

"I'm going to get the flower for you," Lukie replied, rising, stepping to the tree, and, finding the familiar footholds, hoisting herself up and into a climb. In seconds, with her skirt and muslin petticoat flared out about her and her ankle-length pantalets showing a tad more than modesty dictated, she was sitting on the branch right next to the bloom.

Suddenly, unexpectedly—she even caught herself unaware—Engelina laughed. It was a sound she thought she had forgotten how to make, a sensation that felt wonderful skipping across her lips. "You climb like a monkey."

Lukie joined in the laughter, then blushed and hid her eyes, lest her mistress discover the length and breadth of her talent. Because the stem was thick, Lukie had to work at plucking the blossom, but finally she did and tossed it down gently. Engelina caught it with the same caution. It was as perfect as she had believed it. Watching the young servant effortlessly shinny down the tree once more brought a return smile to Engelina's lips.

"You should smile more often, ma'am," Lukie said when she again stood solidly on the ground. "It makes you look as pretty as that magnolia blossom."

Curiously, the comment was sobering, making Engelina realize just how little she had to smile, to laugh, about. As for Lukie, she was reminded of the dark oppressiveness of the house . . . and of the possible impertinence of her remark. She lowered her eyes, collected her shoes and stockings, and said as she started for the courtyard door that led into the parlor, "I'll see about Miss Chloe's breakfast."

"Lukie?"

The servant turned uncertainly. When Engelina said nothing, she felt obligated to ask, "Yes, ma'am?"

Still Engelina hesitated before saying, "If anything were to happen to me—"

"Nothing's going to happen to you, ma'am," Lukie interrupted hastily.

"Of course not, but just supposing something should. Would you . . . I mean, could I count on you to stay with Chloe? Could I count on you to . . . " Here she hesitated again, as though she knew just how telling the next few words would be. "Could I count on you to get her out of this house?"

Lukie's youthfulness vanished, replaced with a maturity that belied her years. "Yes, ma'am. With God as my witness."

Engelina smiled. "Thank you. For being such a good friend."

Lukie nodded, embarrassed by the compliment even as she was pleased by it. She started for the door once more.

"One more thing," Engelina said as Lukie turned back to the dark-haired, dark-eyed lady. Engelina nodded toward the orange-and-black courtyard floor. "Under that chipped brick is some money . . . should you ever need it." She didn't mention the diary she kept there as well. In her absence it would be her voice, explaining what she dared not say now.

Again Lukie nodded. "Yes, ma'am," she said and started for the door but stopped after taking only a few steps. Once more facing her employer, she opened her mouth, started to speak, then paused before saying finally, "Leave the flower in the parlor. I'll take it up on Miss Chloe's tray."

Engelina knew that Lukie had not said what she'd wanted to. She was glad she hadn't. Some things were best left unsaid. In truth, some things dared not be said at all.

Roan was still sitting in the chair, staring up at the portrait and wondering how he was going to track down the woman who was responsible for its return, when, without the least warning, the door leading to the courtyard opened. In a heartbeat, like a carousel spun into time, the room shifted. Furniture changed, was rearranged, and Roan found himself sitting on a sofa rather than the chair he'd occupied seconds before. He had no time to think, no time to react,

before he saw a woman walk through the door:
Engelina.

This time she was not the least transparent. This
time no patches of mist accompanied her. This time
she was as clear, as real, as anyone he'd ever seen.
Before he could even think to question his own visi-
bility, she walked by him, within inches of him, clearly
indicating that she didn't see him.

Ironically, not only did he see her, but he also felt
her skirt brush against his leg. Even more, he felt her
presence. It was a tangible thing that flooded his
heart with feeling, warming it, wrapping it in glazed
ribbons of warm sunshine. Her nearness, like a powerful catalyst, made him feel alive in a way he never
had before. He longed to reach out and touch her,
yet something held him back. What if he touched
her only to discover that she wasn't real, that he was
only dreaming or suffering from some delusional
spell? Worse, what if he touched her and she vanished?

And so he merely watched her, contenting himself
with studying her every subtle detail—the way her
hair overflowed in ringlets even though it was draped
atop her head, the way her neck arched with the delicacy of a swan, the way she bent and gingerly lay the
magnolia blossom she carried on the small table
beside the fan-backed chair. Roan smelled the strong,
heady fragrance of the flower and wondered at the
reverence with which she treated the bloom. Was this
flower something special to her?

Holding a newspaper in her hand, Engelina started toward Roan, scattering all thoughts of the flower,
scattering all thoughts of anything lucid. Her sheer
beauty, the ivory paleness of her skin so markedly
contrasted against her ebony hair, her raven-black
eyes, captured all his senses. She stared right through

him as though he didn't exist, and he had the oddest feeling that maybe he didn't if she couldn't see him, or that, maybe if he did exist, it didn't much matter if she couldn't see him. He would give anything—any-thing!—to feel her eyes on him. But he couldn't. Because they weren't.

Out of curiosity, he leveled his gaze on the newspa-per that she'd just placed on the table before him. The lead article on the front page had to do with the kidnapping of a young girl. As dramatic as the story was, it couldn't hold Roan's attention. He was far more interested in the date on the paper.

June 14, 1880.

1880.

He was sitting here in the parlor of Lamartine House in the year 1880! The realization struck him like a bolt of jagged lightning. What stunned him even more was the fact that he didn't doubt it or ques-tion it. He simply accepted it as truth. Somewhere in the back of his mind rambled the thought that, if he'd gone crazy, he'd done so in a major way.

Roan sensed the presence at the parlor door before he looked up. Furthermore, he knew that Engelina sensed it as well. She whirled toward the doorway, her heart pounding so loudly that Roan would have sworn he could hear it. Roan expected to find Galen Lamartine, but the figure was not he. Even so, Roan knew that Engelina feared this man, or, at the very least, she didn't trust him.

The stocky man, whose muscled arms strained against the fabric of his shirt, was dressed all in black, which only made his shaggy red hair and full-bearded face seem all the more shocking. Something in his amber eyes, something intense and forceful, shouted that he was a man to be reckoned with, a man not to be taken lightly.

"Your carriage, ma'am," he said, his voice deep, dark, atonal.

"Thank you," Engelina replied, adding, "I'll just get my prayer book."

The man made no acknowledgment except for the oh-so-slight nodding of his head. He then disappeared as silently as he'd come.

As though screwing up her courage, Engelina walked once more to the table where she'd laid the magnolia. She picked up her hat, a lacy blue confection, and settled it over a mass of shiny curls. Next she reached for her prayer book. With a haste that Roan hadn't expected, she walked to the doorway. Instinctively he stood and started after her, intending to follow her. Even as he watched, however, she passed through the doorway and disappeared. Or, more precisely, she vanished before his eyes.

"No!" he called out as, with a tremorlike motion, the room reverted back to the present.

In an attempt to brace himself, he grabbed hold of the sofa, but the sofa no longer existed. It had changed back into a chair. The table that only moments before had sat in front of the sofa was gone, along with the newspaper that had reposed upon it. Nothing remained the same. Not a crocheted doily, not a stick of furniture, not a . . . Roan let the thought trail off as his gaze came to rest on a far table. The table was not the same table. In fact, it was vastly different. It was not the difference in the tables, however, that captured Roan's attention, but rather what still lay upon the present table.

In a state of disbelief, he walked forward slowly, half expecting the object to vanish as the room had, as Engelina had. But the object didn't. Instead, its beauty grew with each step Roan took. Reaching out his hand, he hesitated, then braved a touch. The petals of the magnolia blossom felt as soft as satin, as smooth as silk. Their alabaster perfection reminded Roan of Engelina. Beautiful and vulnerable, the blossom, with its perishable petals, nonetheless was resilient. It would survive when far more fragile flowers fell by the wayside. Engelina had the same strength. He sensed it. He saw it. He knew it to be so. Just as he knew that his holding this flower had sobering implications. Not only had he breached the past, but the past had breached the present.

And therein lay an interesting possibility.

One he hadn't thought of until just this fragrant moment.

Maybe it was the magnolia incident, maybe it was the fact that Kay called and reminded him he'd been in New Orleans a week and had only one left to go, maybe it was the control he felt slipping steadily from his grasp—whatever, Roan's obsession mushroomed. It also focused. In a way he couldn't explain but could feel deep in the marrow of his bones, it became imperative that he find the woman who'd returned the portrait. Surely she must know something about Engelina. Surely she was another piece to this confusing puzzle.

Another search of the telephone book proved futile, as Roan knew it would, but he still felt compelled to give it one more try. Afterwards, because he could think of nothing else to do, he paced the house. Downstairs, upstairs, and down again. Cat had shown up earlier and now accompanied Roan from room to room. The animal seemed to sense Roan's tension and to commiserate.

For Roan, everything kept coming back to one fact: David Bell was his only link to this mystery lady. Out of sheer desperation, Roan snatched up the telephone and dialed the overseas number. When the sleepy voice answered, Roan realized the mistake he'd made.

"Oh, no. Look, I'm sorry. I wasn't thinking about the time difference."

"Who is this?" He sounded thoroughly annoyed.

"Roan . . . Roan Jacob."

David Bell immediately recognized the name. It cut through the last dream-fuzzy vestiges of slumber. "Is something wrong?"

"No, no," Roan reassured him. "Everything—the house—is fine."

David Bell's silence asked, "What's the purpose of this call then?"

"I, uh, I was wondering if you could recall anything more about the woman."

"The woman who showed up with the portrait?"

"Yeah. I checked the phone book, but I couldn't find a listing for her. I was wondering if you could remember an address, a place where she worked, anything."

David Bell was clearly having trouble understanding why the strange woman was so important. Roan could hear Bell's curiosity not so much in what he said as in what he didn't.

"I've told you everything I know," he said, adding, "I'm sorry."

"She didn't mention where she lived?"

"No."

"But it was here in New Orleans?" This troubling thought had just occurred to Roan. What if the woman wasn't even from here?

David Bell thought a moment. "I certainly had that impression, though I'm not certain why."

"She didn't mention where she worked, what she did for a living—"

"No," David Bell interrupted.

"Did she mention where she got the portrait? An art gallery maybe?"

"No. I'd intended to ask her where she got it, but she left before I could. As I told you when you called before, she slipped away while I was on the phone."

"I see," Roan said, unable to keep the disappointment from his voice.

"Are you all right?"

"Yeah, sure," Roan lied.

"You haven't been talking to my housekeeper, have you?"

"What do you mean?"

"She insists that the house is haunted and that the portrait upset the ghost." The offhand tone in which the comment was made revealed the credence he gave his housekeeper's belief. The fact that he didn't even wait for Roan's answer indicated that he expected Roan to share his view. "As I said, I really don't know anything except that three weeks ago this woman showed up—"

"Three weeks ago?"

Roan hadn't realized that the portrait had been returned so recently. This revelation sent a shivery tingle galloping down his spine. He wasn't certain as to the tingle's source, but he was well aware of its existence.

"Yeah, about three weeks, give or take a day or two. Why?"

"Do you happen to remember the exact day?" Roan asked, proving that he did, indeed, know the source of the chilled feeling washing over him; he just didn't want to face it. He didn't want to risk hearing what he feared he might.

"As a matter of fact, I do. It was my birthday. I remember thinking that it was a coincidence. I mean, the portrait arriving on my birthday. Sort of like an unexpected gift."

"What day?" Roan repeated, driven by the urgent need to hear what he knew he would.

"May 21. Why? Is that important?"

Roan felt as though he'd been sucked into the vortex of a dark whirlpool. It was the same feeling he'd had on May 21. Then, however, the whirlpool had consisted of water, salty seawater that had yanked at his ankles, pulling him down, down. Now, the whirlpool, if possible, was more insidious. This time it consisted of confusion, disbelief, the sure knowledge that he was neck-deep in something he couldn't begin to fathom.

"Are you all right?"

Roan heard the question and knew that he should answer it..

"Are . . . you . . . all . . . right?"

The words seemed crazy-spaced and faraway. As did his thoughts. The portrait had shown up on the day he'd drowned.

"Hey, are you all right?"

The urgent question snapped Roan back from the churning darkness. "Yeah," he answered, "I'm fine."

Later—how much later he didn't know—Roan sat staring at the telephone. His hand still rested on it. He didn't remember the closing comments. Had he just hung up rudely? Or had he said a socially polite good-bye? The questions were no nearer answers when the phone rang. It continued to ring.

Roan finally picked it up, mostly because courtesy dictated that one answer a ringing telephone.

"Hello?"

"I just remembered something," David Bell began, plunging into the middle of the conversation as though it had never ended. "The woman had wrapped the portrait in a grocery sack that she'd slit open in order to make a sheet of paper. I remember the sack had a big blue heart on it. Underneath it was written Hart's Grocery, H-a-r-t-'s."

"Hart's?" Roan repeated, reaching for a pen.

"Yeah. Like in a play on words."

"Thanks," Roan said.

"It may not be any help."

"Right now I'll take what I can get. Oh, by the way," Roan added, wondering why it had never crossed his mind to ask this question before, "What did the woman look like?"

David Bell told him.

Seconds later, as Roan hung up the receiver, his heart was pounding. A quick perusal of the telephone book netted the information that there was, indeed, a Hart's Grocery in the city. A map showed it in a small residential neighborhood. Roan had visions of it being the friendly mom-and-pop store that had almost ceased to exist because of the bigger chains. Come morning, he'd pay Hart's Grocery a visit.

The lead wasn't much, but it was more than he'd had before. Slim though it was, he'd find the woman. Simply because he had to. Both she and he appeared to be pawns in the same strange game. Maybe she had answers to his questions. Maybe she could tell him something about Engelina. More important, maybe she could tell him why his life had been spared.

The house was two-storied, small, and the color of pink cotton candy. Even though it could have benefited from a coat of paint, the house nonetheless had a quaint charm, which a sagging screen door and a broken wrought-iron trellis couldn't detract from. Maybe it was the ivy that romped playfully over trellis and trim. Maybe it was the colorful array of sassy sweet peas that peeked from the overgrown flower garden. Or maybe it was simply the way the morning sun spotlighted the house.

Roan would have known that this was the place he was searching for even if the aging grocer hadn't told him that it was the pink house at the end of the street. He wasn't exactly certain how he would have known. He just knew he would have, for some inexplicable something drew him to the dwelling.

Roan parked in the driveway, opened the car door and, following the path of seedy grass and cracked concrete, made his way up the chipped steps. The steps ended in a small half-circular porch. Both steps and porch had been painted an unflattering green. The same green paint had been used to print a crude sign that leaned against a front window. The sign read: Cartomancer . . . Learn What Your Future Holds . . . By Appointment Only. The telephone number that Roan had searched high and low for followed.

The lady he was looking for was a fortune-teller? Somehow this didn't surprise him, though the reason might have been as simple as the fact that he was pretty shockproof these days.

Stepping up to the front door, which stood open, leaving only the unlatched screen door to act as a barrier, he rang the doorbell. No one came except a cat as black as sin. The animal gave Roan a look-see, pronounced him unimportant, and with a flick of his tail ambled back into the sultry shadows of the house. Roan rang the bell again.

For a moment it was impossible to tell where the shadows ended and the woman began. Slowly, though, form and shadow separated, and the woman, slipping through a curtain of tinkling beads, walked forward. She was dressed all in black—a collarless, short-sleeved, habitlike dress that fell nearly to her ankles. She wore no makeup, no shoes, and no jewelry, except for a silver cross at her neck. Her hair, the color of a blazing sun, tumbled down her back and slightly dragged the floor as she walked.

She was not a beautiful woman, and yet there was something strikingly dynamic about her—a simplicity, a singularity, a serenity.

"Micaela O'Kane?" he asked.

"Yes," she answered.

"I'm Roan Jacob."

"Do you have an appointment, Mr. Jacob?" she began.

Roan cut her off with, "No. No, I just need to ask you some questions. Some questions about the portrait at Lamartine House."

As though he'd spoken secret and magic words, the woman's eyes narrowed. Silently she stepped back, allowing him entrance. Roan had the curious feeling that she'd been waiting for him; in his heart he knew the absurdity of this, though perhaps it was no more absurd than his being there in the first place.

Again wordlessly, she indicated the room on the right, a small sitting room of sorts. Roan passed into it, noting that the furniture was worn, mismatched, and much of it in need of replacing. Even so, there was a tidiness to the room, a keptness. He seated himself in a chair that had a lacy antimacassar draped across the back. Suddenly, he wondered exactly what he was doing here. And exactly what questions he was going to ask.

Before he could ask anything, however, Micaela O'Kane said matter-of-factly, "You've had a near-death experience." At the surprised look he shot her, she added, "I can tell by your aura."

As she spoke, she seated herself across from him and began to shuffle the cards that lay on the table. She passed them to Roan, glanced up at him with huge topaz-tinted eyes, and said, "Cut the deck." When Roan started to object, to restate that he wasn't there for a reading, she added, "Please."

He did as he'd been bade, cutting the deck neatly and with an arrogant precision that said he put no stock in such foolishness.

At the spot where he'd cut the deck, she flipped over the card, studied it, then, looking up at him, announced, "Yes, you're the one."

Though a ceiling fan swirled slowly overhead, the room was oppressively hot. The heat, plus the words the woman had just spoken, combined once more to create a surreal world. For just a second nothing seemed real. Everything seemed shadowy, as though time had somehow blurred, or perhaps even stood still.

"What do you mean I'm the one?" Roan asked finally.

Again Micaela spoke as she shuffled the cards. Again she spoke as though what she was about to say were common knowledge. "You're the one she's been waiting for."

Something snapped inside Roan. He raked his restless fingers through his hair. "Would you tell me what in hell is going on?"

"Justice," she said simply. She cut another card and, as though the words were written there, she said, "Deliverance of the faithful."

At his confused look, she smiled softly, making Roan think that perhaps she possessed beauty after all.

"I'm sorry," she said. "None of this is making any sense to you, is it?"

"No. But then very little has for the past three weeks."

The mention of three weeks caught her attention and she asked, "What happened three weeks ago?"

"I nearly drowned."

"Ah," she said, as though everything now suddenly fell into place. "I returned the portrait three weeks ago."

"I know," Roan said, adding, "Tell me about the portrait."

She interlaced the cards as she spoke, the action obviously more natural to her than breathing. Occasionally, she glanced up at Roan. "The portrait belonged to my great-grandmother. It's been passed down from generation to generation with the under-standing that at some point someone in the family would return it to Lamartine House. My grandmother, my mother, waited for the sign, but it never came. I waited for the sign, too. Three weeks ago, I saw it . . . in the cards. It told me to return the portrait."

"Why?"

"One does not question the cards."

Roan tried another tack, the one he was most interested in. "What do you know of the woman in the portrait?"

"Engelina?"

Roan nodded.

"I know what I have read. I know what I have heard."

"Which is?"

"That she was a woman greatly wronged."

"By Galen Lamartine?"

"Yes. By Galen Lamartine. The lusty delight of every New Orleans woman. The wicked instrument of Satan himself."

"Go on."

"He was . . . evil. Pure, unadulterated."

"And a sadist?"

Her eyes rose to his. "Yes. He found pleasure only

in the pain of others. Principally in that of his wife.
Though she was unquestionably beautiful, he could
have had his pick of all the women in New Orleans,
many her equal in beauty. But there was a purity
about Engelina, a virginal spirituality that I think
Galen was attracted to. Simply because it is always the
job of evil to tempt goodness. But he couldn't tempt
her. He could not make her turn her back on the
faith that sustained her. And that, Dr. Jacob—"

"How did you know I was a doctor?"

Micaela smiled. "The cards speak, Dr. Jacob. They
speak to those who can hear."

"Why didn't she leave him?"

"Because of her sister Chloe."

"Chloe?" It was the first time he'd had a name for
her sister. The name suddenly made her seem real in
a way she had not before.

"Chloe was a fragile child, an unhealthy child. Her
heart. And Engelina worshipped her. It was only the
two of them, and it had been so for years. Their
mother died when the girls were small, and their
father was killed in a hunting accident when Engelina
was but eighteen. Engelina stayed with Galen because
he threatened that which was most precious to her—
her sister."

"What kind of threats?"

Micaela shrugged. "I don't know for certain. I
know only that Engelina thought them grave. And so
she turned to the only place she could, to her faith.
She waited for God to send a deliverer." Micaela
glanced up again. This time her eyes had deepened
to the color of smoky topaz. "She awaits you."

"That's absurd," Roan said, sanity demanding that
he rebuff the woman's ludicrous statement.

"Is it?" Micaela asked, again with a simplicity that
unraveled Roan's nerves.

"Okay, for argument's sake, let's say that what you're saying is true. Don't you mean she once waited for me?"

Micaela shook her shoulders, sending the cross at her throat into a gentle sway. "Was . . . is . . . what is time, Dr. Jacob? Perhaps it doesn't exist at all. By the time we experience a second, that second is no more. Who are we to say that it ever existed? Or that it doesn't exist somewhere else at the same time that we experienced it?"

At this, Roan stood, walked to the window, and stared out at the first burnished traces of the southern day. Midmorning, and its doleful sighs of suffocating heat, lay only minutes away. He turned, his eyes finding those of the woman.

"I've seen her," he said. "I've even been back to the year 1880." Micaela was silent, prompting him to add, "You don't believe me."

"I believe what you tell me."

The reality of the conversation hit Roan like a hammer to the side of the head. Angrily he cried, "My God, isn't this sounding strange to anyone but me? Has the whole world gone crazy?"

Micaela replied calmly, "You're not crazy. You're just a man with a mission."

"And what exactly is that mission?"

"That I don't know. That is yours alone to discover. My job, my mission, was completed when I returned the portrait." Turning over the topmost card, she said, "I tell you, though, that there is another stranger involved. I don't know the part that he or she will play. I know only that the stranger exists. I know, too"— here she turned over another card, the death card—"that what you do will put you at personal risk. I don't know whether you will survive."

As though just remembering something, Micaela

stood and, with only the admonition for him to wait, walked from the room. He could hear her unhurriedly mounting the stairs to the second floor. Again, the surrealism struck him as the eager rays of the sunlight filtered through the window. Was he really here in this small pink house? Was he really having this bizarre conversation with this strange woman who professed to know the past and to be able to predict the future?

In minutes, Micaela returned with a small leather-bound book. It was cracked and as old as time itself.

"This belonged to Engelina," Micaela said.

Roan recalled having seen Engelina hastily writing in a book—a diary?—seconds before she'd hidden it in the courtyard. Micaela handed Roan the frail volume. It felt . . . real. The world around him felt surreal, yet this book felt real.

Walking Roan to the door, Micaela said, "Read her. Listen to her. *Feel* her."

"And what do I do then?"

"You will know," she said. "You, and you alone, will know."

$\mathscr{N}$ I N E

The phone rang. And rang. And rang. Just the way it had done all evening. Abruptly it stopped in mid-peal, leaving the sound to linger momentarily in the sudden silence. Roan wasn't aware that the phone had stopped ringing, but then he hadn't been aware that it had been ringing in the first place. His attention remained singularly focused on the brittle-paged, dusty-smelling diary he'd been given hours before. Seated in the chair in the parlor, with the portrait above the fireplace and the magnolia blossom on the table beside him, he read.

> *I cannot sleep. I cannot grow accustomed to the heat. Oh, how I miss my fair Rouen. Oh, how I wish I had never entered into this villainous marriage. How could I have been so blind to his wicked ways?*

> *Chloe seems stronger today. What would I ever do without her? She is my sole joy. I would do anything, bear anything, for her.*

> *It rained today, leaving the city to steam like a teapot. Chloe had trouble breathing, and I sat by her bedside all afternoon. Lukie is sitting with her tonight.*

> *The night is long. I listen for his footsteps and think that I hear them in every sound. I loathe the*

wait, I loathe the sounds, yet I loathe the silence more, for it means that all still lies ahead.

We sat in the courtyard today. I love the courtyard, though I hate it, too. While it's true that it means freedom from the house, it is still a prison, a flowery prison, but a prison all the same. He has forbade me to leave the house without him or his Irish henchman.

Chloe has asked for a pet, but he has denied her one. Curiously, for once I agree with him. I could not in good conscience bring body or beast into this house.

The phone pealed again. As before, Roan was lost in the world of Engelina's words. He read every entry, as though each had been written only that he might read it. Sometimes there would be an entry for each day; sometimes a day, or days, would be skipped. Increasingly, though, the entries became blacker in tone. A sense of dread invaded Roan, though he couldn't have stopped reading had his life depended on it.

He grows more insatiable, as though he is ruled by hungry demons. How can one man know so much about inflicting pain? Besides physical pain, the only thing he is better at inflicting is emotional pain. At this he is the dark master.

He is interested only in power, only in controlling me. I do not even think he likes me. I know he doesn't love me. He has no concept of the word. He doesn't even love himself. No, he wants only to control me.

I found a daguerreotype of his mother. He grew angry—at seeing her, at my finding her photograph. He told me that I was never to mention her to him again. He then stormed from the house and did not return till morning.

Roan read this last with interest. Had his mother abused him? Had a little boy longed for love, but had that love denied him? Engelina wrote of his not loving even himself. In a perverse, but understandable way, did he think himself somehow responsible for his mother's lack of caring? Was he unlovable, ergo, not deserving of his mother's love?

Damn! Roan thought. He wasn't a psychiatrist. He wasn't trained to diagnose Galen Lamartine's mental and emotional problems. Furthermore—and this he realized with a start—he was too close to the problem to think clearly. He was personally involved. Personally involved with a ghost? Personally involved with a woman who had lived more than a century ago? Yes. He couldn't explain it, yet he couldn't deny it. That personal involvement compelled him to read on, though with each entry it grew more difficult.

He came last night.

The entry was moving, even frightening, in its simplicity, as was the fact that nowhere in the diary did Engelina refer to her husband by name. Roan longed to know precisely what had happened when Galen came to his wife's room. Nothing had as yet been spelled out. Only hints. Only innuendoes. Surely the truth couldn't be as ugly as the sinister thoughts slithering through his all-too-fertile imagination. Could they?

I grow desperate. Each day I go to mass. Each day I pray until my fingers are raw from reading the rosary. My voice is hoarse from repetitive Hail Marys. God will not fail me. He will send someone to help me. Until then, I will lean on Father John. Though he knows not the cause of my heart's heaviness, he senses my despair. He tells me that he is praying special prayers for me. He tells me to have faith in God.

Only hours before, Roan had been told by Micaela O'Kane that he was the one sent to liberate Engelina. In his heart, it was something he'd increasingly grown to believe as well. Seeing the words in her own hand-writing, however, seeing that she did believe someone would rescue her, that she was waiting for some god-sent someone, did strange things to Roan. Strange as in humbling. Strange as in frightening. He had no idea what he was doing. He had no idea what he was getting into.

His thoughts returned to the red-haired, black-garbed woman he'd seen that morning. Who was this Micaela O'Kane? Who was this great-grandmother she spoke of? And how on the up-and-up was Micaela O'Kane? She was a fortune-teller, for heaven's sake! Maybe all of this was some elaborate ruse, some elaborate scam. What did he really know about her except that she'd returned the portrait with some song and dance about the cards telling her to? In her favor, she hadn't asked for money, though maybe that was down the road. And yet . . .

And yet what?

And yet she'd known things, things about him, things about Engelina. And then there was the uncan-ny fact that she'd returned the portrait on the same day he'd drowned. Was the woman a flawless dia-mond or a flashy rhinestone? Was the woman the real thing or a clever fake? Roan laughed harshly. Real? What in hell would he know about real? Somewhere along the line he'd departed from the path of reality and was taking an overgrown trail to . . . to heaven alone knew where. He knew only that he had to fol-low it wherever it led.

Once more the phone began to ring. Just the way it had all evening. Abruptly, it stopped. Again, Roan paid it no heed. He was lost in the seductive lure of black ink and yellowed paper.

He was in a dark mood.

As always, Engelina had no idea what had caused it, nor was she certain that even he knew its source. Sometimes, like a sickness, a spell just came over him. She did know, though, that she had done nothing to improve the mood. At dinner, she had asked, nonchalantly she'd hoped, if he'd seen the magnolia blossom that she'd left in the parlor. Seemingly it had just vanished, and neither she nor Lukie was able to explain its disappearance. Each had thought the other had moved it. At her inquiry, Galen had turned frosty gray eyes on her and proclaimed that he had things to do that were more important than keeping watch over flowers.

On the heels of that, and to worsen matters, Engelina had spilled her goblet of wine. The clash of crystal, the sight of the ruby-red liquid bleeding across the white linen tablecloth and dripping onto the skirt of her taffy-colored gown had destroyed the last vestiges of his weakening composure. Wordlessly, his eyes cold slabs of granite, he'd risen and, neatly laying his napkin by the side of his plate, walked from the room. He'd gone into his study, locked the door behind him, and proceeded to ply himself with liquor. Engelina knew this because it was his oft-repeated pattern. When the mood consumed him, he sequestered himself with brooding silence and alcoholic spirits. Later, when the demons were full-blown and begging to be set loose, he'd come to her.

At this thought, Engelina's heart thumped within her chest and adrenaline pumped within her veins. Panic clawed at her and she had to fight the natural urge to flee—him, the house, the city. Yet she could not flee. Not with sweet sick Chloe upstairs. Like an animal ensnared in the cruel, jagged jaws of a trap, Engelina was caught, hard and fast.

Maybe he wouldn't come tonight.

Maybe this time would be different.

Maybe she was going to lose her mind!

Reaching for her rosary, she began to pray. *Hail, Mary, full of grace, the Lord is with thee* . . . When that prayer had ended, she began another, and then another, until she had strung together as many as there were pink crystal beads on her rosary. She fingered the silver crucifix, willing its divine form to instill courage and peace within her.

She felt rather than heard the door of her bedroom open. More precisely, despite the heat, she felt a coldness invade the room. Jerking her head toward the door, she saw him standing there, a nightmare come to life. His gray eyes, bright with drink, glistened like the surface of an ice-covered lake. Beneath the ice, however, no emotion shone through. Engelina saw only a frightening emptiness, a soulless vacancy.

"No," she whispered, not even aware that she'd spoken.

Downstairs, with the diary still in his lap, Roan stopped reading. He could have sworn he heard something. It sounded as if someone had spoken the word *no.* Cocking his head, he listened, but nothing more followed, and it was easy enough to convince himself that his imagination had been playing parlor tricks. Without a second thought, he went back to reading the diary.

Her heart beating in her throat, Engelina watched as her husband walked toward her. Her palms grew moist and she clung to the rosary as though it, and it alone, had the power to protect her.

"You don't look glad to see me, my pretty," Galen said in a soft, sinister voice. As he spoke, he brushed his fingertips across her cheek.

The caress was cold, like the chilled kiss of a frost-bitten wind. Engelina willed herself not to flinch, knowing that if she did she'd only anger the beast that dwelled within him.

"Tell me I am mistaken," he ordered. "Tell me you are pleased to see me."

"I am pleased to see you," she complied, playing the game as she always did. Even knowing that she had no other choice, she felt the words stick in her throat, threatening to suffocate her with the lie they told.

"I thought I must be mistaken, for no wife should loathe the sight of her husband." The hand at her cheek trailed higher, one finger teasing an ebony curl dangling about her ear.

"No," Engelina whispered, forcing herself to remain still, even though his nearness sickened her. "I mean, yes. Yes, you were mistaken."

"And as my wife, you would do anything I asked, wouldn't you?"

The question turned her stomach, for she knew that anything he asked would be perverse and painful.

Clutching the rosary until she could feel it gouging her flesh, she managed to say, "Yes."

Galen's lips turned upward into a misshapen

smile. "You are not only pretty, you are also bright."

His smile faded as the sudden light of desire jumped into his eyes. He threaded the fingers of one hand through her hair and, angling her head, lifted her face up to his. She felt, smelled, his whiskey-laden breath burn across her lips. Even though she told herself that she must submit, something inside her rebelled and, just as his mouth would have covered hers, she turned her face away. The instant she did so, she knew that she'd made a grave mistake.

Not a muscle in his body moved, not a tendon twitched. Nothing, except the beating of his hot breath against her cheek. Slowly, torturously, the fingers in her hair began to tighten until it felt as though each hair were being singly pulled from her head. Tears sprang to her eyes. At the same time, a pain tore through her neck when he unceremoniously jerked her head toward his. His misty-gray eyes, blank as a wordless sheet of paper, met hers.

"Don't ever do that again," he said, his voice so silky smooth that one would have thought he was delivering an endearment instead of a threat.

"No," she whispered. "Never."

Then, without another word, Galen slammed his mouth into his wife's. Hurtfully. Punishingly. Without a hint of remorse.

Physical pain mingled with the pain of humiliation, of subjugation. Engelina tasted fear. She also tasted blood. And the crisp sting of a cut lip.

Tearing his mouth from hers, his fingers still roped tormentingly in her hair, he dragged her to a kneeling position before him. A fresh pain, searing and sharp, streaked through her knees as she crashed to the hard wooden floor. The rosary fell from her hand.

"If you ever do that again, my pretty," Galen began, now looking more formidable than usual from the severe angle at which Engelina had to view him, "I'll be forced to punish you for it. You do understand that, don't you?"

Engelina tried to nod her head but couldn't with his fingers buried to her scalp.

"You do understand, don't you?" he repeated, and Engelina realized that he would settle only for a verbal reply.

"Yes," she said, biting back pain, "I—I understand."

"Good. I wouldn't want anything to happen to your sister because of your impulsiveness."

He had threatened Chloe before, but now there was something hatefully insidious in his tone. Engelina's fear leaped higher than ever.

"Digitalis. It's such an unstable drug. A little too much and it can stop the very heart that it helps to beat."

Engelina heard the words but couldn't believe their ugly implication. "You . . . you wouldn't hurt Chloe. You wouldn't—"

"No, no," he interrupted, "I'm not going to hurt little Chloe, because you're going to be a good wife, aren't you?" When she didn't answer, he repeated, "Aren't you, my pretty?"

"Y-Yes."

"You're going to do anything, everything, I ask, aren't you?"

Engelina's stomach churned again, this time rumbling with nausea, but she said, "Y-Yes."

"Good. That's a good girl. That's a good wife." He released her hair, easing some of the pain. "Now," he added, "be a good girl, a good wife, and worship me."

Again, she heard the words, but they refused to merge into anything meaningful. "I don't understand."

"Worship me," he repeated. "You're on your

knees. Worship me. The way you do this god of yours."

Engelina had known since their wedding night that Galen Lamartine was a sick man, a mean man, but his true illness, his true corruption, did not register until this very moment. The nausea she'd felt earlier doubled, and she fought to keep down what dinner she'd eaten. She fought, too, at the panic that rose wave-high within her. Even through her fear and panic, however, her chin tilted in defiance of what he'd demanded. She would not betray the only thing she had left—her religion.

He saw her defiance. It pleased him, for all the greater would be his victory when she did his bidding.

"I won't," she said.

"Oh, I think you will . . . gladly."

"No. Never."

Quicker than lightning, he sailed the back of his hand across her cheek, making her skin pulse with fire, making finger-welts appear instantly. He had never struck her across the face before, and his doing so now took her totally by surprise. In some far corner of her mind, it also told her how desperate, how reckless, he was becoming. All of this she thought as she heard herself a give lung-heavy gasp.

"Say, 'Hail, Galen, full of grace, the Lord is with thee . . .'" he demanded, his voice now hard, his eyes harsh and implacable.

As frightened as she was, Engelina shook her head. "No. What you ask is blasphemous."

"What I ask is my due. I am your lord, your god. I am the one with the power to save you."

"No," she answered, "you cannot even save yourself."

Her reply angered him. She could see it in the narrowing of his snakelike eyes. "Say it," he repeated.

"No."

He simply stared at her. Suddenly he smiled, transforming his face into that of the handsome man whom half the city's ladies secretly lusted after and openly admired.

"Then I suggest that you pray to this God of yours, for Chloe's sake."

With that, he turned and started for the door.

"No!" Engelina cried, hearing full well his threat.

He didn't stop. He didn't even look back.

When his hand was on the doorknob, Engelina begged, "No, wait! I'll say it. I'll say whatever you want. Just leave Chloe alone."

Galen turned, a look of smug satisfaction written across his face. He took one leisurely step, then another, then another, until he stood over her once more. From her kneeling position, he again towered over her. Towered over her in triumph.

"'Hail, Galen . . .'" he prompted.

She had told him that she would say what he'd asked of her. She knew she had no choice. Still, the words would not come. Only tears would be that accommodating. She blinked back the teardrops.

"I will not ask again," he said, his face growing stern.

"'H-Hail . . . hail, Galen . . .'" At the sound of his name on her lips, at the sound of his name used in such blasphemy, something died inside Engelina. She had thought he could hurt her no more than he already had, but she was clearly mistaken. He had forced her to do that which she considered most loathsome. She filled the emptiness she felt within herself with the hollow, monotonous ring of her voice. "'Hail, Galen, full of grace, the Lord is with thee . . .'"

At her prayer's end, Galen stood studying her. It

was evident that he felt a sense of satisfaction. Once more, he'd wielded power over her. Once more, he'd controlled her. Yet he, too, seemed disappointed. Disappointed that he'd been able to break her. Disappointed that she'd complied even though he'd given her no option. Without a word, he left the room.

Engelina, still kneeling, watched him walk away. Again, she felt a tremendous hate well up inside her. This time, however, the hate wasn't confined to her husband alone. This time she equally hated herself. The tears that she'd earlier forestalled would no longer be denied, and she felt them plunge from her eyes and course down her cheeks, one of which still stung with the power of her husband's palm. In slow motion she doubled over, then collapsed onto the hard floor, curling herself into a fetal position.

In the past she'd been so careful not to let Chloe hear her cry. Tonight she didn't care who heard her. Tonight she was so disconsolate that she could think only of herself. She could feel the rosary lying just beyond her fingertips. Reaching for it, she tangled her fingers in it as though clasping the hand of a friend. It was a friend she didn't feel she deserved, not after the sacrilege she'd just spoken, but it was a friend whose strength she needed.

Roan heard sobbing.

This time he knew he wasn't mistaken. This time he knew his imagination wasn't spinning tall tales. Furthermore, the sobbing was so clear that it was without question coming from upstairs. Or did he just intuitively know that it was? Several times in the course of the last few minutes he'd also felt light waves of nausea. He had accepted them as his reaction to reading the diary. What he found written on the pages, what he found implied between the lines, was enough to make anyone sick—heartsick if nothing else. Now he wondered if the nausea had indicated that someone was in pain. Or, more precisely, was Engelina in pain?

This possibility left him feeling colder than cold on an evening that was dripping with heat. Laying the diary beside the magnolia blossom, he stood and started up the stairs. With each step he took, the sound, soft and mournful, became more audible. Yes, someone was definitely crying, and, yes, he knew in his heart that it was Engelina. Hastening his stride, he hit the top of the stairs on something just short of a run. He listened. The sound was coming from somewhere to the left, from one of the bedrooms. But which one?

The question was more easily answered than he dared hope, for, as he started down the hallway, he noticed immediately that one of the bedroom doors stood slightly ajar. A sliver of pale light streamed across the floor. The sight caused his heart to jump to his throat, for he knew there hadn't been a light on in the room for his entire stay in the house. Once he stood before the door, he stopped. What would he find? One part of him wanted to know. One part of him didn't. The part that wanted to know won out. But then, it was certain from the beginning that it would. There was no way he could turn his back on Engelina.

Slowly he pushed open the door.

By degrees the room, pink and rose and green in color, with a gigantic four-poster bed draped in lacy netting, came into view. An altar stood in the corner, while an ivory-colored pitcher sat in an ivory-colored washbowl nearby. A kerosene lantern, perched on a small table, cast a warm smothered light. None of these things drew more than Roan's cursory attention. The only thing he really saw was the woman huddled on the floor. The heart that moments before had jumped to his throat now fell at his feet.

Acting only on instinct, Roan moved toward her. Her back was to him, and the tresses of her long black hair sprawled about her in chaotic disarray. Something in the way she lay—a figure of abject desolation—frightened Roan. As did the heart-deep weeping. It was the kind of sorrowful noise for which there could be no solace.

"Engelina?" he called quietly.

She in no way responded. But then, he hadn't expected her to. He was suddenly uncertain which was more frustrating, his not being able to enter the past or his entering it without really being a part of it.

A sob caught in Engelina's throat, a particularly sad sound, and Roan edged around her and stooped down to face her. She lay curled in a tight ball, wearing a gown with a crimson-red stain smeared across the front. The stain was not the only crimson thing about her. Blood oozed from a cut on her lip, while her cheek, unnaturally pale, flamed with welts that had to have been the result of a slap.

Roan wanted to deny what he was seeing, but, despite the pain it caused him, he could not. He was looking squarely at the heinous abuse of Galen Lamartine. A numbness settled over Roan, as though all emotion had been wiped from him. Slowly, mercilessly, feeling began to return. He felt horror that anyone could be so cruel, especially to someone as delicate, as beautiful, as Engelina. He also felt anger, a red-hot, fiery anger that burned deep within his being. From anger he swiftly moved to rage, a kind of murderous emotion that left him aching for revenge.

The intensity of the emotion frightened him. He had never in his life wanted to hurt another human being. Hurting people went contrary to the healing oath he'd taken, yet in all honesty he had no idea what he would have done to Galen Lamartine had he had the opportunity.

Rising above all these emotions, he felt a powerful, savage need to protect this woman. The creep she was married to had no right to abuse her, not when she belonged to another man. This thought surprised Roan even as it warmed him. In a way he could not explain, he knew that this woman, this broken woman lying before him, belonged to him. She always had belonged to him. She always would.

Unable to stop himself, he reached out his hand and drew a crooked knuckle across her swollen cheek—tenderly, lovingly. He hadn't known what to expect. Would he meet with thin air? Would he feel substance? Would he finally touch Engelina?

Warmth.

Softness.

Both slid across his senses, assuring him that he had made contact with living flesh. The realization was heady, leaving him to feel giddy in a way he never had before. But he also knew a bitter disappointment, for it was obvious that Engelina felt nothing.

"Please," he whispered, drawing his finger across her cheek again.

"Help me," she whispered and for a fleeting moment Roan thought she had, indeed, sensed him, but he realized that she was praying when she added, "Please help me, Father."

Her plea, so poignantly delivered as the tears streamed from her closed, dew-lashed eyes, tightened Roan's heart until it felt like a stone confined within his chest. A heavy cold frustration claimed him. How in hell was he supposed to help her?

As though the question was the catalyst, the room began to shift. Roan sensed it seconds before he felt it. The altar began to disappear, the bed with its netting began to change into another, but quite different, four-poster. Engelina began to fade.

"No!" Roan shouted, reaching for her in an attempt to forestall her disappearance. The attempt was unsuccessful, for even as he tried to hold her, she turned to vapor and vanished before his eyes. "No!" he screamed again, feeling the emptiness of the room, the emptiness of his heart, close in around him.

TEN

"Where have you been?"

Roan heard the exasperation in Kay's voice and deduced that she'd tried to call him earlier.

"I've been here at the house."

"Then why didn't you answer the phone?"

"I didn't hear it."

"You didn't hear it? My God, I've called all evening. How could you not hear the phone ringing?"

"I just didn't hear it. I'm sorry."

"You've had me worried half out of my mind."

"I said I was sorry."

"For God's sake, it's after midnight!"

"I'm sorry I worried you."

"I had visions of a thousand gruesome things—"

"Kay, I said I was sorry."

At the tone of Roan's voice, a tone that said he'd had enough of this conversation, Cat glanced up from the foot of the bed, yawned, then laid its head back on his paws.

Roan sighed, ran his fingers through his hair—the same fingers, he noted idly, that hours before had brushed Engelina's cheek—and said, "I'm really sorry. Honest. Could we just move on?"

A silence ensued during which it was obvious that Kay was considering whether she should let him off

166

the hook just yet. "How are you?" she asked at length, reluctantly giving up the subject of the repeated phone calls.

Relief flooded Roan. "Fine," he lied.

Another silence followed, then, "Are you really?"

"Yes, really."

Something in this third hesitation attracted Roan's attention. He knew that something more was coming even before Kay spoke.

"Stewart called."

And? Roan asked silently.

"He said the guy who owns the house where you're staying called him."

Roan had the feeling he wasn't going to like what followed. "And?" he asked, this time out loud.

"The guy seemed a little worried about you. Something about a portrait. He seemed to think you're fixated on it."

Roan laughed, trying to sound nonchalant, trying not to sound as if he could string David Bell up by his heels. "I don't think 'fixate' is the right word. It's a nice portrait. I called to see where David Bell got it." The silence told Roan Kay wasn't buying his story entirely. "That's all there is to it," he lied, adding, "I got the time difference screwed up and woke him. I think he was pissed."

"Are you sure? I mean about being all right?"

Roan wasn't sure of anything these days, but he answered, "I'm sure."

At least momentarily placated, Kay changed subjects in a random fashion: How was the weather? Was he enjoying any of the city's culinary delights? What day that following week was he planning on coming home?

At this last question, it was Roan who grew silent.

So silent that Kay asked suspiciously, "You are coming home, aren't you?"

"I, uh, I thought I'd stay just a little longer."

This time Kay's silence seemed heavy with disappointment and disbelief. "I thought you were going to stay only a couple of weeks. Two weeks are up on Wednesday."

"There was no absolute time spelled out. The hospital thought I needed to get away for a while."

"You didn't want to go at all," she reminded him. "And you did say a couple of weeks."

"What's a week or two one way or the other?" he asked, thinking that he really wasn't up to this conversation.

"Our wedding. That's what," she answered, her voice now dancing around exasperation. "You do remember that we're getting married at the end of the month? Which was the reason you so conveniently came up with as to why I couldn't go with you. I had to stay here and finalize the plans, which I couldn't possibly do from there, you said." Exasperation had crossed over into anger by the time she'd finished.

"Of course I remember the wedding, Kay," Roan said, aware that he was lying again. Well, not exactly lying, but then not exactly telling the truth, either. He did and he didn't remember the wedding. It was there at the back of his mind; it was just that other more important things were in front.

"Gee," she said sarcastically, "how lucky can a bride get? The groom actually remembers the wedding."

"Kay, don't," he said, suddenly feeling weary beyond words. He didn't want to fight. He didn't have the emotional energy for it.

Silence, then, "Roan, what do you want from me?"

What *did* he want from her? He honest to God didn't know. No, he did know. "Time," he answered. "Just give me some time."

In the end, she apologized and promised him just that. As always, she gave and he took. Ironically, he knew that he was the one being shortchanged.

In a nearby motel, Crandall Morgan lay with his hands stacked beneath his head. To his left the clock announced midnight, or a few minutes past, while to his right the silver moon peeked through a slit in the drapes, giving the dark room its only hint of light. It had been a day of extremes, the highs of exhilaration, the lows of disappointment, and Crandall was reacting to both with a wide-eyed sleeplessness.

The source of his exhilaration was the tunnel. That afternoon at 4:47 he and his teammates had discovered that one end of the tunnel terminated at a spot where the old Capuchin monastery once stood. Centuries before, black-cowled Franciscan monks had quartered there and led worship in the cathedral. It was always exciting to have the past spotlighted, even if it raised more questions than it answered. Who had built the tunnel? Why? And when? And where did its other terminus lead? This latter question would be answered soon, for Wade thought they were nearing a door.

Secrets. They were one reason he loved his job so much. Discovering the past was the unlocking of secrets. In that he felt challenged, challenged to make all the pieces of the puzzle fit until there was a cohesive, coherent whole. Curiously, he didn't like the same secrets in his personal life. *That* he liked neat and tidy and well understood, which was the reason for his disappointment. As much as he hated to have to admit it, he was getting nowhere discovering his new identity. And, furthermore, his resources were running low. He'd searched through everything he could think of, every public record of any kind, but he couldn't find the name of Drexel Bartlett anywhere. It was as though the man had never existed.

Crandall sighed, well on his way to wondering for the thousandth time where he could look next, when a faint tap sounded at the door. He frowned. Who in the world could be knocking on his door at this late hour?

In answer to his question, there was another tap, then a quiet, "Crandall, it's me, Julie."

Surprised, Crandall rolled from the bed. He reached for the pair of jeans that lay carelessly draped across the back of a chair and pulled them on. Walking to the door, he opened it. Moonlight, like liquid platinum, poured about Julie's shoulders, making her long blond hair appear nearly white and softening her sharp features. For the first time, Crandall realized that there was something ethereal about Julie, something intriguingly ethereal.

"Hi," she said.

"Hi," he answered, adding, "is something wrong?"

"No," she said quickly. "I heard you through the wall. I couldn't sleep, either. I thought maybe we could not sleep together."

Crandall smiled and stepped aside. "That's the best offer I've had all day."

He switched on the bedside lamp, causing both of them to blink in the abrupt brightness. Indicating for her to sit down, he rushed ahead of her and grabbed a shirt from the room's only chair.

"Sorry," he said. "My wife—my ex-wife—always said I was a slob, and I guess I am."

Julie sat down. The long tanned legs extending from the cutoff jeans suddenly looked longer. "There're worse things to be."

"Not according to Cindy. Even an ax murderer takes second place to a slob."

Crandall eased to the side of the bed. His unfettered hair, clean from a recent washing, fell almost to his shoulders. He automatically reached for the rubber band that lay on the bedside table by the telephone and began to draw his hair into a ponytail.

"She also hated my hair," Crandall confessed, though he was unsure why he did. Except that sharing this private bit of himself somehow seemed right in a world of midnight, hushed light, and faded motel carpet.

"That's a shame," Julie said. "You have very nice hair." The compliment embarrassed both of them, and Julie hastened to say, "Today was great, wasn't it?"

Crandall sensed her excitement, the same excitement he felt. "Yeah, though I guess you've got to be a little weird to get off on discovering where a tunnel leads."

"Yeah, well, I guess I'm a little weird, then."

"Yeah, me, too."

"Where do you think the other end leads?"

Crandall shrugged. "I don't know, but we should find out soon."

"Yeah," Julie said, clearly invigorated by the prospect. "Don't you think all this secret tunnel business, beneath a cathedral to boot, is wonderful?"

"Or scary," Crandall replied, voicing an emotion he'd felt from the very beginning of the project.

Julie's smile faded. "Maybe that, too. It does make you wonder why a church would have a need for a secret passage."

"Precisely."

Julie's smile returned. "That's what I love about the past. It's filled with delicious mystery."

Crandall's lips curled upward. "That's exactly what I was lying here thinking."

"Does that make us two peas from the same pod?"

"I'd say that makes us two weird peas from the same pod."

Julie giggled, a bright, carefree sound that Crandall found appealing. Almost as appealing as the twinkling light that jumped into her brown eyes.

"I'll tell you a secret if you promise not to tell a soul."

The impish look on Julie's face captivated Crandall. This woman with the impressive IQ, this woman who had to be pushing thirty, suddenly looked like a giddy teenager. Crandall, feeling as young, grinned and crossed his heart.

"Not a soul," he said conspiratorially.

"I sometimes think I've lived before," she stated bluntly, boldly. "You know, reincarnation and all that. I have this obsessive fascination with anything old, and I sometimes think I've seen or said or done something before. I know that everyone thinks this occasionally, but I do all the time. And really strongly. I mean, I just *know* some things. Like I just know that I've lived in New Orleans before. In a big fine house." She laughed. "Why does one always have a grand past life? How come no one is ever poor or ugly or a nobody? How come one is never a servant in a big fine house, but always the mistress or the master?" Her smile disappeared abruptly. "Do you think I'm crazy?"

"No. Though I do think you're one of the most fascinating women I've ever met."

It was obvious that Julie hadn't expected this response. Caught off guard, she spoke honestly. "I thought we had something going there for a while."

"We did. I think we do. It's just that I've got some personal problems I need to work through."

"Are they anything I can help with?"

A part of Crandall wanted to tell her about his recent discovery that he'd been adopted, but he held back. He wasn't certain why, except that he felt so rudderless without a past to steer him. Somehow he didn't feel himself anymore. Right now he didn't have anything to offer a woman, except doubt and confusion.

"No," he said, shaking his head. "At least not right now."

"I'm here," she said, adding, "if you change your mind."

He nodded and the room grew quiet. In the pale light, Crandall thought Julie looked pretty. Not beautiful. But pretty. In an appealing, comfortable, wholesome way. In an honest way. Which was Julie's strength. Everything about her was honest, uncontrived. If she said she had lived before, then, doggone it, he believed her.

"I, uh, I think I'd better go," she said simply as she drew her gaze from Crandall's bare chest, tufted in golden-brown hair.

Both rose at the same time and walked toward the door. Crandall opened it. The night was still firecracker-hot. The moon still shone down with an eye-hurting brilliance.

Julie turned and said, "Good night."

"Good night," Crandall said and watched her start back toward the neighboring room. Suddenly he felt lonely. Lonelier than he could remember feeling in a long time. Even lonelier than he'd felt after the divorce that had stripped him of some of his confidence. "Julie," he called.

She stopped.

He walked toward her, feeling with his bare feet the heat trapped in the concrete. He equally felt the sensual heat trapped in Julie . . . and in himself. Without touching her anywhere else, he lowered his head, dropping his lips to hers. Hers were warm and soft and parted slightly. His moved gently, thoroughly, then pulled away quickly, as though not trusting himself to linger longer.

"Just give me a little time," he said.

Julie nodded and said, "I'll give you all the time you need."

Time.

It was the one thing over which Marie Cambre could not work her magic. She could not stop its passage, nor could she hasten it to her will. Would that she could, she thought as she stared out into the star-spangled night.

"What are you thinking?" the man in her bed asked.

"Wishing I could stop time."

"Why?"

"So that I could stop the evil I feel moving about me. So that I could keep it from worming its way into the future."

"Evil cannot be stopped," the man replied. "It can only be countered."

Marie shrugged. "Perhaps."

"You're still troubled over that girl, aren't you?"

Marie didn't answer, indicating that the man, the man who knew her oh so well, once again had read her like a book. There had been another disappearance in the last week, this one hitting closer to home than was comfortable. Furthermore, it galled her that she still heard the persistent rumors that she was involved.

The man, his burly body powerful and healthy, slipped from the bed and moved to stand behind Marie. She could feel his nakedness. She could feel his hands slip to her arms, where they began a caressing up-and-down motion. She could feel his lips at her neck.

"No one who knows you could believe you are involved," he said, again reading her mind. "A little naughty you might be, but never evil."

Ordinarily the comment would have earned a smile from Marie, but not tonight. She couldn't wrest her mind from the servant girl who had worked in the big fine house owned by Monsieur Desforges. The servant girl who had smiled easily, trustingly. The servant girl who had been almost ethereal with her bright eyes and blond hair. Marie had seen her on several occasions, whenever she'd been engaged in transacting her secret business for the household.

Monsieur Desforges regularly commissioned Marie to carry letters of assignation to the Creole beauty who lived in the white house on Rampart Street. There was also a married woman from the upper crust of society with whom he kept clandestine company. It never troubled Marie to be the instrument of infidelity. If one wanted to stray, one would, and she believed she provided not only a service to the adulterer but also to the adulterer's family in the form of discretion. In the case of Monsieur Desforges, Marie always felt a secret delight, for as she was carrying letters for monsieur, she was also carrying them for madame, whose lusty appetite not only equaled but surpassed her husband's.

"Madame Desforges thinks the servant ran away," Marie said, adding, "But I do not think so. Nor do others." Before her lover could reply, she asked, "Do you believe this Hell-Fire Club exists?"

"If it doesn't, it soon will with all this publicity."

"Are Monsieur Desforges and Monsieur Lamartine still in business together?"

"Yes, and Harnett, too. They own half the companies on the wharves."

"And what do you think of these Messieurs Desforges and Harnett?"

"I think they keep bad company."

"Ah, and so do I." Silence, then, "The disappearances are not over."

"How do you know?"

"I just know."

The man knew better than to argue with her intuition. She was always right.

"I know, too, that it is my place to stop them."

"How?"

Marie shrugged, then smiled as she turned in her lover's arms. "Must I know everything?"

Years away, another woman stared into the primitive night. A black cat with amber eyes stood beside her, as though it, too, sensed the restlessness that she did. The cat meowed.

"I know," Micaela said, her voice soft and soothing.

All the players were in place, the action set to begin. But the cards spoke of deception, betrayal, danger. She saw the bloodred light of a flickering candle; she saw the eerie darkness of a long tunnel; she saw the orange-red flames of fire. She saw death.

Death.

Grim, watchful, unrepentant.

Fingering the cross at her neck, Micaela prayed. She prayed that the wrongs of the past might be righted. She prayed that evil might not triumph a second time. She prayed that love would at last prevail.

The next day, a bright sunny Saturday, the doorbell of Lamartine House rang at precisely three-thirty. Roan, who hadn't slept well the night before, was dozing in the chair in the parlor, Engelina's diary still in his lap. At the sound of the doorbell, he jerked awake. Who in the world could that be? he thought, laying the diary on the nearby table. His footsteps ringing down the hallway, he approached the door, opened it, and, at the sight that greeted him, stood stock-still.

After awkward moments passed, Kay said finally, "Aren't you going to ask us in?"

"Hell, Roan," Stewart said. "We had to come down to see what you're so reluctant to leave."

"You know Stewart and his spur-of-the-moment decisions," Mark said in the way of an apology for their showing up unannounced. Susan, who stood at her husband's side, simply smiled—contritely.

"Well, aren't you going to invite us in?" Stewart asked, echoing Kay's earlier question.

Roan would have given every cent of the money he owned to get rid of his friends politely, but there was no way he could. For the first time in his life, he knew what it felt like to be trapped. Truly trapped.

"Yeah, sure," he said, pasting a smile on his lips and standing back. "You guys just took me by surprise."

Kay was the first to step in . . . and into his arms. "Hi, darling," she said, brushing her lips across his.

"Hi," he said, feeling her lips but not really reacting to them. He did pull her into his arms for a quick hug, but he knew it was because if he didn't do so it would look strange. His reasoning troubled him. Shouldn't he want to hug his fiancée?

In turn, each of his friends passed into the house and, ultimately, into the parlor.

"What a delightful room," Susan said. "Oh look, Mark, what a sweet courtyard!"

Mark joined his wife, and the two of them stood staring out into the enclosed sunlit garden.

"That's a beautiful magnolia tree," Mark said, adding, "Is this a flower from it?"

"What?"

Roan had been concentrating on slipping Engelina's diary into a drawer unnoticed. The battered book was the first thing he'd seen upon reentering the room. The sight of it had prompted another concern. What if something crazy happened while guests were in the house? How was he going to explain the shifting of furniture and the appearance of nineteenth-century figures? Not easily, something told him.

"Is this flower from the tree in the courtyard?" Mark repeated.

Roan glanced down at the blossom that was beginning to turn brown around the edges. "Ah . . . yeah," he answered.

"If you ask me," Kay said, staring out at the courtyard and the tree, "the garden looks positively depressing. That's a hideous fountain."

"I don't know," Susan said. "I sort of like it. I mean, it does look old and all."

"Whose cat?" Mark asked.

"What?" Roan asked, feeling that the conversation was going way too fast for him to follow.

"There's a Siamese cat out here on the patio," Mark repeated.

The fact confirmed what Roan had grown to suspect. There was a break in the wall through which the cat came and went as it pleased.

"It's a stray. The owner of the house asked me to feed it if it stopped by."

"Looks like it's taken up residence," Stewart said, adding, "God, that courtyard is depressing. But then the whole house is."

"It is not!" Susan said. "It's beautiful."

"I didn't say it wasn't beautiful," Stewart said. "I just said it was depressing."

"I agree," Kay said, shuddering. "There's something about this place that gives me the willies. How can you stand to stay here, darling?"

Fortunately, no one gave Roan a chance to answer.

"The place has atmosphere," Mark said.

"It's haunted," Stewart said matter-of-factly.

Roan gave his friends a quick glance.

"What do you mean haunted?" Kay asked, equally interested in what had just been said.

"David said that it's supposed to be haunted, if you believe in that kind of thing. The original house was destroyed in a fire, then rebuilt at the turn of the century, sometime during the twenties, I think, but the guy who rebuilt it lived in it only a year before he moved out. He said it was haunted. It's had a succession of owners, but no one's stayed long. When David bought it, it had been vacant for a while. He's tried to restore it as close as he could to the original."

"Who's supposed to haunt it?" Kay asked.

"I don't know," Stewart answered. "Some woman."

"Can you believe people actually believe all that nonsense?" Kay said, adding, "Have you seen a ghost, darling?"

Again, Roan, who was growing more uncomfortable by the minute, was spared from answering.

"Oh, look," Susan said, excitement once more claiming her as she moved toward the mantel, "that's a petticoat mirror."

"A what?" her husband asked.

"Women checked their petticoats in it . . . discreetly, of course."

Once everyone's attention was riveted to the fireplace, it was only natural that their attention roam upward. To the portrait.

"Good grief, who's that?" Mark asked. "Is she a knockout or what?"

"Watch it, Dr. Hagen," his wife teased, though she couldn't help saying, "She is beautiful, but there's something sorta sad about her, isn't there?"

The mention of the portrait captured both Stewart's and Kay's attention. The latter dramatically so.

Stewart tried to sound nonchalant when he asked Roan, "So, is this the painting you called David about?"

Kay kept her attention focused on the portrait, but it was clear she was listening to Roan's reply with every fiber of her being. It was equally evident she would have preferred that the portrait in question be of someone other than a beautiful young woman.

Roan knew he couldn't avoid answering. He knew, too, that Stewart had made the trip because he'd been worried about him. "Yes," he said, trying to sound as if the question were of no real importance. "Would anyone like anything to drink? I've got some soft drinks in the kitchen, and Dr. Bell's bar is well stocked."

"I'll have a Coke," Susan replied.

"Yeah, me, too," Mark answered.

"Who is she?" Kay asked, ignoring the offer of drinks. Her eyes had never wavered from the portrait.

"She used to be the lady of the house," Roan said, again with what he hoped was nonchalance.

"Did she have a name?" Kay persisted.

Roan hesitated. He didn't want to share even a name with these people in general, with Kay in particular.

Kay turned, pinning Roan's gaze with hers. Her sea-green eyes looked more persistent than usual. "Did she have a name?"

Roan ran a hand into his khaki slacks, as though that gave him a casual look he hoped his voice duplicated. "Engelina . . . I think."

"Engelina Lamartine," Susan repeated. "A pretty name for a pretty lady."

"Is she the ghost that's supposed to haunt the house?" Mark asked innocently.

Suddenly all eyes were on Roan, Mark and Susan just

waiting for the answer to an interesting question, Stewart with a look that Roan couldn't quite define, Kay with a look that he could define even less than Stewart's.

Roan laughed. "Beats me," he lied. "Stewart's the one with all the ghost tales." Turning, he started from the room. "I'll get those Cokes."

When Roan returned, everyone thankfully seemed to have forgotten about the portrait. Laughter and giggles prevailed for the next thirty minutes, with Mark and Stewart catching Roan up on what was going on at the hospital. He listened with half an ear. Kay had seated herself beside him and took every available opportunity to touch him—the back of his neck, his hand, his thigh. He felt himself growing ultrasensitive. Kay's touch was beginning to grate on his nerves. The slightest caress felt like a Mack truck running over him. And her perfume was driving him crazy.

"Well, here's the program," Stewart said, taking his usual charge. "We're going out to eat tonight at one of the fanciest restaurants in town, then we're going to all sleep late in the morning, and then we'll play tomorrow by ear."

Roan had guessed that they'd come for the night, but he'd kept hoping he was wrong. Now, all his hopes dashed, he felt like shouting, crying, throwing them out. None of which he could do, of course. And, strangely, a part of him wanted to see them . . . just not now.

Bedrooms were divvied up, with Roan offering Kay the one he'd been using, the implication being that he would move elsewhere. Which he did. Into the room where he'd witnessed Engelina. As expected, the move didn't please Kay, but this time she said nothing. She simply accepted it as graciously as her disappointment allowed.

According to their plans, everyone was to meet

downstairs in the parlor at seven o'clock so they could leave for Antoine's by seven-thirty. Again, Stewart had managed to get a last-minute reservation. Roan wanted to be the first one down, so he could scope out the room and make certain that it was still in the twentieth century. Not that he could do anything about it if it wasn't.

Cautiously he opened the parlor door. Not now, he thought. Please, not now. As the room came into view, his heart jumped expectantly, then wildly as he saw a man standing at the door leading to the courtyard. Roan feared the tall, lean man was Galen Lamartine. At the sound of Roan's entry, the figure turned.

"You look as though you were expecting someone else," Mark said, a smile on his lips.

Relief rushed through Roan. "No," he said, "I was just expecting to beat everyone down."

"It doesn't take long for me to dress, and I learned a long time ago to get out of Susan's way as fast as I could."

Roan smiled and stepped to stand at his friend's side. Each man, as though it were some tribal rite, slipped a hand into a pants pocket of his suit. Both silently stared out into the enclosed courtyard. The fountain, gilded in the dying rays of the golden sun, gurgled a throaty song.

"I told Stewart we should have called first," Mark said. "But you know Stewart. He's like a freight train you just can't stop."

Roan grinned. "Yeah, I know."

"He's worried about you," Mark said, pulling no punches. "And so is Kay."

"I'm fine."

"Are you?"

Roan started to say yes because it was what he'd

been saying for so long, but he heard himself saying instead, "No. No, I'm not."

"You want to talk about it?"

"Something happened to me in Mexico."

"You had a near-death experience." Roan glanced over at his friend. "It's the only thing that makes any sense."

"I never believed in near-death experiences."

"Our refusal to believe in something doesn't alter reality. What is, is."

"I saw lights, a tunnel. I think I heard a voice, or rather I felt a voice."

"Just accept it as some supreme power in the universe. There is something greater than you, Roan," his friend said with a grin.

"And there's also evil, isn't there?"

"Most cultures throughout history have accepted that premise, along with the corollary that there's goodness."

"And what about justice? Does goodness always win out?"

"I'd like to think that ultimately it does."

Was that what he was caught up in? Roan thought. Was he caught up in the age-old battle of good versus evil? Was it destined that he rectify a long-ago wrong?

He pondered the questions all evening, when he should have been listening to the conversation of his friends, when he should have been responding to the good-night kiss Kay gave him, when he should have been sleeping. He was still pondering the questions at a quarter to one. It was then that he heard the voices, a commingling of muted sounds that came from the parlor.

All else fled from his mind.

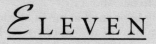LEVEN

The voices grew in intensity as Roan descended the stairs.
What had been soft and subtle when heard from
upstairs now sounded exactly like what it was: party
chatter. My God, was he the only one in the house who
could hear it? Or was he just the first out of bed and
down the stairs? Would his houseguests follow shortly?

At the foot of the curving stairs, he stopped. The
door of the parlor was closed, just the way he'd left
it. From behind the portal he heard the gay notes
of feminine laughter and the tinkling of fine crystal. Turning the doorknob, he paid no heed to the
fact that he wore only a pair of jeans, and these
unsnapped at the waist. Whatever he found beyond,
he knew that no one would be able to see him.

Pushing open the door, he peered inside. Men
and women, all from a past century, milled about in
colorful confusion. Nearby, a couple of women,
dressed to the fashionable nines, giggled behind
spread fans, while two other women spoke of clothes.

"I can find nothing to please me in the city,"
Madame Desforges said, making certain the skirt of
her satin gown billowed just so.

"Nor I. I must have everything shipped from
Paris." Mrs. Harnett pretended to be piqued but
could not hide her pleasure at being able to afford

184

shopping on such distant shores.

Putting out his hand, Roan tested the air for an energy field. Finding none, he stepped into the room and closed the door behind him in an attempt to contain the noise. He tuned out the two clothes-oriented women, whom he recognized as having been here once before—they'd been talking about clothes then, too—and gazed about the room. A group of men, puffing at cigars and imbibing brandy, carried on a conversation in the corner. Galen Lamartine stood in the thick of them. Galen Lamartine with his inordinately handsome looks and his heart of purest black. Again, Roan felt rage. The rage was countered, however, by the realization that, if Galen was in the room, Engelina probably was, too. The need to see her again took precedence over everything else.

He scanned the faces quickly. The memory of what Engelina had looked like the night before, huddled on the floor, a red handprint slashed across her beautiful face and a cut on her lip, burned in his heart. But not nearly as searingly as her tears. Never had he been so moved by anyone's tears. He had about decided she wasn't in the room, after all, and at this he was ready to plunge into despair, when he saw her standing alone, as though she'd slipped quietly to the side for a moment's respite.

She wore the red dress that Galen Lamartine had chastised her for not wearing before, the one she couldn't wear because of the bruises at her throat. It was plain to see why her husband preferred the dress. It was beautiful. No, she made the dress beautiful. Her porcelain-pale skin against the claret-colored dress created images that time could not destroy. The neckline of the dress, low and round, lay off her shoulders, forming puffs of shimmering fabric for sleeves. Beyond the form-fitting waist flowed three voluminous flounces. A ruby necklace, three-tiered, rested at her throat, while her hair, pulled high and piled wildly, contained tiny red rosettes.

She looked absolutely breathtaking. So breathtaking, so exquisitely beautiful, that Roan took a step toward her. If only he could see her more closely. If only he could confirm that she was all right after her husband's brutality of the night before. He had taken a half dozen steps toward her when suddenly, as though she sensed his presence, Engelina raised her head. Her eyes met his. Her soft, sorrowful, soul-dark eyes. He knew it was his imagination or, more precisely, wishful thinking, but he could have sworn that she saw him. For an infinitesimal fraction of a second, he saw some something pass over her face. A recognition. A lessening of the sadness in her eyes.

Madame Desforges and Mrs. Harnett stopped talking abruptly. One of the giggling young women gasped. The other hastened her hand to her mouth in open surprise. Bit by bit, like a wave rolling out to sea, the room grew quiet. Galen Lamartine looked up. Frowned. And started toward Roan. As if a knife had cleaved through his guests, the people parted to allow passage of their host.

They could see him!

The realization that he had at last fully connected with the past hit Roan like a tumbling ton of bricks. He had longed for this. Now, however, he wished it had chosen a more fortuitous moment to occur. He took a step backward. Then another. Galen, his eyes hard and cold, was bearing down on him. The quietness that had descended was now being filled with twitters of stunned conversation. Roan, continuing to back up, took one last look at Engelina. She was still watching him. Closely. As though her life depended on seeing him for as long as she could.

Abruptly, the doorknob pierced Roan's bare back. Reaching behind him, he turned the knob and, without hesitation, opened the door and slipped out into the hallway. He shut the door, and what he hoped was the past, behind him.

He had just taken a relieved breath when he ran square into Kay.

It all happened so quickly that Engelina didn't know what to think. One moment she was standing there wishing she were a thousand miles away from all the noise and gaiety, the next she was looking into the deep dark-brown eyes of a stranger. A stranger who was nearly naked. A stranger who really didn't seem like a stranger at all. Had she seen this man somewhere before? She sensed that some of the women around her feared him, but she didn't. In fact, she had the oddest feeling that he'd come for her, and the even more odd feeling that she would have gone with him—no questions asked. It had something to do with the unwavering way he studied her. It had something to do with the concern she saw in his eyes.

And then he'd disappeared as quickly as he'd appeared.

Engelina felt her husband brush past her as he hurried toward the door. To his cohorts, Desforges, Harnett, and a band of other masculine guests, Galen said, as he yanked open the parlor door, "Search the house."

Run! Engelina silently ordered the stranger. At the empty hallway, she felt her hopes rise, though when she saw her husband speaking with the brawny Irishman, as always dressed in sinister black, the same hopes plummeted. He knew nooks and crannies of

the house that even she didn't. And he was like a
bloodhound, a raven-black bloodhound that never let
go of a scent. Even as this thought occurred, the
Irishman, his beard and hair flame-red, glanced up at
her. At the chilled stillness in his amber eyes, fear
trickled down Engelina's spine. Fear for the stranger,
fear for anyone who got in this man's way.

Galen reentered the room with an ingratiating
smile. "There's no need to worry, ladies. The
scoundrel will be caught."

His remark unleashed a round of comments and
questions, all seemingly made at the same time.

"Who was he?"

"He looked positively mad."

"I'm still trembling with fear."

"He could have killed us, I'm sure."

"Don't be ridiculous. He was unarmed."

"He was unclothed. I've never seen anything so
outrageous."

"I've never seen anything quite so delicious, have
you?" This Madame Desforges said to Engelina and
Mrs. Harnett in a lusty undertone.

Engelina's experience with semiclad men was
decidedly limited. Her experience with men in general was limited, and what she did know about them
didn't endear the sex to her. Even so, Madame
Desforges's comment conjured up an image of cof-
fee-brown hair, tousled as though the man had just
risen from bed, broad shoulders, and a bare chest. To
say nothing of bare feet and pants that hung so low
on the hips one had to wonder how they stayed on.
Despite this powerful physical image, the thing that
most remained with her, however, was his eyes. There
was a strength in them that drew her. Moreover, it
was a strength she needed. Desperately.

"You're incorrigible," Mrs. Harnett said.

The conversation came to a close as Galen stepped back toward his wife. Tactfully, he disengaged her from their other guests.

"Do you know this man?" he asked quietly.

"No, of course not. I've never seen him before." She disregarded the fact, even to herself, that the man looked vaguely familiar.

Galen's hand tightened on her arm. Not painfully. But with the promise of being painful at the slightest provocation. "You wouldn't lie to me, would you, my pretty?"

Engelina tipped her chin. "I don't know the man."

Galen was about to say something more when the Irishman threaded a path through the roomful of guests, making his way toward his employer. Engelina strained to hear what was being said when the two men bent low in conversation. At the words "can't find him anywhere," she breathed a silent sigh of relief. She had no idea who the stranger was, but she knew it was imperative that he escape. She knew one other thing, as well. She knew that she would see him again.

"Kay!" Roan said, his hand still on the doorknob, his heart still pounding in his chest. Whether from what he'd just been through or from what he feared he was about to go through was uncertain.

"What are you doing down here?" Kay asked.

The question implied that she hadn't heard the party sounds. Maybe he, with his ultrasensitive hearing, was the only one who could. But, if that was so, what was she doing downstairs?

As though in answer to his question, she said, "I heard you slip from your room." Before he could reply, she said, forcefully, "Roan, we've got to talk."

Roan released the doorknob, wondering if the

door would now burst open, allowing Galen, and the nineteenth century, to catch up with him. When the door remained closed, Roan breathed a sigh of relief and started for the stairs. "Let's talk upstairs."

He placed his arm around Kay's waist in an attempt to guide her, but she broke free, saying, "I want to talk here and now." With that, she turned the handle of the parlor door and stepped into the room.

"Kay, wait!"

The room lay in darkness, illuminated only by the pale moonlight. Silence, like a hushed summer song composed of still, shrill notes, skipped about, ricocheting off wall and ceiling. Beyond whimpered the fountain.

"What is it?" she asked, obviously confused by his abrupt command.

"Nothing," he said, hoping his relief didn't sound as evident to her ears as it did to his. As always, he felt disoriented. Going from one century to another, one world to another, was unsettling. For a little while following the journey, he seemed to belong nowhere.

"Aren't you going to turn on the light?" Kay asked finally.

Roan did. Kay stepped deeper inside, her gaze going to the portrait of Engelina. Without a word, as though it drew her beyond her will, Kay moved to stand before it. She simply stared at it.

Roan had begun to grow uncomfortable when Kay turned and repeated, "We have to talk."

Roan noted that Kay was as pretty as ever, with her blond hair mannishly short, her nails impeccably manicured, her eyes sparkling the same sea-green. She wore a white negligee, under which he could see the lace of her matching gown and just enough cleavage to be enticing. But he wasn't enticed. And he didn't understand why. There was a time when their bodies fit each other like a glove fitting a hand. There was a time when he couldn't get enough of her. But that seemed a lifetime ago.

"What's wrong?" she asked.

"Nothing's w—" he began.

Kay held up her hand. "Don't! I don't want to hear that nothing's wrong when I know darned well that something is!" She took a deep breath and ran her fingers through her hair, the huge diamond on her finger winking in the light of the overhead chandelier. "Look, Roan, I don't want to shout, I just want to discuss this like two rational adults."

Roan said nothing. The last thing he wanted was to discuss this—whatever "this" might entail—at all, but he saw no way out of it. The best he could hope for was to let Kay dictate its direction.

"Ever since Mexico, you've been different." Roan opened his mouth to defend himself, but Kay stopped him. "No, just hear me out." She hesitated, and Roan could see her trying to assemble her thoughts into just the right words. "I understand that you suffered a severe trauma. I'm not quarreling with that. What I don't understand is why you've shut me out of your life."

Once more, Roan heard the hurt in her voice. "Kay, I—"

"You've always been a private person, and I've tried to respect that privacy. It hasn't been easy, but I've tried. You're just not a person who gives of himself, but . . ." She stopped, once more trying to find the right words. "Ever since the accident, you've been withdrawn. I mean, really withdrawn. Roan, you've been living in your own private world, a world you just won't allow me entrance to."

It crossed his mind to wonder what she would say if he told her that he'd been living, at least occasionally, in a nineteenth-century world. In Engelina's world. In a world that he couldn't take her, Kay, to even if he wanted to.

"Kay, I don't expect you to understand."

"That's just it," she said, a cutting edge to her voice. "I've got to understand. It's time you make me understand. If we're going to go on as a couple."

"That sounds like a threat."

"Not a threat. Just a statement of fact."

"So what do you want to understand?"

"I want to understand why you wouldn't let me stay with you after the accident, why you wouldn't let me come to New Orleans with you, why you won't touch me anymore."

Reacting solely to the last part of her statement, Roan began, "That's not true—"

"It is *so* true. Dammit, Roan, we haven't made love since Mexico! And every time you come near me, I have the feeling that I was just diagnosed with leprosy." Hurt, as it so often does, had given way to anger. A hot, scalding anger.

Roan started toward her, but she held up her hand to stop him.

"No, I don't want you touching me now when an hour ago you could hardly tolerate a good-night kiss. And, God forbid I should share your bed!"

Roan sighed deeply, exhaustedly, and plopped down on the sofa. Everything she was saying was true. He couldn't, wouldn't, insult her by denying it.

"Kay, I haven't meant to hurt you. It's just that I'm going through a difficult time right now. I don't know how to explain—"

"Try."

There was no way he could tell her about what was happening to him. There was no way to tell her how he was caught up in a past world. There was no way to tell

her about Engelina. There was no way he could explain
to her, to anybody, what he himself didn't understand.
Furthermore, he didn't want to share Engelina with
anyone.

"See, that's my point!" Kay cried. "You won't talk to
me!"

"I can't."

"No, Roan, you can. You just won't. And what
about the wedding?" she tossed in.

"What about it?"

"Do you intend to try to be in town for it? Or are
you just going to give me a call that afternoon and tell
me that you need more time here in this godforsaken
house!"

Roan had never seen Kay angry before. It was a
formidable sight, with her sea-green eyes flashing a
storm warning. "Kay, please just give me a little time.
Please—"

"Do you love me?"

The question was simple enough. It was the answer
that was complex. Certainly he cared for her. That he
couldn't deny. Beyond that, however, he couldn't cat-
egorize his feelings. The truth was, he didn't know
how he felt about her. Weeks before, he'd believed
her to be a perfect match for him. But now . . . now
he just didn't know. After all, he was no longer the
man he used to be. Hell, he didn't know who he was
anymore!

"If you have to think about it that hard—"

"Kay, of course, I care for you."

"Do you love me?"

"Kay—"

"Do you love me?" At his silence, a silence that
seemed to have no end, she smiled sadly, mirthlessly.
"Well, I can never say you lied to me, can I?"

Roan stood and stepped toward her. She backed

away and slipped the ring from her finger. She laid it on a nearby table, the same table that had earlier held a perfect magnolia blossom. She then started for the door.

"Kay?" Roan called, his voice choked. He didn't want to hurt her. God, he didn't want to hurt her! But when she turned, he saw that he had.

"Just for the record," she said, her voice soft and oddly composed despite the tears threatening to fall, "is there someone else?"

Again, the question couldn't have been simpler. But, as before, the answer was mired in a complexity he couldn't sort through, for even as he pondered the question, an image of Engelina came to him. He saw her beauty. He saw her unhappiness. He *felt* her as her ghost had merged with his body. The feeling had been exquisite. Painfully exquisite. And more beautiful than anything he'd ever experienced.

"It's not what you think," he managed to say at last.

For long moments, Kay said nothing. Finally her gaze rose to the portrait, then lowered once more to Roan. Without a word, she walked from the room.

In the morning, Roan's houseguests left as unexpectedly as they'd arrived. Roan knew it had everything to do with the silent strain that existed between him and Kay. Though no one said anything, except with furtive looks, it was obvious that Mark, Susan, and Stewart noticed Kay's red, puffy eyes, the absence of her engagement ring, and the way she and Roan were overly polite to each other without ever making eye contact.

When Stewart announced midmorning that they should be getting back, everyone seemed relieved. Particularly Kay. Particularly Roan. Roan's relief lasted until he saw his friends getting into Stewart's BMW. He suddenly felt alone.

"You're sure you won't go back with us?" a concerned Stewart asked as he stood on the shady gallery. The others awaited him in the car. Susan and Mark had already said their good-byes to Roan. Kay had simply, wordlessly, gotten into the car, confirming that something was wrong. Very wrong.

"Yeah, I'm sure," Roan said, though a part of him wanted to take Stewart up on the offer. A part of him was frightened at what might lie ahead. "You don't think your friend will mind if I stay on awhile, do you?" Roan asked, the thought suddenly occurring to him.

Stewart shook his head. "No. I'm sure he won't." Then, tailgating the statement, he asked, as though it was what had been foremost on his mind since arriving, "Are you all right?"

"I'm fine, but thanks for worrying."

The two men stood looking at each other, Stewart jingling his keys, Roan poking his hands into the front pockets of his jeans.

"Well," Stewart said, "we'll see you in a week or two."

"Right. Ya'll be careful going back."

Stewart smiled, though it looked forced. "I've gotta be careful. I've got a hot date tomorrow night."

Roan grinned. "With Jackie O.?"

"Naw. Time to move on."

The two friends stood smiling at each other. Finally, Stewart said, "Well, see ya."

Roan let him get halfway down the steps before calling out. "Stewart?"

Stewart turned.

"Take care of Kay."

At the mention of Kay, Roan again felt his friend's reaction. His loving reaction.

"If she'll let me," Stewart said, every trace of his former grin now gone.

It was all that was said.

It was all that needed to be.

The tunnel was a hot, airless hellhole. Sweat soaked Crandall's back, causing his shirt to stick to him like adhesive tape. The same perspiration dewed his forehead, making the handkerchief tying back his hair sopping wet. Despite the tight enclosure on a broiling summer day, despite the hours-old perspiration that was beginning to smell sour, there was nowhere else on earth that Crandall would rather have been. His two compatriots shared the sentiment.

"You were right!" Julie cried. "There's a door behind all that junk."

"I told you there was a door," Wade said, then shouted, "Hot damn! We've found the other end of the tunnel."

The junk that Julie spoke of was the debris of a collapsed tunnel. Twice the tunnel had caved in around them; twice they'd found a section crumbled. In both cases, they'd had to dig their way through dirt, fallen beams, chunks of brick, and sundry other aged and decaying obstacles.

"C'mon, let's move this beam, and I think we can get through," Crandall said as he grabbed two fistfuls of the rotting wooden post. Wade took the other end of the log and pulled. Dirt fell away as they dislodged the post, causing a minuscule cave-in that sounded loud in the confined area.

"Be careful," Julie said, scraping the clods of tumbling black dirt back with her boot.

"We need to sift through this," Crandall said.

"Yeah, but let's try the door first," Julie said, the brightness that Crandall had seen in her eyes as she'd sat in his motel room once more shining through. She looked like a kid on Christmas morning. Crandall thought she wore her excitement prettily . . . sexily.

"No, we've got to sift this first," Crandall said, trying to hide his teasing grin.

"Ah, c'mon, we can do that later," Julie said, then saw Crandall's half smile. She threw a clump of dirt at him. It hit his chest and exploded. Along with his laughter.

"I think we ought to take a lunch break," Wade said, playing along.

"You're right. It *is* lunchtime, isn't it?" Crandall said.

"All right, you guys!"

Crandall's grin broadened, then died. He nodded toward the door as he glanced at Julie. "Why don't you do the honors?"

Julie now looked like a kid who'd been given a huge, ribbon-wrapped present on Christmas morning. Again, Crandall thought her enthusiasm enchanting.

"Okay," Julie said. She swiped her hands down the sides of her shorts as though cleanliness counted suddenly.

Crunching over uneven dirt, she stepped forward, curled her fingers around the dusty knob and, twisting, pushed against the door. It didn't budge. Not an inch. Not even when she shouldered it.

Swatting at a cobweb, Crandall moved to her side. Together they tried and failed. The door obviously wasn't giving up the room's secrets without a fight.

"Damn!" Crandall said.

"Ouch!" Julie said, rubbing her shoulder.

"Get out of the way," Wade said to Julie. She did and he took her place.

"Ready?" Crandall asked him.

"Yeah."

They pushed and grunted, then pushed and grunted again. The door begrudgingly began to creak open. As though caught on something, it stopped. The two men pushed harder, and the door swung open abruptly on a groan. Crandall grappled to hold on to his footing. Wade cursed.

Darkness, dense and murky, stood before them. For a fleeting second, Crandall had the feeling that the darkness was sinister. He'd never had this reaction before, and he chastised himself for it now.

"Lantern," he said, much as a surgeon calls for a scalpel during surgery.

Julie passed the lantern forward. Crandall took it and held it before him. Slowly, eerily, the room took shape. It was small, probably ten feet by twelve. It was also dank and musty and filled Crandall with a sense of foreboding. He shook this aside, as he had the sinister feeling, and stepped into the room. When his eyes grew accustomed to the semidarkness, shapes began to take form. As they did so, Crandall's heart began to beat wildly, sickeningly. On a back wall, heavy chains were imbedded into stone to serve as human shackles, while on a nearby table, covered with the dust of years, lay iron instruments of torture.

Silence settled, raining down like soundless snowflakes. A rat scurried by, making a squeaking noise. A clod of dirt fell from somewhere in the tunnel. A far-off car horn honked in muted reminder that life was going on somewhere on the surface.

"Good God!" Wade said softly.

Crandall forced himself to be professional. After all, they were there to excavate, not to react or judge. Keeping that in mind, he called out to Julie, "Bring me that other lantern." When seconds passed and no lantern was forthcoming, Crandall looked behind him. "Julie, bring . . ."

He stopped.

Julie stood in the doorway, as though an invisible line had been drawn over which she could not, would not, step. Her face had grown pale, her eyes wide—not with excitement, but fear. Cold, hard fear.

"Julie?" Crandall said, concern causing him to move toward her.

"No," she whispered. "I won't go back in there." Her vehement statement was more than puzzling considering she had yet to be in the room at all.

As she spoke, she took a step backward; Crandall took another step forward. He reached her just as she fainted.

TWELVE

An hour later, Julie lay sleeping in Crandall's bed. He sat in a nearby chair watching her. Her fainting had scared the living daylights out of him. He'd never seen her, or anyone, so pale, so frightened. What in God's name had she meant by not going back into the room? Once she'd come to, he'd tried to question her, but she'd simply stared at him—catatonically, as though what he was saying wasn't registering, as though his voice wasn't penetrating the veil that suddenly seemed to hang around her. When Wade had suggested taking her back to the motel, leaving him to clean up on site, Crandall had concurred. Now, a wet cloth and two aspirins later, she slept. Huddled in a ball as though she were cold. Her eyelids twitching with roving dreams. Her face still paler than it should have been.

Crandall sighed and pressed his eyes shut with his thumbs. He still had the dirt of the tunnel on him. He could smell it, feel it, taste it upon his tongue. He could hear the silence, the door squeaking open, his heavy breathing as he viewed the dark room and its darker contents. Over all this, though, he heard the sound of the sheets rustling. He opened his eyes.

Julie was awake.

"Hi," he called softly.

"Hi," she answered. "How long have I been asleep?"

Crandall checked his watch. "Almost an hour."

Digesting this information, Julie scooted to a sitting position, drawing her legs, which were still beneath the blanket, up under her chin. She hugged them to her.

"How do you feel?"

"Fine, I guess. No, my head hurts." She ran her hand across her forehead. "I've never fainted before. It feels weird."

"I know." Crandall smiled, adding sheepishly, "I fainted once when I gave blood. But don't spread that around, huh?"

Julie started to smile, but it never materialized. Instead, she began to disappear behind the veil once more.

"No," Crandall said, swiftly moving from the chair and to the side of the bed. "Don't leave me again." As he spoke, he tilted her chin, forcing her eyes to meet his. "Talk to me."

She said nothing.

"Tell me what happened back there."

Still she said nothing.

"Julie?"

"I've been in that room before. I don't know how or why or when, but I've been in that room." Her autumn-brown eyes were emphatic and sure. They were also troubled. "When the door opened, it was as though a thousand memories rushed at me. Memories of being held against my will. Memories of being afraid. Memories of—" She shuddered. "Memories of pain."

He pulled her into his arms, whispering, "Shh, it's all right now."

She clung tightly to him. "Don't leave me," she begged.

"I won't," he answered, feeling her breasts flatten against his chest, feeling her breath hot against his neck, feeling her heartbeat slam into his. He had no idea what had happened earlier. He had no idea what to make out of what she was saying. All he knew was that she was frightened. And that it felt right for her to be in his arms. "No," he repeated, pulling her more fully against him, "I won't leave you."

Monday, the day after his friends returned to Houston, Roan felt at loose ends. He didn't quite know how he felt about Kay's breaking their engagement, though relieved and sad, happy and miserable came to mind. He roamed the house, praying that he'd again stumble on the past. Now that he'd entered it, truly entered it in a way that had allowed him to be seen, speaking to Engelina directly became his sole reason for living. He had to see her again. He had to see her eyes seeing him. He had to talk to her. With the vacuum cleaner roaring in the distance, with the housekeeper puttering in pantry and parlor, he decided that now, however, was not the time to pursue the past. And so he grabbed the car keys and left the house, headed where, he didn't know.

In the end, his destination surprised him. Or maybe, upon reflection, it didn't surprise him at all. In her diary, Engelina had written of her daily worship at the St. Louis Cathedral. As the majestic spires came into view, he realized that just the fact that she had stood where he would be standing provided a measure of comfort.

The sight of white candles burning in bloodred votive cups greeted Roan, as did the fragrance of fresh flowers. From the cool, shadowed interior came the hushed sound of tourists moving about. Some few people were privately worshipping in the pews, their heads bowed, their knees bent in supplication. Mass had obviously been said earlier, for a priest, attired in green, collected a book and a silver bowl left over from the service and, genuflecting, disappeared through a side door.

Roan let his gaze roam over wooden pews, stained glass windows depicting Saint Louis at various stages of his life and canonization, the painting of Saint Louis on the wall above and behind the main altar. Moving quietly up the aisle, Roan took a seat on the third right-hand pew from the back. He closed his eyes and simply let himself, and life, be.

Engelina sat in her usual pew in the cathedral. She had missed mass that morning, for Chloe had not slept well the night before, and she had sat by her side until the young woman had drifted off to sleep. Engelina had then gotten the Irishman to drive her to the church for a private moment of worship. He'd simply nodded at her request and silently left to ready the carriage.

She had not gone to confession since the night she had been forced to blaspheme. She would not go again. She could not ask God to forgive her for something so unforgivable. And yet, Engelina suspected that it was she herself who could not forgive the blasphemy she had spoken.

As always, Father John had lightened her heavy heart.

"I did not see you at mass this morning, my child," he had said earlier in his soft, kind, caring voice. The collar of his cassock, a little tight, framed his cherub-round face, making it look even more round than usual and more innocent than a child's.

"My sister is not well."

"I am sorry to hear that. I shall say a special prayer for her."

"Thank you, Father."

"And how are you, my child?"

Engelina concealed the truth. "I am fine."

The priest had placed his hand on hers. The hand, like his cheeks, was etched in fine, reddish-purple veins. Tufts of hair, as yellow-white as that on his head, sprigged his knuckles.

"God is with you," he had said, giving her fingers an understanding squeeze.

Yes, Engelina thought now, he understood that all was not perfect at Lamartine House. She closed her eyes, holding the words—Father John's promise— close to her.

The sun shone warmly through the vaulted stained glass windows. Roan was aware of a lazy lethargy, of an uncommon serenity, of the feeling that time, indeed, had no boundaries. Sighing, he opened his eyes. The cathedral looked the same as it had when he'd closed them. At least, it looked the same at first. Slowly, though, Roan began to notice subtle differences. The altar had changed, shifted in its arrangement, as had the vases of flowers. Roses now resided where day lilies had only minutes before. The sanctuary was still filled with scattered worshippers, but now the women wore frilly hats, while the men were dressed in cutaway coats that looked as if they came straight from the pages of history books.

As this fact soaked in, Roan began to search the pews. Was it possible that Engelina was present? He dared not hope, and yet he did. He spotted a woman kneeling midway. Her hair, piled beneath a summer bonnet of blue, shone with the brilliance of polished onyx. Something in the way she bowed her head—the dip of her chin, a glimpse of the back of her neck— spoke directly to his heart. Again, he was reminded of fragility. Again, he was reminded of strength. Again, he felt an overpowering need to lessen her burden.

With a quickening heart, he watched as she stood, walked the length of the pew and, turning, genuflected toward the altar. She then started down the long aisle toward the rear of the church. Roan stood. He had no idea what he was going to say to her, but he had to say something. He couldn't let this opportunity pass. Not when he didn't know when there'd be another. Or even if there would be.

When Engelina, with her prayer book resting in the crook of her arm, saw him, recognition streaked across her face. The book tumbled to the floor, falling open at her feet. She didn't seem to notice. Neither did Roan. They stared at each other, she with a heart that was thrumming as wildly as his. Curiously, though, a sense of peace swelled through her. Peace, relief, the feeling that she had found a safe haven in a turbulent storm. Just as the one other time she'd seen him, she knew she would follow anywhere this man led. A sudden question came to her. Was this man her deliverer? Was this stranger, in strange clothes, the answer to her prayers?

"I was worried about you," she whispered.

Roan realized the absurd irony of the statement. He wanted to laugh. *She* was worried about him?

"How did you disappear so quickly?"

He smiled. "It was easier than you might think."

She started to smile, but it died when she saw her driver, the flame-bearded Irishman, standing at the church doors watching her.

"I must go," she said, adding, "We must not be seen talking together."

Roan saw the man dressed in black and recognized him. He also sensed Engelina's fear.

"Who is he?" he asked.

"He works for my husband."

"You don't like him." It was a statement.

"I don't trust him."

"Why?"

"He works for my husband," she repeated, as though that simple fact explained everything.

It did.

"I must go," she said again, gathering her skirt in her hand and stepping away from him.

"Engelina, wait!" he called and several worshippers glanced up.

Engelina stopped, surprised, yet not surprised that he'd known her name. She liked the way it sounded coming from him. Forceful, but not sweetly, sickeningly demanding.

He offered her the prayer book she'd dropped. She looked down, as though only now realizing that she no longer held it. She reached for it. Their hands brushed in the transfer.

Roan felt the warmth of her skin. It made him feel as vibrant as the sun streaming through the windows. Engelina, too, reacted to his touch. It was a sure touch, a competent touch, a touch that made her feel protected in a way she could never remember feeling before. Intuitively she sensed a gentleness about this man, this stranger, a gentleness she wasn't certain he even recognized himself. Then, because her driver awaited her, because the stranger's gentle touch, so foreign to her harsh life, threatened to bring tears to her eyes, she wordlessly turned and fled.

Roan followed Engelina from the building, watching as the stocky man fell in beside her. At the black carriage, crested in gold, he assisted her inside.

Engelina never once looked back, though the driver did. His gaze unerringly met Roan's. And then the burly driver hoisted himself into the carriage seat, whipped the animals to motion, and pulled the conveyance into the street.

Roan had no idea how long he stood visually following the carriage's disappearance. He knew only that a horn suddenly honked and a driver shouted an obscenity. The spell broken, Roan looked around him. He stood square in the middle of the street with cars sailing past him right and left. The driver honked again, then shouted, "Hey, mister, are you crazy?"

"Maybe," Roan answered. "Maybe I'm just that."

Roan knew he shouldn't cross over the rope cordoning off the restricted area at the back of the cathedral. He did it anyway, simply because he couldn't help himself. Like a magnet, he felt something drawing him to the spot. He'd been on his way to the car when he'd noticed the statue-dotted garden and the excavation site. He remembered the article that had appeared in the morning newspaper. Something about a secret tunnel and a secret chamber having been unearthed beneath the cathedral grounds. Even more intriguing, however, had been the macabre mention that instruments of torture had been found.

Stepping over the sawhorses, Roan, giving no thought to his freshly laundered pants, dropped down into the mouth of the tunnel. For a fast heartbeat, he remembered another tunnel, one with a bright light at its end. Knowing that he shouldn't, but not listening to the voice of caution, he started down the passageway.

The first step buried his expensive loafers in black dirt. Roan cursed, shook the shoe out, and had the same thing repeated with the second step. He said to hell with it and kept on going. He could barely see before him and in places had to run his hand along the cool wall for guidance. After some thirty to thirty-five feet, he saw a faint light up ahead. He also heard voices. As he rounded a corner, he saw a stretch of the tunnel that was perhaps ten feet long. Behind that was the entrance to a room. The voices were coming from inside the room. Male voices.

At the entrance to the tunnel, with a lantern at her side, sat a young woman. Her hair was long and blond and tied back in a frazzled ponytail. She was abstractedly sifting through the dirt. It was obvious that her attention was on the room. As clear as any emotion he'd ever sensed, he experienced her fear. The woman was afraid of the room. Deathly afraid of it.

No sooner had this woman's fear registered than Roan was besieged with the emotional impressions of other people's fear. Like grisly ghosts, fear floated around him, drowning him in its panicky presence. He also felt pain. Collective pain. So severe was the weakness that overwhelmed him that he doubled over with a moan.

Julie jerked her head toward the sound.

"You're not supposed to be . . ." At the man's bent-over posture, she stopped, then cried as she scrambled to her feet and rushed toward the stranger, "Oh, my God. What's wrong?"

Roan tried to speak but found that he couldn't. The weakness was too great.

"Crandall!" Julie shouted.

Crandall must have heard the commotion even before she called for him, because he instantly appeared at the door of the room. Wade was right behind him.

"Hey, this is a restricted area. No reporters are . . ." Crandall began, only to be silenced by the sight that greeted him.

Julie pleaded, "He's sick or something."

"Get—" Roan took a deep breath. "Get me out . . . of here."

Crandall stepped forward and replaced Julie at Roan's elbow. Wade moved to Roan's other side. The two men, with repeated admonitions for Roan to just take it easy, began to guide him back through the tunnel.

Scraps of conversation drifted to Roan. ". . . your heart . . . maybe a stroke . . . this damned heat . . . what are you doing down here, anyway . . ."

The farther Roan got from the room, the more the symptoms began to abate. By the time he reached the surface of the plundered garden, except for feeling washed out, he felt fine. And, as always, incredibly foolish.

"Do you need a doctor?" Wade asked as Roan collapsed onto the ground. He lay back in exhaustion, not giving a damn about dirt stains.

Roan shook his head. "No."

"I don't know," Crandall persisted. "I think you need to see a doctor. It could be your heart."

"I am a doctor. And it's not my heart." Roan could tell that the three people gathered about him were waiting for him to explain exactly what it was, then. Roan simply repeated, "It isn't my heart. Trust me."

"Would you like some water?" Julie asked.

Roan opened his eyes and looked at the blond-haired woman. She wasn't exactly pretty, but she did have a certain unique attractiveness that somehow seemed enhanced by the dirt streaking her face. "Yeah, please."

Julie started off at a trot for the far wall and a cooler of water.

Roan pushed to a sitting position. Both Crandall and Wade were crouched down before him. For the first time, Roan realized that Crandall looked familiar. It was the ponytail. But where had he seen him? He had no time to ponder the question because of another question thrown his way.

"What were you doing down there?" Crandall asked. "This is a restricted area."

"Sorry about that," Roan said, wishing he could explain. The truth was that he himself didn't know. He'd simply been drawn to the site, as in compelled, as in having all options removed. Maybe it was the same unknown force that had driven him to the cathedral that morning, the cathedral and his first real encounter with Engelina, which had been only ten or fifteen minutes before, but which now seemed longer. Much longer. Again, shifting time planes had rattled him. "I saw the piece in the paper," he said, hoping that explained his presence.

"What happened to you?" Wade asked.

"I'm not sure." At least this was honest, Roan thought. "It's happened before, though."

Crandall cursed. "It must be that room."

The statement piqued Roan's interest. "What do you mean?"

"Ah, hell," Wade said before Crandall could answer. "It's another reporter." This he said as a man appeared from nowhere and started toward them.

"Head him off at the pass," Crandall said, adding, "They've been swarming around us like bees on flowers ever since yesterday."

Wade walked toward the approaching reporter, leaving Crandall and Roan alone. It gave Roan the opportunity to repeat the question he'd asked moments before.

"What do you mean, it must be the room?"

Crandall suddenly looked unsure, as though he wished he'd kept his mouth shut. There was something about the stranger's interest, which was genuine enough, that persuaded him to answer.

"When we opened up the room yesterday, Julie"— here he nodded back toward the water cooler—"had some sort of . . . some sort of I don't know what. She wouldn't go near the room. She then proceeded to faint dead away. She still wouldn't go in the room this morning." He conveniently suppressed the information that Julie had thought she'd been in the room before. He didn't want to get a whole slew of rumors started. Neither did he want anyone thinking Julie was bonkers.

Roan remembered the young woman's fear. It hadn't been a small thing. It had been deep-rooted and bone-ugly. Yeah, he thought as he watched Julie walk back toward him with a glass of water, she had been, and still is, scared stiff of that room.

Julie smiled as she handed him the water.

Roan took the glass. As their fingers brushed, he had a quick inner vision. He saw this woman shackled in chains. He felt her mouth bound. He knew beyond a shadow of a doubt that she'd been a prisoner in the secret underground room.

Thunder rumbled and lightning rippled.

Engelina, her arms hugged about her as she stood in the darkness, stared out into the courtyard. The wind and rain, both fierce in their intensity, lashed at the greenery, beating the fern fronds into the ground, pounding the banana leaves as though they were savage drums, brutalizing the delicate blossoms.

Engelina's mind was a thousand miles away, however. Or, more precisely, the distance of the cathedral away. She couldn't get the stranger out of her mind. She had spoken with him that morning at church. Who was he? Where did he live? How had he gotten into the house on the night of the party?

More important, what would *he* do if he knew she'd spoken with the stranger and the stranger with her? Fear trickled through Engelina. Fear and puzzlement. Why hadn't the carriage driver, Kipperd, reported the incident? True, on the night of the party, Kipperd hadn't seen the stranger, so he didn't know that it was to him she had spoken, but it was his job to keep her away from everyone. Men in particular. Though he didn't love her, though he wanted men to want her, the beast she'd married was jealous of her. So why hadn't the driver mentioned the incident?

A sinister thought slithered through her mind. What if he had? What if the beast was only playing another game with her? What if he came home from wherever he'd gone after supper and proceeded to punish her for this indiscretion?

No, she would not think of him.

She would think only of the stranger.

She would think only of the stranger and of how safe she felt with him.

The day's events, talking to Engelina at the cathedral and stumbling onto the excavation site, kept playing over and over in Roan's mind. That, in addition to the rain thrashing against the windows, conspired to keep him awake. Finally he'd had enough of tossing and turning and wondering if Cat was getting soaked in the name of tomcatting. Barefoot, wearing jeans and a T-shirt, Roan slipped through the darkness and down the stairs. Midway, thunder trembled through the heavens, causing the old house to rattle and shake until the overhead chandelier tinkled threateningly.

Maybe a glass of warm milk would help, he thought, though he knew there was no scientific evidence to support the theory that heated milk aided sleep. He headed in the direction of the kitchen. However, at the closed doorway to the parlor, he stopped. Acting once more on impulse, with a wish in his heart, he opened the door.

At the sound of the doorknob turning, Engelina whirled toward the door. As though on cue, thunder shouted and lightning streaked. The latter illuminated the tall, lean, slim-hipped figure of a man. The man was not the one she dreaded seeing. She knew this instantly because of the way this man's slightly rumpled hair fell onto his forehead, because of the uncommon way this man was dressed, because of the way this man stood in the doorway staring at her.

The stranger.

The very person she most longed to see.

At first Roan thought he was seeing Engelina's ghost. That was how ephemeral the figure appeared in the stark flash of silvery light. Ephemeral and beautiful, so beautiful that the image couldn't be real. No hair could cascade so invitingly about a pair of shoulders. No shoulders could appear the pale color of moonlight. No eyes could, or perhaps even should, appear so piercing. And yet as he watched, he knew the woman was real. Simply because, deep within his own chest, he could feel her heartbeat.

"Don't be afraid," he said quietly.

Afraid? No, Engelina thought, it would never cross her mind to be afraid of this man. Besides, she now knew—she'd known it the moment she'd seen him framed in the doorway, or perhaps the first time she'd ever seen him—that this was the man destined to be her deliverer.

Roan closed the door behind him and walked slowly toward her. Though the room was semidark, he could see her angle her head to accommodate his towering height. When he stood directly in front of her, he spoke again.

"I won't hurt you."

"I know," she whispered.

No, she wasn't afraid of him. Roan could feel this, too. It pleased him. It humbled him.

"Who are you?" she asked. Even in the darkness, he could feel her eyes searching him for this truth.

"Roan. Roan Jacob."

"Roan Jacob," she repeated.

The sound of his name on her lips washed over Roan like heated honey. And it was twice as sweet. Were he to die the next minute, her speaking his name might well be his last request.

"How do you get in the house?" It was always locked. She knew that. *He* always kept it locked. Only he and Kipperd had keys.

Not *my* house, but *the* house. Roan noted this even as he pondered the question he had known she would eventually ask. He just wished that eventuality had been a little farther down the road. "That's, uh, that's not an easy question to answer."

"Why?"

Simple. Direct. What would she say if he answered it as simply, as directly? He was spared from answering it at all—at least for now—by the sudden mewling of a cat. Both Engelina and Roan glanced toward the door leading to the courtyard. A bedraggled Siamese cat, two wet ears pelted to its head, stood at the door begging entrance.

"Oh, poor thing!" Engelina cried softly, her tender

heart taking in the pitiful sight.

"Cat?" Roan asked, uncertain he could believe what he was seeing.

"Is it yours?" As she spoke, she stepped toward the door. Without hesitation, she opened it, allowing the feline to flee inside.

"Yeah. Sort of," Roan answered, analyzing this new development. Not only had he gone back in time, but so had Cat. Interesting, Roan thought. Very interesting.

The cat wasn't concerned with the metaphysical elements of the moment. It was concerned only with getting dry, which it proceeded to do by shaking itself. Water flew everywhere.

Engelina laughed, soft musical notes of a song that Roan knew wasn't played very often. He thought the sound pure magic.

"Obviously," she said as she lighted a nearby lantern, "Monsieur Chat does not like being wet. Perhaps you can dry him with this."

As she turned back to Roan she offered him an apron, which Lukie had left slung over the back of a chair. When her gaze met Roan's, his breath caught. Engelina was beautiful in the flashes of lightning, but she was more beautiful in the muted glow of the lantern. One thing Roan could not fault Galen Lamartine for was his choice of women. He had picked the most beautiful rose on the branch.

Engelina had been equally moved by the sight of Roan. She had thought him handsome, but never had the realization struck her so personally. Looking at him now, he eloquently reminded her that she was a woman. She had forgotten that fact. It was yet one other thing she couldn't forgive the beast for. There was a time when she'd enjoyed being a woman. Now she looked upon it only as a weakness. Now she longed to be physically strong, so that no one would ever take advantage of her again.

Suddenly Roan realized that she was still holding the apron out to him. Engelina realized the same thing.

"Thanks," he said, taking the apron and sitting down Indian-style on the floor. "Come here, boy," he called to Cat.

The animal, once so arrogantly proud, had been suitably humbled by the rain—to the point that it came when summoned, if there was at least the prospect of getting a little drier. Roan thought himself very much like the cat. There was once a time when his arrogance had ruled supreme. The last few weeks had humbled him, however. Perhaps forever.

"It's a strange-looking cat," Engelina said, adding, "Very long and thin. Are there not enough rats in the city for him?" Practically every home in the city owned a cat, a fat cat, specifically to keep the rat population at bay, and yet rats proliferated.

Roan thought of the bag of cat food in the kitchen. "Believe me," he said, "this cat would turn up its nose at a rat. Besides, this breed is long and slender."

Engelina smiled as she eased to her knees beside Roan. The skirt of her ivory dress puffed about her. Stretching out her hand, she rubbed the cat's head. The cat began to purr. "So it is that particular?"

"Yes, it is that particular."

"Does it have a name?"

"Cat."

Again Engelina smiled. So did Roan.

"Its name is not very imaginative," she said teasingly. It felt strange to tease. It felt strange to smile.

"It's a stray. I don't know its real name."

"Ah," she said as though that explained a lot. "Where does it come from?"

"Somewhere in the neighborhood."

"No, where does this breed come from? Where do they grow cats that are slim and that do not like rats?"

Roan considered. "I guess the breed originated in Thailand."

Engelina frowned. "Where is this Thailand?"

"Siam?" he amended.

"Oh," she said, as though this she'd at least heard of. "Why do you dress so strangely?"

The question came out of nowhere and reminded Roan of the delicacy of their conversation. "Where I come from, I'm not dressed strangely."

"Where do you come from?"

He'd anticipated the question, yet he still didn't know how to answer it. "From a long way away."

"From farther away than Siam?"

"Yeah," Roan answered. "From a lot farther away."

"And why have you come here?" Engelina asked, needing to confirm what she knew. It crossed her mind that, although she knew this man was the answer to a prayer, perhaps he did not.

Once the cat had been semidried, it had crawled into Roan's lap, as though needing the same reassurance Roan heard Engelina asking for. She knew who he was. Of that he had no doubt. It had everything to do with the way she was looking at him, as though she would trust him with her life. Which scared the hell out of him because he had no idea what he was doing. He was playing out this game in total darkness. Scared or not, he did know that it was time for honesty. At least a measure of it.

"I've come for you and Chloe."

Engelina said nothing. The fullness in her heart, a fullness that leaped to her throat, prevented communication. At least verbal communication. The tears of relief, the tears of joy, that sprang to her eyes spoke loudly enough, however.

"Don't," Roan whispered, reaching for her hand. Her fingers entwined with his—greedily, hungrily, beseechingly.

"Then take us away. Tonight. Now!"

Her request broke Roan's heart in two. He would give anything—anything!—to do as she'd pleaded. "It's not that simple," he said.

"Why isn't it?"

"I can't stay here, and I can't take you where I'm going."

"Why? I'll give you money. I have some money—"

"I don't want your money!" he interrupted, then forced himself to speak more calmly. "I don't want your money." He searched for a way to explain what was happening without frightening her. "Do you believe in miracles?"

Engelina nodded.

"Then think of my being here as a miracle that hasn't gotten all the bugs worked out yet."

"Bugs?"

"All the kinks . . . all the gremlins . . . all the problems," he said, settling on something she could relate to.

"What kind of problems?"

How did he tell her that he might fade away at any given moment? How did he tell her that he might be in the nineteenth century one second, but in the twentieth the next?

"Engelina, I . . ."

The room began to shift, at first a gentle vibration that quickly turned into a more violent motion. Again, it felt like the tremors of an earthquake.

"No!" Roan shouted, tightening his fingers as though in doing so he could hold on to Engelina and the past.

At first Engelina thought she was imagining the

room's movement. When she realized she wasn't, fear filled her. What was happening? Dear God, what was happening?

"Roan?" she cried, her heart scampering wildly, her hand grasping at his.

"It's all right. Don't be afraid," he said, but even as he spoke, he, the cat, and the apron began to grow dim, to fade, to disappear.

In seconds they had vanished, leaving Engelina to stare at where they—Roan in particular—had once been. Disbelievingly she reached out her hand, but it met with nothing. Absolutely nothing. It was then that the thought occurred to her: maybe she was losing her mind.

$\mathcal{T}$HIRTEEN

"Damn!"

It was two days later, on the Wednesday that marked Roan's two-week stay at Lamartine House. He felt antsy, as though his skin no longer fit him but rather was stretched tight across every nerve ending in his body. He'd felt this way ever since he'd disappeared right in front of Engelina. What in God's name had she thought? Had she been frightened? Had she, as he had his own, questioned her sanity? Therein resided the source of his restlessness. He didn't know what she thought, simply because he'd been unable to return to the past to ask her.

How he hated not being able to control his going back and forth in time! Control. The one thing that was so dear to him was the one thing he didn't even come close to having anymore. It was the one thing he hadn't had since this whole fiasco had begun weeks before. If the events of the past few days had been designed to prove to him how mortal he was, which he sometimes half believed was the case, then the point had been made. Well made. He'd never felt so helplessly human in all his life. Nor had he ever been more confused.

His confusion was centered around his recent disappearance. More specifically, it was centered around an apron. The apron he'd used to dry off the cat. It had been in his lap when he'd been transported back to the twentieth century. It, too, had made the trip. Interestingly, however, the apron had vanished within minutes. Why had the magnolia blossom stayed—its withered remains were still by his bed—but the apron had not? Though Roan didn't have an answer to this question, he knew it was important. If he could figure out this crucial point, perhaps he could visit the past at will. Or perhaps even bring Engelina to the present.

How to bring Engelina forward in time had been on his mind constantly of late, ever since an unsettling thought had occurred to him. He knew there had been a fire, a fire in which Engelina had died. But exactly when had that fire occurred? Nowhere had he read a date. The last entry in the diary was dated June 30, 1880, but that didn't necessarily mean that was the date of the fire. Who would have the answer he was looking for? One person came immediately to mind.

The pink house with the green porch looked exactly as it had the other time. So did its owner. At Roan's knock Micaela appeared, again from out of the dark shadows to the accompaniment of disturbed beads. As before, she wore black, black slacks and a black, high-collared blouse. The color's severity again was relieved only by the silver cross hanging around her neck.

"Hi," Roan said.

She said nothing. She merely studied him with her clear amber eyes, eyes that seemed to see things that other eyes didn't. She didn't seem at all surprised to see him.

"I'd like to talk with you."

Wordlessly she opened the door and let him in. She led him to the room where she'd received him once before. The soot-black cat curled in the middle of the table right next to the tarot cards. The animal didn't even bother to look up. Roan had the odd feeling that not only Micaela but also the cat had expected him back.

Motioning for Roan to be seated, Micaela said, "You are troubled."

"When was the fire?" Roan asked, going directly to the point.

"The summer of 1880," she said, just as point-blank.

Roan had been expecting her to say what she had. Something deep inside him had begun to tell him that what he feared was true, that the date of the fire was approaching. But how quickly? "Be more specific."

"I can't."

"The last entry in the diary is June 30."

Micaela nodded.

"Does that mean—" he began.

"I don't know," she interrupted.

I don't know. The words tormented Roan. Jumping up, he walked to the window and stared out at the midafternoon sun. The mirrorlike glare hurt his eyes. "The thirtieth is roughly two weeks away."

"I know."

Roan turned, his gaze meshing with Micaela's. "Why didn't you tell me when the fire was? Why didn't you tell me time was running out?"

"I knew it would occur to you when it should occur to you."

Something snapped inside Roan. Too many sleepless nights had combined with the feeling of helplessness that plagued him night or day, asleep or awake.

"You make it sound so damned simple! Well, it isn't. I don't know what I'm supposed to do. I can't stay in the past. I can't get her to the present. I can't prevent something's happening from a world away!"

"You were chosen for a reason."

"Yeah, well, to hell with the reason!" Roan said, bounding from the room. "I'm through trying to work the puzzle when I don't have all the pieces!" He slammed out the front door and down the chipped walkway. He was halfway inside the car when he halted and gave a long slow sigh. He glanced over the roof of the BMW. Micaela was standing at the door watching him, just as he knew she would be. "I don't have the answers," he called to her.

Calmly, sincerely, she replied, "You will. When you need them."

Would he? Roan thought. And, if he did, would he have them in time?

Roan spent the evening at the library, frantically searching for the one fact he so desperately needed to know, the one fact that maybe he'd failed to note before. He found nothing new, however. Only that the house had been destroyed by fire sometime in the past century.

It was as he was returning the books to the shelves that he saw the blond ponytail. The instant he saw it, he realized whom it belonged to and why the man had looked familiar the first time he'd seen him. Their paths had crossed there in the library.

"I knew I'd seen you before," Roan said at the man's elbow.

Crandall, his arms equally filled with books,

turned. His look said, "I've seen you, but I can't place you." Suddenly, recognition hit. "Oh, yeah," he said, awkwardly extending his hand as he juggled the pile of books.

Roan did the same juggling act and eased his hand forward. He then glanced toward Crandall's arms. "I guess archeologists dig in books as well as in soil."

"Actually, I'm doing some genealogical research. Of my roots," he added, hoping he sounded casual when, in reality, it was the last damned thing he felt. What he'd feared before, that he wasn't going to be able to find a clue as to his biological father, had come to pass. He knew nowhere else to look. "How about you?" he asked, pointing to Roan's loaded arms.

Roan hoped he sounded casual when he said, "A little historical research."

"I see."

No, he didn't. Not in the least, Roan thought, but he said, "How's the dig coming?"

"Actually, things are getting pretty interesting. After the article appeared in the newspaper, a professor at Tulane, some famous historian of the city, got in touch to say that he's run across a couple of obscure references to a secret tunnel and room beneath the cathedral grounds."

"You're right. That does sound interesting."

"The professor thinks the room and tunnel date back to the late eighteenth century. Though he's not sure what their original purpose was, it's his theory that they represent the site of an attempt by the Catholic church to establish the Spanish Inquisition in the New World."

"That would explain the instruments of torture."

"Right. Seems there was a Capuchin monk sent to

head the thing, but the governor threw him out of the city before he could. They were trying to colonize the area in those days, and the punishing of heretics was hardly going to attract new settlers."

"Hardly."

"Anyway, it's a possible explanation, which we didn't have before. Although," he added with a frown, "it doesn't explain the coins we found."

"What coins?"

"Coins from a century later. Julie found them scattered at the entrance to the room, as if they'd fallen from a pocket or a purse."

"So it looks as if the room was used later than the eighteenth century."

"It had to have been. But for what purpose is anybody's guess."

Roan remembered the young woman's fear, his clear vision that she had been held against her will in that room. He was certain that something sinister had happened there, but he was equally certain that he had enough to worry about. Even so, he heard himself asking, "How's . . . is Julie her name?"

"Yeah," Crandall said, "and she's fine." He was bending the truth. She wasn't fine. Nor had she been since the day they'd opened the room. She still wouldn't go inside it, and sometimes he would catch her just staring into it, as though she were lost in its darkness.

Roan suspected he was lying, but he didn't push. "Well, it was good seeing you."

"Yeah, you, too." On the heels of that, the bizarre episode in the tunnel still fresh in his mind, Crandall asked, "Are you all right?"

"Yeah."

Crandall suspected Roan was lying, but he didn't push. Besides, he had enough to worry about. The dig, Julie, and the elusive Drexel Bartlett were enough to occupy him.

"Well, take it easy," Crandall said.

"You bet," Roan added. As he turned away, an idea struck him. "This professor at Tulane . . . he specializes in New Orleans history?"

The question took Crandall by surprise. "Yeah, I think so. Why?"

"I, uh, I'm trying to find out the date of a fire. You think there's any way he could help me?"

"It wouldn't hurt to ask. Just call the university and ask for Rackley. Bob Rackley, I believe."

"Thanks," Roan said, depositing the books on the table and digging in his pocket for his wallet. "Let me give you my card in case you talk to him before I can reach him." Roan wrote the address of Lamartine House, and the phone number, on the back of the card. He handed the card to Crandall. "If you'd just have him give me a call if you reach him before I do. It's, uh, it's really important that I talk to him soon."

Crandall took the card. "Yeah, sure. Hope he can help you."

"From your mouth to God's ear," Roan said and realized with a start that he, professed athiest that he was, meant the sentiment literally.

Engelina heard Chloe calling her name. Frightened by the rasping sound, she flung her legs over the side of the bed and reached for her wrapper. She was out of the door in seconds and skimming along the hallway. She practically collided with Lukie, who was coming from the bedroom across the way. She, too, was drawing on a wrapper. She, too, wore a worried look.

"She's having a bad night," Lukie said.

Chloe had had more than her share of late, Engelina thought. In fact, as hard as it was to admit, Engelina knew that her sister was worsening. She was visibly losing ground each day.

"When did you last give her some medicine?"

"Three hours ago. I just left her for my room. She seemed to be sleeping soundly."

"That's all right, Lukie. You can't be with her every minute."

As always, Engelina was unprepared for the sight of her sister. Her face was drawn and pale, her lips and fingertips an ice-cold blue.

"I . . . can't . . . breathe," Chloe whispered.

"Of course you can, *ma petite,*" Engelina said as she slipped to the side of the bed and pulled her sister to her.

Engelina sounded far more confident than she felt. In truth, she was frightened. As frightened as her sister. She would give anything if the stranger—this Roan Jacob—were here. He seemed so sure, so certain. But then, maybe she'd only imagined him. There were times, especially in the middle of the night, when she wondered if the brute she'd married had manipulated everything just to make her think she was losing her mind. But how could he have made the man disappear before her eyes? That had been days ago—on Monday night. It was now Friday. She had prayed each day since that he would return, but he had not. What if he never came again? The thought was more than she could bear, and so she simply held Chloe tightly, hoping to alleviate her own fear even as she alleviated her sister's.

"Help . . . me," Chloe choked.

Engelina could feel her sister's erratic heartbeat. Or maybe it was her own. She wasn't sure. "You must remain calm." This, too, might have been as much for her benefit as it was for Chloe's. Glancing over at a wide-eyed Lukie, Engelina said, "Brew some more tea. Quickly."

"Yes, ma'am," the servant said, starting for the door.

Engelina had just turned her attention back to her sister when she heard Lukie's startled gasp. When Engelina looked up, she saw the man standing in the doorway.

Roan had heard someone call out for Engelina, a fractured sound that he'd suspected belonged to her sister. Was he back in the past? Or was he only eavesdropping on it? He'd followed the trail of muted voices and now stood staring into the beautiful black eyes of Engelina, the woman he'd been beginning to think he'd never see again.

Disbelief and relief surged through Engelina. "It's all right," she said to Lukie. "He's a friend."

It was all the invitation Roan needed. Recognizing the distress Chloe was in, he moved to the side of the bed and spoke authoritatively. "Let me see her."

At his command, without the slightest questioning of his right, Engelina disengaged a clinging Chloe and rose from the bed. As hard as it was to leave her sister, she stepped aside. Roan took her place.

At Chloe's frightened, longing look at Engelina, he smiled and said, "It's all right. I'm a doctor." As he spoke, he placed his fingers against the artery in her neck. Her pulse fluttered against his fingertips.

"I . . . can't . . . breathe," Chloe whispered.

"I know," Roan said, adding, "but try not to be afraid. It only makes it harder for you to breathe." Without missing a beat, he ordered, "Pile these pillows higher."

Lukie jumped to do his bidding.

"Breathe slowly . . . slowly . . . slowly," Roan said to

Chloe, his voice hypnotically quiet. "That's good. You're doing fine." To Engelina, he said, "Throw open those windows as far as they'll go. And bring me something to fan her with."

Opening wide the windows, Engelina called for Lukie to fetch a fan from her bedroom. With a "yes, ma'am," Lukie fled on fast feet.

"She has something wrong with her heart," Engelina offered in explanation. "She has ever since she had a high fever as a child."

"Probably rheumatic fever. If so, it damaged the mitral valve. That's what causes the dyspnea and the irregular heartbeat. That's why she's tired all the time."

"What's a mitral valve?" Engelina asked.

"The heart has valves that open and close to allow blood to flow through. One on the left side of the heart is called the mitral valve."

"What's dyspnea?"

"Shortness of breath. Hasn't your doctor explained any of this?" He knew that such technical knowledge was available in the nineteenth century.

"I think that Dr. Forsten thinks women are dull creatures."

Roan glanced up with a slight grin. "Yeah, well, you women got even with the Dr. Forstens of the world." He could see the question forming on Engelina's lips, a question that never materialized because at that moment Lukie returned with a fan, a lovely silk affair that Roan took and began to use to stroke the air in front of Chloe. "Breathe slowly," he admonished again. "This should help." To Engelina, he said, "What kind of medication does she take?"

"Digitalis. In tea. Lukie was on her way to brew some."

Roan glanced over at the servant. "Hurry," he said softly but urgently.

"Yes, sir," Lukie said and left the room.

"You're doing fine." Roan spoke to Chloe, who now leaned back against the fluffed pillows as he fanned the air. Her face was still pale, but her breathing seemed a little more steady.

Engelina eased to the floor beside the bed, her wrapper flaring out about her, and took Chloe's cold hand in hers. "You're doing fine," she echoed. "See, *ma petite*, I told you you could breathe."

The caring tone of Engelina's voice caught Roan's attention. That and the way ringlets of hair strayed about her shoulders in an enchanting, inviting disarray. Inviting? Yes. He couldn't help but wonder what they would feel like coiling about his fingers. Like satin? Like silk? Like he'd died and gone to heaven?

As though sensing his awareness, Engelina glanced up at him. For seconds neither spoke. Then, "I thought you weren't coming back."

"I thought I wasn't, too," Roan said, the week's frustration yet roaming through him.

Now was not the time to go into the subject, and so Roan merely asked what was foremost on his mind. "Are you all right?"

Her eyes spoke first. *Now that you're here,* they said. Verbally, she answered, "Yes."

"Where is he?" Roan couldn't bring himself to refer to Galen as her husband.

Engelina was glad he hadn't. She couldn't stand to hear the word that should be the most endearing in the world to her, but instead was the most hateful. "He's out. I don't know when he'll return."

Roan knew it was already past midnight. The fact that Galen could come back at any moment added an urgency that caused the night to sizzle with expectancy. He couldn't—wouldn't—leave, however, until he'd stabilized Chloe. Assuming, of course, that he could stay in the past long enough to do so. What would happen if he disappeared in front of Chloe? Or in front of the servant, who was just walking back into the room?

"Thank goodness," Engelina said, rising and taking the tray.

As though it were a ritual that had been performed many times before, each with a prescribed part to play, Engelina poured the tea while Lukie walked to the dresser and, opening a drawer, removed a brown bottle. Uncapping it, she returned to the tray and dripped three careful drops into the sweetened tea.

"Put one more," Roan ordered.

Knowing the potency of the drug, Lukie looked to Engelina for consent. They'd been told to administer three drops and no more.

Engelina's eyes went first to Roan, then back to Lukie. "One more," she said.

Lukie did as she'd been told, and Engelina handed the fragile cup and saucer to Roan. They looked strange in such large, powerful hands.

"Here, Chloe, drink this for me."

"I don't like—"

"I know you don't," Roan interrupted. "I wouldn't, either, and I know you're sick of all this medicine, but it'll help your heart." He leaned close to Chloe and whispered conspiratorially, "Plus, it's going to make me look incompetent if you don't start feeling better."

Despite her distress, Chloe mustered a thin smile. She took the cup out of the saucer.

With a skill that Engelina had to admire, Roan coaxed every swallow of tea down Chloe. And halfway had her liking it. Within minutes, Chloe's breathing improved. Another few minutes and her eyelids grew heavy. Engelina didn't minimize the effect of the drug. Neither, however, did she minimize Roan's presence. He'd had the same soothing effect on Chloe as he did on her.

When Roan rose from the bed, Chloe's eyes fluttered open. "Will you come back? I like you better than Dr. Forsten."

"I'll try," Roan promised as he patted her hand. Some of the blueness had faded from her fingers.

"Do you like to play cards?" Chloe asked.

"I love to play cards."

"When you come back . . ." she began, but drowsiness caused her to trail off.

"Go to sleep," Engelina whispered as she turned back the lantern light.

Lukie eased into a nearby chair, where she'd keep vigil for the rest of the night. Engelina, with Roan behind her, stepped out into the hallway.

"She should sleep for a while," Roan said.

Engelina nodded, saying, "Thank you."

"You're welcome," he answered, feeling that he must add, even though it killed him to do so, "She's very ill."

Forcing herself to acknowledge what she already knew, Engelina said simply, "I know."

"I'm going to try to return with some medicine. It's called digoxin. It's digitalis, but a lot more refined than what you're dealing with." At the hopeful light that jumped into Engelina's night-dark eyes, he said, "It won't cure her, but it'll control the symptoms better. The only thing that'll cure her is an operation."

At the words *cure her*, the light reappeared in Engelina's eyes. "But Dr. Forsten never said—"

"He doesn't know. This surgical procedure isn't

even known now. It doesn't come into existence until . . . until much later."

"How much later?" Engelina asked, needing to hear what she had begun to suspect. As crazy as the notion was, as unbelievable as the notion was, it was the only thing that made sense. This man, with his crazy way of dressing, this man who spoke of miracles, this man who'd vanished before her eyes and spoke of surgical procedures that could cure Chloe, didn't look, or sound, like part of the year 1880.

Roan didn't pull any punches. "Until roughly a century from now."

Engelina said nothing. Though she'd asked for the truth, it nonetheless stunned her. "You're from the future?" she said finally.

"Yes."

"But how is it possible for you to be here?"

Roan raked his fingers through his toast-brown hair and sighed. "I don't know. That I haven't the least clue to. I almost died several weeks ago, and all this . . . this strangeness began to happen."

"But you have come for me and Chloe?" The question held an underlying desperation.

"I think so, but—"

"But there's a—what did you say? A bug?—in the miracle."

"Yes. I can't control my fading in and out. I can't stay here long enough to get you out of this house, and I can't take you back with me."

Engelina said nothing. She simply leaned against the wall, as though needing its support.

"You can't stay in 1880, and you can't take us to the future."

Roan saw the confusion, the despair that swirled around her. There was even an element of disbelief, as though she'd fallen asleep and was dreaming. He laid his hand on her arm. "I know. I only half believe what's happening, too."

The power in his hand, the power in his voice comforted her. She forced herself to take a deep, fortifying breath, then said, "I'm frightened."

At her admission, which went though him like a sharp knife, Roan released her arm. It seemed like the prudent thing to do. Especially since he had the almost uncontrollable urge to pull her into his arms. To comfort her. To comfort him.

"Yeah, well, so am I," he said, confused by what he was feeling. He rammed his hands into the pockets of his jeans.

Yes, he, too, was afraid. Engelina could feel it, sense it. She needed his strength, but she now found that his vulnerability appealed to her, as well. It made him seem human, which she'd forgotten that a man could be. She wanted to pull him into her arms, even as she wanted to be pulled into his.

She didn't know what to make of this last perplexing thought, and so she said, "What do we do now?"

"I don't know. Even if I could get you out of this house, your sister isn't well enough to travel any distance."

"No, she isn't. She worsens by the day. I should have left when she was better. But I was afraid he would find us."

She said nothing more, but the stark terror in her face left no doubt as to what she believed her husband would do to her, and possibly even Chloe, if he were to find them after the bold indiscretion of flight. Knowing what he did of the man, Roan believed him capable of anything.

"I should have been strong," Engelina said. "I should have gotten her out of the house when I could." She sighed. "I never should have brought her into it."

Her anguish tore at Roan. "Don't," he said. "You've been strong. Far stronger than anyone I know."

She said nothing, though her eyes glazed over with unshed tears. "He is evil," she said at last.

"I know," Roan said hoarsely.

"Do you?"

"Yes."

She turned away from him then, and Roan had the feeling that she didn't want him to see her cry. He saw her raise her hand and swipe at her cheek.

At length she said, "If ever I was brave, if ever I was strong, those days are fleeing. I am unsure how much more I can . . . withstand." This last word sounded as though it had been cracked in two.

Instinctively, without thought, Roan placed his hand on her shoulder and turned her toward him. His eyes met hers. With his sensitivity, he felt every tormenting emotion that she felt. It was almost more than he could bear.

"Please," he whispered, "don't cry."

His touch, his voice, the empathy he displayed were Engelina's undoing. She'd had no one to lean on, no one to help her share her burden. Her world had been a lonely one. A world of pain, fear, shame. A world in which she tried not to feel anything. And, suddenly, here was this man, a strange man from a strange world, offering her comfort. Moreover, he was making her feel—tenderness, gentleness, all the sweet things she'd forgotten. It was almost more than she could bear.

At the sight of her tears, again without thought, Roan pulled her into his arms. The fullness he'd felt when her ghost had passed through him returned. It was more powerful than anything he'd ever felt. It was so powerful that it was staggering, frightening. As was the knowledge that he might not be able to help her after all.

He would like to be able to tell her that they had time, but he wasn't certain they did. In fact, he was quite certain they didn't. Chloe was ill. Critically ill. And Engelina's death was approaching. He'd contacted the professor, who'd agreed to try to search out the date of the fire, but he couldn't promise anything. Dates were sometimes too elusive to pin down. At best, they had the full summer. At worst, only a matter of tormenting days. He wouldn't add to her worry just now by telling her that history recorded she was about to die.

"Shh," he whispered, folding her closer to him, feeling her plush feminine angles mesh with his hard masculine planes. He stroked her hair, its curls clinging to him as though his touch had breathed life into them. They did feel like silk. Satin. A glorious glimpse of heaven.

Engelina prayed to God not to let him disappear now, to let her know this moment of kindness, this moment of sweetness. It might be her last.

Suddenly, like a frightened rabbit, she raised her head. It was only then that Roan heard the turning of the front door lock. With his acute hearing, he was surprised that he hadn't heard it sooner, but then he seemed to hear, see, feel only the woman in his arms.

"It's he," she whispered, panic racing through her like a strong narcotic. "You must leave. Now. He must not find you here."

"I can't leave—"

"Go!" she said, shoving him from her, though it took all of the emotional strength she had to do so.

The front door closed.

"No!" Roan said even as images flashed through his mind of what Galen would do to Engelina should he find her with him.

"Please," she begged.

Muted footsteps crossed the hall and started up the staircase.

In the midst of desperation, an idea occurred to Roan. It was so obvious, so logical, that he didn't understand why it hadn't occurred to him before. The answer to his problems, to Engelina's problems, lay in the performance of one simple act. All he had to do was kill Galen Lamartine. All he had to do was kill the heartless son of a bitch.

"No!" Engelina cried, seeing the turn of his thoughts as clearly as if they'd been written across his forehead. "He's not worth the sacrifice of your soul."

At that moment Roan was more concerned about Engelina's physical safety than the well-being of his soul. He was equally concerned, though, with the fear that sprang into her eyes, a new fear, not for herself but for him. She would rather endure her husband's abuse that have him risk his soul. This realization warmed his heart in a way that nothing ever had.

"Engelina?" Galen called midway up the stairs. He'd obviously heard the commotion.

"Please," Engelina begged one last time. As she spoke, she took Roan's hand and pulled him toward her bedroom. He went, not because he wanted to, but because of the entreaty in her eyes. The bedroom door opened; he was shoved inside; the bedroom door closed. The last thing he heard before the room began to spin in time was Galen topping the stairs.

"What's going on?" he asked.

"Chloe," Engelina said, her voice composed, but breathless to the sensitive ear. "She had a spell."

And then Roan heard nothing but silence, the silence of a still room, the silence of a century later, the silence of a lone and lonely heart.

$\mathcal{F}$OURTEEN

Engelina sat by Chloe's bedside all the next day. Though her breathing was less labored, she nonetheless appeared chalky pale and drained of all energy. Even so, she smiled at the pink rose that Engelina brought her. Engelina smiled too, though she didn't feel like it. She wanted to weep. For her sister, for herself, for a miracle that had a bug in it. She forced herself to cling to something positive—the medicine that Roan had spoken of, the fact that she was no longer alone, the warmth of Roan's arms. Roan's arms. They were strong yet gentle, leaving her as safe as a kitten cozied against its mother. Ironically, they also left her feeling restless. They made her want more from this man.

". . . the new doctor."

Engelina glanced up guiltily, as though she'd been caught in the middle of some grave indiscretion. "What?"

"I like the new doctor," Chloe said.

Engelina began to straighten the turned-back hem of the sheet, which was already straight. "He's our friend. I mean, he is a doctor, too, but mostly he's our friend." Engelina forced her hands to be still when she realized she was fidgeting. "It would be best if we kept our friend a secret. Just among the three of us."

At this, Engelina glanced over at Lukie, who was clearing away the tray of dishes. The young woman raised her gaze to Engelina. Though not a word was spoken, the look they exchanged was meaningful.

"He will visit us again, won't he?" Chloe asked, sensing that something was a bit strange concerning this new friend of theirs.

"Yes," Engelina answered emphatically.

It was something she not only wanted to believe, it was something she had to believe. If she didn't, she'd go stark-raving mad.

"Send me some digoxin . . . a substantial supply . . . and send my medical bag, too, will ya?"

"What's a substantial supply?" Stewart asked.

"Two hundred or so," Roan replied. "Oh, and send me some antibiotics . . . Bactrim will do . . . and some antibiotic cream . . . Bactroban will be fine . . . something for nausea . . . also some Valium . . . and something for pain . . . oh, and send me some gauze and bandages . . . never mind, I can get those here—"

"What's going on?" Stewart interrupted. Being awakened before dawn on a Saturday morning was puzzling enough, but Roan's shopping list was even more puzzling.

"Nothing's wrong."

"Then why do you need all this?"

"I just want a little bit of everything. In case I need it. You know, some medical staples."

"Digoxin is a staple?"

Roan raked his fingers through his hair. "Okay, I've met someone with a heart problem."

"I thought you went down there to rest, not practice medicine."

"I am resting."

"It doesn't sound like it."

Roan's patience skidded to an abrupt stop. "So are you going to send the stuff or not?"

It was the first time Roan could ever remember a silence this tense between him and his friend. He instantly regretted what he'd said.

"Look, I'm sor—"

"You know damned well I'm going to send it to you," Stewart interjected. "I'll do anything you ask me to. We're friends. And as a friend, I have the right to worry about you."

Contrite, Roan sighed.

"Look," Stewart said, "cut the bullshit and answer me one question straight."

"What?"

"Are you all right? I mean, really all right?"

Roan gave the question the thought it deserved, then said, "Cutting the bullshit, I haven't the foggiest idea."

Roan could tell that his honesty startled Stewart.

"Is there anything I can help you with?" Stewart asked finally.

Again, Roan gave the question consideration. What would Stewart say if he dumped the whole thing at his feet? A part of him wanted to; a part of him feared Stewart's disbelief.

"Not right now," Roan said at last. "Maybe later."

"I'm always here. You know that." Before Roan could reply, Stewart said, "I'll get these things off to you."

"Thanks. Today, if you can. And overnight it, okay?"

"Will do."

Right before he hung up, Roan asked, "How's Kay?"

Another silence, then, "About what you'd expect."

"I never meant to hurt her."

"I know. So does she."

In that second Roan knew that he'd never been in love with Kay. He'd been in like with her, but that was all. It was all he'd thought himself capable of. Now, however . . . He left the thought unfinished, saying to his friend, "Kay deserves someone who can love her all the way. She deserves someone like you."

Another silence followed. This one neither man tried to fill.

A troubling thought occurred to Roan that afternoon as he shopped the drugstore for the dozens of items of twentieth-century medicine that he simply couldn't resist buying on the off chance that Engelina might need them. What if none of this, when taken back to the nineteenth century, stayed? In particular, what if the digoxin faded out the way the apron had? The question was still plaguing him when the digoxin arrived the next afternoon. Roan decided to worry about one problem at a time. Right now, he'd worry solely about getting back into the nineteenth century.

The opportunity came unexpectedly Monday morning. The vacuum cleaner was blaring downstairs to the accompaniment of the maid's off-key humming when Roan, who had kept the digoxin in his pocket since its arrival, felt the stairs begin to shift under his feet. He was midway down when the runner on the staircase changed colors. He was back in time, standing out in the open where anyone, everyone, could see him. Below, he heard voices. Servants' voices, he surmised. Hastening upstairs, he overheard the young black woman—Lukie, he thought he remembered her name being—talking to Chloe. At least he assumed it was Chloe. Lukie was saying something about Engelina being due back from mass shortly.

Roan considered administering the medicine to Chloe himself, but decided against it. It would be better to leave the drug for Engelina. Approaching her bedroom, he prayed that it was empty. It was. He stepped hastily inside. He took in the four-poster bed draped in a lacy fabric that acted as a mosquito net. The bed, still unmade, was rumpled, as though Engelina had slept poorly. The thought of her sharing the bed with her husband sickened Roan, and so he shoved the misery-making images aside in favor of something more comfortable.

At the dresser, a large, mirrored, intricately carved piece of mahogany furniture, he perused the sundry items sprawled across its top—a silver-handled brush, an ivory fan, a cobalt-blue perfume bottle. Unstoppering the bottle, he brought it to his nose and inhaled. The smell of rosewater permeated his senses. His head reeled, making him wonder if he was returning to the present, but he decided he was simply intoxicated with the fragrance of Engelina.

Even so, he was ever mindful that he might be forced back to the present without warning, so he withdrew the plastic bottle of digoxin from his pocket and placed it on the dresser. He'd already enclosed a piece of paper indicating the dosage. No sooner had he placed the bottle on the dresser than he heard footsteps in the hallway. In seconds, just as he slipped into the closet, the door opened. He willed it to be Engelina, but it wasn't. It was a servant, an older woman who moved quickly to the bed and began efficiently to strip it of its linen. Roan watched as she made the bed, then picked up Engelina's wrapper. She headed for the closet. Roan's heart began to pound, and he instinctively stepped deeper inside. The servant had just opened the door when he felt the tiny cubicle beginning to shift. When everything had settled, he was standing knee-deep in projector equipment and dozens of carousels of slides. He was standing knee-deep in another era.

Engelina saw the small brown bottle as she laid her prayer book on the dresser. She knew instantly what it was. Though her heart soared at the sight of the medicine, it did a quick nosedive at having missed Roan. How long ago had he come? How long ago had he disappeared? And why did she feel so heavy-hearted?

Picking up the bottle, she studied it. She had expected it to be made of glass but quickly realized that it wasn't. At least she didn't think it was. Glass was heavier. Whatever this was, it was lightweight. Uncapping the lid, she removed the piece of paper. On it, Roan had written the dosage she was to give Chloe, then had simply signed the note—Roan. Tilting the bottle, she piled the little white tablets into the palm of her hand. As she stared at them, the magnitude of what was happening struck her. Really struck her.

She was staring at medication from the future! The man on whom she was pinning all her hopes was from another century!

For the first time she felt hysteria nipping at her. She fought to keep it at bay. She forced herself to concentrate on returning the tablets to the bottle . . .

and on administering them to Chloe. Roan had told her frankly that the pills were no cure, but they should be an improvement over the medicated tea. She'd start Chloe on the medicine right away. She'd pray that the medicine would, indeed, help her sister. She'd . . .

Engelina stopped short when she saw the man standing in her open doorway.

"And where are you headed in such a hurry, my pretty?" Galen asked, walking into the room on silent feet.

Seconds before, Engelina had fought hysteria. She now fought panic. Even so, she retained enough presence of mind to ease her hand, and the container of medicine, into the folds of her skirt.

"To see Chloe," she answered, forcing her voice to remain calm.

"Ah, yes, Chloe," he said, stepping in front of Engelina. She hated his nearness. It smothered her, making her feel as if a weight sat on her chest. "And how is our sweet sister?"

"She's better," Engelina replied, repulsed by his insincere inquiry. He didn't care how Chloe was. He cared about no one save himself.

Proving her point, Galen didn't even respond but moved on to the purpose of his visit. "I'm leaving early in the morning for Oak Manor. I'll be gone much of the day."

Engelina knew that Oak Manor, located some three hours' drive from the city, belonged to Monsieur Desforges. Madame Desforges refused to visit the mansion, claiming that it was situated too far from civilization. Consequently, Monsieur Desforges used the site for business—whatever his business was. Engelina could never quite determine what, although she knew that Mr. Harnett, and the man now standing far too near to her, occasionally accompanied Monsieur Desforges to the plantation. She relished those times when he, the man she wished she'd never married, was gone.

"You will miss me, won't you, my pretty?" Galen asked, toying with one of his wife's many curls.

Engelina said nothing.

Running his hand along the back of her neck, he tightened his fingers until pain pricked her senses. "Tell me you'll miss me."

Her eyes stung with tears, but she willed them to remain unshed. "I'll . . . I'll miss you," she whispered.

"Of course you will, my pretty. It's the role of a dutiful wife to miss her absent husband. And you are dutiful, aren't you?"

Engelina made no reply. The fingers at her neck tightened.

"Y-yes," she gasped.

Abruptly he loosened his punishing grasp. The unexpected absence of pain was as startling as its presence. It left Engelina feeling confused and wary.

"You're very beautiful," Galen said, his eyes suddenly hazy, his voice suddenly thick.

He lazily drew his finger down the column of her neck, then onto the sheer fabric of her snug-throated bodice. He traced the faint outline of her cleavage. Engelina tried not to cringe.

"You will behave yourself in my absence, won't you, my dear wife?"

How could she not behave herself with his black-dressed, black-hearted henchman watching her? she wanted to ask. Instead, she simply nodded.

"Should I hear of any misdeed, I'd be forced to punish you for it. You do understand that, don't you?"

Again, she nodded.

"You do understand that, don't you?" he repeated, typically commanding a verbal response from her.

"Yes."

"I thought you did." He drew his crooked knuckle across her bottom lip, causing shivers of disgust to ripple through her. "Men may look, but they can't touch." He began to lower his head. Disgust flared into revulsion. "Only I can touch."

Engelina steeled herself against the assault of his lips. When his mouth roughly covered hers, Engelina pretended that it wasn't she at all whom he was kissing. She was standing somewhere nearby watching . . . and wondering what it would be like to be kissed gently and with affection. Wondering what it would be like to be kissed by the brown-haired stranger.

Tuesday morning dawned bright and clear. The fact that Chloe, after only a few dosages of the medicine, was visibly improved, the fact that Galen did, indeed, leave even before the appearance of the morning sun, the fact that the blackguard Kipperd was nowhere to be seen, as well, left Engelina in a rare and gay mood. Though she had only the day to enjoy, she'd learned to appreciate what she had, and so, when Chloe asked for a picnic in the courtyard, a picnic was what was planned.

A pallet was spread beneath the boughs of the magnolia tree and, though it was summer-warm, a breeze occasionally flitted through the leaves, sighing that it was a lovely day for an outing. As Lukie made a pitcher of lemonade and sandwiches of sliced chicken, Engelina helped her sister into a cool chambray dress. Then came the hard part: transporting Chloe downstairs. Lukie, on one side, and Engelina, on the other, lifted her gingerly.

"You would not drop me, would you?" Chloe asked.

"If you don't quit squirming like a worm, that's exactly what we'll do," Engelina answered, delighted that her sister felt well enough to tease. She had been warned by Roan that the drug was not a cure, that Chloe would grow progressively worse even with it, but for today Chloe was better. And for now, today was enough.

Today.

Tomorrow.

Engelina wondered what Roan was doing, in a year so far away from her own that she couldn't imagine what it must be like to live there. Whatever it was like, it had to be better than the world she knew.

"You are dropping me," Chloe said as the trio started down the stairs.

"We are not, Miss Chloe," Lukie said, though she was visibly struggling with the burden she carried. The mocha-colored turban on her head had slipped, while her white apron was hiked to her waist.

"You are!"

"We are not," Engelina chimed in, adding, "Slow down, Lukie."

"Yes, you are—" Chloe insisted.

"Here, let me."

At the masculine voice, three women peered down the stairs. If they were surprised to see Roan, he was equally surprised to see them. Moments before, he'd been taking a walk in the courtyard. Without warning, he'd heard the women coming down the stairs and, observing the pallet, guessed their destination. At seeing no one inside the immediate house, he'd decided to take a chance.

At the sight of Roan, Engelina's heart had begun a merry dance. A smile drifted across her lips. She realized two things simultaneously. One, a good day had just gotten better and, two, this man, whatever else he might be, was not a stranger.

Roan realized two things, as well. The digoxin must have remained in the past, and he'd never seen smiles, the ones both Chloe and Engelina were wearing, that did such crazy things to his heart. As Roan stepped forward and scooped Chloe into his arms, he wished he could always make the two women smile as they now did.

The instant Roan placed Chloe on the pallet, she saw the cat. Roan saw it, too. He'd had no idea that the animal had been in the courtyard and had once more made the journey back in time.

"Oh, look, Sister!" Chloe cried. Though her eyes showed the fatigue her illness caused, they nonetheless shone brightly.

Engelina smiled and lowered herself to her knees. She patted the cat, who rubbed its head against her as though greeting an old friend. "*Bonjour, Monsieur Chat.*"

"He knows you," Chloe said.

"*Monsieur Chat* and I have met. Though he was much wetter then."

"Come here," Roan called to the feline. He picked it up and placed it in Chloe's lap. If Chloe's eyes had shone before, they sparkled now. "Cat, I'd like you to meet Chloe. Chloe, this is Cat."

Cat cast a pair of blue eyes upward and meowed.

Everyone smiled. Engelina and Roan at each other.

"Shall I bring out lunch?" Lukie asked.

"Yes, please," Engelina said, adding, "And our guests will join us."

Roan, who'd been petting the cat, glanced up quickly. His eyes asked the question he could not give voice to.

"He has gone to Oak Manor for the day,"

Engelina said. "That is Monsieur Desforges's plantation some three hours from the city. Our manservant is also gone. It is only the three of us and a housekeeper."

Though her reply resolved one of Roan's concerns, it in no way addressed another. "I, uh, I might have to go unexpectedly."

This had already occurred to Engelina. What if Roan disappeared in front of Lukie and Chloe? How would she explain? On the other hand, would she not risk anything to be with him, if only for a short while?

"If you have to go, we'll understand."

Roan studied her. The truth was that he wasn't certain he could go just because he wanted to. Walking through a door had returned him to the present before, but there were no guarantees. The further truth was that he was uncertain he could make himself leave Engelina.

Engelina smiled suddenly, saying, "Then it's settled, Lukie. We'll take lunch, please."

The sun had never shone more brilliantly, lemonade had never tasted sweeter, laughter had never rung more clearly. After lunch, Chloe insisted that they play cards—poker.

"Poker?" Roan asked in disbelief.

Chloe giggled.

"She is a more accomplished poker player than any in the French Quarter," Engelina said with a smile. "In fact, she is quite shameless."

"She and Lukie are angry only because I beat them. And when they lose, they claim that the squirrels carry off their best cards."

"That isn't true, Miss Chloe," Lukie said, attempting to look offended. "I told you before that sometimes the birds get mine."

Again, everyone laughed.

Chloe proved to be the card shark that Engelina had proclaimed her. Each win delighted her thoroughly. As the afternoon wore on, in seeming proportion to her sister's, Engelina's happiness grew, as well. Though she'd borne so much, suffered so much, there was nonetheless a spark of life still afire within her. Roan longed beyond all else to see that spark ignite into flame. He longed to see her live life to its sweet fullest. He longed to see her live life outside the shadow of pain and fear.

Engelina, smiling at Cat, who alternately spent its time lying in Chloe's lap and foraging in the picnic basket, glanced up to find Roan's gaze on her. A warmth stole through her, a warmth that touched her from head to toe and every spot in between. This man had kind eyes, caring eyes, eyes that saw right through her. He saw all she'd endured. He saw all her fear, all her loneliness. He saw dreams buried so deep within her that she no longer dared to hope they'd come true. Her eyes misted.

She and Roan sat aside on a separate quilt. Above them, birds sang and bees hummed.

"Why are you crying?" he asked so softly that only Engelina heard the question.

"Because I'm happy. For this moment in my life, I'm happy."

Roan's throat clogged with emotion. She asked so little . . . and got so little in return. "I wish I could give you thousands of happy moments," he said, his voice rough with feeling.

"That you want to is more than anyone has given me in a long while." She smiled, a bittersweet smile that tore at Roan's heart. "My *papa*, my *maman* wished happiness for me. Until now, I had forgotten how dear those wishes could be. I shall not forget again . . . for the whole of my life."

The whole of her life. The *brief* whole of her life if he could not alter history. Desperation and restlessness, each as swift as a river rapid, swept through him. Maybe he should take Engelina and Chloe away this very moment. Maybe he shouldn't wait for some Tulane professor of history to search out a date that might not be researchable.

"Is there anyone you could stay with if I helped you escape today, right now?" Roan asked, again quietly.

Engelina had known the question was coming, simply because it had been on her mind, as well. "No," she answered. "He hasn't allowed me to make friends of my own, and I would trust none of his. Furthermore, he has eyes and ears everywhere."

"What if I could get you to another city?"

"How could I ask Chloe to bear so much when she is ill? Excitement, change—each causes her to worsen."

"You must get out of this house," Roan said softly but emphatically. "As soon as possible."

Engelina sensed his urgency. Though it merely echoed her own, it nonetheless frightened her. It was almost as though he knew something that she didn't. What? And, if he did, did she want to know what that something was?

Chloe's laughter, combined with Lukie's, drew Engelina's and Roan's attention. Cat had climbed into the picnic basket and curled up for a nap.

"I wish *Monsieur Chat* were mine," Chloe said wistfully as she stroked the feline. Before anyone could comment, however, she added, "I know he cannot be, though. Galen doesn't like animals."

Engelina's gaze brushed Roan's, and she hastily began to gather up the cards that now lay forgotten. Lukie, as though she, too, suddenly needed to busy her hands, began to stack the dishes.

"No, he doesn't," Engelina said.

"Will you bring *Monsieur Chat* to visit again?" Chloe asked Roan.

"I'll certainly try."

"Where do you live?" Chloe asked with youthful bluntness.

Again Engelina's gaze momentarily touched Roan's. "I, uh, I'm not from New Orleans. I'm from Houston."

"Houston?" Engelina asked, clinging to this tidbit of information.

Roan's eyes once more sought out Engelina. "Yes. That's in Texas."

"I know. I've heard of it. It's far away."

"Not as far as you'd think."

"Does everyone dress as you do in this Houston?" Chloe asked.

Roan smiled. "Many people do."

Chloe sighed, partly wistfully, partly because of a fatigue that was setting in. "I'd like to see this Houston some day."

"Who knows," Roan said, "maybe you will. Right now, however, I think you need to rest."

"I think he's right," Engelina agreed.

"No, I—"

"You need to rest," Engelina insisted.

"I'll carry you up," Roan said, starting to rise. Engelina came to her feet as well, with the assistance of Roan.

She had just smiled her thanks at him when, suddenly, a shadow flitted across the sun, sending an icy chill shivering down her spine. Instinctively, she glanced toward the courtyard doorway. Her heart crashed at her feet.

Even before Engelina's gasp, Roan sensed a presence, a dark, sinister presence. Jerking his head upward, he followed Engelina's gaze. Brown eyes collided with gray, steel resolve with steel resolve.

"Who are you?" Galen Lamartine asked, his voice as cold as a bitter north wind. "And what are you doing in my house?"

ℱIFTEEN

"Galen," Engelina whispered in disbelief.

"Yes, my pretty, it is I. And obviously not expected back so soon." His voice was soft, even gentle, which made the words he spoke sound even more menacing. More frightening yet was the cold-blooded barrenness of his gaze, which first swept over his wife, then over Roan. "I repeat, who are you?"

At the sight of Galen Lamartine, Roan had reexperienced the surge of hatred he'd felt the first time he'd seen the man. The hatred grew second by second until it now threatened to swamp Roan.

Refusing to break Galen's stony stare, Roan answered, "I'm Roan—"

"Dr. Jacob," Engelina interrupted, then rushed ahead with, "He's Chloe's doctor."

The startled look on Galen's face indicated that he hadn't been expecting this reply. "I thought Dr. Forsten was her physician."

"He was," Engelina said. "I mean, he is. I mean . . ." She looked beseechingly at Roan, as though perhaps he could explain what she apparently could not.

"I've been called in as a consultant," Roan said, his eyes still locked with Galen's.

Battle was only ill-chosen words away. Both men felt it, sensed it, as one could feel that the sunny day had taken a turn for the worse. Gauzy threads of vapor now streaked across the vapid sun, suggesting the approach of a sudden tropical shower so common in New Orleans. A brisk breeze fluttered the leaves of the banana tree, while the earth seemed to stand still in expectation of rain or bloodshed. Even the gruesome gargoyles stood poised in goading anticipation.

"Yes," Engelina agreed hastily. "A consultant." She smiled, though it never reached her eyes. Her hands fidgeted with the folds of her dress. "He's prescribed some new medicine. See how well Chloe's doing on it. So well that she pleaded to be brought to the courtyard."

At the mention of Chloe's improvement, Galen's gaze sought out his sister-in-law. The young woman angled her chin rebelliously, as though daring him to disprove her bettered condition. She also, with a subtle discretion, lowered the lid of the picnic basket where Cat slept.

Galen looked back at Roan and smiled ominously. "What kind of fool do you take me for?"

"Galen!" Engelina cried. "You're being rude—"

"Silence!" he said softly, the single, clipped word cutting like the slice of a sharp knife. His gaze never left Roan. "You barge uninvited, and half dressed, into my party, you insinuate yourself into my house when I'm away, and you expect me to believe that you're a physician?"

Roan's hatred was growing by leaps and bounds. "I really don't care what you believe." He instinctively stepped in Engelina's direction, readying himself to come to her aid should it be necessary.

Galen's smile widened, making him dazzlingly handsome. "You should care what I think."

Abruptly Galen's smile died. Abruptly his thinly veiled patience ended.

"Get out of my house . . . and don't come back."
With that he motioned for the man who'd been hover-
ing unnoticed in the shadows to step forward.
"Kipperd, show the doctor"—this last was said snidely—
"out."

Wordlessly, the burly manservant moved to Roan's
side. Something in Roan's imperious demeanor, however, stopped him when he would have taken Roan by
the arm.

"I know the way," Roan said. He glanced over at
Engelina. He saw her fear, her humiliation. He would
have given anything to pulverize Galen Lamartine on
the spot. Though outnumbered, he might have risked
it had it not been for Engelina. He couldn't put her
through any more. He smiled. "It's all right. Thank
you for lunch." Looking over at Chloe, he said, "Take
care." With that, he started for the door that led back
into the house.

"Wait!" Chloe cried.

Roan turned.

"You forgot your basket," the young woman said.
"Lukie, would you please hand it to him?"

Both Lukie's and Roan's expressions said clearly
that they didn't understand why Chloe was trying to
give Roan a basket that wasn't his. When Lukie
picked it up, however, her expression changed.
Realization struck Roan equally the second the basket
was settled in his arms. Inside, he felt a restless feline
shifting positions.

"Thank you," he said. Giving Engelina one last
look, he stepped toward the door.

"If you come back," Galen said softly, so softly that
his voice sounded like the hiss of a coiled snake, "I'll
kill you."

Engelina gasped.

Chloe looked startled.

Lukie unconsciously sought the protective amulet she carried in her pocket.

His head high, his eyes eloquently expressive of his loathing, Roan turned. For long seconds, the two men measured each other. Finally, Roan said, "Be certain you can carry out a threat before you make it."

"Don't doubt my ability."

"It isn't your ability I doubt. It's your courage. Taking on a man can be a little different from roughing up a woman."

A dark red flush stole into Galen's face, though his lips tightened to a thin white line. The look in his sleet-gray eyes was murderous.

On this note, Roan stepped through the open doorway. Kipperd followed at a pace that was steady but slow. Hastening his footsteps, Roan crossed the parlor, opened the door leading into the hallway, then pulled it shut behind him. He heard the doorknob turning just as he, and the basket he carried, disappeared back into the present.

The shower had turned into a storm, with lightning lancing the lead-gray sky and thunder booming its brazen presence.

Her fingers trembled as Engelina held her rosary tightly and tried to concentrate on her prayers. She couldn't, however. Each prayer that was begun soon ended in thoughts of the threat delivered against Roan. She had no doubt whatsoever that her husband—she forced herself to think the word, as though punishing herself for being so stupid as to marry the man—meant what he'd said about taking Roan's life should Roan return. She had no doubt whatsoever that her husband was capable of such violence. If she ever had, the look he'd given Roan at the last would have persuaded her otherwise.

Her fear for Roan took precedence over her fear for herself. Galen had been surly ever since the incident, hours before. He'd said nothing to her, though. That is, until supper.

Seated at the opposite end of the long, elegant table, Galen had drawn the wineglass to his lips, had drunk deeply, then had returned the glass to the linen tablecloth, asking as though about the lightest of matters, "What did you tell him?"

The candle that rested on the table between them flickered just as thunder pealed through the heavens. Engelina's stomach knotted at the question. Even so, she didn't flinch. Nor did her gaze waver. "Nothing," she answered. "I told him nothing."

"Then why did he make the comment about roughing up a woman?"

In answer, Engelina repeated, "I told him nothing."

It was obvious Galen didn't believe her, but she didn't care whether he did or not. A recklessness roamed through her, a recklessness that had not been there before, a recklessness born of the belief that her life could not go on as it had. Even death would be preferable.

Several seconds of silence passed before he asked, again casually, "You do recall that I said I'd be forced to punish you should you not behave yourself in my absence?"

"I behaved myself."

"Then what was he doing in the house?"

"The man is a doctor."

"You believe that?"

"Yes."

"Then you are a fool."

"Yes. A fool for marrying you." It was the closest

she'd ever come to rebellion. It felt good. Very good. She had known then, just as she knew now, hours later, that it was a sedition she would pay for. Perhaps dearly.

That knowledge forced her restless feet to movement, so she walked to the window. Rain pelted the house with huge raindrops, which Engelina fancifully envisioned as tears. The tears she would not, could not, cry. Please, God, give her the strength she needed.

When the door opened, she was almost relieved. At least the waiting was over. Turning, she saw Galen standing in the doorway. His hair was ruffled, his vacant eyes glazed from drink. In the grave gray depths of his irises, however, she saw lust. A lust for violence. A passion for inflicting pain. The black snakelike whip in his hand confirmed this.

Yes, she thought even as her blood ran cold in her veins, she was about to pay for her rebellious comment. In particular, she was about to pay for the afternoon she'd spent with Roan. Regardless of the whip's bitter bite, she didn't regret a moment of her time with Roan. She couldn't, even if forced to bear the wrath of a dozen hateful whips.

Roan lay in bed pondering how the basket had disappeared back into the past just as the apron had, when a wave of nausea barreled through his stomach. So unexpected was it, so strong, that it literally doubled him in two. He groaned.

Engelina!

She was in pain. He knew this as clearly as he knew that this hot summer day had turned as stormy as the day he'd left behind in the past. Rain thrashed against the windows, while wind restlessly rustled

through the eaves of the house. Roan noticed neither. The nausea was so overwhelming that it obliter-
ated everything else. That and the compelling need
to stop what was happening to Engelina.

Throwing his legs over the side of the bed, he had
started to get up when another seizure of nausea
gripped him. He fell back across the mattress, drawing his knees up to his chest. He'd never had an
empathic experience this intense. Did this mean that
Engelina's pain was as strong? If so, what in God's
holy name was that son of a bitch doing to her?

Roan staggered out into the hallway. He had to get
to her! He had to stop whatever was happening!
Rushing to her bedroom, Roan flung wide the door,
but the placid present mocked him. From there, he
hastened to every other bedroom, but in each he found
no passageway back into time. Now frantic, he took the
stairs two by two. Midway down the stairwell, another
round of nausea coiled his gut. He grabbed his stomach, gasped, and tumbled down a couple of steps.
Grimacing, he forced himself upright and stumbled
down the remaining stairs. He threw open the parlor
door.

Nothing.

Dammit, nothing!

After trying every room of the house, the parlor
twice, Roan was forced to accept the fact that he
couldn't go back in time—no matter how much he
wished it.

"Dammit, no!" he cried, dropping to the floor at
the bottom of the staircase. He felt defeated, deplet-
ed, devoid of emotion.

The nausea had ceased. Whatever the bastard had
been doing to Engelina, he had stopped. Roan, however, found precious little consolation in this knowledge. In what condition had he left her? Was she

alone? Was she crying? Was she calling his name? This last thought devastated him.

"Oh, God," he whispered, drawing unsteady fingers through his hair.

Leaning his back against the wall, he closed his eyes. He heard his heart thumping, the rain beating. He heard frustration screaming through body and soul.

Slowly, like an ebb tide returning to the sea, the frustration began to wane. In its place appeared a feather-light feeling, a soft feeling, a warm feeling. It filled him to overflowing with peace, with love.

Love.

He was in love with Engelina.

The fact was breathtakingly simple, as elemental as the changing of seasons. It overwhelmed Roan with its majesty, its beauty. He had been right: Though he'd cared for Kay, he'd never loved her. They hadn't been soul mates. He had been right about one other thing, as well. It was far more important to give love than to take it, for only in the giving did one fill one's own heart.

Roan listened to the sound of his full heart singing this love song. He listened, too, to the rhythmic pulsing of the summer-warm rain. And to soft, heart-wrenching sobs.

Sobs?

Roan opened his eyes and cocked his head. Had he only imagined that he heard muffled cries? No. No, he hadn't! There they were again!

With a relieved start, he realized that he had been transported back in time. He heard a clock chiming the nighttime hour of eleven o'clock. It was followed by silence. Then another sob, which was lost in a crisp crackle of thunder. Standing, Roan hastily headed up the stairs and in the direction of Engelina's bedroom.

The door to her room was shut. Twisting the knob,

he opened the door slowly, cautiously. Though the smell of recently burned candle wax wafted in the air, the room lay in pitch darkness. Only when a bolt of lightning tore through the rain-soaked sky did he notice the crumpled body on the floor.

Engelina!

Roan's heart pounded hurtfully as he closed the door behind him and hurried to her side. Kneeling, he forced himself to be calm, to draw on the detachment he'd learned in medical school. But, dammit, he didn't feel detached! In fact, he felt attached body, heart, and soul to the woman lying at his feet.

"Engelina?" he whispered, touching her shoulder gently.

Like a frightened animal, she shied away.

"It's all right," Roan crooned. "It's me."

His voice penetrated the haze of her fear and pain.

"Ro-an?" she said, the word almost unintelligible because of her hoarseness.

"Yes."

Engelina grabbed his hand, holding it so tightly that her grip threatened the flow of circulation. "Roan?" she said again, as though not daring to believe he was there.

"It's all right," he assured her. "I'm here."

Again he touched her shoulder. Again she flinched, this time not out of fear but pain. How badly was she hurt? He again forced himself to calmness. He had to think rationally, clearly, and right now what he needed was some light.

When he tried to pull away from Engelina, she panicked and clasped his hand so forcefully that her nails dug into his flesh.

"I need to light a candle," he said. "I'll be right back."

Engelina felt his hand slip from hers, felt him edge

from her side. Fear once more engulfed her. She
longed to cry out for him not to leave her alone, not
to leave her at the mercy of her sadistic husband, but
it was too painful to do so. As the whip had cracked
the silence and cleaved her flesh, she'd held the
unshed sobs, the unvoiced screams, deep inside until
her throat burned raw with denial.

Roan fumbled with the items on the small table that
Engelina had set up as a shrine. A votive candle toppled over; a book fell to the floor. Matches. There had
to be matches here somewhere, he thought, trailing
his hands through the darkness. In seconds, and with a
little luck, he found what he was looking for. Striking a
match, he lighted the nearest candle. In the gilded
glow, he saw the bright red blood on his fingertips. As
a surgeon, he'd seen gallons of blood, but all of it put
together didn't affect him as dramatically as the drops
staining the pads of his fingers.

Engelina moaned, a sound half human and wholly
pitiful.

Roan glanced toward her. It was then he saw her
tattered nightgown. It had been ripped as though a
wild beast had attacked her. Lace hung in shreds,
while delicate embroidery lay in fragile ruin.
Stepping forward, his heart in his throat, he kneeled
beside her. Reaching out, mesmerized by the destruc-
tion, he fingered the gown's mangled sleeve.

Engelina moaned again, this time shifting her
weight from her side to her belly. The action exposed
her back. At the sight of the welts, Roan stared. In
horror. In disbelief. In denial. No, he thought. He
wasn't seeing what he thought he was. No one, not
even someone as demented as Galen Lamartine,
could be so cruel. But the open wounds seeping
blood didn't lie. Neither did Engelina's tormented
cry.

"Lie still," Roan whispered, sick at heart. He knew he had to get her off the floor—he couldn't just let her lie there—but moving her would hurt. Nonetheless, it had to be done. Slipping his arm beneath her neck and knees, he rolled her toward him.

She groaned.

"I know," he whispered, feeling her pain as if it were his own.

Even though Roan fought to keep his arms in place, he brushed her back, bloodying the sleeve of his shirt and sending scorching spasms of pain erupting across her skin. She cried out.

"I'm sorry," he said, gently laying her on the soft bed.

Engelina tried to thank him, but no sound escaped her cracked lips.

"Shh. Be still."

Be still. It was such an easy command to obey because, when she moved, every muscle in her body protested. Yes, she would lie still. Very still. And maybe the fire searing her back would cease. As the gown began to fall away from her shoulders, Engelina forced her eyes open even as she reached for the front of the gaping garment.

"I have to take this off," Roan explained, unfastening one last button that by some miracle had managed to survive Galen's wrath. "I have to see how badly you're hurt."

Roan waited for her acceptance of this intimacy. When her eyes closed again, when her hand fell away from her bodice, he was unsure whether she had acquiesced or simply slipped back into her pain-ridden world. Whichever, he peeled the gown down. As a doctor, as a man, he'd seen his share of women's bodies, but none had ever seemed so perfectly formed. Sweetly sculpted shoulders, a tiny waist spannable with two hands, breasts that were small but full. Breasts with chocolate-dark crowns that, like her ebony hair, contrasted markedly with her porcelain skin. As had happened once before, a possessive feeling overcame Roan. This woman was his. For now. For forever.

Easing her to her side, he stripped the gown from her back, leaving it to bunch at her waist. Three angry-looking gashes, the ghastly handiwork of a whip or a belt, he surmised, had sliced open her tender skin as though it were nothing more than a side of raw beef. In places, blood still oozed, while in others it had begun to dry into a crimson crust. Roan tried not to think of how the marks had gotten on her back but rather concentrated on doing what needed to be done.

It was then that the irony hit him. His medical bag, his fully equipped medical bag, was more than a hundred years away. In view of that, what could he do to help Engelina? Water. At least he had water. If nothing else, he could cleanse the wounds and apply a cool cloth to them.

He spotted a pitcher sitting in a washbasin. He prayed that the pitcher contained water. Thankfully, it did. Pouring some into the bowl, he looked around for a cloth. When he could find none, he finished tearing the sleeve from the gown.

Engelina stirred at the disturbing motion.

"I'm sorry," he whispered, adding, as he wet the cloth, "This won't sting. It's only water. It'll make the cuts feel better."

"Cuts," she repeated, keying in to what he'd said, but then giving in to the sweet coolness dissipating the burning pain. She moaned, this time in relief. Suddenly, as though the water had revived her, she grabbed his hand again. Her eyes were wild with desperation when she said, "Don't let him whip me again!"

"No, I won't."

Then, forgetting about herself, she pleaded, "You must go! He'll kill you!" The strength with which she held him was yet another irony of the evening. She was telling him to go, yet clinging to him as though he were life itself.

"I'm not going."

Roan quickly cleansed the cuts as best he could. Through it all, Engelina whimpered, crying out softly when the pain became unbearable. She realized, however, that sometimes she whimpered not because of the pain, but because of the gentleness of Roan's touch. It was so at odds with the brutality she'd just suffered. It was so at odds with her husband's barbaric touch. She longed for this tender sweetness to go on forever. Somehow she knew that in time it could make her forget all the ugliness she'd known.

Easing her to her side, Roan quickly, modestly drew the sheet about her. When their eyes met, hers still glazed from tears, Roan's heart again swelled with love.

A drizzly, heated emotion tugged at Engelina's heart. It surprised her that she could feel anything. Or maybe it had just been a long while since she'd cared to, dared to.

What passed between them was as steamy as the rainy southern night.

So caught up in the darkness of Engelina's eyes was Roan that he didn't hear the door open. All he heard was a surprised gasp. Jerking his head toward the sound, he saw Lukie standing in the doorway. From the roundness of her eyes, he had startled her as much as she had him.

"It's all right," he called softly.

His words, the tone of his voice, were obviously encouragement enough, for the young servant stepped into the room. She was carrying something bundled up in a kerchief.

"I brought something for her," she said, moving into the room and to the bedside. To Lukie's credit, she didn't flinch at the sight of Engelina's lacerated skin. "He's whipped her before, but never this bad." As she began to untie the kerchief, she added, "She doesn't want anyone to know, especially not Chloe, but everyone does. It's just that nobody says anything."

"Even Chloe knows?" Roan asked.

Lukie looked over at Roan as she removed a jar of a foul-looking substance from her bundle. "I think she pretended she didn't know, because she didn't want to believe it, but after tonight . . ."

She left the sentence unfinished, forcing Roan to conjure up his own horrible images of what had happened that evening. The most horrible part was the reason Engelina had been whipped. He knew, but he had to have it confirmed.

"He beat her because of me, didn't he?"

Lukie glanced up. She didn't whitewash her reply. "Probably. But then, he doesn't need much reason."

"Where is he now?"

"He left the house, like he always does after he beats her. He'll probably be gone all night." She made the sign of the cross. "Pray to God that he is."

By now the lid was off the foul-looking substance. It smelled as vile as it looked.

"What is that?"

"Goose grease. It has magical properties. My aunt . . ." Lukie suddenly looked sheepish. "She's not an evil voodoo like everyone claims. She's not. She can work magic, that's all."

Roan took the jar from Lukie, saying, "We could use a little magic."

Between the two of them, they smeared the grease onto the gashes on Engelina's back.

"This'll help," he said, not having the foggiest idea whether or not it would. He reasoned that at least it couldn't hurt. "I wish we had something for pain." This he said to Lukie.

"I have some laudanum."

Opium. There was opium in laudanum. "Get it."

In minutes, Lukie returned with a bottle, from which she began to pour a liquid into a teaspoon. Roan deferred to her judgment concerning the dosage.

"Here, take this," Roan said to Engelina. "It'll help to ease the pain."

As he spoke, he poured a glass of water from the pitcher, then helped Engelina to a sitting position. She took the laudanum that Lukie offered and the water that Roan did. Afterward, he settled her back into the bed.

"Go," she repeated. "He meant it. He'll . . . he'll kill you."

"Shh," Roan ordered, sitting once more on the side of the bed and taking her hand in his. He meshed their fingers together. "He left the house."

"But he'll be back. Please, go . . ."

He tightened his hand in hers. "Let me worry about him."

"Roan, please—"

"Go to sleep," he said softly but emphatically.

She closed her eyes simply because they would no longer stay open. The pain that had cruelly embraced her was slowly beginning to recede, leaving her to drift on a cloud of blessed oblivion. Somehow, some way, Roan would take care of everything. Somehow, some way, God would work a bug-free miracle.

"That's it," Roan said. "Just go to sleep."

"Lukie?" Engelina whispered.

"Yes, ma'am?"

"Chlo-e . . ." she began, but the word died away.

"I'll take care of her, ma'am."

Lukie's eyes met Roan's, and he asked softly, "Is Chloe all right?"

"She's worried about her sister."

Roan was well aware of what Lukie was avoiding saying in Engelina's presence. Namely, that the stress was taking its toll. "If her heart acts up, you can give her an extra pill."

Lukie nodded, then started for the door. Halfway there, she stopped, dug in her pocket for the dirty red cloth tied with twine, and, walking back, handed the bundle to Roan. "It's my aunt's special gris-gris. It'll protect you." The servant left before Roan could do more than say thank you.

Engelina stirred, and Roan, after laying the amulet on the bedside table, stroked the hand held within his. It was small and delicate, yet, like her, strong, too. He studied the rest of her—the pale shoulders illuminated in the flickering candlelight, the striking beauty of her face, the sublime entanglement of hundreds of raven curls. Outside, lightning struck again, while thunder scrambled swift-footedly behind.

Engelina moaned.

"Shh, it's only thunder," he said.

"Go," Engelina whispered dazedly, adding, "Please go . . . please . . . please . . . don't go."

This last heart-truth squeezed Roan's chest until he thought he would burst. He tightened his hand.

"No," he said in a voice saturated with emotion, "I won't go."

He sat thus for several minutes on the side of the

bed, holding her hand in his as rain hurled itself against the house. Grim visions of her flayed back still taunted him. Even now, he didn't want to believe that she'd suffered as she had. The very thought repelled him, sickened him. Perhaps what repelled him most was the fact that he so easily could be reduced to the likes of Galen Lamartine. Already he was only an opportunity away from the same violence.

As he looked at the woman before him, violence was the last thing on his mind. Unable to stop himself, he traced the tears that had dried at her temple. Engelina sighed and turned her head into his wrist. Her warm breath brushed against his skin. As though it was the most natural thing in the world, he cradled her cheek. Again, as though it was the most natural thing in the world, she nuzzled her cheek into his palm.

"Roan?" she called softly, then said something that he couldn't make out.

He leaned forward. "What?"

". . . yourworld," she said, slurring the two words together.

He leaned closer. "I can't understand you."

". . . take me . . . to your . . . world."

For the rest of his life, Roan would never forget the agony, the ecstasy, of her plea.

SIXTEEN

*That same night, Crandall heard Julie's cry between the ear-*splitting claps of thunder. Grabbing his jeans from the back of a chair, he yanked them on as he hobbled across the worn carpet. He didn't give shirt or shoes the slightest thought. Zipping the jeans with one hand, he turned the doorknob with the other. Once the door was opened, the wind-driven rain lashed at him, dampening denim and wildly whipping his blond, shoulder-length hair about him.

Sidestepping one puddle on the poorly draining concrete, he squarely hit another. He cursed as he knocked on the door of the adjacent room.

"Julie?" he called, twisting the doorknob.

The door didn't budge.

"Julie?" he tried again, this time slapping his open hand against the metal door. Someone two doors down told him what to do with his knocking.

"Crandall?" came a whisper-thin voice.

"Yeah. Are you all right?"

The door opened an inch, then, after a hesitation during which Crandall wasn't certain whether Julie was confirming his identity or trying to decide whether to let him in, the door opened all the way. He stepped in. He noted that every light in the room was on—the ceiling light, both lamps, even the bathroom light.

"I heard you cry out."

Raking her hand through her long straight hair, which was noticeably moist from perspiration, she said, "I'm sorry I woke you." There was a distance in her voice, her demeanor, that he hadn't experienced before. He didn't like it. Mainly because it hurt.

"I don't give shit that you woke me. I just want to know if you're all right."

"I'm fine," she said, though her wide, fear-tinged brown eyes indicated she was lying. Her breathing, which fell in an uneven rhythm, confirmed this as well. "It, uh, it was just a bad dream."

Crandall studied her. Of all the people he knew, she was the last one he would pick to be scared spit-less over a dream. But then, she'd hardly been herself of late.

"What kind of dream?"

"Just a bad dream," she said as she headed for the rumpled bed and climbed into its middle.

The fact that she wore nothing but an oversized T-shirt proclaiming that archeologists did it in the dirt, and a pair of skimpy panties, seemed in no way to bother her. It bothered Crandall—in the nicest possi-ble way.

"You know," Julie added, giving a false little laugh, "dreams in which the bad guys chase you, and you can't run fast enough." She shivered suddenly, though it was stuffy-warm in the room. "It's this damned rain. And this damned job. I'm ready for this damned job to be finished!" Without missing a beat, she asked, "So when are we going over the records?"

Though the church archives had already been checked in vain for maps showing the secret tunnel and secret room, Crandall had obtained permission to go through the church business records for the

years 1870 to 1880. His request had been based solely on the coins found scattered at the entrance of the
room. Four of the coins had been dated 1873, one
1877, and one 1880. Working solely on a hunch,
which the textbooks didn't teach, but which a lot of
archeology turned out to be based on, Crandall
wanted to know what was going on in the cathedral
during those years. Perusing the records would take
them out of the field for a while, which he thought
was a good idea for all three of them. Especially for
Julie.

"In the next day or two," he said, answering her
question.

"So what do you expect to find?"

He shrugged. "I'll tell you when I see it." Easing
to the side of the bed, he asked candidly, "Do you
want out of this project?" Before she could miscon-
strue what he was saying, he explained, "I don't
mean just the records. I mean this whole cathedral
thing. If you want, you can pack your bags and get
out of here tomorrow morning. Hell, tonight, if you
want to."

That she even considered his offer told Crandall
how desperate she truly was. Finally, she said, "No. I
don't want out." She smiled, mirthlessly. "More to the
point, I can't get out." She played with a loose thread
of the oft-washed blanket, then glanced up. "I can't
explain it, but I'm supposed to be here. None of this
has been coincidence."

That she was echoing something that Crandall
himself had already thought set him back a second.
In fact, it made him feel downright spooked. From
the very beginning, he'd had the feeling that unseen
hands had been guiding him back to the city of his
birth. From the very beginning he felt there was
something that he had to learn about his true lin-

eage. It crossed his mind that maybe all of this—the room, Julie's bizarre behavior, his unexpected discovery of his birth—were interrelated. But how? How could such a thing be possible?

Crandall focused his attention back on what Julie was saying, something she seemed uncomfortable sharing. Perhaps because she wasn't certain of the reception she'd get. "I've, uh, been having dreams ever since we opened up the room."

"What kind of dreams?" Crandall asked when she was reluctant to offer more. She'd never elaborated on the room, other than the fact that she felt as though she'd been in it before, that she felt she'd been held there against her will. Crandall had naturally been curious but had respected her privacy.

Crandall saw her swallow. "Nightmares, really," she said quietly, as though saying the word too loudly would be a bad omen.

"Like what?" When she said nothing, he repeated, "Like what?"

"You'll think I'm crazy." She raked her hand back through her hair. "You probably do already."

"I don't think you're crazy."

"You should. I do."

"Let me be the judge of what I think, okay?"

After one last consideration, the words began to tumble out, as though they had to be said all at once or not at all.

"I'm a prisoner in the room. Chained to the wall like an animal. There's this candle glowing in a red votive cup, casting all these eerie bloodred shadows. And there's a Bible on a table, which I always think in the dream is strange. Then there're these men, just looking at me as if I'm some sort of chattel to be bought." She glanced down at the blanket, absently noting that she'd worried a thread loose. When she looked back up, tears glazed her eyes. "They hurt me."

Without invitation, without explanation, Crandall pulled her into his arms. She clung tightly.

"I'm scared," she whispered.

"Shh," he soothed, smothering her in a close embrace. With only the thin fabric of her T-shirt between them, Crandall could feel every soft curve of her feminine body. It felt good to hold a woman this close. Better than it ever had before. It crossed his mind that maybe this time he was holding the right woman.

"Don't leave me tonight," Julie pleaded, folding her arms about his neck, burrowing deeper into him. "Please don't leave me."

Because it felt good, right, Crandall slipped his hands beneath her T-shirt, smoothing the satin skin of her back. The same hands skimmed her rib cage, then found the fullness of her plush breasts. She rasped his name as her eager mouth sought his.

And then they were lost to the heated fury of love-making.

Through it all, Crandall couldn't shake the feeling that he was scared, too. Scared of sharing his heart again. Scared of disappointing Julie the way he'd already disappointed one woman. Scared of what he might discover before this investigation was completed.

Roan was scared.

It was two days later, on a hot and humid Thursday afternoon, and he had no answers to the questions that plagued him. He didn't know the date of the fire, he didn't know whether to tell Engelina about her impending death if she didn't get out of the house, he didn't know how to get her out of the house. He still could stay in the past for no more than a few hours. The night of the beating, he'd sat by her side until dawn dappled the sky. He had then disappeared back into the present. As always, he'd felt helpless. Even angry.

Neither did he know what to do for Chloe, who had slipped into another decline. He suspected that Lukie had been right about the young woman. She'd probably known about Galen's brutality all along but had chosen to believe that she must be wrong. Confronted with the truth, she'd become morose. Once more she was having trouble breathing. Once more she was pale and drawn.

Roan had promised Chloe that he'd take care of her and Engelina. He hoped to God he hadn't lied.

Only two things made the days bearable. First, Galen, who had stormed out of the house after beating Engelina, had not returned. Rumor whispered that he was at Oak Manor with Messieurs Desforges and Harnett. Roan didn't care where he was as long as he stayed there, but he feared that at any given moment he would return. What would happen then?

The second thing was a supposition he had struck upon. While he couldn't be absolutely sure of its validity, every time he'd tested it, it had proven true. He thought he'd found the key to entering the past at will. Not staying there, but entering it. He'd been thinking about why he'd finally been able to return to the past on that fateful night when he'd known Engelina was in pain, and after he'd frustratingly tried everything to reach her. It came to him like a bolt out of the blue that maybe his realizing he was in love with her had effected the journey. Since then, each time he'd allowed the warm feeling of love to fill his heart, he'd been transported back in time.

What would happen if Engelina realized that she was in love with him?

"Your back looks much better," Roan said.

While the goose grease, supposedly imbued with magical properties, had been a halfway decent medication, the antibiotic ointment he now brought with him on each visit far outperformed it. As he applied the ointment, Roan tried hard not to think of the softness of Engelina's skin. Or how the smell of her perfume, the sweet, subtle scent of rosewater, seemed to enslave his senses.

"What is this called again?" Engelina asked.

She sat on the stool before the dresser, her wrapper draped discreetly about her in a way that allowed exposure of her back but nothing more. She vaguely remembered, or thought she did, his having pulled her gown completely from her on the night of the beating. It was strange how she could think of the beating so calmly. Far more calmly than she could think of Roan's seeing her body. The latter made her feel hot and flushed in a way she'd never felt before. Very much the same way she felt every time he touched her. Like now. And so she asked an inane question to curb her own runaway thoughts.

"Antibiotic ointment," he answered absently, wondering for the thousandth time how anyone could inflict pain on anything as perfect as this back, this woman.

"Antibiotic ointment," she repeated, lazily closing her eyes to the heavenliness of his caress, a caress that she could so easily grow accustomed to. Though she was not even aware that she did so, she sighed.

At the softness of the sound, at its unexpectedness, Roan glanced up and into the mirror. Engelina's head lolled to the side, while the weight of her hair, drawn from her back, cascaded about one shoulder like a black velvet waterfall. Ebony eyelashes, long and spiky-thick, edged her eyelids, as always forming a striking contrast to her pale cheeks. Her lips were parted slightly. She looked, at least in Roan's humble opinion, more beautiful than any woman had a right to.

Perhaps it was the sudden silence, perhaps it was the fact that his hand stopped in mid-stroke, perhaps she sensed his attention—whatever, Engelina opened her eyes. Her gaze met his in the mirror.

Her heart stopped.

As did his.

Time, whatever it was, however one chose to measure it, stood still. Stock-still. With not a second left to beat.

"You're so pretty," Roan whispered, uncertain how she would react to this frank remark, but unable to keep from making it. He simply had to say what he felt or die on the spot.

At his words, Engelina's eyes misted, and she whispered, "Please don't say I'm pretty. I don't want to be pretty."

Bewildered by her reaction, he stepped to her side and kneeled down beside her. When she angled her head to face him, he had to admit that she was even more beautiful than her reflection in the mirror.

"Why don't you want to be pretty?" Roan asked, forcing himself to keep his hands from her when all he wanted was to pull her into his arms.

"My—" She tried to say the word *husband* but couldn't, although Roan knew whom she was talking about. "He wants me because I'm pretty. He wants to possess me only because other men will covet what he has." Though she clearly fought it, a tear slipped from her eye and ran down her cheek. "I would rather be plain. Plain and loved."

Roan was uncertain whether it was what she said or the single tear despoiling the flawlessness of her beauty that caused his heart to burst wide. With anger for her husband, with love for her.

"Not all men are like him," Roan said, his voice scratchy with emotion.

A warm, candy-sweet feeling erupted in Engelina's heart. She knew this man spoke the truth. "No," she whispered, "you are not like him."

"No," Roan said. "I would never hurt you. I would never punish you for being beautiful."

As he spoke, he brushed aside the tear with the pad of his thumb. It was his undoing. With a will of its own, his palm cradled her face.

Engelina closed her eyes, luxuriating in the exquisiteness of Roan's caress. She had wanted him to touch her. Perhaps more than she'd ever wanted anything. When he touched her, she forgot the vileness of Galen's touch, the ugliness of his heartless possession.

At her pose, as vulnerable as that of a trusting child, Roan's composure slipped. Or rather it fell away completely. With a low moan, he slowly drew his hand across her cheek, absorbing the softness he found there. His knuckles caressed her chin, then trailed down the column of her neck, which she angled without even knowing she was doing so. At the indentation of her throat, he stopped, allowing his thumb to rest in the precious hollow.

Engelina sighed and unknowingly let her hands loosen their hold on her silken wrapper. It fell away, exposing her shoulders and hinting at a hidden cleavage. Roan's heart scampered wildly.

"Engelina," he whispered.

Engelina heard her name gently falling from Roan's lips. It was a sweetness she'd never thought to hear. It was a sweetness she didn't even know existed. With her eyes still closed—her lids felt far too weighty to control—she opened her mouth to say something.

She wasn't sure what. Perhaps she wanted to tell him
how sweet her name sounded. Perhaps she wanted to
tell him to never stop saying her name. Perhaps she
merely wanted to call his. Whatever she would have
said, she never had the chance, for Roan's lips
brushed against hers.

At this intimacy, her composure skittered into the
shadows.

His mouth but skimmed hers, momentarily commingling their breaths, more than momentarily commingling their desire. Roan told himself he shouldn't
do this. Engelina told herself she should stop him.
Both were aware that, even though her husband was a
tyrant, she had taken vows of fidelity. At the moment,
however, those vows seemed as fragile as the thinnest
crystal, as fragile as Roan's control.

Unable to help himself, he brought his lips back to
hers. He kissed her softly, swiftly. She sighed, indicating her receptiveness even though her lips had moved
but slightly beneath his. He kissed her again, this time
more slowly, more leisurely. Like a clumsy novitiate, she
moved her mouth, seeking more of what he was offering, seeking to give even as she took. Participation was
new to her. She'd been kissed before—cunningly, bru-
tally—but she'd never been asked to be part of a mutual
sharing. She'd never wanted to, before now.

"That's it," he whispered.

Bracketing her face with his hands, he worked his
mouth over hers and encouraged her to respond in
kind. She did. Tentatively at first, then with more
boldness.

Engelina could never remember feeling this way
before—both hot and cold, weak and strong. She felt
as though she could fly as high as any bird had ever
soared in the sky. More important, she felt secure.
This man would not betray her by inflicting pain. This

man would die before he hurt her. She knew this. She knew, too, that she was breaking her vows. Though her marriage was a travesty, it had been based on vows solemnly sworn before God. Surely, though, something that felt so right could not be wrong.

Could it?

Roan sensed her hesitation. He knew its source. Though it took all the strength he had, he pulled his mouth from hers. They simply stared at each other. Their breathing was unsteady; their hearts beat erratically. Though neither was sorry for what had just happened, one basic fact couldn't be ignored: She belonged to another man.

That same afternoon, Marie Cambre lay with her lover. The sweat of passion sheened her skin, making it gleam like a gemstone. Her lover's breath rasped unevenly against her ear, while her breath fell in unsteady, syncopated sighs. She never felt quite so alive as she did during lovemaking. She never felt her powers were stronger. In that moment of surrender, she understood that life and death were but different shades of the same color, and that sex, elemental and primary, tinted the whole.

It would never cross her mind to feel guilty about giving her body to a man who wasn't her husband. Guilt was for those without the confidence to make their own rules. Besides, vows remained valid not because they were recorded before a priest, in some book of church and state, but rather because they were recorded in a heart. In that sense, the man who'd just spilled his seed into her was her husband.

Her lover rolled from her, easing to her side at the same time that a lazy smile came to his lips. "I believe you have slipped me one of your love potions. I think of nothing but bedding you."

"You don't need a love potion, my pet. It is I who need help keeping up with you."

The man's smile faded as he ringed the round crest of her breast with his finger. The dark nipple beaded, as though reveling in his touch. "Ah, my little vixen, you have no trouble keeping up."

His mouth found hers. The sweetness of his kiss pierced her soul, and she panicked. What if he didn't like the news she must soon tell him? She had put off her secret for a while, but it would not long be denied. She had prayed at the cathedral for a special blessing from the Virgin Mary. Father John had treated her kindly as he always did. Many in the church did not. Father Ignatius seemed only to tolerate her heathen presence, as did many of the parishioners. Her reputation always preceded her. And in the past days, rumors of her involvement in the Hell-Fire Club had heated up. Another young woman was missing, and everyone was saying that it was time the police made an arrest. Another wave of panic washed over Marie. What if one day soon the police showed up on her doorstep?

"What is it?" the man beside her asked, sensing the change in her mood.

"Nothing," Marie lied, forcing a smile to her full, sensual lips. Adroitly changing subjects, she asked, "And how is Chloe?"

"Not well."

"I shall make her a stronger gris-gris."

"I'm not certain that it will do any good." Before Marie could respond, the man added, "I'm not certain that all the gris-gris in the world will help any member of that household."

"What do you mean?" Marie asked, her thoughts

going first to her niece. "Is something wrong with Lukie?"

The man kissed Marie's brow. "No," he said, "she is safe."

"Then—"

"Something strange is happening in the house."

"What do you mean?"

"A man has shown up. A man named Roan Jacob. He claims to be Chloe's doctor, but . . ."

"But what?"

Marie's lover shrugged. "I don't know. The man is . . . strange. The way he comes and goes is strange."

"And what of Galen?"

"That is strange, too. He has disappeared. To Oak Manor with Desforges and Harnett."

Seconds passed before Marie said, "Another young woman is missing."

The man tightened the arm lying across Marie's waist. "I know."

"The police are growing desperate to arrest someone."

Sensing Marie's fear, the man said, "They have no evidence of your involvement."

"If they are desperate enough, they will need no evidence."

The man tilted his lover's chin until Marie's eyes met his. "I would not let them take you."

"Perhaps you couldn't stop them."

"I would stop them," the man said emphatically, defiantly. His eyes softened as his hand slid to her stomach. "I could not let them take the mother of my child, now could I?" At her startled look, he smiled. "Did you think I didn't know?"

Her eyes unwaveringly on his, she asked, "And does my carrying your babe in my belly please you?"

The kiss he gave her was answer enough.

* * *

A century away, in a small, single-windowed room of the St. Louis Cathedral, Crandall and Julie sat poring over volumes of dry historical data. They had been thus monotonously engaged since the day before. Wade had thrown up his hands that morning, announcing that, if he didn't get back to the dig and away from the books, he was going crazy. Crandall wondered how far behind his friend and colleague he was.

"I've got to take a break," he said, standing and stretching cramped muscles.

Julie needed no encouragement to follow suit. Shedding her reading glasses, she asked, "If we don't know what we're looking for, isn't it possible we've already found it and just don't know it?"

"We'll know it."

"Speak for yourself."

Crandall didn't know how to explain the feeling he had. He simply felt the need, as though some unheard voice were whispering in his ear, to look through the church archives. He knew he would know what he was looking for when he saw it. *If* he saw it, he thought on another rough sigh.

"Ah, hell, maybe I'm just fooling myself," he said, drawing his fingers through his hair, which he hadn't worn in a ponytail since the night he'd spent with Julie. Letting his hair hang loose and free was symbolic of the way he was feeling these days, of the way Julie made him feel.

"Hey, hey," she said, obviously sensing his flagging spirits, "if you think you'll know it, you'll know it." She stood and walked toward him, brazenly placing her arms around his neck. She smiled. "And, if you say I'll know it, then I'll know it."

Crandall slid his arms about Julie's waist and drew her close. "I know I'm crazy about you. And that's all I really need to know."

Like the first star of evening, it dawned on Crandall that what he'd said was the truth. He'd spent the last few months obsessed with finding his roots, obsessed with learning about a man he hadn't even known existed until then. Was it really important that he find out about this Drexel Bartlett? When he stared into Julie's eyes, the way he now was, he didn't think so.

"The past—yours, mine—doesn't matter," he said.

"No," she answered, as mesmerized by the present, by the future, as he.

Crandall lowered his head, uniting his mouth with Julie's. The kiss was long and deep and filled with promises that both would keep. When their breathing was labored and their bodies heated, Crandall pulled his mouth from hers.

"I, uh, I think we'd better get back to the books," he said.

Julie grinned. "I think so, too, unless you want to give a passing priest a coronary."

Another hour of tedium passed. Crandall perused three volumes, disclosing everything from the budget of 1879 to a list of christenings to the mundane notation that someone had forgotten to purchase candles. There was even a poem in French written by a nun, extolling, as best Crandall could decipher, the virtues of her habit. Interesting, but hardly what he was looking for. One more, he thought. He would look at one more volume and that was it. Enough was enough. He reached for the nearest book. At this point, inspiration had deserted him, and he didn't much care which book he picked up.

The book, dealing with church transactions in the

year 1880, seemed a hodgepodge of information—none of it of any value. Crandall flipped through it. More hastily with each passing page. On the next to the last page was a list of names. Obviously people serving the church in that year. Out of habit, he scanned the listing. He was midway through it when the name jumped out at him.

Father Jonathan Drexel Bartlett.

At first Crandall didn't believe what he was seeing, but the longer he stared at the long-ago dried ink, the more he had to accept the written reality. In the year 1880, a man by the name of Jonathan Drexel Bartlett had served as a priest at the cathedral. The man had to be a relative of the Drexel Bartlett Crandall had been searching for. It would simply be too coincidental, otherwise.

Coincidence.

Crandall was left feeling once more that his being in New Orleans, at the cathedral, was far from coincidence. Just as his opening this volume had not been coincidence. He had found what he'd been looking for. He had found what it had been destined for him to find all along. The question now was, exactly what did it all mean?

Micaela, with the sleeping cat at her feet, studied the tarot cards, wondering what they meant. They conjured up visions in her fertile imagination, visions of a votive candle casting a bloodred glow, visions of a holy book—a Bible?—resting on a table. Pain was all around. Pain and fear and betrayal.

In the middle of it all was Roan Jacob. He was in danger, with death hiding in the shadows. His life rested in the hands of the second stranger, whose presence she'd sensed all along. Engelina was in danger, too, though for her Micaela could see no reprieve. Though she'd read the cards a hundred times of late, the outcome was always the same.

Engelina D'Arcy Lamartine was destined to die.

SEVENTEEN

Roan lost all track of time.

He spent every waking moment, of which there
were many, slipping back into the past to keep a
watchful eye on Engelina. Now that he had the key to
travel—he simply concentrated on his love for her—
he went several times a day and even more frequently
at night. These nocturnal visits she sometimes wasn't
aware of because she was asleep. Nor did she question how he now was able to visit the past so often.
He was grateful she didn't. He wasn't certain he
could lie about his feelings for her, but equally
uncertain that she could handle hearing about them.
She had too much else on her mind and heart—
Chloe's deteriorating health and the return of
Galen.

This latter event occurred two days later, on a
Saturday afternoon. He stormed into Lamartine
House as unexpectedly as he'd stormed out. Lukie
rushed to tell Engelina, who pleaded for Roan to flee
to the future. He had, but only because Engelina had
been nearly hysterical with worry for him. While back,
he made a decision. Leaving the house, he went in
search of a gun. It took less than an hour for him to
realize that one could illegally purchase anything in
the French Quarter.

That night he made a startling discovery.

Unwilling to leave Engelina at the mercy of her hellish husband, regardless of the personal danger involved, he returned. He had concealed the gun within the medical bag. Hastily making his way to Engelina's bedroom, he found her pacing the floor.

At the tap on the door, at the twisting of the doorknob, Engelina whirled. Though she was unaccustomed to Galen's knocking, her heart nonetheless jumped to her throat. Perhaps it was a new and diabolical tactic of his. At the sight of Roan, she fought rushing across the room and throwing herself into his arms. Ever since the kiss they'd shared, a fine tension had existed between them. It was as though neither knew quite what to do now or, more to the point, it was as though neither knew what they were morally free to do. What she wanted to do, however, had never been more clearly defined in Engelina's mind. She wanted to be in Roan's arms again. She wanted to taste his lips. She wanted to experience once more the addictive feeling of being cherished.

But she forced herself to remain standing where she was.

"Are you all right?" Roan asked, shutting the door behind him. Every instinct told him to cross to her and take her in his arms, but, following the kiss, he'd sensed her moral confusion. Consequently he'd kept his distance. Even though it had been the hardest thing he'd ever done. Even though he didn't know how much longer he'd be able to manage it.

"Yes," she answered, her heart still thumping wildly. This time from Roan's nearness.

"Where is he?"

"In his study. He locked himself in there hours ago." At Roan's unspoken question, Engelina volunteered, "He hasn't been up to see me."

Roan's relief was obvious.

"You shouldn't be here," Engelina said. "He could come at any second."

"I won't leave you."

"Please—"

"I won't leave you," Roan insisted, the gun within the medical bag giving him confidence. Before she could plead again, he shoved a straight-backed chair beneath the doorknob of the lockless door. He was on the verge of announcing that the chair would at least forestall Galen when a slight knock sounded.

Engelina's gaze flew to Roan. Roan's hand tightened on the medical bag. Slipping to a position behind the door, Roan opened the bag, expecting to see the gun where he'd left it. Instead, he saw nothing except the usual medical paraphernalia. The gun had not been transported to the past. Why? Roan didn't have time to consider the baffling question, for a second knock followed the first.

"Ma'am?" Lukie called.

Engelina's relief almost brought her to her knees. Roan was left in little better condition.

Engelina eased aside the chair wedged beneath the doorknob. She opened the door, discreetly, so as to keep Roan hidden from view. Lukie, her hair wrapped in a red kerchief, looked as relieved as her mistress.

"He just left, ma'am," she said.

Engelina sighed. "Thank you, Lukie."

"He told Kipperd to stay close." The tone of Lukie's voice said that she didn't trust the red-bearded Irishman any more than Engelina did.

Engelina nodded her silent understanding. "How is Chloe?"

"Resting quietly. I gave her the new medicine that Dr. Jacob brought." Days before, when Chloe's condition had worsened, Roan had brought something to calm her and make her sleep.

"Stay with her, please," Engelina said.

"Yes, ma'am." Lukie smiled. "She said she would dream of the magnolia blossom you brought her this morning."

Engelina wished her dreams would be as pleasant, though, the truth was, she doubted that Chloe's would be either. Her sister was frightened. Engelina sensed it. Furthermore, she didn't blame her. She was frightened, too. Though she was less frightened with Roan by her side. In seconds, when the door was closed, she turned to him. Their eyes met. Hers said clearly that, though she'd begged him to go, though she still knew that was best for him, she was glad he was here.

"You need some rest," he said quietly, hearing every silent word she'd just intended. He knew she was glad he was there. That knowledge was enough to make him tackle the devil. Singlehandedly. Without a gun.

This brought his mind back to the question of why the gun hadn't made the time journey.

"What's wrong?" Engelina asked.

"Nothing," Roan said, hiding his disappointment, his puzzlement, as he set the medical bag on a table and wedged the chair against the door again. "Nothing," he repeated.

Engelina wasn't sure he was telling her the truth, but, when he once more insisted that she rest, it was an offer she couldn't refuse. It seemed like forever since she'd lain down, forever since she'd closed her eyes in peace.

When he drew a chair to the side of the bed, she whispered, "You mustn't stay long."

At her concession to letting him stay, Roan smiled.

"No, I won't stay long," he said, reaching for her hand.

It was the first contact they'd had since the kiss. His taking her hand seemed so normal that he did it before he thought. Perhaps because it had been so long since they'd touched, perhaps because of his ultrasensitive tactility, her skin burned his. With his imagination gone wild, he could actually feel her hands moving over his face, his body. At each point along the way, he seemed to burst into flames. Fearing an outright conflagration, he released her hand.

"Rest," he ordered, his voice rough.

At the removal of his hand, Engelina felt bereft. She had longed to touch him, to have him touch her, and, now that he had, her appetite had only been whetted. At the sudden loss of what she craved most, she wanted to beg him to take her hand again. She wanted to beg him for more, for intimacies that should have shamed her but didn't. Baffled by her brazenness, she tucked her hand beneath the pillow and closed her eyes. As unlikely as she thought it under the circumstances, she instantly fell asleep.

Roan watched her—the way her hair waywardly, temptingly lay about her, the way her chest, beneath the bodice of a pale pink dress, rose and fell with her even breathing, the way her lips were parted slightly. Once more Roan's heart filled with love. He had to find a way to save her from the fate history had written for her. He had to!

But how?

Especially when he didn't even know the date of the fire that would sweep through Lamartine House. Though he knew he was making a pest of himself, Roan checked daily with the Tulane professor. The man had been unable to come up with any information, and the tone of his voice the last time Roan had spoken with him had implied that he couldn't understand such a dogged interest in something so trivial. After all, the house hadn't been that important in the history of the city. Roan had pleaded with him to continue looking.

No, Roan thought as he gazed at a sleeping Engelina, the fire was important only to one woman from the past . . . and to one man in the present who'd been commissioned to save her. He wondered if his falling in love with her had been part of the grand scheme, as well. Or had he managed to do that all on his own?

The smell of smoke wafted through Roan's dreams.

Some lucid part of his sleeping brain told him that he was only having another sensory hallucination. Hadn't he had them a dozen times since moving into the house? Yes, he had, but this time the smoke smelled so real. It burned his nostrils. It pricked his lungs. It frightened him.

Roan jerked awake. He still sat at Engelina's bed-side, but sometime during the long night, he'd laid his head on the bed and had fallen fast asleep. The first thing he noticed was that Engelina slept soundly, the second that, indeed, he did smell smoke. Instinctively, he realized it was coming from behind him. Whirling, he saw that one of the votive candles on the altar had been left burning. Golden shadows danced on the wall as the candle burned low, sending spirals of smoke into the hot air. Relieved, Roan stood, crossed to the altar, and blew out the candle. The room was pitched into darkness, except for a splash of moonlight stealing through the open window. Roan stared out at the night, wondering what he would have done if the house had been on fire.

Suddenly, the burden he carried became too weighty. Suddenly, his impotence became more than he could bear. He cursed silently, the word as hot as the weather. He'd told Micaela O'Kane that he had no answers. She had told him he would have them when he needed them. She had told him that he, and he alone, could save Engelina.

But, dammit, how could he when he couldn't stay in the past and couldn't bring her to the future? How could he when he hadn't a clue as to why some things transported back in time and stayed, while others vanished? And then there was the gun. It hadn't transported back at all. Why?

As though ordained, his gaze followed the platinum path of moonlight. It illuminated the magnolia tree in the courtyard as though the tree were the only thing of value at that moment. Magnolia tree. Magnolia blossom.

"She said she would dream of the magnolia blossom you brought her this morning."

Lukie's words to Engelina, spoken earlier that evening in regard to Chloe, filtered into Roan's thoughts, leaving him to pose a question that abruptly seemed like the single most important question in the world. Had the magnolia blossom that had been transported forward in time, the one that remained to this day, been plucked by Engelina for Chloe?

Okay, assume it had, Roan thought, knowing somehow that it had been gathered by Engelina for her sister. For someone she cared deeply about. Maybe she even made a regular habit of bringing Chloe flowers. Hadn't he seen flowers several times in Chloe's room? Okay, okay, back to the assumption, Roan thought, the excitement of discovery flowing through his veins. The flower had been picked out of love. The medicine he'd administered to Chloe equally had been given out of caring, as had the amulet Lukie had given him. Those things had stayed, while the basket, the apron, both articles that had no emotional ties attached, had faded back into the time plane from which they'd come. And the gun . . .

Roan's heart took a giant leap. Yes, yes, he was on the right track! He could feel it! The gun hadn't transported back in time because it had been associated with hate. Yes, that made sense. Emotions had to be the key. Especially in view of the fact that his realizing he was in love with Engelina gave him at-will access to the past.

He frowned.

But what, if anything, would allow him to remain in the past? That was the crowning question. That, and could he find a way to bring Engelina to the present? And for neither of these questions did he have anything even remotely resembling an answer. Nor was there any guarantee Micaela was right. Just because he needed answers, and desperately, didn't mean he would find them. Now. Or ever.

"Tell me about your world?"

Engelina asked the question the following night. She had awakened in the wee hours of the morning to find Roan sitting in a nearby chair. It had never crossed her mind for a single instant that the man in the candlelit shadows was her husband. She knew he wasn't. She *sensed* Roan's presence. Just as she'd sensed that he'd been there dozens of times over the past days watching over her even as she slept. She wanted to tell him to leave, to go back where he was safe, but she didn't have the strength to do so. As selfish as it was, she wanted him with her. Near her. So near her that they were one. This realization no longer shocked her. It was fact. And wasn't it just as much a sin to lie as it was to have such adulterous thoughts?

"You need to sleep," Roan said, studying her from beneath steepled fingers.

As he often did, he had been staring at her, and the way her white gown fell so intriguingly, so sexily, about her, when she'd unexpectedly awakened. That she had known so unequivocally that it was he warmed his heart. As for the rest of him, it was hot. As hot as desire could make a man.

She shook her head, causing the thicket of her black hair to sway invitingly on the pillow. "No, talk to me. Tell me about your world."

Suddenly, he liked the prospect of doing so. He wanted to give her the gift of the future. It was a gift he wanted her to like. But what tack should he take? A philosophical one? A scientific one? Would she believe the changes that had taken place? Would he? Would anyone?

"A lot of things have changed," he said.

He proceeded to tell her about automobiles and airplanes, medical cures and cinemas, rock and roll and a United States that now numbered fifty. He spoke of radio, of television, of microwave ovens and computers. Through it all, Engelina said nothing but rather stared at him with a wide-eyed innocence, a childlike fascination. When he came to the moon walk, however, innocence and fascination gave way to incredulity.

"You tease me," she accused with a smile. She was now sitting up, though she refrained from leaning against the headboard because of her tender back. Though dramatically improved, it was far from healed.

Roan grinned. "I'm not teasing you. Men have actually walked on the moon."

"That isn't possible."

"It is. I promise you. The men are called astronauts."

"And how do these astronauts get there?" she asked, playing along with his game. "In airplanes?"

"Sort of. They travel in a spacecraft." At her disbelieving look, he added, "I'm not putting you on."

She frowned at his modern choice of words.

"I'm not teasing you," he clarified.

Slowly her smile died. "You're serious?"

"Yes."

Overwhelmed, Engelina said nothing. Roan longed to move to the side of the bed, but he didn't. Mainly because he didn't think it a good idea. Or, perhaps more to the point, he thought it too good an idea. He noticed that Engelina hugged her arms about her and wondered if she, too, was fighting temptation.

"I know my world sounds strange, but it isn't. Not really. It's just different. Though maybe not so different, after all. People are still the same. Some are good, some are bad."

This last comment set both minds in the direction of Galen, who had once more mysteriously, but thankfully, disappeared from the house. As usual he had left his henchman Kipperd in charge.

Engelina chose to ignore the subject of her husband. Instead, she said, "Would I like your world?"

Roan heard the unspoken wistfulness of the question. He remembered, and vividly, her asking him to take her to his world, to the future. He could think of nothing he'd like more.

"I honestly don't know. But I hope you would."

"You work in a hospital?"

"Yes."

"You live in a big house?"

"A condominium."

"A condominium," she repeated, trying out the unfamiliar word.

"Yes."

"You have an automobile?"

"Yes."

"An airplane?"

He smiled. "No."

"A woman?"

His smile died. The two of them sat staring at each other through the flickering candlelight. The question had just popped out, surprising Engelina as much as it had Roan. She knew that she had no right to wish it, but she didn't want him to belong to another woman. His kiss hadn't felt as though he did, but then neither had her kiss, and she very much belonged to another man. When he didn't answer, Engelina's heart fell to her feet.

Hugging her arms more tightly about her, she said, "You have a woman."

"I did. I was going to be married at the end of the month."

The realization that the once-arranged wedding was only days away stunned Roan. As it did Engelina, though she tried to focus on the fact that he'd used the past tense of the verb.

"You did have a woman?"

"Yes."

"But no more?"

"No, no more."

Was that relief he saw streaking through her coal-black eyes? God, he had no right to hope it was, but he did!

Although she had no right to feel it, relief flooded Engelina.

Why? Her eyes asked why he'd changed his matrimonial plans.

"Because of a portrait," he said quietly, frankly, knowing he was opening up a topic that might best be left unopened. He needed, though, to share some of what was in his heart, before its fullness drowned him.

She didn't know what she'd expected to hear, but what he'd said certainly wasn't it. "I-I don't understand."

"When I arrived at this house, I found a portrait in the parlor." His eyes piercing hers, he added, "It was of a woman. The most beautiful woman I'd ever seen. From the moment I saw her, I became obsessed with her."

"I still don't under—"

"It was a portrait of you. The same portrait that hangs in your parlor."

Engelina heard the words but couldn't make them form into anything coherent. What did he mean he'd seen the portrait, her portrait?

"My portrait still hangs in the house?" she asked, intrigued, even pleased, by the prospect.

"Yes," Roan answered. He saw no need to go into the fact that it had been recently returned, nor the circumstances under which it had. Neither did he want to mention the ghost that haunted Lamartine House.

"You saw it and . . ." Engelina let the words trail off, but they both remembered his usage of the word *obsessed.*

"Yes," he answered, his eyes never leaving hers.

She glanced away first, as though she were melting in his heated stare. "My portrait survived all those years?" she asked again, bewildered by the fact.

"Yes."

Survival. For all of its sturdy meaning, it was a fragile word. Both Engelina and Roan knew this. Just as Roan knew the sudden direction of Engelina's thoughts. It was a natural direction, but one that the two of them had been ignoring for days. Roan wanted to ignore it forever. Engelina wanted, needed, to face it at last.

"It's strange knowing that I died before you were born," she said, glancing up at him again and trying to make the statement sound casual.

Speaking of her death caused a shadow to pass over Roan's soul. Because he couldn't sit still, because he couldn't continue to gaze into the most beautiful eyes he'd ever seen, eyes that were asking of him something he didn't want to give, Roan stood and crossed to the window. He ran his hands into the back pockets of his jeans.

He knew. Engelina saw in his face, his eyes, that he knew when she died. She saw, too, that he didn't want to tell her. Her pulse quickened, for his reticence could mean only one thing. Strangely, it was something she'd suspected all along.

"When?" she whispered, sounding far braver than she felt.

The single word slashed at Roan, severing a chunk of his heart. He would have bet every dime he had, every dime he ever hoped to have, that she knew her death would be soon. Had she simply sensed it, or had his reluctance tipped her off? Maybe both.

"Roan?"

He turned, because he couldn't do otherwise when she spoke his name softly, urgently. Her eyes had darkened until they appeared fathomless. Even so, he saw the fear, the resignation, within their ebony depths. He wasn't certain which touched him more.

"I was sent back to save you. And I will. I swear to you I will."

The fervor in his voice made her believe. Almost. "And what if you can't?" she asked.

"I will!" Roan crossed the room, took her hand in his, and held it tightly. So tightly that it was painful for both her and him. He forced himself to lighten his grasp. He couldn't, however, force himself to let loose her hand entirely. Not if his soul had burned in hell for it.

"I won't let you die," he whispered, splaying her fingers across his and fervently entwining them together. "I swear I won't let you die." This last was said as he brought her hand to his lips and kissed the back of it. Closing his eyes, he prayed that he hadn't lied to her.

"Roan?"

He opened his eyes, his gaze instantly connecting with hers.

"Don't tell me," she said. "Don't tell me how much time I have left. And you must promise me something," she added. "Promise me that you won't blame yourself if . . . if things can't be changed." When he said nothing, she commanded, as though his emotional well-being was far more important to her than her possibly impending death, "Promise me!"

"How can I promise you that?" Roan asked, his voice thick.

"Because I ask it of you," she said simply.

Roan had never known anyone as unselfish as Engelina. His heart had never been so swollen with love. Nor had he ever wanted, needed, to express that love so badly. But he couldn't. Because it was the most tormenting of hells to be near her and not be able to show her his love, he had to put some distance between them. He started to pull his hand from hers at the same time he started to rise from the bed.

Gripping his hand, she whispered, "No."

His eyes met hers.

"Please," she whispered, now slowly bringing his hand to her face. "Don't go."

She heard his sharp intake of breath. She knew she was playing with fire, a fire that could consume them both, but a restlessness, a recklessness, roamed through her that she couldn't deny. As insistently as the beat of a savage drum, she was reminded over and over that her life was possibly on the verge of being cut short. Did she want to die without having ever lived? Did she want to die without knowing the exquisite tenderness that could exist between a man and a woman? In answer to her own questions, she closed her eyes and cozied her cheek into the palm of his hand.

"Engelina," Roan whispered, feeling her breath, like the pastel wings of a butterfly, beat against his wrist.

Both were aware of the night's sultry heat. It blasted through the open windows, causing the summer air to shimmer like desert sand. The mosquito netting, a froth of lace, had been pulled aside in deference to any heaven-sent breeze. Roan's shirt, moist with perspiration, clung to his back, while Engelina's gown, high-necked and long-sleeved out of modesty, chafed her damp skin. It was not this heat, however, that ruled supreme. It was the heat of their passion.

"Engelina," Roan repeated, his hand coming alive to the feelings rushing through him. With both hands, he caressed her—her cheeks, her temples, her forehead beneath the tangle of her hair. As though trying to memorize even the smallest feature of her, he brushed the pads of his thumbs across her closed eyelids. He then trailed his eager fingertips across her lips, parting them in the sensual journey.

"We shouldn't do this," Roan said, his gaze feasting on her as his thumb gently played with her lower lip.

What his thumb was doing seemed more intimate than anything Engelina had ever experienced before. It sent shivers of pleasure scampering through her.

"No," she whispered, "we shouldn't do this."

"It's wrong for us to do this," he said, leaning forward and rubbing his nose against her chin.

"Yes, it's wrong," she said, feeling his breath against her neck. His fevered breath. It felt heavenly, wonderful, and made her feel alive.

"It is wrong, isn't it?" he asked.

"Yes . . . no . . . I don't know . . . Roan?" she called softly, confusedly as she raised her mouth to his.

For heartbeats, they stood poised at the flaming abyss. Once they'd toppled over into it, there would be no saving them. They would be consumed, burned alive, in the bonfire of their passion.

"Stop me," Roan pleaded one last time, his raspy breath rushing headlong into hers.

"I can't," she whispered, her heartbeat thundering like a mad litany in her ears. "God help me, I can't."

The fire consumed them.

Her mouth was softer, sweeter than he remembered, though these thoughts barely registered. Nothing registered, really. He was too busy burying his lips in hers.

No, this wasn't wrong, she thought. She knew this as intuitively as she knew that her heart was beating. No, it wasn't merely beating. It was flapping in her chest, like a giant bird longing to be free. She had been Galen's prisoner, confined to house and courtyard, but Roan was the key to her freedom. Only in his arms could she escape. Only in his arms could she feel all she was meant to feel.

Though it was the most difficult thing Roan had ever done, he forced himself to make love to her slowly, gently. She knew nothing of lovemaking, a fact that was pitifully obvious, though she kissed him, touched him with an honesty of emotion that was more endearing than all the practiced lovemaking in the world. Nor did she shy away from him, either out of modesty or fear. When his tongue sought hers, she sought his in return—tentatively, then more boldly. When he unbuttoned her gown, she unbuttoned his shirt. When he slipped the gown over her head, ever careful not to hurt her back, she lifted her arms in assistance. Only once did she flinch. When his mouth, following in the wake of his hands, brushed the tip of her breast, she whimpered and pulled away, darkly remembering how teeth could punish.

His eyes found hers.

"I'd never hurt you," he said with such fierceness that her eyes filled with tears. "Never! I'm not like him."

Feathering her fingers through his hair, she whispered, "This I know."

To prove her point, she angled her head and grazed his mouth with hers. She nibbled. He nibbled, then impatiently latched his mouth on to hers. He took the controls, which she willingly surrendered, and deepened the kiss. After tenderly ravaging her lips, he trailed kisses along the upturned column of her neck, then kissed her breast. This time she didn't shy away. This time she simply savored the thrilling feeling.

It was almost more than she could withstand—the feel of the hot night, the feel of Roan's hot mouth, the feel of her skin blistering everywhere he touched. She'd never known that lovemaking could be so sweet. She'd never known that touching a man— sculpted shoulders, hair-dusted chest, bare belly— could be so wonderful, yet so maddening. Her body begged for a completion that she would have done anything to attain.

She whimpered and called his name.

Lowering her carefully to her back, Roan followed her down, his body covering hers in an age-old fashion. And then it was happening. Soul-deep kisses. Damp skin slicking across damp skin. Sighs mingling with sighs. Legs entwining. Bodies searching. Need appealing to need. Heart calling to heart.

Slowly, gently, to the accompaniment of her soft, sexy cries, Roan eased his body into hers. Deeper. Deeper. Deeper still.

Suddenly, he stopped. Dead. Disbelief written across his face. How was it possible? How could it be? How could the woman beneath him be a virgin?

EIGHTEEN

"I don't understand."

Roan made the comment much later, after their breathing had returned to normal, after the candle had burned low and sputtered out, after the moon had risen to its highest and now sat preening itself in the clear, cloudless sky.

Engelina, from the crook of Roan's arm, angled her head toward him. She had known that the subject couldn't be avoided, and so she didn't play coy. Even so, the words didn't come easily.

"He cannot . . . he cannot bed me."

"You mean he's impotent?" From the blank look on her face, it was obvious that she had no knowledge of the word. "He can't maintain an erection?"

Engelina tried to look away. Roan caught her chin in his hand and kept her eyes trained on his. There was just enough moonlight to allow him to see her embarrassment.

"We have to talk," he said softly, encouragingly.

"Yes. I mean, no he can't. He tried on our wedding night, but he couldn't. I thought . . ." She stopped, visibly garnering courage. "I thought that was why he beat me that night. I thought I had caused him to shame himself, but . . . but I soon discovered that he just likes inflicting pain."

Roan tightened his hold on her, placing a kiss at her temple. He denied the rage that wanted so fervently to flare at any mention of her abuse. He didn't want to feel rage. Not now. Not with her lovingly tucked at his side.

Engelina closed her eyes, fighting tears at the beauty of this man's touch. He was so gentle, so caring, so kind. Aside from Chloe, he was the only good thing in her life.

"Has he ever tried to have sex with you again?"

She shook her head. "He makes me undress sometimes, sometimes he kisses me, touches me"—this last caused her to shudder—"but he's never tried to bed me again. Every time he hurts me, he leaves the house afterwards. I think . . . I think he relieves himself with other women."

The thought had crossed Roan's mind, as well. The infliction of pain might well be Galen's aphrodisiac and, once aroused, he culminated his need with another woman.

"He told me once that I was too pure to bed. He hates my faith, yet I think he envies it. I think he punishes me for believing in what he can't."

"You might be right," Roan said. With Engelina's face only inches from his, with her bare body flush with his, a wave of possession swept over Roan. "Why didn't you tell me you'd never been with a man?"

"Did it matter?"

"No—Yes, it did. I would have . . . I would have been slower, gentler, something!" He ended on a note of frustration, that he might have hurt this woman who already knew far too much about pain.

Engelina bracketed his cheek with her hand. "You could not have been gentler. For however long or short my life might be, I will remember your gentleness. I will remember tonight."

At her words, Roan experienced a myriad of feelings. The reminder of her looming death knotted his stomach in fear, while the sweetness of her sentiment melted his heart. He also felt guilty. Guilty for compromising her principles. Mostly, though, he just needed to lose himself once more in her. On a low moan, he speared his fingers through her long, flowing hair, drawing her face up to his. His breath fanned across her cheek seconds before his mouth connected with hers.

Engelina returned his moan. With a will of its own, her body molded itself to his. She sought out the hardness of his muscle-toned chest, the tautness of his trim thighs. Breast to chest, belly to belly, she tried to merge their bodies into one. This time their loving was fast and laden with a furiousness born of desperation. Each felt time slipping away, life slipping away. Each tried to grasp a handful, a heartful, of both.

"I hurt you."

It was the first thing Roan said when he could speak, though even then his voice was reedy and short. Curiously, his temper was also short. He was tired of worrying about Galen, tired of worrying about how, or even if, he could change history, tired of having to love Engelina on the sly.

"No, you didn't hurt me," Engelina said, her voice as unsteady as his, her feelings as unsteady as his.

She was tired of the emotional carousel on which she was trapped. She was tired of fearing the heartless man she was married to and tired of worrying about her sister. Mostly, though, she was angry. Angry that she'd only now discovered the beauty that could exist between a man and a woman, angry that she might not live long enough to know it again. Her eyes glazed with tears.

"I did hurt you," he said in self-reproach.

"No, you didn't."

"Then—"

"I don't want him ever to touch me again!" The curt words had come from out of nowhere. They were filled with fear, and a hate that she fought but couldn't win the battle against.

Roan tightened his arms about her. "No, he won't touch you again. I won't let him!" Again he wondered if he was promising something he couldn't deliver. Again, he felt a desperation so keen that it threatened to consume him.

"I don't care if God does punish me for tonight." Her thoughts had begun to ramble, skipping from one subject to another without any logical flow. Roan sensed in her a desperation as deep as his own.

"God doesn't punish the good."

"I don't care!"

"I shouldn't have compromised your principles."

"I knew what I was doing."

"I don't want you ever to regret—"

Her fingertips silenced him. When she spoke, her voice was fractured with feeling. "I would rather spend eternity in hell than never know what we shared tonight."

At her admission, Roan's heart burst wide. His love, which he'd once found so hard to express, poured out. "I love you," he whispered, peering into her obsidian-dark eyes. "I love you more than I ever thought it possible to love anyone or anything."

His declaration humbled Engelina, making her feel warm, making her feel as though she'd climbed to the highest mountain and now stood looking down. Curiously, that lofty position gave her a vantage point that she hadn't had before. Because she wanted to come to him whole or not at all, she said, "I am not free to say the words. I am not free to think the words."

As much as he wanted to hear her say she loved him, he understood her silence. There was so much unsettled in her life, so much that he'd already asked her to compromise. He couldn't help but wonder, however, if her personal realization of her love would not have given her access to the future, just as his for her had given him access to the past. Whether it did or not, he knew that it had to come from her—spontaneously and in her own time. Time. It was something they were running low on. Her next words confirmed that she, too, knew this.

"Maybe I never will be free to think or say the words."

"I won't settle for never. I'll find a way for us to be together."

As his lips closed over hers, Engelina allowed herself the momentary luxury of belief. She also allowed herself one small admission. Though she wouldn't think of the word *love,* there was no way she could deny that she belonged to this man. She belonged to him wholly, completely. She always would. She always had.

That night, unlike all the other nights, Roan didn't vanish back into the present. Waking at daybreak, he unexpectedly found himself still in Engelina's bed with her still in his arms. He had no idea what to make of the fact, but he had the strangest feeling, as he slipped from the past to the present only seconds before the housekeeper showed up at Lamartine House, that he could have remained in the past had he chosen to. If that were so, had his verbal declaration of love made it possible? It was an intriguing thought, which he entertained over the rocky course of the next few days.

* * *

Wednesday morning, the phone rang.

"Hello?" Roan said, wondering who could be calling so early.

"This is Bob Rackley. Over at the university," the man added for clarification.

None was necessary. Roan had recognized the name immediately. The history professor had never called before. Roan had always had to contact him. Surely, this must mean that the man had something to tell him.

"Have you found anything?" Roan said, cutting right to the chase. He tried to keep his voice steady. In the brief interim between question and answer, he thought he was going to faint from all the blood rushing to his head.

"As a matter of fact, I think I have."

Roan closed his eyes and leaned back against the wall.

"Dr. Jacob, did you hear me?" he heard the professor ask.

"Yes," Roan answered, hesitating only slightly before asking the single most important question in the world, "Have you found the date of the fire?"

"I found a book that mentions a fire in a mansion in the Garden District. The description matches Lamartine House."

"When?" Roan asked.

"The date is 1880. Just as you thought. The book gives no confirmation as to the fire's source, although it speculates that it resulted from—"

"Do you have a specific date?" Roan interrupted, trying not to sound testy.

"July 2. July 2, 1880."

The blood in Roan's head rushed faster. "Are you certain?"

Bob Rackley laughed. "You don't understand the

nature of historical research, Dr. Jacob. Few things are absolutely certain, but that's the date recorded in the book I found. Frankly, at this point, I don't think we can afford not to accept it as gospel. It is, after all, more than I've been able to come up with before now."

"Yeah. Look, thanks for everything."

"You're welcome. Glad I could help."

In seconds, Roan heard the buzzing of a dial tone. His head buzzed, too. With his back to the wall, he eased to a sitting position. He was relieved to have a date at last, but filled with despair at the realization that, unless he could come up with a plan of action, Engelina had but three days left to live.

"I have to get you and Chloe out of here."

Roan's announcement came later that evening as he and Engelina spoke quietly in her bedroom. The tone of his voice brooked no opposition, yet she felt compelled to point out the obvious.

"Chloe isn't well. She can hardly breathe—"

"We no longer have an option." At the argument he saw coming, he said, bluntly, "We can no longer afford to wait."

Engelina stood and walked to the window, where she stared out at the courtyard canopied by the clear night sky. She understood the significance of what he was saying.

"I see," she said. "And exactly how long do we have before we must make this move?"

"I want to move you out tomorrow. No later than the day after. You must be out of this house by . . . You must be out of this house soon."

Engelina turned, her eyes finding Roan's. He saw fear flash across her face seconds before she willfully reined it in.

"I was hoping we had more time," he said, explaining his sudden haste. "I learned this morning that we don't, however." When she said nothing, he repeated a question he'd asked once before. "Isn't there anyone who can take you in? Just temporarily?"

Engelina shook her head. "No. No one I trust."

"Then we'll have to come up with another solution."

He began to pace the floor, but with a confident stride. Curiously, he once more felt in control. Finding out the date of the fire had symbolically untied his bound hands. He still wasn't certain what he was going to do, but he'd do something. He hadn't been sent on this bizarre quest just to sit helplessly by. Nor had he been sent back to fail.

"The ultimate goal is to get the two of you out of the city," Roan said, as though talking to himself, "but that's too ambitious for now. Besides, unless I can stabilize Chloe, she can't travel a long distance. So, what we're looking for is a place nearby where you can hide out." A sudden thought occurred to him. "Doesn't Lukie have an aunt?"

"No," Engelina said quickly, amending her answer to, "She does have an aunt, but we cannot go there."

"Why?"

"I don't know her, but she's evil."

"If you don't know her, how do you know she's evil?"

"She's heathen."

"That's not evil—"

"I won't take Chloe there."

"All right, all right," Roan said. "Well, that leaves only one choice. You do have places in the city that rent rooms, don't you?"

"Boardinghouses?"

"Yes."

"Yes, we have boardinghouses."

"Then I'll go tomorrow and find us a room in one."

"But—"

"Engelina," he said firmly, "we no longer have a choice."

Saying nothing, she turned back to the window. Roan crossed to her and placed a hand on each of her arms. She closed her eyes and leaned back into him . . . into her lover.

"Exactly how long do I have?" she asked, knowing that, for Chloe's sake, the question could no longer be avoided. It was not only her life she was playing with but possibly Chloe's, as well.

"We have until July 2."

The fear she felt at hearing the exact date of her death was tempered by his usage of the word *we* and by the feel of his arms closing around her. The prospect of not feeling those arms should she move out of the house prompted her to ask, "And will you be with us?"

"Every step."

"But how can you, when you fade in and out?"

"I think I've found a way to stay as long as I want."

She turned in his arms. Her eyes were alight at this possibility. "You've found a way?"

"I think I have."

"How?"

He trailed his fingers across her cheek. "Just trust me. Just trust my love for you."

Seconds later, when his lips found hers, Engelina realized that she did trust him implicitly. She trusted him with her and Chloe's very lives. She trusted him with her very heart.

* * *

The following day, Roan, whose jeans and tennis shoes collected more than one curious stare, rented two rooms for six bits a week apiece at Mrs. Fedder's Proper Boarding House, a plain white-shingled establishment located on the edge of the French Quarter. Though the price included meals, plump, penny-pinching Mrs. Fedder was quick to point out that it didn't include meals for four, especially those for a servant, however indispensable she might be in the care of her eccentrically dressed employer.

Assuring the woman that he understood her generosity must have its limits, Roan spent the better part of all afternoon outfitting the room with food and other necessities. The task took longer than he thought it would, causing him to change his plans for moving Engelina and Chloe. He had intended to do so that very day, but, because it was nearing eight o'clock, and because Galen had once more disappeared, Roan decided that the next day—July 1— would do as nicely. All that mattered was that Engelina be out of the house by July 2.

Besides, Roan had one last errand that he must run. Slipping back into the present, on what he knew might well be his last time to do so, he pocketed the letter he had written and left Lamartine House. He headed for Micaela O'Kane's. Some fifteen minutes later, again expressing no surprise at seeing him, the flame-haired seer wordlessly opened the door to him.

When Engelina opened the door of her bedroom a little before nine o'clock, she heard the voices. In and of itself, hearing voices was not unusual. After all, the servants talked among themselves. Hearing several masculine voices, however, was startling. Especially since she'd thought she and the servants were alone in the house, especially since the voices were furtively low and seemingly angry with one another.

Holding her billowing skirt in her hands in order to stifle any rustling, she tiptoed down the stairs. Midway, as she recognized one of the voices, she stopped. Galen! When had he returned? She'd heard no one arrive, although she had been occupied in Chloe's room during much of the evening. And to whom was he talking?

"You're a careless fool!" Galen hissed.

A second voice, vaguely familiar, said something that Engelina couldn't understand.

"Well, perhaps you do not mind being found out, but I do," Galen retorted. "Hanging does not suit my noble neck."

"Noble?" the vaguely familiar voice said. A chortle followed. "You're no more noble than I."

"Gentlemen, gentlemen," a third man interjected. This French-accented voice Engelina recognized as belonging to Monsieur Desforges. Which no doubt made the vaguely familiar voice Mr. Harnett's. "This discussion is getting us nowhere. We must concentrate on the decision before us."

"He's right," Galen said, though Engelina could tell that the concession had been made grudgingly. "So what do we do?"

"I say the Hell-Fire Club is getting too hot. I say we need to cool it down for a while."

Hell-Fire Club? At the words, Engelina's stomach coiled like a barrel of serpents.

"I agree," Galen said. "What started out as secret is now on the lips of every person on the street."

"But it's all speculation," Harnett said. "No one can even prove that the club exists."

"Many dead men have been strung up by speculation," Galen said, adding, "But none of this would

have become speculative if you had used some dis-
crimination. For God's sake, you took every young
woman you saw. For God's sake, you took Desforges's
own maid?"

"She was comely," Harnett said, defending himself.
"She will fetch a handsome price. And, furthermore,
I have seen you look at your Lukie with lustful eyes."

"Gentlemen—" Desforges intervened.

"And I didn't notice your turning down
Desforges's golden-haired miss," Harnett threw in.
"You rutted with her as did the rest of us."

"Gentlemen—"

"You're swine," Galen said, not bothering to hide
his contempt.

"And you are Satan himself."

"Gentlemen, keep your voices down!"

In the crackling silence that followed, Engelina
thought she might actually retch. Surely she wasn't
hearing this. Surely these men were not involved in
the notorious Hell-Fire Club. Surely Galen could not
be that wicked. Yet, even as this last thought crossed
her mind, she knew, indeed, he could be that wicked.
That wicked and a thousand times more.

"What we need to do," Desforges said, again the
voice of reason, "is transfer the women we're holding.
Get them aboard the ship. Let them set sail for the
brothels of Galveston. And then, let the Hell-Fire
Club rumors die down, which they are sure to do
once young women stop disappearing. And if the
police are looking for a scapegoat, let them continue
to look in Marie Cambre's direction. With the right
word in the right ear, we might get her to hang for
this yet."

"I agree with all you've said," Galen said. "We must
move the women. Tonight. Then, we must sit easy for
a while."

"It's settled," Desforges said. "We'll do it by the light of tonight's moon."

"So be it," Galen said, adding, "Our friend in black will help us."

Kipperd! So he was involved in this, too. Engelina was not surprised. She had no more time to consider the Irishman's participation, because she heard chairs scraping back as the men obviously rose.

She scampered up the stairway, turned the corner, and hid flush against the hall wall. She was aware of nothing but a cold numbness settling over her body. She waited, poised for flight should she hear Galen start up the stairs, but he didn't. Instead, she heard the three men exit by the front door. The last thing that was said was Desforges's admonition that Harnett go to the wharf, tell the captain to ready the ship for sail, then rendezvous with them. Where was not mentioned.

Still huddled against the wall, Engelina tried to think. She had to do something, but what? She had to tell someone, but whom? Roan. Sweet Mary, Mother of God, where was he? He had not been there since early morning. There was no way she could reach him, and she needed help now. Suddenly, an idea occurred to her.

Hastening to Chloe's room, she found Lukie sitting by the sleeping woman's bed. Lukie rose at her employer's entrance.

"She's sleeping," Lukie reported softly.

"Good," Engelina said, adding, "I must go out."

Lukie's dark brows knitted in concern. "At this hour?"

"I must," Engelina said.

"But—"

"I must. Should Roan—Dr. Jacob—come, tell him I'll be back as shortly as I can. Tell him to wait for me. Tell him that it's very important I talk to him."

"Yes, ma'am," the young servant said, though it was clear she didn't much like what she was hearing.

In minutes, Engelina had fled down the stairs and out the back door to the stable. As she had expected, the carriage was gone, driven she was sure by Kipperd. Saddling the only horse left, she flung her leg over in a most unladylike fashion. A whip to the horse and she was gone. Headed for someone who would help her. Someone who would advise her in this grisly matter.

Fear rumbled deep inside Lukie. Something was wrong. Very wrong. She had felt it for a long while. She had known that the master of the house was evil. But now, some new evil was afoot. She sensed it from her mistress's strange behavior. Where had she gone at such an ungodly hour? And why did she, Lukie, have this awful feeling that something terrible was about to happen? Fear once more shuddered through her. She eased to the side of the chair and watched Chloe sleep. Miss Chloe, Miss Engelina, even she herself—no one was safe in this house. Could she afford just to sit idly by and watch whatever this terrible something was happen?

No!

Jumping from the chair, Lukie checked Chloe before slipping quietly from the room and down the stairs. From the servant quarters in the back, she rallied the already-sleeping housekeeper, whom she ordered to remain with Chloe until her return. She then started off at a run for the outskirts of the city. Her Aunt Marie would make a powerful, protective gris-gris.

The man in black noticed the young woman fleeing into the night only because his amber eyes were as sharp as an eagle's. The carriage, which he drove and which was hidden in a copse of magnolia trees, pulled slowly into motion. Discreetly he followed Lukie, who ran so fast that she threatened to outdistance him. Only occasionally would she stop, rest, then race onward. Near the outskirts of the city, she disappeared into a narrow alley. Bringing the carriage to a halt, Kipperd followed on foot.

Lukie had the spooky feeling that she was being followed, yet each time she glanced backward she saw no one. Perhaps she was only imagining it. Perhaps she felt vulnerable only because she had no protective amulet. She'd given hers to Dr. Jacob and, though she didn't regret her action, she fervently wished she had it right this moment. The howling of a nearby dog did nothing to settle her jangled nerves, and so she ran onward, her feet barely skimming the ground beneath them.

She had just turned a corner, her aunt's house only minutes away, when she ran square into the man. Her first thought was that he'd been waiting there for her. Her second was that she recognized him. And then she thought nothing, for a blunt blow to the chin rendered her unconscious.

As always, the cat looked not so much asleep as unconscious. Roan watched as Micaela, her black robelike dress flowing about her, her feet bare, the curls of her brilliant red hair trailing the floor, gently swished the feline from the table. She seated herself, motioning for Roan to take the chair opposite her. Neither had spoken a word since he'd shown up on her doorstep.

Micaela shoved a deck of cards toward Roan, indicating for him to shuffle them. When he had, she began to deal. The cards revealed nothing to him.

Apparently they spoke volumes to her.

Her eyes, the uncanny color of a golden sun, found his. "You are going on a journey."

"Yes. I'm going back into time. And I'm going to stay there until I can find a way to bring Engelina to the present." He had been right. Ever since the verbalization of his love, he'd been able to stay in the past as long as he chose to. Intuitively he knew the power was his for as long as he wanted it.

"And what if you can't find a way to bring Engelina to the present?"

Roan knew that possibility existed. He knew it only too well. "Then I'll stay in the past."

"You would give up all you have here?"

"Yes," he said unequivocally and without hesitation.

Micaela studied him, then said, "Danger surrounds you."

"So you've told me."

Micaela nodded in acknowledgment of their previous conversations. "Yes. But the danger was always ahead of you. It now surrounds you. Like a cloud ready to rain down its poison. You may not survive."

This, too, Roan knew. Curiously, his survival mattered less than Engelina's. "And what of Engelina? Will she survive?"

Micaela said nothing. She stood and walked to the scarred mantel above the fireplace. She turned, wondering if she should tell him that the cards foretold his failure, that the cards foretold Engelina's death. "I know only that her life depends on you. And that yours rests in the hands of a stranger."

"You mentioned a stranger before."

She nodded, thinking of the bloodred candle she kept envisioning and of the Bible. She had no idea what either meant. "I know only that the stranger's presence balances the scales. His, her, presence balances out an evil. His, her, presence atones for the sinfulness of someone else."

"And you know nothing more of this stranger?"

For the first time, Roan saw frustration in Micaela's usually impassive face. Her fingers touched the cross at her neck, as though seeking its strength. "No. I know nothing more. Except that I sense betrayal."

"What kind of betrayal?"

She shook her head. "I know nothing more."

"The fire occurred July 2," Roan said, remembering one of the reasons he'd wanted to see Micaela this last time. "At least that's the only date that can be found."

"I sensed that it was soon."

The two of them looked at each other.

"What will be, will be," Micaela spoke finally, softly.

Roan couldn't argue the point, so, silently, he stood. "Thanks. For everything."

"God be with you."

"Yeah," Roan said, starting for the door. He stopped midway across the room when he realized the envelope, addressed to Stewart, was still in his shirt pocket. Taking it out, he started back toward Micaela. She still stood in front of the mantel. "Would you mail this if I don't contact you within a couple of weeks?"

"Of course."

Roan laid the envelope on the mantel. As he did so, he saw the picture, an old tintype of a man and a woman. What struck him forcefully, like a baseball to his gut, was that he recognized the man. He had a red head of hair and a red beard that grew out of his face like a brambly brier patch. Both his hair and his eyes, the latter as brilliant as a bar of gold, matched perfectly those of the woman before him, and, like

Micaela, the man wore only black.

Betrayal. Hadn't Micaela just spoken the word? Roan threw a questioning glance at her.

"My great-grandparents," she said with pride and deep affection.

NINETEEN

The St. Louis Cathedral had already been locked for the night. Engelina, her heart weighted down from what she'd earlier heard, her breathing fast and shallow from her furious ride, pounded upon the massive door. When no one answered, fear and desperation drove her to pound again. This time her effort was rewarded. A nun, her benign face peering out of a black veil, a swinging crucifix chain at her waist, opened the door a crack and peeped out.

"The cathedral is closed till morning," the woman said kindly.

"I know," Engelina answered, trying to corral her renegade breath. "But I must speak with Father John."

"Father John has retired for the evening. Could you not wait—"

"No!" Engelina interrupted, placing her hand on the door as though fearing it would be closed in her face. "Please, I must speak with him. The matter is of the gravest urgency."

Either Engelina's dishevelment or the sincerity of her plea spoke to the nun's caring nature. She opened the door, the very gesture inviting Engelina to enter the sanctuary.

"If you'll wait here," the woman said, "I'll try to rouse Father John."

Engelina was relieved beyond words. She simply nodded and leaned back against the door for support. Silence cloaked the huge empty cathedral, causing the nun's footsteps to whisper hollowly, respectfully, but with a strange loneliness. In the stillness, Engelina heard the jingling of the chain at the nun's waist. She heard, too, her own heart thumping in her chest. Like unholy demons, the words she'd overheard in the parlor crept back to haunt her.

Even now, the grim reality was almost more than Engelina could bear. The stealing and selling of women was more than she could comprehend. And the fact that her own husband was involved made her sick. A stomach-caving nausea had just spread through her when she saw Father John approaching from the rectory.

"Father!" she cried, pushing from the door and hastening toward him.

As always, just the sight of him soothed her, everything from his cherub-round face to his clear and compassionate blue eyes. His cheeks seemed even more red-veined than usual, but Engelina wondered vaguely if the scarlet glow from a nearby candle wasn't to blame. The glow, crimson and eerie, cast shadows on his white-blond hair and on his long close-fitting black cassock. In one hand, he carried a worn Bible. Something about the sacredness of the Bible contrasted with the profaneness of the crimson light made a fleeting impression on Engelina, but it was just that—fleeting—for the mission that brought her to the church took precedence over everything else.

"My child," Father John said, taking her hand in his and directing her to a pew. He sat down beside her. "Whatever is the matter?"

His voice, gentle and kind, enveloped her like a

warm fire on a cold winter's night. Yes, she thought, she had done right in coming here.

"Father . . ." she said, then stopped. She suddenly didn't have any idea of how to say what she must. The words were too hideous to repeat, the images they conjured too awful to view.

"Are you all right, my child?"

Engelina nodded, slinging rebel curls about her perspiration-dewed face.

"Then you must tell me what brings you out so late."

Engelina had no idea what time it was, but it had to be past ten o'clock. How long did it take to move imprisoned women? And from where were they being moved? These unknown women's safety prompted Engelina to speak.

"I'm sorry to bother you, but I didn't know where else to go," she said, tightening her grip on the priest's hand. His skin felt soft and smooth, falsely suggesting that the saving of souls wasn't all that hard work.

Out of the corner of her eye, she saw Father Ignatius, swarthy and lean, looking curiously at the two of them as he approached the chancel, then disappeared through a side door. Engelina didn't know where the door led, but then there was much of the cathedral not open to worshippers. There was also much about Father Ignatius that remained a mystery to her. He was quiet, darkly so, and she had the curious feeling that he was more condemning than forgiving.

"I, and God, are always here for you," the cleric at her side prompted.

Father Ignatius was forgotten. "Oh, Father," she said, the words tumbling out, "I know about the Hell-Fire Club. I know about the women who have been kidnapped. I know they are being sold into brothels—"

"Wait, wait!" Father John interrupted. The Bible in his hand fell to the floor. "What are you saying, child?"

Engelina gathered her scattered wits. "I overheard talk about the Hell-Fire Club—"

"Everyone in town has overheard talk. It's but a figment of everyone's wild imagination."

"No! It's real, Father. I swear it's real. I overheard Messieurs Harnett and Desforges and . . . and my husband talking about it. They are members of it."

"Surely you are mistaken," the clergyman said, kindly but forcefully.

"No," Engelina countered, adding, "They've been kidnapping young women—even Monsieur Desforges's maid—and using them . . . vilely, then selling them to a brothel in Galveston. They are moving the women now. This moment. I don't know from where, Father, but they are carrying them to the riverfront." With each word her speech had become more hurried and her eyes wider. With each word, her hold on the priest had become more frantic. "We must do something to stop them. Should we not go to the police?"

"No!" At the sharpness of his retort, Father John repeated more calmly, "No. We must think this through carefully. These are serious allegations."

"Do you think I don't know that?"

He didn't reply, at least not directly to what she'd said. Instead, he asked, "Are you sure—"

"Of course I'm sure," she answered, impatience creeping into her voice. "I heard them talking. As soon as they left the house, I came here."

"Desforges? Harnett? Your own husband?"

"Yes." Shame spread through Engelina, shame at her husband's involvement.

Pulling his hand from hers, the priest placed an elbow on the back of the pew in front of him. As was

his habit, he wedged his face into his palm, squaring
his chin. His pose was one of deep contemplation.

"Shouldn't I go to the police?"

The more she thought of this, the more certain
Engelina became that it was the path she should follow. So certain was she that she couldn't understand
Father John's not immediately agreeing with her. In
truth, though, he said nothing, neither in agreement
or disagreement.

"Yes," Father John said at last in answer to her
question. "That is what must be done. But," he said,
taking her hand again, "you must let me do it. The
task is an unpleasant one. No woman should have to
face it. Your husband? Are you certain? Could you not
have made a mistake?"

"No, Father," she said softly. "I am not mistaken."

The priest sighed. "I have not been blind to your
unhappiness. Nor have I been blind to its source. I
knew it had something to do with your marriage."

"He's an evil man, Father."

"Then you must pray for his soul."

"God forgive me, but I'm not sure I can."

He squeezed her hand. "Do what you can, and
God will forgive the rest. Now," he said, releasing her
hand and standing, "you return home. I'll take care
of everything."

As Father John walked Engelina to the door, she
felt a burden lift from her shoulders. This trustworthy
man would take care of everything.

"Oh, Madame Lamartine?"

Engelina turned, facing the clergyman once more.

"I think it best if you say nothing to anyone."

She nodded. Other than Roan there was no one
she could tell. Shame would see to that.

* * *

Something was wrong.

Roan sensed this as soon as he reentered the past.
Finding the house empty of Engelina and Lukie only
confirmed his suspicion. When he spoke to the servant sitting with a resting Chloe, he became more certain. Even the woman, whom he'd startled within an
inch of her life, found it odd that Lukie had left the
house so late, and, no sir, she had no idea if the mistress of the house had gone out, too. Nor did she
know if Mister Lamartine had returned.

All in all, as Roan made his way down the curving
staircase, he felt uneasy. And not only about the disappearance of Engelina and Lukie. He felt uneasy about
the photograph he'd seen at Micaela's. The fair-
skinned, red-bearded Irishman who worked for Galen,
Galen's henchman Engelina called him, was Micaela's
great-grandfather. That fact, and the word *betrayal*,
which Micaela had used more than once, worried
him. Was Micaela's great-grandfather destined to be a
betrayer or, and this thought congealed Roan's blood,
was it Micaela herself? Would she wittingly or unwit-
tingly betray the trust he had placed in her?

Roan was approaching the foot of the stairs, with
not a single answer to any of these perplexing questions, when the front door burst open. Roan stopped
dead in his tracks with one foot hesitating on the last
stair. His gaze rushed forward, colliding with not one
but two startled gazes. For a split second, Roan had
the feeling that he was once again staring at the photograph on Micaela's mantel. The Irishman, his hair
and beard aflame with color, looked precisely as he
had in the tintype, while the dark-skinned, dark-
haired woman beside him, looked as tall, as stately, as
beautiful. In truth, so like the photograph did they
appear that Roan could easily have believed the couple had just come from sitting for it.

Except their expressions weren't the same. In the photograph they'd been smiling. They now appeared grim. The Irishman also appeared wary.

"Is Madame Lamartine in?" the man—Kipperd, Roan believed his name was—asked.

Roan drew his foot from the stairway and said, just as warily, "No."

"Do you know where she is?"

"No."

"We must speak with her," the woman said. She wore a fashionable pheasant-brown dress and carried a matching crocheted reticule.

Once Roan's attention was directed solely to the woman, he saw that she was upset. Extremely. Even as Roan made the realization, Kipperd's arm went around her waist in a consoling gesture. He ushered her forward and closed the front door.

"We must speak with her," the woman repeated, adding, "It's about my niece, Lukie."

Lukie. Niece. This woman was Lukie's aunt? This was the woman who made protective amulets? This was the woman Engelina thought evil?

"Lukie may have been kidnapped," the Irishman said, coming quickly to the point.

Roan was still reeling from learning the woman's identity when this last piece of information was thrown at him. He felt as if he caught it square in the stomach.

"Kidnapped?"

"We're not certain," Kipperd said, explaining further. "I followed her into town but lost her several blocks from Marie's house. She never showed up there, although I'm certain it was her destination."

"But why do you suspect kidnapping?"

"With all the kidnappings that have occurred, how can I not suspect foul play?" Marie asked, obviously agitated by the very thought. "I swear, if Galen

Lamartine is involved, I'll kill him myself!"

"It's all right," the man beside her soothed. "We'll find her."

Kidnappings? Roan had no idea what she was talking about, although her words did jar his memory slightly. Didn't he once see an 1880's newspaper headlining a young woman's disappearance? And what was this about Galen Lamartine being involved? This last he heard himself voicing aloud.

"The man is a devil!" Kipperd said. "I would put nothing past him."

"Wait a minute! I thought you worked for him."

"Aye," the Irishman said, unknowingly reverting to his native tongue in his anger, "but only so I could keep an eye on Lukie. This house is evil from foundation to roof. I would not leave a mouse unprotected here."

"I can't argue with your assessment of Galen Lamartine," Roan said. "Nor the evil of this house."

The two men looked at each other, appraisingly, critically, as though seeing each other for the first time.

Finally, the Irishman extended his hand, saying, "I'm Kipperd O'Kane."

"I'm Roan Jacob," Roan said, offering his hand in friendship.

"This is Marie Cambre," Kipperd said.

The woman had but nodded when her knees suddenly buckled. She would have fallen had it not been for the quick arms of her lover.

"She carries my babe," Kipperd said candidly but proudly. "The excitement of tonight has been too much for her."

"Bring her in here," Roan said as he ushered them into the parlor.

In minutes, Marie was sipping water and having her pulse taken by Roan. She was also proclaiming that she was fine and would not be pampered. At the steady beat of her pulse, Roan concurred that she was, indeed, fine. At her steely disposition, he suspected she was equally right about the pampering.

"So," Roan said, sitting in the chair opposite the sofa when the couple sat, "what do you know of Galen's being behind these kidnappings?"

"I know little," the Irishman said, "but suspect much."

"Then tell me what you suspect."

Kipperd O'Kane did. He told Roan about the rumored aristocratic but brutal Hell-Fire Club, about how the disappearances of the young women were believed to be related, about how Marie, because of her practice of voodoo, was being associated with the latter. He spoke, too, of how he'd grown to suspect Galen and, only recently, his cronies.

"Desforges would have to be involved," Kipperd said, "because I suspect that his plantation, Oak Manor, plays some part in the club. Perhaps it's the meeting place."

"It's certainly well situated," Marie said. "It's miles out of town."

"And Galen goes there often," Roan said. "Especially lately."

"Indeed," Kipperd said.

"So what happens to these women after they've been used by the aristocratic club members? Are they killed?"

"I don't believe so," Kipperd said. "Not that these men wouldn't kill if they wanted to. I believe they think they're above the law. No, I think they sell them into some kind of slavery. Probably to brothels."

"All the men own wharf property," Marie said, her spirits once more fully revived. "It would be easy to carry the women aboard a ship without being seen."

"Especially if they used the middle of night to do it," Kipperd said.

"And Galen is out many nights," Roan said.

"Yes," Kipperd agreed, adding meaningfully, "Not that his wife minds, I'm sure."

Again the two men studied each other. Just how much did this man know about what had gone on between Engelina and her husband? And did the Irishman know that he, Roan, was in love with Engelina? Perhaps. Perhaps more than perhaps, Roan thought as he looked deep into the man's farseeing amber eyes.

The Irishman came to his feet, bringing the conversation back to the issue at hand. "Galen and his cronies returned to the house tonight."

At this news, combined with Engelina's disappearance, the hair on the back of Roan's neck stood up. "Are you certain?"

"Yes. They seemed upset. At least Galen did. I didn't dare try to overhear for fear of being discovered. They had barely arrived when out they came. They stood talking in the yard for a while, then Galen and Desforges left in Desforges's carriage. Harnett had his own horse and he, too, left in the direction of town. I let him get sufficiently ahead of me. I was on the verge of starting out after him when I spotted Lukie. I followed her, instead, when I saw Harnett veer off in the direction of the docks."

"What about Engelina? Did you see her leave the house?"

Kippered shook his head. "No. But if she'd taken the back way, I might not have. In fact, I probably wouldn't have, with the thick copse of magnolia trees."

"If she's not here," Marie said, logically assessing the situation, "then she must have gone out."

"But where?" Roan asked, a feeling of desperation setting in.

"And where is Lukie?" Marie asked.

Roan, too, stood and, for a reason he couldn't explain, a vision of the woman archeologist flashed through his mind. Julie. That was her name. He had sensed strongly that she'd been held against her will in the room beneath the grounds of the St. Louis Cathedral. Had she been one of the kidnapped women? If so . . . Roan's mind began to race with possibilities, all of which culminated in excitement.

"If everything you say is true about the Hell-Fire Club and Oak Manor," he began, "wouldn't they have to have some place here in town to hold the women until they were ready to transport them to the plantation or to the docks?"

"That possibility has crossed my mind," Kipperd said.

"That must be it," Roan whispered.

"What must be it?"

Roan looked over at the couple. "I might know where that holding point is." Before either could make a comment, he added, "Don't ask me how I know. You wouldn't believe me if I told you."

"I don't care how you know as long as we find Lukie," the Irishman said.

Marie came to her feet. "Let's go."

"You stay here—" Kipperd began, but she cut him off.

"No. She's my niece. And it's my neck threatened by the hangman's noose."

When neither man could dissuade her, they gave in. Minutes later, with Marie seated within the Lamartine carriage and Roan and Kipperd at its lead, they were headed in the direction of the St. Louis Cathedral.

En route, Roan had a troubling thought. If the

cathedral was the holding point, wouldn't it be logical to assume that someone at the church was involved? And, if so, who?

The phone rang in Lamartine House. Only a Siamese cat, curled at the foot of Roan's bed, was there to hear it, however. After eight rings, silence once more descended.

The cat seemed pleased.

Bob Rackley, who'd made the call from the Tulane University library, was annoyed. He wanted to talk to Roan Jacob. What he had to tell him probably didn't amount to a hill of beans, but, nonetheless, he wanted to tell him. In fact, in some inexplicable way, he felt it was his duty to tell him. As though his passing on this information was ordained. In much the same way, he'd felt compelled to go on researching Lamartine House even after he'd found a date for the fire. Ordained? Compelled? The history professor smiled, passing his hand over his bald pate. Lord, he had to get his hairless head out of these books once in a while. It was beginning to sound as if he was walking on the thin edge.

Bearing a crimson-cupped candle in one hand, a Bible in the other, the black-cassocked figure hurried along the subterranean passageway. Candlelit shadows, like red, hostile creatures, leapt against the dark walls, creating a bone-chilling atmosphere even though the tunnel was stifling hot.

They had been found out, the man thought, his heart flickering with fear. This wasn't supposed to happen. He'd been told, promised, that it wouldn't. They'd been careful, so careful, and now they'd been found out through their own carelessness.

Overheard! Sweet Mary, Mother of God, now everyone would know!

As the man turned the last twist in the tunnel, he heard voices. Angry, raised voices.

"You're not only a fool, you're a crazy fool!" Galen shouted, the accusation spilling out into the tunnel, as though the room were too small to contain it.

"I tell you she was following me," Harnett said.

"Following you?" Galen countered. "You on horseback, she on foot, and she's following you?"

"She saw me. I know she saw me."

"And what if she did? She's seen you at the house before, on dozens of occasions."

"She was following me," Harnett insisted, like a petulant child.

"She was most likely on the way to her aunt's. She's been slipping out of the house for amulets ever since she's been with us."

The black-cassocked figure came to an abrupt halt when he saw the young black woman sprawled on the packed-down dirt floor, her mouth gagged, her hands bound behind her, her eyes wide with terror. Chained against the wall were four more young women, three white, one black, but their eyes, their minds, were dulled by drugs.

"My God," the clergyman said, his eyes finding Galen's, "she's your maid."

Four sets of eyes—Desforges's, Harnett's, Galen's, and Lukie's—leveled on the priest who stood in the doorway. His round face was the personification of innocence and kindness.

"Good, you're here," Galen said, callously ignoring his remark about Lukie.

Father John stepped into the room, deposited the candle and the Bible on the table, then rushed to kneel beside Lukie. One of the women chained to the wall, a woman with long flowing blond hair, looked at the candle with its scarlet flame, then at the Bible, then closed her eyes, once more deadened by the drugs coursing through her body.

"Leave her be," Galen said, gesturing toward Lukie. "There's no help for it now. She'll have to be sold with the others." The cold look he threw Harnett said that it was all his fault.

Lukie whimpered, her eyes pleading with the priest.

"We'll need the church's carriage," Galen said to the clergyman. "We have to get rid of these women tonight. Things are growing too hot."

"Hotter than you know," Father John said, adding, "We are found out." His dark blue eyes, which could be so compassionate-looking, now glowed with a mixture of fear and anger.

Galen, who had started toward the chained women, whirled around.

"Your wife," the cleric said, taking great delight in announcing the source. "She just left after asking me to advise her on what to do with her newfound knowledge."

"She can't know," Galen said.

"Oh, but she can," Father John said.

"But how—" Harnett began.

"She heard the three of you talking."

For a second the room was deathly quiet. One of the chained women moaned into the silence. The sound, though pitiful, attracted no one's attention.

"Jesus Christ!" Harnett cried, throwing his hands into the air.

"I told you to keep your voices down!" Desforges said, his fists balled tightly. "I told you—"

"Silence!" Galen thundered. "There are ways to handle her."

"But are there ways to handle those she confides in?" Desforges asked.

Galen looked back at the priest, who had come to his feet and was now standing beside Lukie. "Has she told anyone?"

"I don't think so. She was too upset to know what to do, whom to tell, though she thinks I'm going to the police."

"What if she tells this mysterious physician who has come into her life?" Desforges asked.

"Yes, what about him?" Harnett chided, knowing he'd found his partner's Achilles' heel and taking full advantage of it.

As though the name of the devil had been mentioned, Galen's eyes glazed over with an icy coldness. His handsome face contorted. "I will handle both of them. In whatever way is appropriate. For now, however, these women must be moved. Get the carriage." This last he said to Father John.

"No."

Galen's expression showed that he doubted he'd heard correctly.

Father John pulled himself to his tallest, which was only a few inches beyond five and a quarter feet. "I am finished with this unholy adventure."

Galen's eyes closed to slits, while his voice was as frigid as freezing sleet. "I will tell you when you're finished and, as for this being an unholy adventure, it did not seem to matter when the money crossed your palm."

Digging into his pocket, Father John pulled out a handful of coins, paltry in value. "This," he said, "is the extent of my gain. I gave to the Church, to the poor."

As quick as lightning, Galen stepped forward and, striking the priest's outstretched hand, sent the coins tumbling to the dirt. Father John shrank backward, cowering against the wall.

"Don't play at piety," Galen hissed. "You but attempted to bribe your God. And tell me, good Father, did He look the other way when you had your way with the maidens?"

Father John's face flamed carmine, for once concealing the shallow veins that networked his fair cheeks. "I never—"

"Did you think we didn't know that you slipped down here at night?" Before the priest could answer, Galen added, "Drugs make one mumble. They also strip speech to its basic honesty."

Father John looked as though he'd been struck. He also looked sick with guilt and shame.

"Get out of my sight, you sanctimonious lecher," Galen said, dismissing the priest as though he no longer mattered, as though perhaps he never had. To Desforges, he said, "We'll have to use your carriage. I'll pull it around. Meet me at the shed with the women." To Harnett, he added sarcastically, "And see if you can make the journey without taking another prisoner."

Harnett looked as though he could kill his compatriot.

Desforges was already moving to unshackle the drugged women.

Father John, with tears gathering in his blue eyes, picked up the Bible, which he painfully clutched to him, and slunk quietly back through the tunnel. There was one plan of action left to him. If only he had the courage to perform it.

A work shed covered the opening of the tunnel door. Galen, minutes behind the priest, had just thrown wide the tunnel door when he heard voices.

"The opening has to be somewhere near here," Roan said. "Somewhere in this area."

"Are you sure?" Kipperd asked, searching the ground for any trace of unevenness.

"At this point, I'm not sure of anything," Roan answered.

"What about the shed?" Marie asked.

Both men glanced in the direction of the small wooden building.

"That's a possibility," Roan said. "That would be a perfect place to conceal the tunnel door."

As Roan spoke, to the accompaniment of a loud creak, he pulled open the shed door. A shaft of moonlight rushed inside, immediately illuminating a man—a handsome man, a man with a gun held fast in his hand.

"Welcome to the Hell-Fire Club," Galen said, his voice rich, warm, and full of dark excitement.

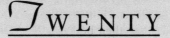WENTY

"Our plans have changed, gentlemen," Galen announced minutes later to his partners in crime as he ushered his three unwilling guests into the underground room at gunpoint.

It would have been hard to say whether Desforges or Harnett was the more surprised. Whichever, neither spoke but simply stared.

Meanwhile, Roan, Kipperd, and Marie seemed not the least surprised by what greeted them. Calmly, and with all the dignity in the world, Marie stepped forward and kneeled before Lukie. At the sight of her aunt, tears gushed to the young woman's eyes.

"There, there," Marie cooed, wiping at the tears. "Everything's going to be all right."

Galen laughed. "Your optimism is admirable, Miss Cambre."

The quiet, piercing look Marie gave her captor suggested that, if she did have supernatural powers, he might well be in for a peck of trouble. With typical arrogance, Galen only seemed to relish the prospect. His patience suddenly wore thin, however, and he began to bark orders.

"The women will have to wait," he said, directing his remarks to his cohorts as he looked over at the chained prisoners. "We must carry these three to the docks first."

"And?" Harnett inquired.

"Use your imagination," Galen said, his words rich in sarcasm. "What do you think would be wise to do with three people who could hang us?"

"We could dump their bodies at sea," Desforges said. "Nobody would ever find them and, if they did, nobody could identify them after the fishes had dined."

Galen sighed as he stared at Marie, who still kneeled beside her niece. He stroked her cheek with the back of his hand and said, "What an inglorious end for such a beautiful woman. And you would have brought such a handsome price, too. Though you're no longer a maiden, many would have paid to sample your experience."

Kipperd, who along with Roan and Marie had managed to hold on to his composure, took a step toward Galen. Languidly, Galen raised his gaze from Marie to Kipperd. The gun followed, stopping Kipperd in midstep.

"I overestimated you," Galen said quietly, smoothly to the Irishman. "I thought you could be trusted."

"Aye," Kipperd returned, "you overestimated me."

"You, on the other hand," Galen said, glancing in Roan's direction, "I didn't overestimate at all. I knew you were trouble the first time I saw you."

"You haven't the foggiest idea just how much trouble I can be," Roan said, his eyes glued to Galen's.

Galen laughed again, macabre notes of a dark symphony. "Leave him for me," he ordered his two cohorts. "I want the pleasure of killing him myself." Again, as though the games had grown tiresome, Galen sobered. "Get them to the wharf, and I'll meet you there." As he spoke, he handed the gun to Desforges, adding, "I'm taking Harnett's horse."

"Where are you going?" Harnett asked, his tone reproachful.

Galen's gaze met Roan's. It was obvious that he took pleasure in what he said next. "I have some unfinished business at home. I need to teach my wife how to keep her mouth, and her legs, shut."

Roan tasted the bitter bile that rose to his throat. He forced himself to swallow it. "If you touch her again, I'll kill you."

Galen's face broke into a broad smile. The smile then gave way to laughter. The laughter grew fainter and fainter as Galen disappeared from the room and down the tunnel.

As the last notes died, Roan realized that he'd been taught a valuable lesson. He now knew the true, and grim, meaning of the word *hate*.

Outside the night closed jealously about them. Harnett had been assigned the task of bringing the carriage around, while Desforges escorted the three prisoners along the tunnel and out through the shed entrance. With only the inquisitive moon as a spectator, they awaited the carriage's arrival.

No one had spoken a word, not Desforges, not his prisoners. Marie had not even said good-bye to Lukie. She had simply, quietly glanced in the young woman's direction, her very look reassuring and calming. Even Roan, who'd been privy to the wordless exchange, had not been unmoved by it. It was plain to him why the beautiful woman was known as a priestess, for she did seem possessed of unnatural powers. It was also evident that Micaela was her great-granddaughter.

Now, standing, waiting in the dark for their fate to unfold, Roan sensed a serenity blanketing Marie. He saw, too, that she and Kipperd traded subtle glances, as though they could communicate silently. Roan would sell his soul for some of Marie's composure, for he could never remember a time in his life when he felt less composed. At the thought of what Galen would soon be doing to Engelina, fear choked his chest. He couldn't stand idly by and do nothing. He had to try to escape. Dammit, he had to try to reach Engelina!

As though she'd read his mind, Marie laid her hand on Roan's arm. Her look said for him to bide his time.

At last the carriage arrived. Even the two snorting horses seemed restless, as if they didn't like being part of such a nefarious deed. One of the animals reared up, pawing the simmering summer air with its hooves.

"Hold them steady!" Desforges rasped.

"Just get everyone aboard!" Harnett ordered.

Desforges opened the carriage door and, using the gun, signaled for Marie to enter. Casting a quick glance in Kipperd's direction, she put her foot upon the first rung of the steps. In so doing, she dropped her reticule. Roan could have sworn it had been done on purpose. With the serene elegance that characterized her every movement, she stepped back to the ground and, her skirt flaring about her, kneeled to pick up her purse.

"Get aboard!" Desforges called. "Now!"

"A woman goes nowhere without her reticule," she said calmly as her hand slipped inside the frilly crocheted bag. Her hand was still in the bag when she stood and faced Desforges. "Certainly not to her death," she added.

"Those amulets won't protect you now," Desforges sneered.

Marie smiled and said, "Mayhap. Mayhap not."

A shot rang out, pricking the stillness like a pin pricking a balloon. Concurrently, a puff of smoke rose from Marie's dainty handbag. Without a word, with nothing more than a startled look on his face, Desforges dropped to the ground, a bullet in his heart. He was dead before he landed.

"Hey—" Harnett cried.

It was uncertain whether the word expressed his surprise at the firing of the gun or the fact that the burly Irishman, his massive hands guided by rage, yanked him from the carriage. Kipperd, by application of a sharp right twist to the neck, killed Harnett with the same decisiveness Marie had shown moments before.

"Quick!" Kipperd said to Roan. "Take the carriage and go to Lamartine House." Even as the order was being given, Roan climbed aboard. He had no idea how to drive horses, but the circumstances left him little choice. "We'll follow you as soon as we send for the police and collect Lukie."

"How will you get there?"

"Lamartine's carriage should be where we left it. Here, take this with you," he said, handing Roan the gun that Galen had given to Desforges. As he spoke, he slapped one of the animals on the flank.

The carriage lurched forward, almost unseating Roan. Throughout the nightmare drive, Roan's only consolation was that at least he didn't have to worry about the fire. That was yet a day away.

The phone, sounding like a gunshot, blasted through the drowsy stillness of the motel room. Crandall groaned, while Julie, who had been asleep in his arms and in the midst of the recurring dream about the bloodred candle and Bible, bolted upright. Her sexy cotton tank top, the color of raspberry, was wet with perspiration.

"What the hell!" Crandall grumbled as another ring exploded in the night. Groping for the switch to the lamp, he found it and twisted it on. He grabbed the phone on the third ring. "Hello?" he growled at the same time he glanced at the clock. It was fifteen minutes till midnight. Who in hell would be calling at this hour?

"Mr. Morgan?"

"Yes."

"This is Bob Rackley. Forgive me for calling so late, but I've been trying to reach Dr. Jacob all evening. You wouldn't happen to know where he is, would you?"

Crandall switched the phone to his other ear as Julie crawled from the bed. "No, I don't," he said, watching as she whipped the sweat-soaked tank top over her head. Her full breasts jumped into view, as did the curve of her hips when she unceremoniously discarded her matching, cut-high-on-the-thighs panties. She headed for the bathroom. In seconds, Crandall heard the shower. "Is it urgent that you reach him?"

"No. Yes. Actually, I'm not certain. As you know, he asked me to do some research for him. More precisely, to research the date of a fire that damaged Lamartine House back in 1880. Well, I discovered a date, July 2, but now . . . Well, I've found another book that mentions yet another date. I have no idea which date, if either, is right." The professor's voice once more grew apologetic. "I know that this is a god-awful hour to call you, but the date seemed so important to him. In fact, he seemed downright obsessed with it. I would just feel better if I could tell him about this recent finding."

Bob Rackley didn't mention that getting the information to Roan was bordering on an obsession for him, as well. He didn't mention that he'd lost track of how many times he'd called Roan that evening.

"I don't know what to tell you," Crandall said. "Dr. Jacob and I are really more acquaintances than friends."

"I see. Well, I'll just have to keep trying. Look, I'm sorry I woke you."

"No problem."

"Well, good night."

"Good night. Hey, wait a minute!" Crandall heard himself saying. "What is this new date of the fire?"

"July 1."

Crandall gave a small laugh. "Bit of a coincidence, isn't it? I mean, it'll be July 1 in"—he glanced at the clock—"roughly ten minutes."

"Yeah," Bob Rackley answered, "a bit of a coincidence."

Neither would have sworn that it was coincidence at all, although neither would have sworn exactly what it was. After Crandall hung up, he stared into space for a full minute. He had an odd feeling that he couldn't account for. It was the same odd feeling he'd had upon learning that a relative of his had been a cleric at the cathedral. The feeling had only intensified when he'd learned that the relative had mysteriously committed suicide. From the very beginning, Crandall had felt that his working on this project had been . . . the only word that came to mind was *ordained*. His finding out about his relative had equally been ordained. And now . . . He glanced over at the phone. Dammit, he had the feeling again! But what was he supposed to do with the knowledge? How was he supposed to reach this Dr. Jacob when Bob Rackley couldn't? Hell, he didn't even know where the man lived!

No, that wasn't true. Springing from the bed, he searched through his pants for his wallet. Roan

Jacob had given him a card with both his phone number and his address on the back. After checking several pockets of the wallet, he finally found the card. Yeah, there was the information. Without considering why he was doing it, he reached for the phone and dialed the number. No one answered and, after a dozen rings, he hung up. He hesitated only a second before grabbing his jeans and shinnying into them.

"Where are you going?" Julie asked, walking back into the room draped in a towel.

"This isn't going to make any sense, but I've got to go over to Roan Jacob's house." He looked at the card. "Lamartine House."

"Why?"

Crandall laughed. "I'm not sure. I just know I've got to go." At Julie's confused look, he added, "Come with me, and I'll explain on the way."

She went with him.

He explained. As best he could.

And then they both fell silent. Though neither knew how to account for the feeling, time seemed of the essence.

As though a hot, hellish wind were blowing across her, Engelina sensed Galen's presence. Halting her pacing of the parlor—she'd been walking out her frustration at not knowing where either Roan or Lukie could be—she whirled, her gaze clashing with Galen's. Her first thought was that she hadn't expected him back so soon. She hadn't expected it to take so little time to move the imprisoned women. Her second thought was that Galen's eyes, gray as a morning mist, shone with an unnatural brightness.

"You always seem so surprised to see me, my pretty," he said, sauntering into the room as though he owned the world and merely leased it to the rest of mankind. He walked to the liquor cabinet and deftly poured himself a generous brandy.

"I-I thought you were out," Engelina said in response to his comment. As always, his presence induced fear. She tried to keep it tamped down.

"Obviously I was out."

"I mean, I thought you would be gone longer."

"Oh, did you? And just what did you think I was doing?" When she said nothing, he added, "Come now, dear, loyal wife, venture a guess."

The fear Engelina was trying to control slipped its restraints. She suddenly had the feeling that he was playing with her, much as a cat toys with a mouse before the kill. She hastily told herself that he couldn't possibly know what she'd overheard. He couldn't possibly know of her visit to Father John.

"Then let me venture a guess for you," he said as he swirled the ruby-red brandy. His gray eyes glittered like diamonds. "I'll bet you thought I was out doing Hell-Fire Club business. Maybe out ravaging all those captive women before we sold them into slavery."

The color drained from Engelina's face, leaving it pasty-white.

Galen smiled. "I see I'm right, though I feel obligated to tell you that Father John never went to the police. If it's any consolation, I doubt they would have believed your story, anyway. After all, I am a fine, upstanding citizen of this fair city. As are Desforges and Harnett and the other select members of the club. More important than our reputations, however, is our money. It's interesting how those with money are always believed."

Engelina's knees weakened, forcing her to clutch

the back of the sofa for support. She couldn't believe what she was hearing. "How did you know about Father John?"

"Simple, my pretty. He told me."

"I don't believe you," she said, her voice barely more than a whisper. Father John would not betray her. Of this she was certain. Wasn't she?

"As you choose." After taking several sips, he drained the glass in one long swallow and set it down. "Actually, as you overheard, I was out doing club business. That is, until a more pressing matter arose. Did I tell you that we have Lukie?" he asked, demonically throwing in this bit of news.

"What do you mean you have Lukie?" Suddenly, nothing seemed real. Not the floor beneath her feet. Not the light coming from the kerosene lantern. Certainly not what she was hearing. Father John? *Had* he betrayed her? Lukie? Did they have Lukie?

Galen gave a look that said he was profoundly sorry. Engelina didn't believe the look for a minute.

"Harnett got carried away and thought she was following him. Of course, she wasn't. She was merely sneaking out to go to her aunt's. Did you know that she sneaked out to go to her aunt's?" He didn't wait for her answer. "Anyway, Harnett bagged her and, well"—he shrugged—"as you can see we have no choice now but to sell her, as well."

Engelina dug her fingers into the back of the sofa. "My God, you can't be serious."

Galen had turned and was studying her portrait above the fireplace, as though he was suddenly mesmerized by it. For a moment, Engelina thought he hadn't even heard her. Abruptly he turned to face her.

"Of course I'm serious," he said, as though the conversation had not lagged at all. "Just as I'm serious about having to kill Kipperd and Lukie's aunt. You know, I think those two are amorously involved." Galen frowned. "I don't mind telling you that I was disappointed in Kipperd. I thought he was loyal to me." Galen looked reflective. "Though perhaps I didn't at that, because I never entrusted him with club business." His eyes turned meaningfully icy. "One should pay attention to one's instincts, don't you think, my pretty?"

Engelina was no longer thinking. At least not coherently. She was caught somewhere between Galen's pronouncement that he intended to kill the Irishman and Lukie's aunt and that Lukie's aunt and the Irishman were lovers. Nothing, no one—not even her beloved Father John—was what he seemed to be, lending even greater credence to the fact that the world around her no longer seemed real. The only thing that seemed real was the cold, threatening way her husband was looking at her. Yes, threatening. His remark about trusting one's instincts had been said to frighten her.

He stepped toward her, terrifying her even more. She forced herself not to cower, which meant the exaggerated elevation of her chin.

"You know what my instincts tell me about you?" he asked softly, his crooked finger playing at the corner of her mouth. "They tell me that, like Kipperd, you have been disloyal."

"I-I don't know what you mean," she choked out.

"Of course you do," he said endearingly. He continued to stroke her mouth as though they were intimate lovers in the throes of an all-consuming passion. "Tell me the truth, and I won't punish you. Lie to me, and I'll make you sorry you were ever born."

Fear, blacker than the night, enfolded Engelina, though she bravely kept her eyes glued to his. "I don't know what you want me to say."

"Are the two of you lovers?"

"Lovers? Who—"

His fingers now formed a vise, his thumb resting at one side of her mouth, his forefinger at the other. The vise tightened. "Are the two of you lovers?"

Though speech was almost impossible with her mouth so grotesquely misshaped, she managed to say, "I don't know what—"

He clamped his hand until his fingers bit deep into her flesh. She cried out, though she hated herself for the weakness.

"Are . . . the two of you . . . lovers?" he repeated slowly, distinctly. Engelina sensed it was the last time he was going to ask the question.

"No," she whispered, the sound barely edging past her lips. She prayed that God would forgive her lie.

Abruptly, Galen released her. As though he accepted her answer without reservation, he turned away, took a step, then whirled back around, sailing the back of his hand through the air and striking her full across the cheek.

"Liar!" he rasped as the force of his blow sent her sprawling on the floor.

A spider-web blackness journeyed through Engelina's head, and she fought to hold on to the last shreds of the light that grew dimmer and dimmer. By sheer will, she chased unconsciousness away. She couldn't chase away the pain, however. It was all-consuming—her cheek, her hip where she'd landed, her very pride.

Using the sofa as leverage, she tried to pull herself up, but couldn't, and so she fell back to the floor, assuring herself that she'd get up in a minute. She had to get up. She'd dismissed the housekeeper from sitting with Chloe, and she must go check on her. She had to keep Galen from her, should he choose to take his wrath out on her. Galen. Where was he?

"You lying whore!" she heard and raised her head in time to see him rip her portrait from the wall above the fireplace. He threw it to the floor, knocking over an end table and scattering the bric-a-brac atop it.

At the loud crash, Engelina's hand flew to her mouth. Her fingers came away bloodied. She also heard Chloe calling her. She had to get up. Please, God, help her to get up. This time, when she tried, she pulled herself to her knees, then to her feet.

As though the action reminded him of her presence, Galen once more turned toward her. His gaze softened, as though seeing her for the first time since arriving home. He seemed oblivious of her disheveled hair, oblivious of the blood trickling from the corner of her mouth.

"Did I tell you, my pretty, that I have also taken your lover prisoner?"

He was lying. Engelina knew he was lying. He had to be lying, although the truth was that she couldn't understand why Roan hadn't come to her. He was to find them a room, then come for her, but, as yet, he hadn't.

"It's true," he said. "He'll be killed along with Kipperd and Marie Cambre. Even as we speak, they're being taken to the wharf."

"No," Engelina said, still denying the possibility because her sanity depended on it.

"Yes," he said, "and I intend to do the honors myself." He smiled, as though a most pleasant thought had just occurred to him. "Would you like to go to the wharf to see me kill him?" Before she could answer, he added, "Yes, I think that would be a good idea. Then, you can be the last thing he sees. See how generous I can be?" Galen's smile broadened as he once more stepped toward her. "And I'll make you an even more generous offer. If you tell him that you never loved him, I'll kill him quickly." He now stood directly in front of her. "What do you think of that, my pretty?"

The hate that had festered inside her since her marriage now opened into a raw, pus-oozing wound. The stench of the odorous emotion seemed everywhere about her. "I think you are the most despicable human being on earth."

Galen's eyes glinted with malice. "And I think you are foolish to say so."

"No," she said, "my only foolishness is that I have not said so before now." Before he could reply, she continued. "And I will no longer bow to your dark bidding. Kill me if you will. I welcome it."

Into the silence, Chloe once more called for her sister.

Galen's eyes turned ice-cold. Across the frigid landscape of his irises, Engelina saw his intent the moment his evil mind conceived it.

"No!" she cried. "You stay away from her!"

As she spoke, she lunged toward Galen, knocking him and the table behind him to the floor. The lantern toppled over, spilling both kerosene and flame. Engelina didn't notice as she bolted from the room and rushed up the stairs. She was midway up when she felt Galen grab a handful of her skirt.

Roan opened the door to the smell of smoke and to the sight of Engelina and Galen tussling on the staircase. Earlier, Roan had experienced nausea. He hadn't questioned why. He'd known. And his knowing had caused him to push the already frothing horses harder and faster.

"Let her go," he said softly but menacingly.

Startled by a voice he recognized, but one he certainly never expected to hear, Galen released Engelina and whirled around. Instantly, his gaze connected with the steel pistol aimed at him, then slid upward to take in Roan's dark, intent eyes. Seconds passed as the two men simply gauged each other. Roan had known, the very first time he'd seen Galen, that the two of them were destined for combat, bound for battle. Both knew the war had arrived . . . and there'd be but one victor.

"Roan!" Engelina whispered, half swooning with relief.

At the sound of his name, Roan raised his gaze to the woman standing several stairs above Galen. He noted that she held on to the banister as though it, and it alone, provided her the support she needed to stand. Her hair fell about her in a shamefully bedraggled state, while her cheek, already purpling into a bruise, had begun to swell. A thin stream of blood flowed from the cut at the corner of her mouth. The hate that Roan felt for Galen Lamartine turned to loathing, a loathing so complete that it left no room for any other feeling.

"You goddamned son of a bitch," Roan said, his voice quivering with the storm-black emotion.

Galen smiled and climbed a step in Engelina's direction. So slow, so fluid was the motion that it was barely discernible, particularly to a man ravaged with the need for revenge, particularly to a woman who hadn't taken her eyes off the man who stood in the doorway.

"God need not bother to damn us, for we damn ourselves."

Galen's hand snaked out, capturing Engelina by the

waist and hauling her down the steps to stand in front of him. Stumbling, fighting for balance, Engelina cried out as her body was crushed against her husband's.

"Unless you're a marksman with the pistol," Galen said, "you'd be well advised to put it down."

Angry at his naiveté, Roan held fast to the gun. The truth was, though, that he wasn't a marksman. He wasn't even anywhere close.

"Put it down," Galen repeated, adding a new threat, "or I'll hurt her."

Still Roan held on to the gun. Instinct refused to let him part with it.

The arm slung about Engelina's waist tightened cruelly. At the same time, Galen snatched a handful of his wife's hair. He yanked, angling her head backward at a painful angle. Engelina winced but managed to stifle a cry.

Nausea tore through Roan, almost doubling him in half. "All right! All right!" he said, stooping and laying the gun on the floor. "Just don't hurt her."

Galen grinned as he took a step upward, towing Engelina behind him. "I see you can be reasonable, after all."

Slowly Roan walked toward the staircase, easing his foot onto the first stair. "C'mon, Galen, let her go. This is between you and me."

Keeping his back to the second floor, Galen inched onto another stair, again taking Engelina with him. He said nothing in response to Roan's remark, though his eyes never left Roan's.

Behind Roan, at the foot of the stairs, fire spilled from the parlor and flirted with the staircase runner. Bright orange flames also teased the Aubusson carpet near the doorway, flaring higher and higher until the fiery tongues licked at the lacy curtains hanging at the narrow window. Smoke circled in and out among the pieces of furniture like swamp fog.

"Let her go," Roan ordered again, aware of the spreading fire, aware that their time, Engelina's time, was limited.

He didn't understand how the fire could be occurring now—by the clock, it was only minutes past midnight, only minutes into July 1—but he knew this was the fire that would destroy Lamartine House.

"Or do you need a woman's skirt to hide behind?" Roan asked.

Galen said nothing. He just kept backing up the stairs, drawing a stumbling Engelina with him. For each stair that Galen gained, Roan gained another.

"Even your cronies died like men," Roan goaded, pleased to see Galen's surprise at the fate of his cohorts.

Galen's surprise was only momentary. "They were but fools," he said.

"And you," Roan said, "are but another."

The handsome man smiled. "Time will tell."

Having arrived at the top of the stairs, Galen veered to the left. He watched as Roan completed the steps, moving to the right. Cautiously, carefully, Roan kept his eyes on Galen. They were like two animals of prey stalking each other, with the fire below tracking them both.

The pain in Engelina's neck was unbearable, her fear equally so. She feared not only for herself—surely this was the fire destined to mean her death—but for Roan, as well. Galen would kill him if given only half a chance. She had to do something to help Roan. If not, they were both lost. As was Chloe, whom she now heard calling her once more. Fear was evident in her sister's voice.

"It's all right, Chloe," Engelina called out in reassurance.

Galen's hand clamped over Engelina's mouth. "Shut up!"

Guided by instinct, Engelina sank her teeth deep into Galen's flesh.

Startled, he released her, crying, "Damn you!"

Roan recognized the moment for what it was: the only chance he might get. Ducking his head and leading with his shoulder, he charged forward, hitting an unsuspecting Galen in the stomach. The force of the impact knocked Galen backward, sending him into the banister. The sound of cracking wood rent the air. As did the hiss of the fire as it jumped hither and yon, as though applauding the drama unfolding on the second floor.

On a deep growl, Galen pushed from the broken railing and lunged at Roan. He, too, hit his mark, felling Roan as though he were a rotten tree. Pain scurried through Roan, making him gasp for his next breath. At the kick he saw coming, he rolled to his side and forced himself up. Staggering, Roan nonetheless struck Galen full in the face, bloodying his own knuckles even as he cut a gash in Galen's mouth. Galen retaliated by punching Roan, once more knocking him to the floor. A swift kick to Roan's ribs followed.

"No!" Engelina cried as Roan bent over in pain.

Galen kicked him again. This time Roan grabbed Galen's foot in midair, sending him backward to land on the floor.

"Get out of the house!" Roan shouted to Engelina.

"Not without you and Chloe."

"Go!"

"No!"

The fire, like a precocious child at play, had begun to hopscotch its way up the staircase. The first floor now swam in a sea of flames; smoke surged upward to attack lungs and eyes. As though it were feeding on the evil within the house, the fire took sustenance, growing hotter and higher. From seemingly everywhere came a deafening crackle and pop.

Galen came to his feet. A wide, malevolent grin spread across his face. "I think the three of us shall arrive in hell together," he said.

Galen once more began circling, circling, a step, a half step at a time. Roan had no choice but to play the game, the sinister ring-around-the-rosy game. Abruptly Galen halted. Roan stopped, too.

"Tell the devil hello," Galen said and grinned as he rushed in for the kill.

Roan stepped backward . . . and felt the broken unsteady railing behind him. He saw the man closing in on him. Suddenly, Roan knew Galen's deadly plan, which he'd been stupid enough to fall for. He had no choice but to counter. Quickly. Though not so quickly. Forcing himself to wait until the last moment, he edged aside, allowing Galen to plow headlong into the railing. The sound of splintering wood rose above everything else. A long, loud, agonized cry followed as Galen tumbled over the balcony. Seconds later, there was a mighty, bone-crushing thud. Then silence. A silence filled with fire-song.

Engelina closed her eyes in horror but with relief. She wanted to savor her newfound freedom, but the reality was that she was trapped again, held prisoner again, this time by the dreadful conflagration spreading inexorably closer. Gray-black smoke, thick and endless, spiraled up the staircase, causing her eyes to sting, her lungs to burn.

"C'mon!" Roan shouted, pushing her toward the stairs. There was a wild look in his eyes when he said, "Go on. I'll get Chloe." When Engelina hesitated, he shouted, "Go on!"

The imperious tone of his voice brooked no opposition. Wending her way through the budding flames, through the billowing smoke, she started downward. All of a sudden, she remembered something and turned to retrace her steps. She practically ran into Roan, who was carrying Chloe, whom he'd wrapped in a quilt.

"Dammit, Engelina, get out of the house!" he bellowed.

"I can't. Not without Chloe's medicine."

"We'll get more."

"I'll only be a minute," she said, hastening past him.

"Sis-ter?" Chloe called. Because of her fragile breathing, she was already choking on the smoke.

"Get her out of here," Engelina called, racing back up the stairs.

"Here, let me have Chloe."

The voice came from out of the viscous smoke. It belonged to Kipperd. Glancing downward, Roan saw Lukie standing in the doorway and Marie at the foot of the stairs. He hadn't heard them enter, though he thanked God for their timely arrival. Without hesitation, he passed Chloe to the strong-armed Irishman and fled back up the stairs to find Engelina.

As though the demons of hell had been unleashed, the fire now seemed everywhere, in every nook and cranny, in every hall and room. It seemed eager, greedy even, to destroy, to devour, the house.

"Get out of here!" Kipperd called to Marie.

Instead of obeying, however, as though she were drawn beyond her will, the priestess walked to the doorway of the parlor. Engelina's portrait lay on the floor. Bright flames danced about it and yet, as though it had been carefully planned, a clear, fireless path led to it. Like a siren, the portrait called to her.

Unable to stop herself, not questioning the why of it, she stepped into the parlor. In seconds, with the portrait in hand, she returned to the foyer.

"My God, woman," Kipperd yelled, "are you mad?"

"No," she said calmly, "only fulfilling a destiny."

Upstairs, Roan searched frantically for Engelina. He found her in her bedroom, where she kept the digoxin he'd prescribed for Chloe.

"Come on!" he said, taking Engelina by the arm and rushing for the stairs. Engelina stumbled. Roan pulled her to her feet.

As they stood at the top of the stairway, it suddenly burst into wildfire, flames shooting upward toward the ceiling. Engelina screamed as the candent fingers pawed at her skirt. Roan pushed her out of the way.

"Take off your petticoat!" he shouted.

She didn't question his command. Stripping off the underwear, she handed it to him. He draped it over her head, saying, "We'll have to make a run for it!"

She nodded, her heart pounding in her chest.

Without hesitation, he took her hand and started down the stairs. Unable to see before him, he felt his way, slapping at the flames that threatened to ignite their clothing, holding his breath. Still, the fire consumed them; the smoke overwhelmed them.

The realization that they weren't going to make it came gradually to Roan. Or perhaps it came in one crystal-clear moment of truth, the way the nearness of death often proclaimed itself to him in surgery. Whichever, it came—as smoke blackened his face, as it forced him to shield his eyes, as it filled his lungs. When Engelina tripped, her hand falling from his, he panicked. If they were going to die, he at least wanted them to die together. Strangely, he didn't fight their fate. He'd always known that he might die in his effort to save her. He didn't fear death. He only feared living without her.

Scrambling back up the steps, he felt for her body. He found it, searching for her face in the thick blackness. When their eyes connected, he saw that she, too, knew they were about to die.

They were about to die. Engelina accepted it as God's will. In truth, He had blessed her. Though her life would be short, though it had been filled with unspeakable cruelty, she had also known a love that few ever knew. For that, in these last moments of life, when breath was more precious than jewels, she would be grateful. She vowed that the last thing she would see would be Roan's face.

Through the hot, searing smoke, she smiled, brushed her fingertips across his soot-streaked face, and silently admitted what she'd known all along. She was in love.

In seconds, his body protectively covering hers, a blackness descended, first hers, followed by his. And then they both, together, saw a bright-white light beckoning.

Kipperd O'Kane, with Chloe's quilt draped over his head for protection, stood in the open doorway, disconsolately watching the fire burn away his hope of rescuing Engelina and Roan. He knew they were trapped on the stairs. He knew, too, that they had collapsed. And that they were dead or dying. And then he saw it. Or thought he saw it, though for the rest of his life he would not speak of what he thought he saw, except once to Marie many years later in the dark of night. His lover did not chide him, did not tease him, did not tell him that he must have been mistaken.

She was perfectly willing to believe that Engelina, and the strange man known as Roan Jacob, had vanished into thin air.

$\mathcal{T}$WENTY-ONE

"Oh, my God!" Crandall cried as he saw the smoke rising from the house.

Before the car had even come to a complete stop, he slung open the door and started running toward the building. The fact that a car, presumably belonging to Roan Jacob, was in the driveway hastened Crandall's feet. Taking the gallery steps two at a time, he threw wide the front door. He could hear Julie's footsteps behind him.

What he saw, however, stopped him cold. Fire burned everywhere—from lace curtains to authentically duplicated rugs to irreplaceable furniture. Flames, brilliant orange and sanguine red, ate voraciously at the carved ceiling, the paper walls, the curving staircase.

"Holy hell," Julie whispered, her choice of words accurately describing what she was witnessing. Even as she watched, a beam crashed nearby, sending sparks flying.

"Get out of here!" Crandall cried.

Julie, however, didn't move. She couldn't. She was too captivated by the beautiful horror unfolding before her.

Cupping his hands to his mouth, Crandall hollered, "Jacob? Are you here?"

There was no answer.

Coughing, Julie said, "He couldn't survive this smoke long."

"I know," Crandall said, then realized that Julie hadn't obeyed him. "Will you get the hell out of h—"

"Look!" Julie cried, pointing in the direction of the stairway.

A Siamese cat, fearless of the fire, stood staring upward at the stairs. The animal mewled pitifully. Crandall stepped to the animal's side, seeing the stairway from another angle. This angle allowed him to see the couple.

"It's him!" Crandall shouted. "And a woman!"

Though the stairway was ablaze, Crandall started upward. Flames leapt high, hungrily, about him.

Grabbing Crandall by the arm, Julie shouted, "You can't go up there!"

"I can't let them die!"

"They may already be dead!"

"I've got to see!"

Glancing frantically about, Julie spotted a quilt at the base of the stairs. The quilt looked old, as though it belonged to another time. She snatched it up.

"Here, put this over you!"

Crandall did, hiding his long blond hair from the greedy blaze. He started up the stairs. In seconds, he'd disappeared behind a veil of gray-white smoke. He was gone for what seemed like forever, but then appeared with a woman slung over his shoulder.

"Is she alive?"

"I don't know."

"Put her down and I'll drag her out," Julie said, freeing Crandall to rush back for Roan. The woman was dressed strangely, as though she belonged to the same era as the quilt. While Julie pulled her away from the house, the cat followed, as though it needed to see the job well done.

In minutes, both Roan and Engelina lay stretched out on the front yard, with the cat looking on. Neither registered a pulse. Swearing and sweating, Crandall began CPR on Roan. Julie began the same on Engelina. But to no avail. Despite their concerted efforts, there was still no pulse for either of them.

"Keep going!" Crandall shouted.

Crandall and Julie were still performing CPR when the wailing of sirens sliced through the hot July night. Within heartbeats a fire truck arrived, accompanied by an emergency medical vehicle. From everywhere, people began to appear. A van sporting the call letters of a local television station pulled into the driveway. A man with a minicam jumped from it, as did a local newscaster. From nearby houses, sleepy-eyed neighbors began to gather.

Slicker-dressed firemen, with long snakelike hoses, went to work, while the medical team, carrying a bevy of modern equipment, including oxygen masks, replaced the tired, discouraged couple. Released from their awesome duties, the two of them clung together as though they had something very personal at stake.

From that night on, for reasons that neither could explain, Crandall never again searched for his roots—he didn't feel the need—nor did Julie ever again experience the terrifying nightmare. It was as though the power of the past had ended that evening for them, there on the lawn of Lamartine House. It was as though the bizarre occurrences of the previous weeks had reached a closure.

No! Roan pleaded as oxygen filled his lungs. With a sputtering cough, life was sucked into his body.

"All right!" Crandall cried.

With teary eyes Julie cheered, as she wondered at the depth of her feelings for this virtual stranger. In some inexplicable way, though, he seemed connected to her, she to him.

Dazed, Roan wondered what all the noise was about. He wondered why he was lying on the hard ground. He wondered why strange faces were staring down at him. No, not all of the faces were strange. He recognized Crandall and Julie and thought it peculiar that they should be here in the year 1880. 1880? No, this wasn't 1880. He could tell by the way the people were dressed. But he could smell the fire he'd left behind. Fire? Engelina? Oh, my . . .

". . . God!" he said, jackknifing to a sitting position.

"Easy, easy," one of the medical workers called out.

Ripping the mask from his face, Roan looked about him. He didn't have far to search for Engelina. She lay beside him—deathly pale, deathly still. She, too, wore a mask. Even as Roan watched, one of the medical assistants shook his head at the other and removed her mask.

Something wild and savage erupted within Roan. He hadn't endured all that he had, Engelina hadn't endured all that she had, for history to write this cruel ending. Why in God's name had he been sent back? Why in God's name had he been allowed to live if she must die?

Pushing the fireman aside, he frantically began to perform CPR on Engelina. He pushed upon her chest. He breathed his life into her mouth. He prayed. Minute after dark minute passed.

Finally, the fireman spoke softly, consolingly to Roan. "I'm sorry, sir. She's dead."

Ignoring him, Roan continued with the life-saving

procedure. When the fireman touched his arm, Roan glanced up as though ready to fight.

"Leave me alone," he barked, never breaking the rhythm of push and breathe, push and breathe, push and breathe . . .

Hope, however, can survive only so long. Reality, with its oftentimes grim message, is all too eager to squelch it. She was dead. He knew it, felt it, hated it. He stopped pushing on her chest. He stopped breathing into her mouth. He stopped living. For long moments, he stared down at her. Soot blackened her face, a face that was swollen from the recent abuse she'd suffered. Blood, as red as a rose, still trickled from the side of her mouth. He touched the cut at her lip. He touched her swollen cheek. He touched the thick-lashed eyelids.

"Noooo!" he keened into the night, the sorrowful animal-like sound carrying far and wide and touching every heart that heard it. Carefully, tenderly, Roan pulled Engelina's lifeless body into his arms. He began to rock.

Time ceased to be. There was no yesterday, no today, no tomorrow. There was only an endless, eternal ache. The summer night whispered its condolences as quiet tears slid down Roan's cheeks.

He heard someone say that the house was a total loss; he heard someone else ask another just how long he was going to hold the woman; he heard himself silently answer forever—forever in his heart.

The cat, as though sensing Roan's sadness, sat a quiet, sad vigil beside him. Roan recalled the first time he'd seen the cat. The first time he'd seen Engelina's ghost. The first time he'd breached the past. He remembered the first time he'd kissed her. And the first time they'd made love. He remembered this last so vividly that even now he could feel her warm breath beating against the hollow of his throat. It seemed so real. So hauntingly real.

Thinking that he must surely be going crazy, Roan peered down at Engelina. Her face had turned from pale to pink. Her mouth was parted, emitting a sweet, shallow breath. Even as he watched, her eyelids fluttered open to reveal the darkest eyes he'd ever seen.

"Roan?" she whispered, reaching for his face with her fingertips, but lacking the strength to complete the journey.

Roan's heart sang, soared, burst wide in two. He tried to speak but couldn't. Instead, he brought her hand to his face and held it there, kissing it softly, letting salty, unashamed tears seep upon it.

Noticing the people about her, she asked, "Where are we?"

"My world," he said.

"Your world?" she asked, the possibility already bringing a shadow of a smile to her lips. As soon as the smile appeared, however, it faded. "Chloe?" she whispered.

"We'll go back for her." At the fear that claimed Engelina, he added, "I promise you that."

This last was so passionately said that Engelina believed him. But then, she'd always believed him. He was the worker of miracles, the keeper of promises, her deliverer. He was the man she loved.

"I love you," she whispered, saying the words for the first time and, in so doing, freeing herself from the past.

Wordlessly, Roan pulled her to him, holding her close against his love-filled heart. A prayer of thanks, heavenbound, winged its way through the star-studded southern sky—Roan's prayer, Engelina's prayer, a prayer that gratefully acknowledged a love strong enough, binding enough, to defy time.

Sandra Canfield has written more than twenty books under her name and under her pseudonym, Karen Keast. She has won many awards, most recently the Romance Writers of America Award for Best Romantic Suspense Novel of 1990. She lives in Louisiana with her husband.